THE
NUGGET

THE
NUGGET

P. T. DEUTERMANN

ST. MARTIN'S PRESS

NEW YORK

Published in the United States by St. Martin's Press, an imprint of St. Martin's Publishing Group

THE NUGGET. Copyright © 2019 by P. T. Deutermann. All rights reserved. Printed in Canada. For information, address St. Martin's Publishing Group, 120 Broadway, New York, NY 10271.

The Library of Congress Cataloging-in-Publication Data is available upon request.

ISBN 978-1-250-20588-9 (hardcover)
ISBN 978-1-250-20589-6 (ebook)

Our books may be purchased in bulk for promotional, educational, or business use. Please contact your local bookseller or the Macmillan Corporate and Premium Sales Department at 1-800-221-7945, extension 5442, or by email at MacmillanSpecialMarkets@macmillan.com.

First Edition: October 2019

10 9 8 7 6 5 4 3 2 1

THE
NUGGET

PROLOGUE

I was staring out the window at the crowded expanse of Pearl Harbor below when the court members, three commanders and one four-striper, filed solemnly into the room. My defense counsel cleared his throat to get my attention. I turned around and walked back to the defense table. The members took their seats up on the dais with the captain in the middle. One of the commanders was a JAG officer. He sat right next to the captain, who was president of the court. The other two were line officers but neither of them was an aviator. The investigating officer, somewhat analogous to a prosecutor, was a lieutenant commander JAG officer. The clerical yeomen took their seats, but I didn't see a court reporter. There were no spectators.

The captain banged his gavel once. "This Court will come to order," he announced in what sounded to me like a weary voice. I thought he looked pretty old but he had a lot of ribbons on his uniform. Maybe the war had aged him, just like me.

"This court of inquiry," the captain continued, "has been convened by the Commandant of the Fourteenth Naval District, Rear Admiral Draper, to inquire into the case of an individual claiming to be Lieutenant Robert T. Steele, formerly of the carrier squadron Bombing Six, who was recovered from the Philippine island of Talawan after being missing for almost two years. I remind members and the subject of this court that a court of inquiry is, under Naval Regulations, an investigating body—a sort of grand jury, if you will. It is only authorized to ascertain facts and report them for consideration by the convening authority. It can also offer opinions, but they must be relevant and related to one or more facts. Its proceedings can be used as evidence in any subsequent court-martial, if one is deemed appropriate. In this case we will begin by taking testimony of the individual before you who is claiming to be Lieutenant Steele."

He turned to look directly at me. "You, sir: are you in fact claiming to be Lieutenant Robert T. Steele, USN, who was declared missing in action from USS *Hornet* and your bombing squadron following the sinking of the *Hornet* during the action off the Santa Cruz Islands, October, nineteen forty-two. Is that correct?"

I stood to respond. "Yes, sir, that's who I am."

The captain nodded. "So you say, sir. I must say you don't look much like a lieutenant in the US Navy."

I had to smile. That was the understatement of the year. I had a full beard and my hair was long enough to have been tied in a bun if I'd wished. My face and neck were nut brown, from my forehead right down to my collar line. There was a long, white scar on the right side of my head. I had wanted to wear dress khakis to the court, but since my identity was in question, they wouldn't let me wear the uniform until the court made its findings. They'd cleaned up the Filipino native clothes I'd been wearing when they finally retrieved me from Talawan, and that's what I was wearing today. Surrounded by all these officers in uniform, with their black ties, shoulder boards, glistening collar devices, and pressed shirts, I felt like the impostor they thought I was.

"I was on Talawan for just over twenty months after the sinking of the submarine *Hagfish*," I replied. "The Japanese were searching hard for me and my gunner, so the local resistance leader advised me to have my face stained. He failed to tell me that it might be permanent. I can demonstrate, if you wish, that the rest of me is definitely white."

The captain raised his eyebrows. "That won't be necessary, sir. Perhaps the simplest thing to do here is for you to tell your story, right from the beginning."

"How much time do you have, Captain?" I asked.

"Whatever it takes," he said, getting comfortable in his chair. "From the beginning then. Where and when was that, by the way?"

"Right here, Captain," I said. "Right here in Pearl Harbor. On one noisy December morning, back in nineteen forty-one."

ONE

I awoke to the sounds of machinery. Ventilation fans, to be specific.

Where am I? I wondered.

I opened one eye and quickly clamped it shut. My mouth felt like it was filled with a wad of bitter cotton and I now knew how many brain cells I had because every one of them hurt. Maybe I should have used some of them last night. A tiny Greek chorus of some of the less badly dehydrated cells began a chant: You can not drink. You can *not* drink.

I took a deep, painful breath, still wondering: Where the *hell* am I?

There were other noises, now: a distant rumbling of some very large machinery, the clatter of a swab and bucket being used out in the passageway. Sound is vibration. My cells and I really didn't need vibration just now. Like we've been saying since about 2200 last night, chirped the brain cells: you can *not* drink.

Then it came to me: passageway. I was on a ship. A very big ship. I opened that eye again and winced when I saw a bright white line stretched under the door to where I lay in bed. I sat up, carefully, and my stomach rewarded the effort with a lurch of nausea. And then I remembered the night before.

It had started innocently enough. Upon graduating from the Operational Training phase of flight training, I'd received orders to the USS *Enterprise* (CV-6), where I'd be assigned to the air group's dive-bombing squadron. I debarked off the transport ship and slogged my seabag over to the base personnel office, where I got to hurry up and wait. Where's my carrier? The Big E was at sea, somewhere, one of the clerks told me. Due back, well, sometime. I'd drawn myself up to my full height of five foot nine, okay, eight, inches and demanded more precise information. I am Ensign Robert Tennille Steele, United States naval aviator, and I need to know when and where I'm supposed to meet *Enterprise*.

The tired-looking personnelman was underwhelmed. You and about a hundred other guys, Ensign, he'd said. Here's a voucher for the base BOQ. I suggest you go there now and get a room before they're all gone. You'll know your ship's back in port when you see a big crowd headed down to the Ten-Ten dock. Join them. When you get there, look up. She's a *big* gray bastard, you know? Uglier'n a stump, if you ask me, not beautiful like one of our battleships. Here's your orders packet. When you *do* see the carrier, grab your seabag and your orders and report to the OOD on the officers' brow, that's at the back end, Ensign. Next.

I'd stomped out of there with as much dignity as I could salvage, which wasn't much. The after brow. That's at the back end. Wiseass. I'd been at sea for two years. I damned well knew which was forward and which was aft. This was the curse of having those lonely gold bars on your shirt collar: everybody assumed you knew absolutely nothing, even though I was an academy graduate, had completed two years at sea in a cruiser, and after that, just over a year at Pensacola and other flight-training fields. In the Army they called their second lieutenants shavetails, whatever that meant. In the Navy all it took was for someone to say the word "ensign" and you were immediately lower than whale dung. It was almost like being a plebe again. It reminded me of what one of the chiefs had said when I reported aboard my cruiser: the three most dangerous things in the Navy are a boatswain mate with brains, a yeoman with muscle, and an ensign with a pencil.

That evening I'd gone to the O-club to get a beer but mostly to sulk. Just before leaving San Diego at the close of advanced flight training my girlfriend back in Omaha sent me a Dear John letter. She'd understood that, as a brand-new naval officer, I wouldn't see much of Omaha, or her, once I graduated from Annapolis. Added to that problem was the Navy's rule that new ensigns could not marry for two years after commissioning. My application for flight training at the end of those two years was apparently the final straw. We broke off our unstated engagement, promising to remain friends and maybe try again once I completed my Navy obligation. I got more mail from my folks back in Omaha than I did from her, and the Dear Bobby wasn't much of a surprise. I still felt like sulking.

I'd of course asked around the O-club bar if anyone knew when the Big E was coming back in. That got me several suspicious looks and headshakes, even though I was in uniform. The bartender pulled me aside and explained that the movements of important ships like the *Enterprise* were secret, especially with all this war talk going around. In other words, stop asking or some people in suits will show up and take your ignorant ass away in irons.

I guess I should have known that. He'd been friendly enough about it, but that was probably because I was an ensign and he felt sorry for me. He'd even topped up my beer for free when he saw how crestfallen I'd looked. Then Ensign Mick McCarthy, one of my classmates, showed up. It seems he was stationed on the battleship USS *Oklahoma* as 3rd Division officer. He immediately ordered me a second beer and we got caught up. Long story short, before I knew it I was pee-lastered. Mick, being Irish, was of course just getting up a head of steam. The last thing I remember about the club was that Mick ordered me a Me Tie, or something like that. Mick called it dessert. The bartender cut me off after one after I dropped the empty glass.

How or why we ended up on the battleship *Oklahoma* remained an annoying mystery, right up there with getting in consecutive breaths of air without hurting my lungs, or, worse, having that other eye open suddenly. Apparently the first eye had spilled the beans on how much pain that slim band of white light could inflict.

I can *not* drink. I must *never* drink.

At that moment, the ship's announcing system switched on with a snap and a crackle. Then the Antichrist started blowing a bugle. An *amplified* bugle, no less, telling us that reveille was upon us. I covered my face and ears with a pillow against the hateful noise, which finally, mercifully, stopped. To be replaced with the braying of a boatswain mate who wasn't aware there was an amplifier present. Apparently it was time for sweepers to start their brooms and give the ship a clean sweep-down, fore and aft. That was followed by detailed instructions as to where to sweep (all interior decks, ladders, and passageways) and *how* to sweep again: give the ship a *clean* sweep-down, fore and aft, with every raspy syllable drilling into my poor head. During the next thirty minutes I stumbled down to the officers' head where I embarrassed myself, and then I slunk back to the stateroom, got my uniform back on, and then my shoes—socks were hard, shoes a bit easier.

I collapsed back into the desk chair. I needed the chair to properly hold my aching head in both hands, eyes closed again, while the entire ship was treated to even more amazing announcements: mess gear; breakfast for the crew; all hands to quarters, officers' call, and all this on a Sunday when any civilized aviation outfit would simply have piped holiday routine and been done with it. The final insult came when some evil bastard blew a *police whistle* over the announcing system, meaning: attention to morning colors. I did see colors, but not of the national kind. *Gawd*, I was hung over.

Then a surprise. Instead of actually saying, Attention to colors, the bosun said: What?

I echoed him. What?

The bosun was still holding down the switch on his 1MC microphone when somebody near him up on the bridge yelled: Hit the deck! loud enough to make *me* roll out my desk chair and hit the deck. At which point said deck, that solid battleship *steel* deck, punched my whole body so hard it knocked the wind out of me, followed a tenth of a second later by a truly thunderous roar from somewhere way down in the guts of the ship. I felt her roll ten degrees to port and then back over to starboard, where, even scarier, she stayed. The stateroom's built-in desk and bureau set had been dislodged by the blast and was leaning out of the bulkhead and wedged on the desk chair right over my head. I tried to disentangle myself when all the lights flickered out. Then we got hit again, somewhere farther aft. Same gut-punching, knee-banging booming explosion, followed quickly by what sounded like the ship's antiaircraft guns beginning to hammer away topside.

Suddenly I got myself clear of the chair and the trash can. As I tried to scramble to my feet I realized I was wrong about that: the chair and the trash can had gotten clear of *me*, rolling across the stateroom deck all by themselves, along with all the other loose gear. The ship was now listing by at least fifteen degrees, maybe even more. My hangover evaporated, extinguished by adrenaline.

Gotta get out of here, I thought. Then came a third hit, this one definitely underwater, the sound muffled but the impact no less mortal. I could literally hear and see the bulkheads and the door frame deform under the impact. I crawled to my feet, felt for the stateroom door, and tried to get it open. No dice: it was wedged shut. I kicked and pulled at it in the darkness until it gave way, wrenched it open, and saw light: battle lanterns were glimmering all along the passageway, their smoky yellow beams revealing at least a foot of water rushing down the passageway.

Water. Running down the passageway? No. No. *No!*

The deck was now tilting over even more, piling that water up against the outboard bulkhead as I scrambled down the passageway toward a watertight hatch visible about 40 feet aft. Where *was* everybody? The main steel girders of the ship were groaning now, accompanied by a thousand cracking and pinging noises as rivets were pushed out of the metal like cold bullets. There were no more guns banging topside but still lots of explosions, some close, some distant now, as if our unseen attackers had tired of *Oklahoma*, and little wonder. I finally reached the watertight door which someone had dogged down, but only partially. By then I was almost walking on the bulkhead as the ship's list had increased to over thirty degrees. Despite the warm harbor water swirling past my knees, I felt a cold chill: the *Oklahoma* was going to capsize. She was going to turn turtle and go completely upside down.

I grabbed the hatch-operating handle and twisted it upwards as hard as I could. I couldn't budge the damned thing. The water was piling up on my side of the hatch and for the first time I thought I was going to drown here. I hit that operating handle again but with no better results. I saw a fire extinguisher mounted on the dry-side bulkhead. I grabbed it and used it as a hammer, striking upwards on the handle. I thought I could hear panicked shouting in the next compartment. Then the top of the extinguisher snapped off and the stink of acid foam filled the flooding passageway. I recoiled from the acrid cloud, tripped, and went underwater for a moment. I bobbed back up, eyes stinging, fighting a rising panic.

Suddenly the handle moved, and then swung all the way up. The hatch popped open, knocking me once again back into the passageway. Somebody grabbed my shirt and hauled me through the hatch into a companionway, the place where a double ladder from the next deck up reached down to the deck I was on. The two ladders were covered in dungaree-clad sailors, some only partially clad, all trying to fit through the two hatches up above at the same time. My rescuer dropped me into two feet of water on the dangerously sloping deck. I was about to say something when a blast of boiler steam began roaring up the stack, which must have been right behind the companionway. The noise drowned out all the shouting around the ladder. The crowd streaming up the ladder thinned out, as if encouraged by that tremendous roar of escaping high-pressure steam.

One of the last men on the ladder saw me just sitting there. He yelled something at me, but all I could hear was the thunder of escaping main steam. He gestured at me with both hands: C'mon, Ensign. C'*mon*. Then he was gone, disappearing up the ladder into a sudden waterfall that began to come back *down* the ladder.

That finally registered.

I bolted for the empty ladder and went up like a striped-assed ape, taking every third rung, steel treads skinning my shins as if to say: Faster, faster! She's going. And she *was* going. She was beginning that final ponderous roll. I caught a slim glimpse of daylight over on the high side and lunged for it even as a huge cascade of water came through a main deck hatch. I don't know how I got through that but I did. I slid down the hull, bumped off the armor belt, and dropped into the harbor, joining a swarm of men who were frantically trying to get away from the capsizing giant.

Why get away? Weren't we safe now? Then I remembered: if she went all the way down, sank out of sight, she'd suck anybody in the water nearby down with her. I struck out in the away direction, vaguely aware that there were fires everywhere along battleship row accompanied by the drone of unfamiliar aircraft engines. A titanic explosion erupted somewhere down the Ford Island waterfront, closer to the inner harbor. It was so big it punched my eardrums. By then most of us realized we weren't getting anywhere as *Oklahoma*'s massive 26,000-ton hull displaced an equal amount of harbor water when she capsized. All of that water was now flowing back *towards* the upside-down ship. It swept us up onto the barnacle-covered hull and then dragged us back down in a succession of waves. On the next surge those who could tried to scramble up the hull itself, grabbing rivet heads, ridges of armor plate, and even protruding barnacles, which were sharp as knives. I was so frightened that I don't remember clambering all the way to the keel but I did, my bare hands stinging from a thousand cuts. Somewhere back aft a mighty geyser of air and water was shooting a hundred feet into the air from one of the torpedo holes as the ship flooded. There'd been about thirty of us who'd gotten out, but I was the only one who'd made it to the keel.

Exhausted, I lay spread-eagled along a section of the ship's keel and tried to regain my wits. I now knew what people experienced during a large earthquake: when the earth itself moves, your brain can't process it. It was terrifying. Then I smelled fuel oil, lots of it, followed by a hot gust of flame as the oil ignited back down by what had been the waterline. Instinctively, I started crawling backwards to get away from those grasping flames and worse, the choking clouds of oily black smoke that threatened to displace all the breathable air. Then I heard the broken screams of those still down in the water as the flames reached them, driving them underwater and then, inevitably, back up, lungs bursting, to the surface, there to inhale superheated air, flame, and smoke.

I wish I could say that I bravely held my ground or tried to rescue some of them, but the truth was I simply pressed my face down onto the battleship's keel, squeezed my eyes shut in sheer terror, and tried to ignore the continuous sounds of explosions nearby, the chatter of machine guns as the Japs came back on strafing runs, and the screams of the men down in the water, which one by one subsided into a sickening silence. At some point my brain had had enough. Everything went mercifully black.

TWO

Someone was lifting me into an upright position and then patting my face, none too gently.

"Sir? Sir? You wounded?"

I opened my aching eyes. Two grimy sailors in wet, oil-soaked dungarees had ahold of me. I blinked several times and then looked over their shoulders at the spectacle of the entire Pacific Battle Fleet either aflame, upside down, or barely afloat.

"What the hell happened?" I croaked.

One of the sailors, a petty officer third class, stared at me with frightened eyes. "The goddamned Japs, that's what happened," he said. "Now: we gotta go. Are you injured?"

"No, I don't think so. Except for my hands," I said. I looked around at the mountain of steel on which I was sitting. "I was inside. *Jesus!*"

"Okay, sir?" the petty officer said. "C'mon, we gotta get you down into the P-boat. Then we gotta get over to mainside. We got lotsa casualties in the boat. You ready?"

I blinked a couple of times. Ready? Ready for what? Then the pair of sailors took me by the shoulders and we all three slid down the hull of the overturned battleship to the personnel boat that was waiting for us. Barnacles ripped my khaki trousers

and the backs of my legs. The personnel boat was grossly over-
loaded, its gunwales only inches from the oily water. Inside lay
about thirty casualties in various states of crisis. A chief petty officer was standing at the conning console. He pulled a lanyard
once, sounding one bell, and the boat surged up against the steel
hull long enough for the two sailors to pull me into the back of
the boat. Somewhere behind us, out of sight because of the steel
mountain which had been *Oklahoma*, something blew up with a
hard, ear-compressing blast. Moments later large things began to
pepper the water around us. The chief pulled the boat away from
the hulk of the *Oklahoma* and turned it towards the other side of
the harbor. He looked over his shoulder at me.

"You injured, Ensign?" he asked, his voice betraying carefully
restrained fear as he struggled to maintain some form of command composure.

"No," I replied. "I was—"

He cut me off. "You're an officer. You know first aid. How's
about going forward and helping with the wounded?"

"Certainly," I replied and then crawled into the passenger compartment just forward of the coxswain's console as the chief carefully turned the boat and headed for the Ten-Ten dock across from
Ford Island. Two white-hats were trying to tend to the wounded
with the P-boat's tiny first-aid kit. I was shocked by the carnage:
men whose every inch of visible skin was roasted black and weeping serum as they tried to breathe into seared lungs. One man
right in front of me was holding up his right arm which ended just
above his wrist in a bloody tourniquet composed of a broken mop
handle and the sleeve from someone's shirt. The man's eyes were
closed as he cursed the Japanese through clenched teeth. The man
next to him had a gaping chest wound and was obviously dead.
Another blast from the direction of Ford Island made everyone
cringe, but we kept at our clearly hopeless task, trying to stop
bleeding and help burn victims breathe. I joined in their frantic

efforts even as I realized we weren't going to be able to do much more than try. For a few seconds I had to close my eyes and take a deep breath. Then I shook it off and jumped back in to help.

Ford Island across the harbor had disappeared behind towering clouds of black smoke by the time we reached the shipyard. Two destroyers that had been in dry dock just forward of one of the battleships were blackened wrecks. There were dozens of ambulances, utility trucks, and even private vehicles swarming around the base of the pier. Another P-boat was unloading wounded ahead of us, so the chief throttled back and waited. Soon there were two more boats behind us, and more coming out from under the smoke cloud covering the harbor. When we finally nudged our way to the landing, a gray-faced nurse met us and did a quick, visual triage. She noticed me as I was holding up a sailor whose back was probably broken.

"You injured, Ensign?" she called down to the boat, staring at the blood all over my khaki uniform.

I shook my head. I'd tried to answer her but my mouth was too dry.

"Okay," she said. "You can help me. Everybody's going to the triage station, right over there. The docs decide who's going to the hospital, and who isn't. Any more able-bodied in this boat?"

Four sets of bloody hands rose.

"Organize it, Ensign," she told me and strode back to the main triage station.

I did. As soon as all the passengers had been lifted by hospitalmen to the pier and onto stretchers, the chief backed the P-boat away from the landing and headed back out into the harbor. I saw to it that the stretcher cases were attended to, and that the dead were moved away from the survivors. I could hear sirens going all over the shipyard. There were many fires blazing on this side of the harbor as well. The first thing every wounded man wanted was water, which was in short supply in the noisy chaos around me. I, myself, was desperately thirsty. Then one of the base fire trucks showed up, covered in soot and with bullet holes in the cab doors. Three firemen got out and rigged a 2.5-inch hose down to the triage station. One of the firemen cracked open the nozzle, allowing all the triage medical personnel to wash their hands and faces for the first time. The cries for water from the dozens of stretcher cases became louder.

I noticed a trash skip nearby that had a case of empty Coke bottles in it. I gathered up six of them, got in line for the nozzle, rinsed them out, and then filled all six. I went back to the ever-growing triage line and began offering sips of water to as many of the wounded as possible. I'd gone through five of the six bottles when a nurse yelled at me to knock it off, pointing out that the water could kill patients with abdominal wounds. There was an audible groan from the crowd of wounded, but I did as I was told. Ensigns did not argue with Navy nurses.

I drank the last bottle myself and then sat down on one of the bollards lining the big Ten-Ten dry dock. Across the shattered harbor there were huge oil fires and even bigger clouds of intensely black smoke flickering with boiling red flames. The tops of some of the stricken battleships would be visible for a few moments before being enveloped again, swallowed up by their own funeral pyres. I looked for the *Oklahoma* but was unable to make her out, only then remembering she'd capsized. There was now an even longer line of boats waiting at the landing. The air along the waterfront stank of burnt oil and blood.

I decided to get out of there. I'd survived. I'd helped, as best I could, and I'd been yelled at anyway. Now it was time to find my seabag and the Big E.

THREE

The next morning there were seven other newly minted pilots in the dining room of the bachelor officers' quarters, which had escaped damage in the Japanese attack. One of them told me he'd heard *Enterprise* was due in port that afternoon to refuel, rearm, and then get back out to sea. I finished my breakfast and went back to my room. I'd slept poorly Sunday night, getting up twice to take a shower, as if that would cleanse my shocked brain from the things I'd seen that day. I finished packing my seabag and made sure my orders packet was in good order, and then lay back down on the single bed.

I wasn't exactly proud of myself. Getting drunk Saturday night. Waking up in a "borrowed" stateroom with a sick hangover. Then the attack. Instead of running topside to find a machine gun to man, I'd bolted like any other rat escaping a sinking ship. I could have gone back down to the waterline and helped some of those guys get out of the water before all that ignited. Instead, well. Shit.

People talking in the hallway outside woke me up. I looked at my watch but then remembered I no longer had one. I peered out the window and saw that it was late afternoon. I jumped up, grabbed my seabag and orders packet, and went downstairs to check out. I waited out front for a shuttle bus that made a circuit of the base once an hour. The air outside was even worse than on Sunday; it reminded me of the smell coming from the rendering plants out in the Omaha stockyards. There didn't seem to be as much smoke over the harbor, but that only made the scope of the destruction even clearer. I was glad when the gray-painted school bus showed up and I could get aboard and avert my eyes.

By 1700 I was down on the pier watching a gaggle of tugboats push the USS *Enterprise* into her berth. Her gray paint had a dark cast to it, as if in deference to what had happened only yesterday. The closer she came to the pier, the bigger she got: almost 26,000 tons, just over 800 feet long, and with 2,200 officers and men onboard. She carried ninety aircraft of different types and had three elevators and two catapults. She could run 32 knots at full power and her sides bristled with antiaircraft guns. That wall of steel alongside the pier made the sound of her starboard side ventilation exhaust ducts reverberate against the pier buildings. I could see several khaki-clad figures with one lone white pith helmet of the harbor pilot standing among them way up on the structure called the island amidships. I had to back away from the pier's edge as a harbor crane came down the waterfront, clanging its warning bells. It was bringing the first of two brows to the after elevator sponson. It looked like there were a couple hundred men on the pier waiting to get aboard. Working parties had already begun to wrangle the heavy black fuel hoses to the pier's edge in preparation for refueling.

It was another hour before I approached the aftermost brow and started climbing. The brow next to that one was already filled with a steady flow of repair parts, replacement equipment, and white-hats with seabags balanced on their shoulders. Up forward on the pier there was another concentration of working parties, cranes, and even a steel conveyor belt structure that was carrying what looked like bombs up to the forward sponson. The ship's aviation crane was also in action, lifting the fuselages of planes from flatcars on the pier up to the hangar deck. When I reached the sponson deck, which was a platform that extended out over the ship's side beneath the actual flight deck, I saluted in the direction of where the national ensign ought to be, out of sight because of the overhanging flight deck. I presented my orders packet to the officer of the deck.

"Ensign Steele reporting for duty, sir," I announced to the harried-looking lieutenant who had the misfortune of being the OOD on the day of arrival in port.

"Which squadron?" the OOD asked, noticing the gold wings on my uniform shirt.

"Bombing Six," I said, wincing as a blast of steam came out of the main stack way up above the sponson. To my embarrassment, no one else seemed to even notice it.

"Messenger!" the OOD called, and a young sailor in dungarees and a white hat trotted over. "Take the ensign to Bombing Six's ready room." He turned back to me. "Welcome aboard," he said, mechanically, looking over my shoulder. "Next."

The messenger grabbed my seabag and led me up into the hangar bay from the sponson and into a world of barely controlled pandemonium. The hangar bay was a cavernous room beneath the flight deck where planes were stowed, maintained, fueled, repaired, and then sent up on one of three large elevator platforms to the flight deck. The hangar bay was a place of non-stop noise populated by hundreds of men working on planes or moving them around the bay to make room for new arrivals. Two of the ship's elevator doors were open to provide some fresh air and sunlight, but the atmosphere was still filled with welders' smoke, oil fumes, and the clatter of machinery. Some of the squadron ready rooms were on the deck right beneath the flight deck, so we had to go into a ladder companionway on one side of the hangar bay and climb three more sets of ladders. We finally reached an athwartships passageway and then turned left down a centerline passageway, where we had to step over heavy steel frame risers, fondly known as knee-knockers, every ten feet.

The Bombing Six ready room was arranged like a small movie theater, with rows of seats facing a stage area. The back of the stage was covered in heavy, fireproof curtains because the ship was in port. I knew that there were large area maps mounted behind those curtains, and I could hear men talking and working back there. The ready room was empty except for a harassed-looking chief petty officer, a yeoman second class, and a lieutenant commander with dark circles under his eyes. He was dressed in working khakis—long-sleeve shirt, black tie, khaki trousers, and brown shoes. The chief looked up when the quarterdeck messenger dropped my seabag and then backed out into the passageway.

"Nugget alert," he growled, causing the officer and the yeoman to look my way.

"Ensign Bobby Steele, reporting for duty, sir," I announced, hopefully, stepping forward with my orders packet. The yeoman took the brown envelope while the lieutenant commander gave me a handshake and a quick once-over. Something large clattered on the flight deck above, causing me to jump.

"You'll get used to that, Mister Steele," the lieutenant commander said, quietly. "I'm Wade McClusky, CAG. Welcome aboard. You were here when the Japs attacked?"

"Yes, sir. Actually, I was aboard the *Oklahoma*. Barely got off before she turned turtle."

McClusky gave me another, more appraising look. "That must have been bad," he said.

I blinked as I recalled the scenes of bloody horror I'd experienced the day before. I felt tears in my eyes, which surprised me and embarrassed me at the same time. I tried to think of something to say, but McClusky waved me off.

"We're all sick about it," he said. "The only good news is that when it comes time to get even with the yellow bastards, *we're* going to be at the point of the spear. Yeoman Sykes will get you signed in. Tell me: did you get the training program that covered *all* the carrier aircraft types, or did you specialize early?"

"I was in the last one-year course, sir," I said. "I have five hundred fifty flight hours all in, with a final operational training tour for the SBD, dash two."

"Okay, good. We'll need to get you qualified on this deck as soon as possible. You fancy yourself a good stick back at field carrier landing school?"

"Well, yes, sir, I did. But somebody told me a real carrier moves around a little bit more than the FCLP did." I put on my sincerest straight face. "Is that true, sir?"

"It just might be, Ensign," McClusky said, eyeing the chief and the yeoman, who now seemed to be struggling to contain themselves. Then the CAG realized I was fooling with him.

"Aw, shit," he said with a grin. "*God*damned ensigns." Then his face sobered. "But I'm serious about your deck quals. We're gonna be going out soon and Bombing Six will be fifty percent nuggets."

That news surprised me. I'd assumed I'd be the only nugget in the squadron. "I'll do my best, sir," I said.

"And you'll do it in at least two types of aircraft, Mister Steele. I'm a fighter guy, myself, but once we go after the Japs *every*body may need to swap aircraft types once we start taking losses, so stay flexible."

"Aye, aye, sir," I said, automatically, and then followed the yeoman down to the squadron office. On the way, as we descended ladders and made our way through what seemed to be yet another labyrinth of cold steel passageways, Yeoman Sykes gave me some friendly advice.

"Commander McClusky is the carrier air group commander, in case you didn't catch it," he said. "He's the CAG: runs the whole show—the torpedo guys, the fighter guys, the dive bombers and the scout bombers. He is *every*body's senior officer and a great guy to boot. He laughed when you joked with him, but don't try that with our CO or XO. They take themselves a whole lot more seriously than the CAG does."

"Got it," I said. "And thanks for the tip."

The yeoman stopped in front of the Bombing Six squadron office. He turned to face me. "You mean that?" he asked.

"Absolutely," I said. "I may be a nugget, but I'm not stupid."

"Well, I'll be damned," the yeoman said, wonderingly, as if he couldn't imagine such a thing.

That evening I managed to find my way to the main officers' wardroom after getting lost three times. *Enterprise* was big, really big, and getting lost was not hard to do. Nothing like my first ship after graduation, the light cruiser *Helena*. Any academy grad wanting to go aviation had to spend his first two years of commissioned service at sea in a "real" ship, as the cruiser-destroyer set called them. Carriers, and, indeed, the whole idea that naval aviation would amount to anything, were dismissed as a pipe dream by the big-ship, big-gun clique: bunch of hotshots zooming around, bragging about their wings of gold as if they could make a difference in a real shooting war.

I had the sense that the Pearl Harbor disaster had put a massive hole in that construct. Six Japanese carriers had slogged their way through the far north Pacific in December, under weather conditions which any experienced Pacific Ocean mariner knew were simply atrocious. We would later learn that they'd left a cargo ship anchored back in Japan, stuffed with actual radio transmitters taken from the carriers, manned by radiomen from the carriers, themselves. As the Jap fleet left for Hawaii, Admiral Yamamoto told them to talk, but sparingly, as if they were afraid of being intercepted. Then they were to go silent. Then one of them was to transmit, but quit in mid-transmission, as if they'd been yelled at. Then they all went silent again, and while the American radio direction-finding nets were still going nuts trying to figure it all out, the six radio-silent carriers appeared out of the squalls and the December fog above Midway Island to launch a massive strike.

That's what carriers did: strike. Our battleships were their objective. Even the Japs apparently were still in thrall to their battlewagons. I imagined there were a lot of hurt feelings at very senior levels in our Navy just now. I later heard a story that the commander of the Pacific Fleet had been standing at his office window, watching the immolation of his battleship force, when a spent bullet plinked through the window and hit him in the chest, bouncing off his tunic. Later he was reported to have said, I wish it had killed me. Just like those six carriers had killed off forever more the notion that the sacred battleships, not those ugly carriers, were the queens of the sea. All of us aviators were of course horrified by what had happened at Pearl Harbor, and yet, I was willing to bet that at least some of us harbored an I-told-you-so somewhere in our breast. Although: even as an ensign, I knew better than to say anything like that out loud.

The next morning I woke up to find that we were at sea. *Enterprise* was so big that someone in the wardroom had had to tell me we were at sea.

FOUR

That someone was my roommate, Ensign Chuck Snead. He'd been aboard for two months now and thus was an "old" hand, although still technically a nugget. He laughed when he saw my surprise.

"Happens to everybody," he said. "Even in shitty weather, this big beast doesn't move around much."

"Where we headed?" I asked.

He shrugged his shoulders. "We'll find out at morning brief in the ready room. The word is that we're going out for CarQuals for a couple days, then back into Pearl to refuel and pick up some more planes. SBD Three-A's, I'm told. You landed on a big-deck yet?"

"Have not," I replied. "But I figure if I could land on the training decks, this oughta be a piece of cake."

He rolled his eyes and attacked his scrambled eggs.

"Okay, okay," I said. "What'd I say wrong?"

He wiped his face with his napkin and then poured us both some more coffee. A steward came by and relieved us of our plates.

"In one sense, you're right. In good viz, calm seas, it's a piece'a cake. They call it a big-deck for a reason. But here's the thing. We've got almost ninety birds on this ship. So launching and landing is a really complex dance up there on the flight deck: spotting the guys preparing to go off; recovering the guys coming back *and* getting them out of the way of the next guy in the pattern? That requires precision flying. Launching, well, you go when they tell you to. Landing, on the other hand, means you get called in to a specific landing slot. You don't dawdle, you don't delay, you fly downwind, turn onto final, and get your bird down. You have about ninety seconds to do that before the next bird is on final right behind you."

"Ninety seconds."

"Yeah," he said. "It's not like the training command, where they wait until the nugget gets the setup right and then lands the thing. And another thing: the LSO is in charge. You set the plane up for the landing, but it's the LSO who decides whether or not you will actually land or go around."

The landing signal officer, known as Paddles, was an experienced carrier aviator who stood at the back of the carrier flight deck and watched your approach. He held what looked like oversized Ping-Pong paddles in his hands, festooned with brightly colored ribbons so the approaching pilot could see them, and gestured with them to correct the approaching pilot's altitude, attitude, and speed as he closed on the flight deck from astern. The pilot could see the deck and analyze his approach on the invisible glide slope leading down to the arresting wires. The LSO could see the approach *and* whether or not the pilot was anywhere near that invisible glide slope. What looked like a perfect approach from the pilot's point of view might look like a mid-deck crash well beyond the arresting wires to the LSO.

"Paddles is king," Chuck said. "If he waves you off, you firewall the throttle and go around. You disregard his instructions, even if you make a perfect landing, they'll take your wings."

"But—"

"No buts, Bobby. That's because Paddles is in direct comms with the Air Boss up in PriFly. *He* may know something about the deck you don't, like there's a plane stuck on the roll-out area. You land, you'll collide with that plane and kill you, the other pilot, and the arresting gear crew."

"Well, yeah, they taught us that in flight school and advanced. *Always* take a wave-off. But there must be circumstances where—"

"No, there aren't. And that's because there will be lots of aircraft up there in the pattern. When's the last time you ever flew with ninety aircraft?"

"Um, never?"

"There you go." He looked at his watch, which reminded me I *had* to go buy a watch in the ship's store. "Time to hit the ready room," he said.

Two hours later I was strapped into a brand-new Dauntless model 3A dive bomber, waiting for a signal to start the engine. Sitting behind me in place of the gunner was the Bombing Six flight officer, the third most senior officer in the squadron after the CO and the exec. He was Lieutenant William C. Quantrill, from the class of 1937. When he'd introduced himself I'd done a double take. When he saw it, he said, yes, I am, and then launched into his briefing for the training we were going to do that morning. He was black-haired, eagle-eyed, and sported a hatchet-shaped nose. Chuck Snead, my roommate, had told me to watch my p's and q's around Quantrill. As flight officer, he was directly responsible for the professional qualifications of every pilot in the squadron. When he's around, Chuck had told me, everything you do—and say—is under inspection.

Quantrill was flying back seat today because I'd never landed on a fleet carrier before. I had many hours of advanced training, both in field carrier landing practice and also aboard some of our older proto-carriers. Flight school had involved mostly biplanes, but advanced training let us fly the early models of the actual Dauntless dive bomber. Today's hop was going to be pretty straightforward. Take off, circle the carrier once at 2,000 feet, get into the landing pattern, and then land. Taxi forward, set up for

launch, and do it all again. There were ten of us flying this morning. My earphones crackled.

Pilots, start your engines.

Immediately my plane's aircrew appeared in front of my plane
and gave me the signal to make sure the starting circuit was off
and then to show them both my hands. That way they could be
sure the engine wouldn't actually start until they'd done their
bearing-wash turns, where they walked the big prop around twice
to ensure all the engine bearings were wet with oil. Lieutenant
Quantrill and I went through the pre-start checklist, and then I
fired her up. The Dauntless had a 1,000-horsepower engine; when
you started that mill you knew you had your hands full.

We were first to go. As I turned up the engine while standing
on the brakes I saw that the airspeed indicator was showing almost 50 knots. Perfect. The shooter gave me the signal, I released
the brakes, and then we were off the bow and climbing to the
right. I cleaned her up and then climbed to 2,000 feet. Out of the
corner of my eye I saw the next plane launch and follow us up into
the pattern.

"Continue outbound for five miles and then start your landing checklist," Quantrill ordered. Once again he played the part
of my gunner and read me through the list. Wheels, flaps, heat,
mixture, barometer, hook, and a final engine instrument scan.
When I reported checklist complete he told me to turn left, set us
up in the approach pattern, and then land. The Dauntless almost
landed itself with that stiff wind coming over the bow. I was proud
to notice that the LSO mostly just stood there, watching my approach with nothing much to say. After dropping the arresting
wire, I followed the signals of the wing-walkers and headed back
up to the bow.

The second circuit was much like the first, with only one cor-
rection from the LSO. Once on deck we taxied to one side of the
flight deck and shut down. I slid the canopies back, suddenly aware
that I was sweating. Landing on a carrier is a tense experience, but

the Navy had cleverly reduced a lot of that anxiety with its check-lists and standard procedures. By the time you walked through all of that you were out of time to be scared. You just landed. But that didn't mean nobody was watching. Everyone from the captain on the bridge and the Air Boss up in the tower, to the LSO, all the way down to the deck crews watched and graded every landing, every time. They even stationed two cameramen up on the back of the island to film each landing. The old hands would tell you that if you saw one of them jump up and begin filming, you were doing something wrong.

"That was okay," Quantrill announced as he unstrapped. I was too busy watching one of the other nuggets get a wave-off and execute a go-around, but then I realized I'd been given a compliment. "Okay" was the top grade. I thanked him.

"Don't take it personally," he said. "These are perfect land-launch conditions. That said, you've obviously got the feel for it. Your next job is to pick your gunner."

The plane captain slapped the wing to get my attention. Time to disembark, Nugget, so we can get this bird struck down below and out of the way. I realized Quantrill had already climbed out and was walking aft to pick up his next check-ride. I nearly fell out of the cockpit after catching my flight suit on something. The crew waited patiently for me to figure it out. Once I got down on the deck, the plane captain asked me what Quantrill had had to say.

"Okay," I reported.

"There you go, Ensign. He gives maybe three okays a year. Go that way, and watch for props."

That afternoon I did two more hops, this time with one of the more experienced pilots riding the back seat. We launched at sun-down, flew around for a while, and then came back aboard just as darkness settled on the ocean. Compared to the training carriers, the deck lighting system on *Enterprise* looked like a Hollywood opening. I greased it in again, dropped the hook, and headed forward for the second round. By the time I got back astern of the ship, they'd turned the lights down to wartime condition. No more brightly lit glide path, but rather a dim stream of red lights extending down the deck. The brightest thing I could see was the LSO paddle-set. For a moment I was taken aback as I came in at 110 knots, intently watching both my lineup and the LSO's paddles. It looked good, but then it didn't. The LSO furiously waved his paddles and I applied power and bent the plane to the left, over and away from the flight deck. I flew out front for five miles to gather my wits, and then turned around for another try. The plane's radio intercom crackled on.

"Your sink rate was too high," my back-seater said. "Use power to control your descent, not the stick. Cut when Paddles tells you to. Let's do the checklist again."

My second approach was much better and we banged down on the deck like we were supposed to. We taxied over to the deck edge to clear the landing area. My back-seater said not to worry about it. "You lose three-quarters of your visual cues at night," he told me. "Think of a night landing as an instrument, not a visual approach, with the LSO's paddles being the primary instrument, and it'll get easier."

I was reminded of something one of my flight instructors had told me: one aw-shit undoes 10,000 attaboys.

I make this sound like Bombing Six was the only squadron training and qualifying nuggets. Not true. Torpedo Six, Scouting Six, and Fighting Six were all in the same boat, literally, anxious to deck-qualify their new guys. The Big E stayed out for five days, hurling nuggets into the sky and hoping to get most of them back aboard. I had thought we'd have been roaring west to repay the Japanese for their treachery on December 7th, but then something happened that made things clearer. Bombing Six had the day off, so I'd gone up to vultures' row, way up on the island structure, to watch flight ops. It was amazing to observe the carefully controlled chaos of the flight deck, with planes landing, re-spotting, launching, or being struck below on one of the elevators. Today Fighting Six, our fighter squadron, was putting their nuggets through their paces.

It was a perfect day for flight ops: a brisk, 25-knot true wind, light whitecaps, and no appreciable swell to make the ship pitch or yaw. Our three plane-guard destroyers were happily blasting sheets of blue-white spray over their decks as they kept up with us at 25 knots. Two cruisers were nearby, sliding through the light chop as if it wasn't even there. With 50 knots of relative wind streaming over the bow, a launch should have been a piece of cake. It was, until one of our fighters, an F6F Hellcat, wound up to full power, released the brakes, and bolted down the deck and into the air, just like he was supposed to. Except one second later, his engine stopped. Just stopped, its propeller blades snapping to a rigid freeze. The pilot probably was still trying to comprehend what had happened when his Hellcat dropped like a stone directly into the path of the oncoming carrier, disappearing without a trace. They probably tried to turn the big ship to keep from running over him, but a carrier at 25 knots doesn't turn on a dime. In fact, it doesn't *begin* to turn for almost a third of a mile. I found out later that main engineering control had called the bridge to report a brief vibration on the two port shafts. That did not bear thinking about. The three destroyers searched our wake for an hour, but we all knew they were mostly going through the motions. The decision was made to end the flight qualifications and go back into Pearl.

That afternoon our skipper, Lieutenant Channing Cox, got the whole squadron together for what turned out to be my first all-officers' meeting. We nuggets had seen the CO but not had any interaction with him as yet other than a formal welcome to the squadron. He was a pleasant-faced man with prematurely gray hair. He was polite, reserved, and apparently a man of few words. When he did speak people tended to pay attention as my roomie pointed out. Cox was an expert in the grim trade of dive-bombing and had won several all-Navy bombing competitions, principally by holding his dive down to 2,000 feet before releasing. Fleet doctrine at the time called for release at 4,000 feet. We nuggets kept our distance because we had the impression that he was waiting to find out from the flight officer which ones of us were going to make the grade.

Usually the entire air group flew off to land ashore before the carrier went into port, but not this time. Lieutenant Cox walked up to the podium in the Bombing Six ready room accompanied by our exec, Lieutenant Francis X. Corrigan, and Lieutenant Quantrill, our stern-faced flight officer. The usual ready-room chatter was absent after what had happened earlier. The skipper surprised us.

"Let us stand and pray," he announced.

We all stood and bowed our heads, not quite sure of what was going to happen next.

"Almighty Father, we pray for the soul of Ensign Croswell, lost today to an engine failure during flight training operations. He did nothing wrong. His engine failed, as engines sometimes do. We commit his soul and his valiant memory to your care and compassion. Amen."

We stood for a moment of silence. Then he ordered seats and continued.

"When you went through flight training, you saw operational accidents. That's the nature of flight training because you are learning how to defy an irresistible force called gravity. That same force lives out here, too. I don't know what caused that mishap today and we may never know. Maybe there'll be some useful film. But either way, here's the important lesson: I believe Ensign Croswell was *surprised* by what happened today. Why? Because when his engine locked up, he pulled his nose up, so high in fact that he flipped over backwards and sliced straight in. You will remember your instructors back at P-Cola taking you up for a syllabus hop and then, when you least expected it, *especially* if you were focused hard on the lesson of the day, he'd snatch the throttle back to idle to simulate an engine failure. And what's the first thing you were taught to always do? Push the nose down to maintain airspeed while you figured out what to do and where to land if you had to.

"An engine failure will always happen at the worst possible time, whether through mechanical spite or the efforts of Zero trying to shoot it and you to pieces. So you *always* reserve a little bit of brainpower, no matter what you are doing in the air, to prepare yourself for an engine failure. Our dive bombers can take a lot of punishment, especially these new models. They have some armor protection for the crew and those new self-sealing gas tanks. But that irresistible force called gravity never goes away. We even make use of it when we try to bomb ships, which is why we're called *dive* bombers. *Always* be prepared for that mill to fail on you, like right at the moment you pull out from a bombing run and every ship in the Jap formation is shooting at you."

He paused to scan the room, especially we new guys sitting in nugget row, like misbehaving children being seated in the very first row in church.

"I'm not telling you be afraid of your airplane. I *am* telling you to review your training and first-response actions every time you're doing *any*thing except sightseeing. Especially as you approach one of those worst-case scenarios for an engine failure, like landing, launching, bombing, or dogfighting. Here endeth the lesson. Lieutenant Quantrill will now tell you where we're going and why."

The skipper stepped down off the stage and sat down. Quantrill reached behind him and pulled the curtains apart. The wall behind was covered in one big ocean chart, with several small islands scattered all over it. I couldn't make out the map's scale, but it looked huge.

"We're going into port tonight to refuel and reprovision," he announced. "Then we're leaving tomorrow night to head for the central Pacific to an area known as the mandated islands. We'll go in company with the *Yorktown* to, at long last, take the fight to the Japs. Admiral Halsey will be in command so it won't be boring. *Saratoga* was supposed to go but she ate a Jap torpedo last week and is laid up in Pearl. This briefing will be just an overview. Things like what 'mandated islands' means. Later this afternoon the air intel people will be here with detailed briefs and threat assessments. No one will be going ashore tonight. So: let's take a smoke break, get some coffee, and then we'll get to it. Ten minutes, please."

While Quantrill conferred with the exec and the skipper, the rest of us took care of head calls, fresh coffee, and cigarettes if needed, which included almost everybody. When we reassembled, we nuggets found ourselves the proud owners of thin clipboards, on which we were supposed to take notes. Three hours later we all had hand cramps and really thick clipboards. There was simply too damned much stuff to get our feeble brains around. When the skipper finally called time and sent us to chow we were instructed to leave our boards behind—they could not leave the ready room. Cheer up, he told us. You won't have to memorize all that good dope. We smiled in relief until he told us why. It would all change by tomorrow, and every day right up to the day we went after the Jap bases far to the west. Oh, yay.

After chow we went down and out onto the hangar deck for a smoke and some fresh air. The ship was so big that we hadn't even been aware that *Enterprise* had entered port and was now alongside the Ten-Ten dock, busily on-loading truckloads of stuff. As long as we stayed out of the way of all the whirling forklifts, bomb-trains, and cargo elevators, we were allowed to hang out. We'd all looked once across the harbor at the silhouettes of blasted ships illuminated by a hundred welding torches. Just once, though. The sight still made us sick to our stomachs and we unconsciously blew cigarette smoke at each other just to hide the persistent stench from the harbor water.

FIVE

The next week at sea offered a blistering operational pace as we headed west to the Marshall and Gilbert Islands. The entire air group spent its mornings doing flight training, the afternoons in intel briefs, and nights practicing night landings until almost midnight. Fighting Six suffered another accident, but this time the pilot, who was not a nugget, got the plane down into a good ditch and one of the destroyers picked him up, shaken, chastened, but alive. I felt my own confidence growing as I went through all the legs of the training program and I really fell in love with the Dauntless model 3A. She was a powerful bird and each launch felt like she wanted to go out there and kill something. Responsive, protective, stable, a dream to fly and land, with those 1,000 horses in the mill, big flaps, and the knowledge that we were sitting in front of some armor. It was also comforting to know that our gasoline tanks, unlike those on a Zero, probably wouldn't turn into fireballs at the first hit.

I had finally been assigned my gunner, an aviation communications specialist second class by the name of Bill Perry. Each Dauntless carried a crew of two: the pilot up front, and right behind him, his rear-facing gunner, who manned a twin .30-caliber machine gun mount and also handled all the long-haul communications, checklists, and anything else I might need help with. The

Dauntless had two sets of guns: two .50-caliber machine guns embedded in the nose and that twin thirty stinger in the back, which made life dangerous for any fighters who got on our tail. The twin thirty had a firing cutout which prevented the gunner from shooting our own tail off, but otherwise he had a wide field of fire.

Our current mission was to hit the Jap bases in the central Pacific. It wasn't going to win the war, but it would put them on notice that as long as we had carriers, none of their bases were safe. The islands were small and scattered, with some being nothing larger than a circular coral reef surrounding an anchorage suitable for seaplanes. Others were large enough for an airfield and possessed harbors deep enough for cruisers and destroyers. Given the vastness of the Pacific Ocean, *any* harbor was a godsend: a place to shut down, make repairs, refuel, rearm, and sleep, without having to worry about enemy submarines or high seas. Our intel people said the Japs had fortified most of the islands with heavy anti-aircraft guns and even fighter planes. This was going to be no cakewalk, but our blood was up. Just the sight and smell of Pearl Harbor was enough to make every one of us want to go out there and kill as many Japs as we could find.

On strike day, we held reveille at 0300, followed by a breakfast of steak and eggs. One last intel briefing and then we manned up in the dark. Our planes had been spotted on the flight deck the night before, arranged in order of takeoff, with full fuel tanks and a mix of bombs hung underneath. The standard Bombing Six Dauntless load for ship attack was a 1,000-pounder centerline and two 100-pound incendiaries on either wing. Fighting Six's Wildcats would come with us to deal with any Jap fighters who came up, while Torpedo Six bombers would be ready to go in and attack any anchored warships. Since we knew where the islands were, Scouting Six's Dauntlesses, which were normally reserved for long-range find-the-enemy missions, were each armed with two 500-pounders. Between the two carriers, we were sending in nearly sixty planes against five island bases.

For once the weather cooperated, handing us relatively clear skies, albeit with winds from the east. That meant the two carriers had to steam away from the target to get the planes off and back on. I thought it took much too long to assemble the strike group once airborne. The first to launch, the fighters, had to wait for as long as an hour for all the rest of the planes to get off and into formation, wasting precious gas. On the other hand, I couldn't have told you how to do it any differently. The strike couldn't head for the target until everybody was assembled in formation. Still, with Bombing Six going second, we seemed to spend an awful lot of time boring holes in the sky waiting for the rest of the gaggle.

The air group formations finally settled out on a western heading. The target islands were 120 miles away. Torpedo bombers stayed relatively low, at 8,000 feet. Dive bombers and the Scouting Six formation flew at 15,000 feet, and the fighters cruised at 20,000 feet. Somewhere to the south of us, the *Yorktown* air group was also en route. In theory the Japanese should have no warning that an American carrier air strike was inbound. That said, we soon got a reminder of what some German general said back in 1880: no plan survives first contact with the enemy's main force. Or the vagaries of open ocean navigation, he might have added.

The first island atoll that came into view was empty. Absolutely nothing there. Apparently our skipper had taken us to the wrong island. Same deal with the second island. Our redoubtable leader turned northwest, which brought us to a much larger island. This one had an airfield. It wasn't much of an airfield, but there were planes parked along the taxiways, and they weren't ours. There were also seven of those big *Kawanishi* flying boats anchored out in the harbor, as well as a half-dozen transport ships. No warships, however, but that was okay with me. For the first time in my life, I was going to get to roll in on an actual Japanese target, along with eight of my squadron mates.

The skipper led the way down and put his 1,000-pounder right alongside a tanker, which bucked, rolled, and then caught fire.

The second guy down was Tom Whitley, one of the other nuggets. He put his 1,000-pounder on the same tanker, but his bomb *hit* it. The ship exploded in a balloon of fire. The third guy down was Quantrill, whose big boy went wild, exploding in the water a quarter mile from a freighter. I was the fourth one rolling in. I chose a fat freighter anchored close to shore. As I pulled out, Bill Perry shouted into the intercom. My crowd-pleaser had hit the front end of the freighter and blown away one-third of the ship. I pulled out of the dive, holding a deep breath against the g-forces, and looked around for the skipper and the planes that had gone before me. I finally found them up and to my left as they circled back to begin strafing runs against those *Kawanishis*.

A sudden cracking shock wave startled me as I circled back around to follow the boss back up and then over and down to tear up the seaplanes. We'd caught the Japs flat-footed, but they didn't stay that way very long. AA bursts were peppering the air around us, close enough that I couldn't disregard them. The little island was covered in winking red flashes, and only after three more hurtful bangs in quick succession did I react and start jinking. One final ear-cracking bang right behind us caused Bill to yell and then start cussing but by then the skipper was slanting back down from up-sun to make a strafing run on that clutch of seaplanes, using his forward-firing .50-calibers. We all followed suit, leaving five of the seven flying boats aflame. The other two had managed to light off a couple of engines and were trying desperately to get airborne, which is when Fighting Six showed up and smoked the both of them.

The skipper then made a high banking turn and headed for the airfield, where we could see Jap planes already taxiing to the end of the runway in a frantic effort to get airborne and come after us. Most of us still had our 100-pound incendiaries on the wings, so we came down on the field strafing and dropping those onto hangars and parked planes. I toggled mine too late and put them onto a pier near the end of the runway, where they did absolutely nothing. By then, however, several Jap fighters were climbing after us, and the Zero had one of the fastest climbing rates in the business. Fortunately Fighting Six attacked them from above as they strained to get some tactical altitude. That turned into a fur-ball of slashing fighters, ugly black bursts of AA fire, tracers burning up the air, and some of the combatants pitching down into the sea in huge balls of gasoline fire. That was the signal for we dive bombers to get the hell out of Dodge and head back to the carrier. We could see columns of smoke rising from distant atolls, so Scouting Six and Torpedo Six must have done some damage, too.

During the time it had taken us to get to our targets, the carrier had been advancing west at 27 knots, so the trip back took much less time. In theory the entire air group was supposed to have joined up for the flight back, but once the Jap hornets' nest woke up, discretion absolutely became the better part of valor. I turned on the homing beacon receiver and got a solid tone, joined up on the skipper at 15,000 feet, and only then noticed we were shy two SBDs. I asked Perry if he could tell who was missing, but he didn't answer. I asked him again and then swiveled my head around to see what he was doing. I saw blood spatter on his section of the canopy. He appeared to be taking a nap, his eyes closed and his body relaxed. Much *too* relaxed. His clipboard notes and some of the nav charts were whirling around his cockpit like trash on a city street. I realized there must have been one hell of a hole back there. All the excitement and adrenaline rush of the attack drained away and I felt a wave of nausea as I realized he was probably gone.

I landed in turn with a lead weight on my heart. As soon as I was clear of the wire I signaled to the deck crew that I needed a medic. They pushed my plane to the deck edge and then two hospitalmen were scrambling up my wings. I nodded in the direction of the back seat. A moment later, the senior medic looked back at me and shook his head. Once I was down on the flight deck I was shown a two-foot-wide hole in the hull of the aircraft just to one side of the main keel girder. Another foot to the left and that shell would have blown the tail right off. One of Perry's bloody feet was dangling into the hole, minus his flight boot. The entire underside of the aircraft was slick with black blood. I just stood there, speechless, when a third medic grabbed my arm and escorted me away from the plane. He headed me forward to the island and the ready room, asking me if I was hurt. I said no, I was okay, physically, anyway. Good, he said. Because you're all going back. Halsey wants a second strike.

Good for Halsey, I thought, as the hospitalman showed me into the ready room before disappearing back out onto the flight deck. Quantrill caught the expression on my face and came over.

"What happened?"

"Lost my gunner to AA fire," I said. "I need to make a head call. Then I want to sit down."

After taking care of business I went back to the ready room and dropped into one of the nugget chairs, glad to just close my eyes. I couldn't believe it: Perry was dead. The other pilots in the ready room were talking about the strike, some bragging, some cursing, some just babbling with excitement at having conducted the squadron's first wartime strike. Lots of "Remember Pearl Harbor, you bastards" and stuff like that. Somebody sat down next to me. I opened my eyes. It was Lieutenant Cox, the skipper.

"Tough luck," he said. "Perry was good troops."

"I hardly got to know him," I said wonderingly.

"You hardly got to know the other two nuggets, either," he said. "Now they're officially missing."

That was another shock. I tried to cycle up their names and couldn't. One of them was my *roommate*, for Christ's sake. What was his name? Chuck Snead, that was his name. *Damn!*

"You did well out there," the skipper said. "Good bomb work. Good formation work. You smacked that one freighter really good."

I nodded. "Thank you, sir," I mumbled.

He looked at his watch. "Halsey's ordered another strike. The

Japs will be fully alerted this time, so I gotta ask: you up for another go?"

I stared at him, wide-eyed. Just like that? Your gunner's dead. Your roommate's missing. No biggie. We'll get you another gunner and another airplane. Ready for round two, there, Ace?

Amazing myself, I nodded and said yes, sir.

"Attaboy," he said. "Think of it this way: a second strike is a chance for revenge. Even *more* revenge. You need a drink?"

I shook my head, remembering reveille on the *Oklahoma*. "No, sir," I said. "I need a clear head."

"Okay, Nugget. Oh, and by the way: welcome to the first team. Brief in ten minutes."

He got up and hurried off while I tried to collect my thoughts. I felt another wave of cold nausea as it all sank in. My gunner had bled to death without saying a word and I had been oblivious. Two other aircrews were simply missing. There was a chance that we might get some seaplanes out into the area to search for them, but even I knew that wasn't really going to happen. We'd been deep into Injun territory. If a seaplane *did* find them, it wasn't going to be one of ours. And if the Japs did pick them up, they'd interrogate them and then cut their heads off.

My reverie was interrupted by the general quarters alarm and then the Big E began to accelerate, her massive bulk settling to one side as she turned back into the wind. Everybody stopped talking in the ready room. The 1MC, the ship's announcing system, came on to report enemy aircraft inbound and for all pilots to man their planes. There was a general rush out to the flight deck, the intel brief forgotten, which I joined until I realized I didn't have a plane. I stood there, pressed right up against the sheer steel sides of the island, and then jumped when the five-inch batteries opened up. Engines were starting up in big blue clouds of smoke out on the flight deck and the first planes, fighters, were trundling forward to the launch position on the flight deck. A hand grabbed my arm in all the noise.

"You Mister Steele?" he shouted.

I nodded and he pointed to an SBD that had just come up from the hangar bay. The message was clear: There's your bird. I ran over to the plane where three flight-deck crewmen were hustling to tow it clear of the elevator. She was sporting a 1,000-pounder centerline, but no 100-pounders out on the wings. I nearly collided with a heavily built, redheaded enlisted man in a flight suit who arrived at the wing root at the same time I did. The noise of aircraft engines by now was overwhelming; we both had to duck as another SBD taxied by, its wingtip three feet over our heads. Both the fore and after five-inch guns were going full bore by now, adding to the din. The redhead gave me an after-you signal, so I scrambled up onto the wing and into the cockpit. He was right behind me, lifting himself awkwardly into the gunner's cockpit. There was no time for checklists: the flight deck guys were frantically making the signal for crank-it-up, and I did. The engine bearings were apparently on their own this time. Moments later, with both of us still strapping in, we were taxiing up towards the bow. I caught a momentary glimpse of the forward five-inch mounts spitting fire out towards the starboard bow but then I had to stand on the brakes to avoid colliding with the plane in front of me. One minute later we went howling off the bow.

I wasn't sure who was up or even on what frequency, so I followed the guy in front of me who was also sporting a 1,000-pounder centerline. The fighters all appeared to be scrambling northwest, where the sky was filling with black puffs from the formation's AA batteries. Pretty soon we rendezvoused with another two SBDs, one of whom flashed us a hand signal with the tactical frequency. We climbed to 15,000 feet, away from all the shooting behind us, and headed due west on slow cruise to let the rest catch up. The skipper joined up a few minutes later and gave everybody a quick, off-the-cuff brief on where we were headed. I never did see any Jap airplanes. Then I remembered my passenger, whom I assumed was flying temporary gunner for me. I switched to intercom.

"Bobby Steele here," I said. "Welcome aboard."

"Rooster W. Baynes, radioman second, at your service, suh," he said in a Southern accent. "We gonna go kill us some Jappers?"

"I certainly hope so," I said. I had barely met all the pilots, so there were lots of the enlisted I didn't know by name. "You done this before?"

"Oh, hell yes, Boss," Rooster said. "At least twice."

I laughed. At least he was game, I thought. "You got me by one," I said. "This is my second real strike. First one didn't end so good."

"I heard about Bill Perry," he said. "Damn shame. Boys said he was good with these here guns."

At that moment the skipper started issuing orders for our formation assignments into two-plane divisions. Then he broadcast corrected navigation data to the target island, whose name was unpronounceable. Rooster got busy with charts and calculations on fuel consumption. I paid attention to my formation flying, noting that the weather was starting to thicken. My division leader was Lem Worth, an aviation chief petty officer out of the NavCad program. At that time, nearly a third of the Big E's pilots were enlisted. Lem took station on the skipper, and I took station on him.

Checklist, I remembered suddenly. You forgot to run your checklist, especially armament. We had about a half hour. I told Rooster what I was doing, and he proceeded to check out his twin .30-caliber machine guns by firing a burst off to one side of the formation, undoubtedly scaring the hell out of the divisions above and below me. I explained to Rooster that we tested guns when ordered to do so, and only armed the big bomb just before we began our dive.

"Got it, Boss."

I ran through my takeoff and bombing checklists while keeping one eye on my division leader. We were flying just south of west through some gathering cumulonimbus cloud formations. I'd missed one item on the takeoff list, which was to cycle the dive brakes. I wouldn't be able to do that while flying tight formation. I was reaching for my canteen when a Zero slashed by the formation's right side, machine guns blazing, just as somebody yelled: Bandits! on the tactical freq. Wide awake now, I nestled in closer to my division lead, wondering where our fighters were. Back at our carrier dealing with *their* bandits. Suddenly my lead got rid of his 1,000-pounder and began a turn to the right. A stream of tracers was starting to envelop him as I turned with him.

"Dive brakes, Boss," Rooster yelled. "Hit the brakes, then smoke the bastard."

It's fighter time, I thought. This was what my two .50-cal. machine guns were for. I pulled the engine power to fifty percent and deployed the dive brakes as we turned together to get away from the Jap fighter. That stream of tracers got uncomfortably close and then, as we slowed sharply, the Zero whipped past me, which allowed me to bank into position behind him and loose a long burst of .50-cal. right at him. I firewalled the throttle, retracted the brakes, and stayed with him. Suddenly I was flying through thick black smoke, and then the Zero mushroomed into a huge ball of orange fire, went inverted, and slanted down towards the sea.

Rooster was cheering me on with a variety of rebel yells, until he stopped abruptly and started shooting at yet another Jap fighter that was making a high side pass on us. I could see Rooster knew his business because he didn't shoot *at* the Jap fighter but out in front of it, directing his stream of bullets on an intercepting arc that shattered the Jap's canopy in a spray of blood. Rooster let out some more rebel yells, but then I realized we were alone. I looked around for my division leader but couldn't find him—or anyone else. I couldn't hear them, either. One moment the Bombing Six freq was a case study in audio pandemonium, the next a scary, static-filled silence. I swiveled my head around but couldn't see anybody else. I checked my altitude: 17,300 feet. We'd been flying at 15,000. All I could see up ahead were huge, ice-white clouds, boiling up towards the edge of the atmosphere, bent on cooking up one big-ass thunderstorm.

And an island. One lonely atoll, bigger than the one we'd hit this morning but not by much. The reef was the usual volcanic circle surrounding bright blue water. With ships.

"Rooster," I called. "I think that's our target."

"Well, hell, Boss, let's go bomb the bastids. Ain't nothin' else to do."

I looked to see where the sun was, which was almost overhead, so it didn't matter from which direction I hit them. I made a 360 sky sweep, hoping to see more bombers, but it looked like we were alone with the thunderclouds. Just then an updraft rocked us pretty bad, so I slipped down to 10,000 feet to get out of the cloud boil-up. There were five or six ships down there, but one bigger than all the rest. From this altitude I couldn't tell what they were, other than they didn't appear to be moving.

Anchored, then. My kinda ship.

"Okay, here we go," I told Rooster. "Feel free to strafe when we pull out."

"Hell with that, I'm gonna strafe in *and* out, Boss. Just like they did at Pearl, remember?"

"Too well, Rooster. Much too well. Here we go."

I reached down and armed the thumper. Then I rolled in, throttling back and extending the dive brakes to stabilize the plane as we dropped down through two miles of increasingly un-settled air. The SBD had a crude telescopic bombsight mounted above the instrument panel. Normally in a ship attack, you had to calculate the lead angle and basically aim ahead of the ship so that the bomb arrived where the ship *would* be, not where it was right now. But if these guys were anchored, and I could see no signs of a wake on my target, then I could aim right at him, which is what I did. Rooster started calling altitude from his bare-bones instrument panel in the gunner's cockpit, while I concentrated on lining up my dive. When he called 2,500 feet I let her go and began my pullout, changing course to the left to make it harder for any AA gunners. I pulled back on the stick and experienced the familiar press of g-forces. I had to be careful here: pull too hard and black out, which meant a crash. Pull too light and you'd hit the water, with the same results.

I thought I felt some AA fire, but then there was a large explosion behind us. Rooster started up with the rebel yells again as I leveled off at 500 feet and began a banking turn to get back upstairs.

"Yee-*haw*, Boss," Rooster shouted. "Had to be an ammo ship. Lookit that, *lookit* that. God damn! Burn, you yellow-bellied cowards. Remember Pearl Harbor, you mangy dog sonsabitches!"

I looked over my shoulder and saw a titanic cloud of smoke and fire, laced with arcs of fiery debris dropping all over the atoll. The cloud was big enough to obscure the harbor and all the ships that were in it. I added power to get the hell out of there, punching through bright white clouds on the way up to cruising altitude. I realized I still hadn't heard anything on the Bombing Six frequency. Where the hell *was* everybody?

"Rooster—that radio working?"

"Yes, suh, I see a—whoops. I lied. No green light. Radio is tits-up, Boss. Sorry."

"Rooster, turn on the homer."

"Homer *is* up, Boss," he announced a moment later. "Mother bears one four five, good tone."

Well, I thought: our mission had been to bomb that harbor, and bomb it we did. So now it was time to go find the Big E. Getting into the pattern with no radio comms might get interesting, though.

SIX

We were intercepted 30 miles out by one of our fighters. I gave him the hand sign for no radio. He rocked his wings, flew ahead of us, and led me safely over and through all those trigger-happy cruisers and destroyers right into the approach pattern. We weren't alone. It looked as if most of the catch-game strike had made it back about twenty minutes before we did. The fighter-biter banked away and headed back to his CAP station. I had plenty of time and gas to go through the landing checklist with Rooster, and then I joined a holding pattern of three SBDs five miles off the carrier's starboard bow. The western horizon behind the carrier was getting darker and darker as all those thunder-bumpers got organized. We were orbiting at 2,000 feet and those storms were probably 30 to 40 miles away, which meant that their heads were bumping up against the stratosphere. Fortunately the land-launch course for max winds over the deck was still almost due east.

My landing was uneventful, although I was surprised to see quite a bit of white fire-fighting foam on the port side of the flight deck, and what looked like some big gouges in the wooden flight deck. The flight deck crew directed me to a spot over on the starboard side and then signaled for me to shut her down. Once in the ready room we got the full story from the other pilots. Formation discipline had become the first casualty when the Jap fighters jumped the unprotected Bombing Six gaggle. The SBD is a bomber, not a fighter. Doctrine called for dumping any heavy ordnance if the bandit problem was bad enough, just as my division lead and most of the others had done. Apparently I was the only one who'd held on to his bomb and actually used it.

Rooster and I huddled with the post-strike intel officers and told our story. We were claiming two Zeros and an ammo ship. They'd have to take that on faith as the SBD didn't have a gun camera forward like fighters did. Once the ship secured from flight quarters the skipper called a quick meeting. We'd had one loss, one of the NavCad pilots and his gunner, who'd been seen to crash and blow up in the ocean after two Zeros shot it up. Otherwise, the SBDs had given good account of themselves, knocking down several Zeros.

"That's a pretty good showing," the skipper began. "Considering we had no fighter cover. They were all back here around *Enterprise*, fighting off a formation of Bettys. One of the Bettys lost half a wing and was on fire when he elected to car-qual onboard the Big E. That's all the foam you saw topside. CAG was wounded in the left forearm and leg, but he's determined to get back in the cockpit, and knowing him, he will."

"Are we gonna try another strike?" one of the guys asked.

"Negative; it seems that the *Lexington* took two torpedoes from a Jap sub. She's still afloat and under her own power, but you saw what those Jap torpedoes can do back in Pearl, so she's probably Bremerton bound. *Saratoga* is getting fixed up in Pearl, so for right now, it's the Big E and *Yorktown* to cover the whole Pacific.

"There was one bright spot: Nugget Bobby Steele here," he said, pointing at me. "Flamed one Zero, and his gunner made a second Zero's canopy turn all red for a possible. Then he ducked into a cloud and took his thousand-pounder to Malawit atoll and parked it in an anchored ammunition ship, which blew up in spectacular fashion. Well done, Nugget."

There were noises of approval from my squadron mates, grateful that someone had managed to uphold the honor of Bombing Six on what was supposed to be an air group strike. I reminded myself to make sure that Rooster received appropriate recognition. I would have never thought of that hit-the-dive-brakes tactic, even though we'd been taught that back in flight school. I had to admit it: I'd clutched up when those tracers began to envelop my cockpit.

The post-attack meeting broke up and we all headed for the wardroom, not having eaten anything since very early this morning. Now that we were at war, the wardroom remained open on a round-the-clock basis and that night was no exception. Lieutenant Cox stopped by my table as I was finishing up.

"I meant that 'well done,'" he said. "It allowed me to report that we sank at least one substantial ship, which was enough to mollify the admiral. How'd you manage that?"

"A Zero got on my tail. I deployed the dive brakes and cut power, which forced the Zero to bust past me and then I flamed him. After that, I couldn't find anybody in all those big clouds, but I could see an island, so I decided to head for that. There were some ships and they were all anchored, so I chose the biggest one and got lucky."

"Dive brakes," the skipper said. "That's fighter stuff. They teaching that in SBD operational training?"

"They are, but I kinda froze up. It was my gunner, Baynes, who yelled for dive brakes."

"*The* Rooster Baynes?" the skipper asked. I nodded.

"That boy is a genu-wine piece of work," he said with a smile. "You want him for your permanent gunner?"

"If that's possible, yes, sir, I would. Why's he called Rooster?"

"Go on liberty with him one time. You'll see. Heavy-duty skirt chaser. He still do that rebel yell bullshit?"

"Often," I said. "And loud, too."

"I wish the Japs could hear that just once," he said. "I'll see if I can get him for you. Again, good job today."

I went back to my stateroom, suddenly dead tired. Chuck's stuff was all still there. I wondered what they did in this situation. He hadn't been declared killed in action, just missing. There was a knock on the door. It was Yeoman Sykes, the squadron admin officer.

"We've got word Mister Snead is officially MIA," he announced. "When you get time can you gather up all his stuff? You'll know what's yours and what was his better than anyone else. We'll come get it when you're ready."

"What happens to it?" I asked.

"Gets boxed up and stored aboard until we get definite word. On a regular strike they'd have had some ships looking, but that deal today, well . . ."

"So if they do get recovered, it's gonna be by the Japs?"

He nodded, a dismal expression on his face.

"Right," I said. "I'll call you."

"Thanks, sir. Sorry."

"Me, too," I said.

The next morning we were still a ways out of Pearl, so I had time after breakfast to gather up Snead's personal effects and cram it all into his seabag. The word around the breakfast table was that there was no word. One guy said that translated to no chance, and then looked embarrassed for saying it. I realized I'd have been one of the missing if it hadn't been for Rooster. I went back to the stateroom and called Sykes. He came and got Snead's seabag. I told him I wanted to write Rooster up for a commendation. He told me he'd get me the paperwork. Neither of us could think of anything else to say, so he just left.

I sat down and jotted off a note to my folks back in Omaha since we'd have mail going off in Pearl. Home seemed a million miles away after my first taste of war. I was born in Omaha, Nebraska, the second of three children. My father was a mechanical engineer at the Union Pacific Omaha Works, which was a major repair and overhaul facility for the railroad. We lived in north

Omaha, not far from Fort Omaha, where Custer had lived before he went west to teach the Indians a lesson. My upbringing was pretty traditional, attending local public schools, participating in Scouts, and, once old enough, accompanying my father and older brother on pheasant-hunting trips out near a town called Hastings. My older brother, Geoff, went east to college, where after a year he succumbed to the ravages of the influenza outbreak of 1934, the year I graduated from high school.

I had always assumed that I'd follow my dad into the railroad engineering business, starting at the bottom as he had done, but there was a depression on and one of the ways the railroads were hanging on was by cutting their employee levels to the bone. My father was by then a senior engineer so his job remained relatively safe. He solved my problem by sending me to Creighton College, a Jesuit school, to get a start on an engineering degree. I'd always been good in math and science, so at first it was a good fit, but after a year of the mandatory review courses for the benefit of all the freshmen who were *not* that good in math and science, I was bored. I'd been dating a pretty girl from Council Bluffs at the time, and her older brother had won an appointment to the U.S. Naval Academy. Being from the Midwest, I was completely ignorant of what the Navy was all about, but I met him when he came home for Christmas leave and found out that Annapolis was quite the place.

Long story short, I went through the admissions process and then the political appointment winnowing, both of which were by competitive examination. I ended up as the first alternate for our congressman's appointment quota, and when the principal failed the physical examination, I became a lowly plebe, the purposefully degrading term for a first-year midshipman. Everything about the academy was foreign to me except the high academic standards and a truly nose-to-the-grindstone work ethic demanded by the academy. That was nothing new for me, having enjoyed a year under the gentle tutelage of the Jesuits. One-third of my entering class had "bilged out" by the end of my second year, either by resigning because they hated it or because they'd failed on the engineering-heavy academic side. Those who remained became a fairly homogenous cadre of prospective naval officers, known as the class of 1939. Prior classes during the Depression had had the option of graduating but delaying acceptance of a commission. The Navy changed that policy when the war clouds gathering over Europe began to look like a repeat of 1914, especially after Hitler revealed his ambitions by invading Poland.

I had opted for the aviation career path upon graduation and was tentatively accepted, but there was a catch. I had to complete that required two years of sea duty first. Naval aviation was still the bastard child in the minds of many senior officers. More maddening to the battleship navy was the fact that naval aviation was beginning to absorb serious budget money, which they thought would have been much better spent on yet another battleship. Going aboard my sea tour cruiser was an exercise in being very circumspect about my future flying career. The aviation board members who'd approved me for flight training actually told me to say things like: I haven't made up my mind yet, because I want to see what the "real" fleet is like before I commit. That would ensure that your ship would treat you as a prospective career surface guy and act accordingly.

I did enjoy my sea tour in *Helena*, although not much of it was spent at sea because in 1939 there was little or no money to send the fleet to sea. There were a couple of annual fleet exercises, but otherwise, the big ships spent most of the year swinging to the hook or moored to concrete buoys in the various ports. In sharp contrast was the local Army airfield, where we saw planes going up every day of the week. To get a squadron of battleships to sea cost millions; to send up a biplane for a training hop cost about twenty-five dollars in aviation gasoline, if that.

In the spring of 1941 I received orders to report to Pensacola and began flight training. It hadn't been quite two years, but there were straws in the wind about what might be coming for the United States in Europe, and those straws were glowing, every one. From within the military establishment we could see that President Roosevelt was executing a careful balancing act with respect to the German onslaught across the European continent. The American public was dead set against a repeat of the ghastly casualties of the first go-round with Germany. In retrospect it seemed a little stupid, but there were still a whole lot of families who'd lost sons and husbands "over there."

Flight training was enjoyable. I had no trouble with ground school, avionics, aircraft engineering, and the like. The flying was great, made more so by the undercurrents of unspoken urgency that permeated Pensacola. About the time that most of my class was getting a little cocky, the Navy sent down a pilot who'd been secretly seconded to the RAF during the Battle of Britain. He soon knocked the wind out of our sails with his quiet but fearsome stories of going up against the Luftwaffe. I finished training in late '41 and then went to advanced training at San Diego in October. And now, here I was: an honest-to-God carrier pilot, or, nugget first class.

Now I wanted to reassure my family that I was okay and also tell them some of what we'd been doing. That, of course, was not allowed. All letters had to be read by the squadron censor, who, inevitably, was Lieutenant Quantrill. He'd explained in detail what we could say and what we couldn't, so my note home was filled with platitudes about being on a great ship, the good chow, being really busy, meeting exceptional pilots, and the fact that we were taking the fight to the treacherous enemy. The rest of it was made up of questions: how's my younger brother, is the Omaha Works doing well, are you getting enough to eat now that there's rationing, any tornadoes yet, etc.

I'd left my academy ring with them when I headed west for San Diego. That had been a precarious moment, with all of us understanding the reason for doing that but no one willing to express it in words. A lot of the other pilots who were married had left their rings with their wives. Some had even written final letters to be sent in the event that they were declared killed in action. I'd looked in Snead's stuff, but hadn't found one. I finished my letter with some upbeat, "I'm fine and my squadron is great" words. Then I'd just sat there at my little fold-down desk, my mind in neutral, until I realized I needed to get my unsealed letter to Quantrill's basket in the squadron office if I had any hope of getting it off in Pearl.

Pearl was in such a shambles that the usual routine of an air group fly-off wasn't possible. Most of us stayed aboard the ship and got some sleep. There was an island-wide sundown-to-sunup curfew so the fleshpots of Honolulu, such as they were, were in limbo. The officers' club had finally been cleared of wounded but now would require a couple weeks' worth of sanitizing and re-painting. The *Enterprise* ship's company (the crew) faced the usual round-the-clock flurry of on-loading everything conceivable in the way of supplies, food, bunker oil, aviation gasoline, ordnance, and replacement aircraft.

Getting some much-needed sleep was enough for most of us, but our "vacation" didn't last long. On the third day in port we got some more nuggets to replace our losses. We also received six replacement aircraft, which meant pilots were needed to check out the new SBDs that had arrived, in sections as usual, via cargo ships. I thought there might be competition to get one of the new birds, but more experienced hands remembered what it was like to take what they called a "factory bird" up for the first time. There were sometimes unpleasant surprises, so we nuggets were assigned to take our pick and then to join the mechanics in physi-cally mounting the wings and testing the avionics, the hydrau-lics, and the gun systems. It was during this period that I really got to know the SBD, working alongside the mechs, finding loose wires, unconnected piping, flat tires, and even dinged propeller blades. Apparently the Douglas Aircraft Company was producing the dive bombers so fast and the need was so urgent that the new planes were never test-flown. They left that to the operational flight crews, who, after all, had the biggest stake in the plane performing to specs.

Rooster Baynes joined me on the second day of the delivery process and pitched right in wherever he could help. He'd been told I'd asked for him as gunner and was apparently pleased with that assignment. I think he'd also heard that I had put him in for a commendation. The SBD gunners were special people. They came from the various enlisted ratings but their role was as much co-pilot as gunner. Rooster had a colorful reputation, which included some dramatic run-ins with shore patrols in various ports. He was a dedicated bachelor and apparently a master escape artist, a useful talent when an unsuspecting husband came home unannounced. He was a wizard with carrier plane avionics, a speed-key with the Morse code, and he loved his guns, as evidenced by his efforts to trade the carrier's ordnance chief our SBD's twin thirty for a twin fifty. The chief just laughed and told Rooster to get lost.

That night the skipper called a meeting in the ready room to inform us that we were going back out, this time to attack Wake Island. The Japanese had invaded Wake Island four days after they hit Pearl. The first time they were driven off by the small but determined Marine garrison; the second time they sent two carriers, whose bombers and fighters overwhelmed the vastly outnumbered Marines and Navy defenders. Wake was 2,300 miles away from Pearl, and actually closer to Tokyo, which was "only" 1,990 miles away. According to naval intelligence the Japs were bulking up their logistics capabilities on Wake. The scuttlebutt on the Big E, however, was that the real reason we were going out was because Halsey wasn't happy with our last outing and was itching to bomb something. There was no thought of retaking the island, so the plan was to make a surprise attack, and then run back to

Pearl. Everybody had an opinion about the mission, but I agreed with the skipper: he thought it was more a case of showing the Japs that no place in the Pacific was safe from American carriers.

The strike date for the Wake attack was set for February 24th. It turned out to be a costly effort with very little to show for it. Basically, the intel was all wrong: there was just about nothing there. We made the first strike, went back to the carrier, rearmed, and then hit Marcus Island, another godforsaken outpost in the vast emptiness of the central Pacific. The AA fire was more intense and we lost more planes and pilots. We had little to show for it except more forlorn seabags in storage.

Back in Pearl, the air group went ashore and *Enterprise* went into the shipyard for some mysterious "configuration changes." None of us knew what that meant, and we spent the next month and a half integrating replacement planes and pilots, training more nuggets, and taking some time off down at the Royal Hawaiian Hotel. Each squadron got a long weekend on Waikiki and the chance to behave like aviators ashore. My sojourn to the *Oklahoma* kept my drinking limited to two beers a night. I caught a lot of static over that but I couldn't erase the memories of sitting on the battleship's overturned hull, watching sailors burn in the harbor right in front of me. She was still there, although now we'd heard they were trying to pull her carcass upright.

At some point, *Hornet* slipped out of Pearl, which gave rise to all sorts of rumors. The carrier was going to sea—but without her air group? Only towards the end of our six-week stint ashore did we learn that the Big E had hosted the Doolittle Raid over Tokyo, launching a clutch of stripped-down Army Air Corps B-25 Mitchell bombers that proceeded to strew bombs all over downtown Tokyo at rush hour. They then flew over Japan and into China, where some of them made safe landings. In terms of wartime damage, the strike was more like a stunt than a real bombing attack, but all of us could imagine the consternation in the Japanese capital at the sight of American bombers roaring low overhead and dropping bombs in downtown Tokyo.

Following the shock and shame of Pearl Harbor, the Doolittle Raid was an amazing morale booster at home. Morale needed boosting: the Japanese had conquered the Philippines, Burma, Java, Singapore, the Andaman Islands in the Bay of Bengal, and the Solomon Islands. They'd destroyed the last effective Allied naval fighting force in the western Pacific at the Battle of the Java Sea. They'd bombed Darwin, Australia, and taken Guam. Our pinpricks in the Marshalls and at Wake didn't look like much in comparison.

SEVEN

The *Hornet* came back from the Tokyo raid and was joined in Pearl by *Enterprise* and *Yorktown*. While the Big E and *Hornet* began the familiar process of restuffing their guts, *Yorktown* went into dry dock for battle damage repairs. The rumor mills began to grind in earnest when all the air group skippers were called to a big-deal meeting at Admiral Nimitz's headquarters up in the Makalapa crater. Three carriers in port at the same time *had* to mean something big was up, but as mere pilots we were not being consulted. One thing for sure—we were all more than ready to stop training and go do something for real, like killing Japs. We didn't have long to wait.

In the last week of May 1942, all three carriers set out from Pearl, accompanied by every cruiser and destroyer able to get up steam and come with us. We went out and turned southwest at 16 knots, as if headed back to the Coral Sea for the benefit of the Jap spies in Honolulu. One day later we turned due north and kicked it up to 25 knots. We hoped the first day's track had thrown off any Jap sub surveillance stationed near Pearl. All hands were told that the task forces were maintaining radio silence, including aircraft radios. No transmissions, not even to test repairs. Complete silence. All message traffic between ships was by flashing light. Fighting Six flew protective combat air patrols, called CAP, over the formations. Surprisingly, Scouting Six flew no search missions. Their planes were all reconfigured as full-fledged dive bombers. The only disappointing note was that Halsey wasn't going with us. He'd come down with some horrible skin disease called shingles and had been hospitalized. In his place were *two* rear admirals: Frank Jack Fletcher, an aviator who'd won the Medal of Honor at Veracruz, and Raymond Spruance, a battleship admiral but considered one of the smartest flag officers in the Navy. We chuckled when we thought about that: it took two rear admirals to replace one Vice Admiral Halsey.

By the first of June we were meandering somewhere north and west of Pearl. At noon the admirals' staff intelligence officers fanned out to the ready rooms to tell us what was going on. It seemed that the Japanese had decided to take Midway Island, a tiny speck in the ocean manned by a detachment of US Marines. As its name implied, Midway was a strategically located atoll that was perfect for ships making the big jump all the way across the Pacific to refuel and get fresh water. The Japs apparently figured that if they could occupy Midway, they could harass any US Navy forces headed west. Subs could base there and then lay siege to Hawaiian waters. They were bringing four of their fleet carriers to the party, having learned at Wake that carrier air made the difference between success and failure. Our mission: to attack and sink those four carriers.

The intel guys made one thing perfectly clear: we would have to achieve surprise to pull this off. We had three carriers; they had four. Some of theirs had made the attack on Pearl last December. The Japs had been victorious throughout most of their efforts across the entire western Pacific. We would not be dealing with nuggets; we would be dealing with their first team, which they called the *Kido Butai*. To keep our presence a secret, locating the enemy carriers would be entrusted to a squadron of Catalina flying boats, called PBYs, which were much smaller versions of the

Japs' *Kawanishi* seaplanes, operating out of Midway. The three American carriers would not send out long-range search planes but would depend on the Catalinas to find the Jap carrier force for us. If it all worked, they'd have no idea there were three American carriers out there waiting to ambush them when they attacked Midway Island.

The timing would be precarious. The Japs would launch strikes against Midway before sending in their amphibious corps to land, take, and occupy the island. The PBYs were based on Midway. They would have to locate the Jap carriers *before* their home base fell into Jap hands. While the Japs were busy falling upon hapless little Midway, we would fall upon them. That was the plan.

The intel officer finished his brief and we just looked at him. Even we nuggets, which included one "medium old hand," namely me, and all the new nuggets, understood that somebody was making a really big gamble here. The three American carriers, *Enterprise*, *Yorktown*, and *Hornet*, were all that we had left in the Pacific. The Japs were sending only half their fleet of *nine* carriers. We'd have to sink them *all* if we were to prevent the seizure of Midway. That was a tall order.

"I know," the briefer said, sensing the doubt in the room. "Lotta ifs and maybes. But, look: working for us is the fact that we know they're coming, we know their objective, and thus we know the general area where there ought to be four Jap fleet carriers, who do *not* know we're anywhere nearby. If we can put strike forces over their decks while they're busy beating up on little Midway Island, we can hurt them really bad. Working against us is what we've learned in the southwest Pacific: that once opposing carriers become aware of one another, *every*body's gonna get hurt. So the side that gets the first strike in has the best chance to actually destroy the other side's carriers. After that, you end up trading strikes."

"Sounds like everything depends on finding them before they find us," the skipper said.

"Yes, it does," the intel officer said. "So, for planning purposes, we have to assume that's how it's gonna work out."

"Why aren't *we* looking for them, again?" the skipper asked.

"If they see a PBY overhead, they'll assume it's from Midway. If they see an SBD, they'll know there's an American carrier out there somewhere. That's why *we're* not searching. That's also why Scouting Six is being hung with bombs. They're not going to be scouting this time. They're all SBDs, so they're gonna be bombing. Think of it: if we could sink all four of their carriers, over three hundred aircraft and as many front-line, highly experienced pilots would have nowhere to land."

The ready room went silent. In a way it was all clear enough: if three American carriers could get the jump on four Jap carriers, we might change the entire situation in the Pacific. Right now the Japs were winning everywhere. Take out almost half their carrier fleet and we might even put them on the defensive.

"Which carriers, again?" the Skipper asked.

"*Kaga*, *Akagi*, *Hiryu*, and *Soryu*," the intel officer replied.

Quantrill put up a hand. "How in the *hell* do we know all this?" he demanded to know.

"Spies," the briefer said, quickly. "More than that I can't tell you, but we do feel the intel is solid. We'll find out when the Catalinas sound the alarm."

For the next three days we bored holes in the north Pacific Ocean, staying under the cover of some truly shitty weather in case the Japs did put out scouts. We spent our time trying to fully absorb the strike plan, which envisioned all three carriers launching everything they had to make a coordinated attack on the Japanese flattops. It was a great plan. Everyone thought so. On the other hand, none of the carriers had ever attempted a simultaneous launch of three entire air wings.

Questions began to surface as we learned more. Things like: the bombers and the fighters will head to the target at 15,000 feet. The torpedo bombers, on the other hand, needed to be down low when they got to the target. Were they to go first, while we bombers waited to see what they accomplished? Or did the admirals envision torpedo bombers skimming the waves on their way into the carrier formation while SBDs, both Bombing Six and Scouting Six, fell on them from high altitude. The reaction from the admirals' staff seemed to be: Gee, those are really good questions.

The first Catalina flying boat sent out on the third came up and announced he'd found a Jap formation while we were still struggling to figure out the details. Immediately we started to make our strike preps, only to be told, no, wait, those *are* Japs, but we think it's the Midway invasion force. That's not who we're looking for. Stand down but stay ready.

Stay ready? We'd been ready for a week. More Catalinas fanned out into their sectors, searching 200 miles from Midway with no results except more crappy weather. Then came reports from Midway that *Jap* snoopers had been sighted. Marine fighter air went up after the reconnaissance planes only to watch as Jap carrier bombers arrived and descended on the island. Then silence.

We now knew that their carriers were close enough to Midway to make a strike. But where? The range of possibilities covered several thousand square *miles* of ocean. All of us stayed up late on the night of the third, but if our bosses knew anything, they weren't telling us. For all we knew in our sweaty little ready rooms, our carrier task force might run smack into theirs in the middle of the night. Finally the skipper told everyone to hit the sack. I'm confident they'll call us when they need us, he said with a perfectly straight face.

They called at 0330 the next morning, which was the 4th of June. We wolfed down the traditional steak and eggs in the wardroom, then suited up and went to the ready room—to wait some more. We could feel the Big E's huge hull rumbling as she pressed into the night, surrounded by destroyers and cruisers busy keeping station. A briefer showed up and told us the Catalinas had located the Jap carriers and that they were 230 miles away. *Enter-*

prise and our other two flattops were burning up the ocean in an effort to close the distance between us. That many miles meant that our heavily loaded SBDs could make it out there, but having enough gas to get back was an open question. One thing the staff briefer said got our attention. Admiral Fletcher, he said, wanted a coordinated strike by the three air groups. He intended to launch everything he had, but he wanted that huge gaggle to arrive over the enemy flight decks simultaneously, so as to overwhelm the enemy's defenses. The skipper put up a hand.

"That means we'll launch our CAP fighters, our escorting fighters, then our bombers, then our torpedo bombers, in that order, right? All three carriers?"

"Correct."

"That means we will all have to wait, orbiting the task force, burning precious gas, until the last plane from the slowest carrier gets airborne, right?"

"Um."

"That won't work, Commander," the skipper said, as we digested the prospect of orbiting for an hour, or more, before heading out to do business. "You need to go back to flag plot and point that out to everyone who'll listen to you. Otherwise, you're talking about sending the whole air group on this wonderful coordinated strike with gas tanks half empty. We might get there, but ain't nobody coming back."

The briefer didn't know what to say. The skipper pointed him toward the door and off he went, a visibly worried man.

EIGHT

The *Enterprise* air group consisted of four squadrons for this mission: one each of fighters, dive bombers, scout bombers, and torpedo bombers. Standard procedure was to launch the fighters first. Their job was to set up a protective combat air patrol on stations around the carrier formation. These were F4F Wildcats. The next to go were the long-range dive bombers, which now were all SBD3As, armed with 1,000-pound bombs centerline and a 100-pound incendiary bomb on each wing. They were to be followed on this strike by the scout bombers, also all SBDs. Normally scout bombers, as their name implied, were sent out ahead with lighter bomb loads, because their primary mission was to locate the enemy. If they found them, they would report and then attack, using a 500-pound bomb hung centerline and two 100-pounders on the wings. This time, they would be armed like us. The torpedo bombers, each carrying a single Mark 13 torpedo weighing 2,200 pounds, were the most heavily laden, and thus the last to launch in order to have enough fuel to make it out and back. The bombers would travel at high altitude; the torpedo guys would fly much lower, and would sometimes get to the target before the heavy attack planes did.

The torpedo bombers were something of a special case. The word in the air group was that their Mark 13 air-dropped tor-

pedo basically didn't work. The planes that carried them, Douglas
Devastators, had to fly straight, low, slow, and level in order to
spin up the torpedo's gyro guidance. Only then could they drop
their weapons. Unfortunately, in far too many cases, the damned
things would break up, run erratically, porpoise up to the surface,
sink, or run circular, unlike Japanese torpedoes which were *always*
lethal. That long, slow, straight approach to an enemy target presented the enemy's defense gunners a big, fat, non-maneuvering
target. It was such a suicidal maneuver that the Navy came up
with a bizarre smoke tactic. A fighter or a bomber would fly perpendicular to the torpedo bomber's approach line, emitting a
smoke cloud. Once the smoke settled on the ocean, the torpedo
bombers would begin their approach to the target, and then, at
the last minute, burst out of the smoke cloud, launch their fish,
and escape. Talk about a Rube Goldberg idea. Unfortunately, war
at sea is a come-as-you-are situation. That's what we had, so that's
what we sent out.

The fighters got off in good order, and our SBDs all made it
off the deck without incident except for one, whose engine began acting up, forcing him to get back onboard. And then, like
through so much of the Midway operation, we waited. We waited
for the Scouting Six guys to get airborne, and then for the carrier
to bring up the Devastators with their ponderous one-ton torpedoes slung centerline. We'd been orbiting over the task force,
burning up our fuel, for an hour and fifteen minutes before the
last torpedo bomber got off. And then we were told to wait some
more, while the *other* two carriers got their warbirds sorted out
and up in the air. After almost a two-hour wait, our admiral,
Raymond Spruance, had had enough. He ordered his two CAGs
to get going. We were given the best estimated position of the
enemy carriers and told to go get 'em. The coordinated, all-in-
one strike was history.

Off we went, already aware that we probably didn't have enough
gas to get back even *if* we found them where they were supposed

to be. If we had to go looking for them, then we *knew* we wouldn't have enough gas to get back. It was not a great way to start off on a mission. Our CAG, Lieutenant Commander Wade McClusky, took us up to a cruising altitude of 15,000 feet and told everyone to set up their engines to max conserve. At that altitude we could still breathe without tapping oxygen supplies and our engines didn't have to scavenge for air, either. Somewhere out behind us were dozens of airplanes intent on the same thing, but hardly in a coordinated manner.

Personally, I was still excited as hell. We were going after some of the carriers who'd brought all that death and destruction to Pearl, *and* there was a fair chance they didn't even know we were coming. There were fifteen of us, all carrying half-ton bombs, and supposedly thirty more bombers from the other two flattops. If only two of us managed a direct hit, that carrier would be a sitting duck for all the planes coming behind us. Rooster was singing Civil War hymns back in his cockpit, Union and Reb. I kept going over the pre-attack checklist: Arm the bombs. Just before rolling in on the target, squirt a shot of ephedrine into each nostril to keep my eardrums from bursting as we tore down out of the sky. Check to make *sure* I'd armed the bombs. Dive brakes out to stabilize my trusty SBD as we came down on the near-vertical from three miles up, holding her steady as I watched to see where the guy before me had planted his bombs. Remembering the most important rule: aim for where that big boy is gonna be, not where he is right now. If the guy ahead of you missed to starboard, then there was probably a wind coming from port: allow for it. Don't screw up: this is the Big Time, Nugget.

Once we got to the last, best estimated position of the enemy carrier formation, we found a whole bunch of empty ocean. High white clouds at various levels, bright sun, and no goddamned Jap carriers, or anything else for that matter. Nothing. Miles and miles of empty ocean, and fuel tanks indicating below fifty percent. For the first time I was scared. Had the same staff planners who'd en-

visioned a coordinated, three-air-group strike blown the target location as well? Our CAG came up on the tactical net. Box search,
he said in a calm voice, as if nothing was wrong. The entire air
group followed him around as he began the classic box search pattern: fly north 10 miles, then fly east 15 miles, then fly south 20
miles, then west 25 miles, inexorably expanding the box. My heart
sank. A box search was the last resort, and at some point, we'd
have to face facts: fuel state would demand that we head back for
the carrier.

Then we caught a break: the CAG saw something down on
that vast, fluid desert: a ship's wake—a bright white scar pointing northwest. It was a warship. Had to be, moving at that speed.
And he was on a mission, going as fast as he could to—what? The
CAG had probably deduced that he was trying to rejoin the carrier formation, having been sent out to do something or other.
The CAG turned the entire group onto a course matching that
ship's course, and ordered us up to 20,000 feet, attack altitude.
Sure enough, fifteen minutes later, we saw more white scars on
the ocean, four miles down.

"Target in sight," the CAG announced in a satisfied voice,
which was the signal to arm our bombs and prepare for an immediate attack. He led us straight toward that formation, not having
to worry about getting the sun behind us—it was going on noon.
There were lots of patchy clouds, so our view of the Japs came and
went, sometimes blotted out by white clouds, then crystal clear as
we closed in on them. Something else became apparent: there were
swarms of aircraft, down low, which seemed to be pursuing other
aircraft. I saw three fires on the water, tiny yellow blazes from this
altitude, but unmistakable: those were the fires made when a plane
went into the water and exploded.

"I see three carriers," the CAG announced. "Bombing Six
takes one, Scouting Six takes another one."

Our skipper came up. "Supposed to be four," he said. "And
what about Torpedo Six?"

"I think they're already down there," the CAG said.

That was a sobering observation. All those fires on the water and Zeros twisting and turning everywhere. By now we were close enough to see tiny black bursts of AA fire all over the Jap formation. The CAG and our skipper were talking the situation over as if this was just another fleet exercise. The bad news was that it looked like our torpedo bombers had run into a buzz saw. The good news was that the Japs were busy shooting down planes flying fifty feet off the water. Hopefully, none of them was looking up as we shifted into right echelon formation. I caught my first glimpse of Scouting Six behind us, also setting up the stairway formation.

By now we could make out the carriers, and after countless hours studying enemy carrier recognition photos, we could even name them: *Kaga, Akagi, Soryu.* Rooster told me the CAG's gunner was sending out precise locating information for the other two air groups, assuming they'd ever gotten off and come after us. I looked down at my fuel gauge, and then back out the canopy windows. I didn't want to dwell on where I'd seen that needle pointing. The CAG made his assignments:

"Bombing Six takes *Kaga*; Scouting Six take *Akagi*. We'll leave *Soryu* to *Yorktown* and *Hornet*. And then we gotta find that fourth carrier. Rolling in in sixty seconds. I will lead Bombing Six down."

That must have irked our skipper, but the air group commander had the right to start the fight if he wanted to. Some CAGs stayed at altitude to direct the attack. Our CAG was not one of those. It was a little strange, actually, since our CAG was a fighter guy, not a bomber pilot. The fact that he had chosen to fly an SBD should have told us he was going to make the first dive. I checked my arming wires for the umpteenth time and told Rooster to sniff his joy juice. I did the same, and then watched as first the CAG and then our skipper rolled left and then pointed their noses down and into a steep dive toward IJN *Kaga*. Two more SBDs from Bombing Six's Section 2 went next, and then it was my turn.

"Here we go, Rooster," I said, and then threw the stick over and down. That got me a yee-haw. I had a ringside seat for what happened next. The CAG released his bombs at around 3,000 feet, but it was clear that he'd aimed right at that big beast instead of leading it. Fighter guy mistake. His bombs fell behind the ship, which actually was bigger than *Enterprise*. The skipper did a better job, but still missed, close aboard, but close enough to have probably scared *Kaga*'s main propulsion engineers to death. The third bomber in the stack planted a 1,000-pounder on the last 100 feet of the carrier's flight deck, right where a clutch of aircraft were spotted. The ship's entire back end erupted into a huge fireball. The fourth guy missed to starboard, but, again, close enough to rattle the boiler rooms.

I focused on that big red circle up on the front end of the carrier's flight deck. By now the wake behind the flattop was bright white and really broad, which meant she was up at full power, 30 knots. She had a small island structure compared to *Enterprise*, and her smokestacks came out the side of her hull and pointed downward. I glanced at my altimeter as we dropped at 200 knots, and then back at where I was pointed. Altimeter. Aim point. Altimeter. Aim point.

Move it forward.

Altimeter. The air was screaming through the holes in my dive brakes now as I gripped the release handle.

Altimeter. 2,500. Okay. I jerked the release handle and felt the plane buck as a half ton of fun, love, and joy left the belly, followed by the two incendiary bombs, their tails waggling like eager puppies as they followed the main event down. I wanted to stay in the dive to see if I hit her, but the ocean was coming up horribly fast and I was already pulling on the stick for all it was worth. I could feel the skin on my face sagging as the g-forces piled on and my vision narrowed down to a red-rimmed tunnel.

Pull *harder*, clean up the flaps, pull, pull, *pull*. I thought I felt a bump, as if the bottom of my plane had actually touched the surface, but then, dear God, *finally*, I saw the sky-ocean interface rising into view ahead of me and I could relax the pull. Then Rooster was yelling something and opening fire with his twin thirties. I saw tracers whipping by at an angle on our left side so I jinked right, opening up Rooster's field of fire. The tracers stopped as I clawed for altitude. I never saw the Zero who'd jumped us. I turned harder to the right and was rewarded by the sight of a huge fire on the front end of *Kaga*. Huge doesn't really describe it: the almost 900-foot-long carrier itself was barely visible underneath the enormous bolus of 100-octane aviation gasoline–fueled fire rising into the air above the formation.

"Nice one, Nugget," the skipper said from somewhere above me. I was about to say thank you, sir, when two blasts of AA fire hammered us on either side. I almost lost control as I dived, twisted, and turned to evade the gunners on what looked like a battleship I'd made the mistake of overflying. Then I added power, still twisting and turning, to get back up to where the rest of the squadron were regrouping. Off to one side of the formation I could see what looked like another carrier in the same shape as my target, more fire visible than carrier. Even farther away I could make out yet another tall column of black smoke, but what was burning was obscured by all that smoke. The skipper called a heading to return to *Enterprise* as I climbed to 15,000 feet. The big white clouds were still around, so I simply turned to that heading and went to max-conserve. I was afraid to look at my fuel gauge.

Twenty minutes later another SBD joined up on me, and then two more appeared out of a cloud about a mile north of us. The squadron re-formed in bits and pieces for the next half hour before the first plane ran out of gas. The pilot, a skinny, older guy with a heavy Maine accent, came up on the tactical net and announced he'd run dry and was going down to ditch. I told Rooster to mark the chart with our estimated position. I knew all the other pilots were doing the same thing in case the admiral spared a destroyer to go out and search for the crew.

"How we stand, Boss?" Rooster asked. He sounded nervous. He should have been.

"Touch and go, Rooster," I said. "If we can go straight in and land, we'll make it. But just in case, find the ditching checklist and start making preps."

The skipper came up and asked everyone for his fuel state. The replies were not encouraging, and ten minutes later yet another SBD began a slanting dive down to the ocean three miles below, his propeller clearly no longer turning. We marked the chart again. At about this time two *Enterprise* fighters showed up and turned to lead us back to the Big E. Their heading was ten degrees to the right of the one we'd been flying. The SBD3A carried a homing beacon receiver, but it was only accurate to ten degrees. We must be close, I thought, but there were enough clouds ahead of us that I couldn't see anything down below. Finally the skipper came up and ordered us down to get into the land-launch pattern. I looked at my gauge. Between twelve and ten gallons left. Fortunately we were gliding down at low power. Now everything depended on the order of landing.

We finally could see the carrier when we broke through 4,000 feet, and she was blasting east into the prevailing winds, surrounded by what looked like dozens of aircraft. The whole air group had gone out; the whole air group, minus Torpedo Six, now wanted to land, with everyone anxiously asking to be me-first. The pattern, which was an imaginary oval 5 miles long and 2 miles wide at 3,000 feet, had three levels at 1,000-foot intervals, from which planes were being called down to the flight deck in the order of how desperate they were for fuel. I watched a half-dozen planes peel out and ditch while we were orbiting in the highest level of the pattern, quickly pursued by plane-guard destroyers.

Between eight and ten gallons left, and now the pointer was bouncing around.

"*Boss! Traffic!*" yelled Rooster. I looked up and quickly pointed my nose out of the pattern to avoid running into a fighter directly in front of me, his tailhook dragging about 25 feet from my nose.

"Thank you, *Rooster*," I squawked, easing us back into the circling crowd. He had realized I'd become distracted by the fact that we weren't turning anymore. Facing to the rear, he'd had to unstrap, lift himself, and turn completely around, which is how he'd spotted the guy right in front of us. I'd been busy watching how well the guys who were ditching landed. Not everyone was achieving a nice belly landing down there. Some of the planes hit flat, bounced back into the air, and then nosed hard down and disappeared like a razor blade dropped into the water, the top of the plane just barely visible as it shimmered out of sight, seeking the bottom three miles down. By then I was on the downwind leg of the pattern, headed towards the back end of the carrier while keeping her on my port side.

The Air Boss came up on the land-launch net. "Anyone at five or less?" he asked.

I waited for a second and then replied. "Two one six is at five."

"Two one six cleared to make an approach."

"Two one six," I replied and then began the long, 180-degree turn to line up with the flight deck. 216 was my sail number, painted on the fuselage. I called for the checklist and Rooster read me through it. Wheels down. Check. Flaps down. Check. Hook down. Check. Full pitch. Check. There was one guy about a mile out ahead of me. He settled down to the deck but then something happened. He yawed left as he came over the round-down, prompting the LSO to dive for cover into the catwalk. His left wing hit the left edge of the flight deck, flipped over, and then he crashed into the sea, disappearing immediately in a boil of foam and smoke.

I expected the LSO to wave me off and was reaching for the throttle, but he didn't. He jumped back up to his platform and extended his arms, paddles fluttering in the 45-knot wind over the deck. I swallowed hard and then concentrated on putting her down, centerline, nose up to force the hook into the wires, cutting the engine on the LSO's command, and feeling the grunting stop as a wire caught my hook and brought me to a stop in about 100 feet. Instantly there were two wing-walkers in front of me, their hands crossed, telling me to hold still until my hook was cleared, and then directing me to taxi off the centerline so the next guy could get down.

"God*damn*, Boss," Rooster said softly over the intercom.

"God loves us, Rooster," I replied as I shut down the engine. We had between zero and three gallons left before all the instruments subsided onto their pegs. "He surely does."

NINE

There was jubilation down in the ready room and on the flight deck in general. *Three* Jap carriers in one morning. Never mind that the strike had been as screwed up as Hogan's Goat. The individual claims began to expand exponentially, with everyone claiming credit for at least two out of the three sinkings. Underlying all that, however, was the solemn knowledge that many of our casualties and missing in action were the result of our own mistakes, like holding an entire air group overhead for so long that many guys departed knowing they never had a chance to make it back, even before we departed. The skipper joined us finally after having spent a half hour up on the flag bridge, along with the CAG and the skipper of Scouting Six, briefing the admiral in detail. The elephant in the pilothouse was that there was no one briefing for Torpedo Six, because they had been wiped out. The skipper joined in the backslapping for a few minutes, but then signaled for silence.

"We missed one," he announced. "Intel says *Hiryu* was out there. We'll have to go back, and pretty quick, because—"

At that moment the Big E began leaning into a hard turn, sharp enough to put any unsecured aircraft out on the flight deck in danger of rolling off. That was followed by the GQ alarm, and the announcement that Jap planes were attacking *Yorktown*, which was about ten miles away from us to the south. Most of us went up on deck and sat in the starboard catwalk. *Enterprise*'s AA batteries all trained out to make sure that any Japs who saw us would get a hot reception. The sky over *Yorktown* darkened with AA bursts, interspersed with the fiery trails of dying Jap planes as they arced into the sea, pursued in some cases right down to the crash by *Yorktown*'s Hellcats. Even so we saw bomb hits on the wildly maneuvering carrier, followed eventually by the white waterspouts of torpedo hits. Unlike our torpedoes, Jap fish worked, as all of us knew. *Yorktown* began to slow way down, and we could begin to see more and more of her flight deck as she listed.

Big E spit off six fighters to join the ones we already had up, but the Japs seemed not to know we were there. Perhaps it was because they were busy killing *Yorktown*. In any event, once the raid was over, the ship secured from GQ and we were ordered to get chow and then prepare for an afternoon strike. If there'd been any doubt that *Hiryu* was out there, she'd clarified the situation for all to see. *Yorktown* was badly hurt, and soon some of her surviving aircraft started landing on *Enterprise*. I didn't know where *Hornet* was, but the admirals had dispersed the formation just in case the surviving Jap flattop did seek revenge.

The wardroom was not the scene of jubilation I'd experienced in the ready room. There were far too many empty seats and the pilots were eating with the grim determination that preceded a dangerous mission. It was more like we were refueling than eating lunch. A final coffee and a cigarette, one last head call, and then back to the work of killing carriers. Both *Enterprise* and *Hornet* would be sending strikes, but there'd be no waiting to gather up a coordinated strike this time. Each air group was directed to launch as soon as possible and get bombers over the one surviving Jap carrier before the Japs figured out they were facing not one but three American carriers and ran for home. We learned that there would be no torpedo bombers going on this one, because there weren't any left on *Yorktown* or *Enterprise*. *Hornet*'s torpedo bombers had missed the show this morning when they couldn't find the Jap fleet. Low on fuel like everyone else, they had opted to return to the ship rather than start a search, a decision that certainly had saved their lives. By 1330, our first planes were going off the bow. The air group's fighters were being kept back in anticipation of yet another *Hiryu* strike. Who could blame the *Hiryu*?

Bombing Six launched around 1400, some 150 miles from where we thought *Hiryu* ought to be. The orders were clear: as soon as a squadron, or what was left of it, was airborne, they were to head for the target. As I looked around at our somewhat tattered formation, I realized Bombing Six and Scouting Six had sustained much heavier losses than I had thought. I wondered at the time why we weren't waiting for the rest of our planes. Then I figured it out: there weren't any.

"I didn't know it was that bad," I told Rooster as we climbed to 15,000 feet.

"Lotta scuttlebutt going around, Boss. 'Specially about guys running out of gas and going in the drink. Mister Franklin went in before we even got there."

"Damn," I said. "I didn't know that."

We flew on for a while, thinking our thoughts. Three Jap carriers destroyed. Had to be, with fires that big. They might still be afloat, but they'd be nothing but burned-out hulks. Maybe we could get a fourth this afternoon. But at what cost? It had been a big celebration back in the ready room, but now I was embarrassed to think that I hadn't given a single thought to the crews we'd lost. Man, I had a lot to learn.

"Smoke," somebody said over the tactical net. "Three three zero."

"Angels twenty," the skipper ordered. We followed him up into the thin air. Bombing country. Rooster and I went through our attack checklist. I felt under my seat for the arming handle. It was right where it was supposed to be. We were carrying the standard ship-buster centerline, with the two firebombs, one on each wing. The theory was that the big boy would tear the target open and rupture the fuel lines rising to the flight deck. Then the little boys would light it up. We finally could see two columns of black smoke down there on the silver sea, surrounded by smaller dots. Should have been three, I thought, and then realized one of them had probably gone down. But where was Number Four? We hadn't seen her this morning, so she must be somewhere distant from the *Kaga-Akagi-Soryu* formation. And then we looked down and saw a line formation of planes coming down from the north, headed towards *our* carrier formation. They were probably 6,000 feet below us. *Hiryu*'s last stand?

The skipper came up on our Bombing Six tactical net. "She's north of here, somewhere. I want to fly northwest by north to get up-sun, and then we'll kill her. Those bastards down there won't have anywhere to land. I'll send out the heads-up. Come to three three zero."

Normally we would have been formed up in echelons of divisions, two or three aircraft in each division, with rigid control on where you were supposed to keep station. Not this afternoon. Bombing Six and Scouting Six were basically intermingled, bombers all. We were flying in the flattest echelon I'd ever seen, two half-strength squadrons, mindful of our dead, what these Japs had done at Pearl Harbor, and intent on murder.

It took another fifteen minutes before one of the planes called target in sight, zero one zero. Off to our right, one big and a lot of smaller white lines in the ocean, heading southeast, following their planes so that they'd have a shorter distance to fly to get home.

Not today, you sonsabitches, I thought. Ain't gonna be no home for you.

"*God*damn right," Rooster said. Apparently I'd said it out loud.

"Arm the fun," the skipper ordered. "And follow me."

I shot my ephedrine capsule, rolled in, and followed the skipper and two more planes down. Hard roll to the left, then pitch the nose down, so that the centrifugal forces pushed fuel towards the engine and not away from it. Split the flaps to get stability as the airspeed ramped up, and then reach down and pull the arming handle. I was the fourth plane down so I got to see what the first three accomplished before it was my turn. First two hit close aboard, close enough to have cracked some seams on her under-water hull. Number three, a pilot from Scouting Six, flew through an alarming cone of increasing AA fire, planted a 500-pounder on the back of her flight deck in the midst of a dozen parked planes, and then knifed straight into the ocean on the carrier's starboard quarter.

I swore at the sight but then it was my turn. That cone of fire was swinging my way about as fast as I was dropping. Hand it to those Japs: here came a possible 1,000-pound bomb aimed right at them but not a one of them was running for cover. Suppressed by the rising whine of my dive were clacks and small bangs as some of that fire hit my plane. *Hiryu*'s after end was burning pretty well by then so I touched the stick left just a bit and let baby go at 2,500 feet. Then turn and pull, pull, *pull* as more of those bullets smacked my wings and fuselage. I chose to fly straight out and away from the carrier's port bow, not jinking hardly at all, on the theory that distance from all that AA fire was my friend. Doing that worked fine unless there were some Zeros waiting for you at the bottom of the roller coaster.

Then Rooster, facing aft, got a look at *Hiryu* and treated me to a truly enthusiastic yee-haw. Now level over the bright white-caps, I could begin a spiraling turn back up to altitude. As I did, Lieutenant Quantrill planted a big boy smack in the middle of the *Hiryu*'s flight deck. It punched what from my angle and altitude looked like a small wedge-shaped hole in the flight deck, and then there were two huge explosions jetting out her hangar bay side doors under the flight deck, followed by a huge hump bulging up in the flight deck itself. But what got my attention was what *my* fire-baby had done for us. I'd hit her in the forward one-third of the flight deck and the resulting blast had peeled her flight deck and the forward elevator smack up against her island like a ripped-open can of stewed tomatoes.

"Break it off, break it off," the skipper called. There was no longer any point in wasting bombs on the clearly wrecked carrier, which was now subsiding out of sight beneath the huge clouds of smoke and flames. The skipper ordered anyone else with bombs to go after a battleship that was following astern of the carrier, still shooting every one of her AA guns in our general direction. Then the *Hornet* air group arrived, and conducted its own strike against *Hiryu*. I shook my head. What would they be aiming at, I wondered? You could see her rapidly diminishing wake, but that was about it. What you *could* see were *Hiryu*'s remaining aircraft, milling about the disaster like wasps whose paper ball nest has been torn open, which was just about what had happened.

Nothing much was accomplished against the battleship. She was escorted by some cruisers and destroyers and their combined AA curtain almost obscured the heavy. Five pilots dropped, but prudently, from about 6,000 feet, and mostly killed a lot of fish. There were two heavy cruisers trailing oil, so maybe someone got to them in all the excitement. More of the *Hornet*'s air group arrived. Having missed the morning's festivities, they brought greater numbers than our badly depleted group, so our CAG ordered us to leave them to it. We turned out to head back to Mother *Enterprise*.

We settled out at 12,000 feet and counted heads while dealing with the adrenaline crash and its immediate result: a great wave of weariness flooding through our veins. I was aware that Rooster was babbling away on the intercom about what *our* bomb had done, as if none of the other hits had counted, but I almost couldn't make out his words. I shook myself out of it, did an instrument scan, and then sucked down some water from my Thermos. The water helped. Then something on the instrument scan jarred me even more awake.

"Rooster," I called. "We losing fuel?"

It took a moment for him to inspect the wings. "Uh, yes, sir, Boss, I think we are. Right wing's weepin'. It ain't *too* bad, but . . ."

My master fuel gauge showed enough to get back to the carrier, but obviously some of that AA fire had done the Japs' bidding. The 3A model of the SBD had self-sealing fuel tanks, but if you put enough holes in the rubber lining, you'd begin to lose fuel, which showed up as a fine white mist contrail behind the affected wing. I reported my problem to the skipper, who calmly asked if I could make it back. I told him I thought I could. Okay, he said. That was all I needed to hear, because it told me he'd set me up to be one of the first ones back aboard. I let Rooster know that "they" knew about our problem, but I watched the fuel gauge all the way back.

We were fourth to land, not first, because there were three planes ahead of me who had bigger problems. One of them ditched alongside a destroyer, which quickly plucked the crew out of the sea. Our destroyers had that business down to a fine art by now and it was always a great comfort to know one was already coming to get you if you had to make a water landing. Landing itself was a bit hairy for once, because there were a lot more airplanes parked up front than usual which meant a lot less landing room. We later found out that *Yorktown* had been abandoned for fear she'd blow up like the *Lex* had. All her surviving planes had been dispersed among our two remaining decks—*Enterprise* and *Hornet*. The two squadron skippers went topside to tell the admiral that *Hiryu*, while not actually sunk, had been wrecked and would probably sink that night.

The rest of us went to the ready room and dropped, exhausted, into our assigned chairs. The squadron doctor came around amid the babble, offering a shot of bourbon to each pilot. This time I grabbed it eagerly and threw it down. He tipped the bottle to ask if I wanted a heeltap but I shook my head. I closed my eyes and let the whiskey and the buzz of excited chatter do its work, trying to ignore the poignant fact that, of the four nugget chairs positioned right up front in the briefing room, mine was the only one occupied. My fellow new guys were now just part of the wreckage and oil slicks floating out west somewhere, where four aircraft carriers and literally thousands of Japanese sailors had met their doom in the cold waters above Midway Island.

Four carriers. Great God.

Four carriers and *all* their aircraft. Had to be hundreds of them. No dispersing their surviving airplanes to the remaining decks, because there weren't any remaining decks. Yes, we'd apparently lost *Yorktown*, but most of her people and planes were still with us, and there was nothing the Japs could do about that now. Remember Pearl Harbor, you sonsabitches, I muttered, but it didn't seem to have the kick it used to. There was a noise in the ready room. The skipper was back. I sat back up and tried to look enthusiastic, but the scale of the past two days was overwhelming. Every time I closed my eyes I saw that image of *Hiryu*'s flight deck curled up against her bridge windows. Then I heard people dropping into their seats and the room going quiet.

"We're withdrawing from the area," the skipper announced. "The admiral said that because the Japs still had battleships and cruisers out there, he thinks they'll come for us in the night if we make the mistake of hanging around. One of their battlewagons could sink both *Hornet* and *Enterprise* in five minutes."

"What about the *Yorktown*?" a voice behind me asked.

"They've put a damage control team back aboard and taken her under tow. She swallowed two torpedoes and a couple of bombs. If the Japs also withdraw, we might get her back to Pearl, but at least most of the air group and ship's company are safe for the moment. The admiral wants another strike tomorrow morning to make sure somebody's not trying to tow *Hiryu* out of the area. The other three have been confirmed sunk. Gentlemen, we have achieved a fantastic victory over the Japanese navy. Two of those carriers were part of the sneak attack on Pearl. The admiral says this will put them on the strategic defensive, which will give us time to rebuild our fleet and then really take the war to them for a change."

Nobody said anything. I think most of us were still a bit numb and not much interested in high strategy *or* taking the war anywhere just then. The skipper leaned over the podium. He was pretty damn tired, too.

"It's not like we got a free ride," he said with a sigh. "Just look around."

None of us looked around. We didn't have to. I wondered if any of the other guys were, like me, feeling just a little bit guilty that we were still alive while so many were . . . For some reason, I spoke up. Nuggets weren't expected to say anything unless spoken to, but I wanted to say something.

"Nugget wants to speak," the skipper announced.

"Today," I said, "when I was diving on *Hiryu*, I could see the Jap AA gunners running all over the flight deck trying to get to their stations. When they started up, it was *damn* clear that they could see me, too. Think about it: here came a dive bomber with a serious bomb who probably wasn't going to miss, and yet I didn't see a single one of them running for cover or diving down into the catwalks. Today was goddamned wonderful: four carriers. But I think this war's gonna take a while."

There was silence in the ready room for about ten seconds. Then the skipper nodded. "Nugget's right," he said. "Amazing as that is."

There was general laughter. Picking on nuggets was still fun. Then the skipper continued. "The Japanese got cocky here at Midway. I hate to think of what they'll be like when they get backed into a corner." Then he looked up and beamed. "By the way, I need to congratulate the nugget here for making two direct hits on two different carriers. In that regard . . ."

He stopped and nodded to Yeoman Sykes, who went to the ready room door and admitted two flight deck aviation boatswain mates. They wore the shirts of the arresting gear crew, and between them they were carrying a tailhook from an SBD. They stood a little nervously in front of the hollow-eyed pilots in their chairs, many of whom still looked like they wanted to kill something. The skipper went over and removed something shiny from the ring at the top of the hook where the bolt holding it to the tail went through. He held it up and wrinkled his nose.

"This is the head of a flying fish," he announced. "See the little wing fins on the side? Yesterday when Mister Steele here got back aboard, the deck guys found the fish embedded in the base of the hook. Apparently Mister Steele had a close encounter with the Pacific Ocean on pullout, yes, Mister Steele?"

I remembered that bump, and nodded sheepishly.

"This was just after he'd put a crowd-pleaser into *Kaga* that turned her into a moving volcano. Therefore I hereby decree that Bombing Six is now a nugget-free zone, and that 'Fish' Steele is hereby officially named."

I started laughing. All the pilots had nicknames, or call-names as they were usually referred to. You never got to choose your call-name. Something had to happen that inspired the rest of the squadron, led by the skipper, to anoint you with your forever name. If it arose from something embarrassing, that was even better. I had hooked a fish by pulling out too low. Fish it was.

I was able to brush over the other reason we were a nugget-free zone in the general hilarity, but I'd noticed something. We did dangerous work. I remembered reading about Ulysses Grant calmly asking Sherman after the battle of Shiloh: What was the butcher's bill? There were going to be casualties. We could mourn, but on our own time. Our professional face required that we get up the next morning and go back out if we had to as if nothing significant had happened.

As the meeting broke up I sat there in my chair for a moment, trying to make sense of everything. Lieutenant Quantrill walked by.

"Chow time," he announced with his usual stern face.

"Not that hungry," I replied.

"That's too bad. Get down to the wardroom and eat. We may have to do a night launch if the Japs press their case with those battlewagons. You'll need fuel, *Fish*, just like your airplane."

The way he said "Fish" made it clear that I was not on his best-buddy list. He'd missed with his bombs on the first attack; I hadn't. Could that be it? I knew that was a petty thought, but it wasn't as if I'd just been along for the ride.

Hell with it, I told myself, and went below to get some of that green-glaze ham and powdered mashed potatoes.

TEN

The next day a final strike *was* called. A Catalina from Midway had reported seeing a carrier and two damaged cruisers in the vicinity of yesterday's strike. There'd been no confirmed sightings of the big support fleet that had come out with the four flattops with the invasion force for Midway Island. Despite that fact, they might still be nearby. The distance was just over 250 miles, a long run, but if the Catalina's report was correct, there wouldn't be very much opposition at the other end, and certainly no Zeros. My main concern was that we were missing some of our most experienced aviators due to the previous day's action. We'd lost thirty-one planes from our air group alone.

The flight out to the target area took us into fog and mist about halfway there. We were flying at 13,000 feet. When it was clear, we could see. The converse was also true. We finally got to the estimated position and found empty ocean. It turned out that the *Hornet* had also launched an earlier strike on the news that *Hiryu* might still be afloat. They'd found a lone destroyer in the area where we'd torn up *Hiryu*, but were unable to land a bomb on it. We got to that location as the *Hornet* guys were headed back and we tried our luck. Nobody could hit that feisty tin can and he never stopped shooting at us the whole time, even taking down one of our planes. We finally gave it up, and, with no sign of

Hiryu, headed back to the Big E, arriving after dark for the major fun of night carrier landings. At least this time we had fuel left.

The following day brought more reports of Japanese ships to our northwest. *Hornet* sent out a strike that found two heavy cruisers, apparently damaged and leaking a lot of oil, along with two destroyers, but no carriers. They promptly attacked. Big E had sent out a morning scouting mission looking for any threats to our northwest, but they'd found nothing. Everybody assumed that the Jap admiral had decided that, without any air cover, it was time to get his much diminished fleet out of there. Then in the afternoon we got the order to put a strike together and go after those two cruisers. The *Hornet* after-action report said that they had heavily damaged both of them.

When we arrived they certainly looked damaged, but from the volume of AA fire that came sizzling up at us this wasn't going to be a routine mop-up mission. We had come to the party with 500-pounders so that we could carry more avgas because of the long range. The first three guys to roll in achieved one hit and two very near misses. It helped that neither cruiser could maneuver. I was number four and planted my bomb centerline behind a cruiser's main smokestack. It didn't diminish her AA fire as I pulled out, though, and I clearly heard the snaps and pings of Jap metal bouncing off my plane. Still, I was satisfied that my bomb *had* to have gone off down in a main machinery space. When we left, both ships looked like goners, smoking from every orifice, topsides wrecked, the gun barrels of their turrets drooping over the side as if exhausted, and white plumes of steam bleeding out of the hull instead of the stacks. I told Rooster that if they did get them home, they'd be used for scrap steel.

"They ain't *never* gonna get them pogues home, Boss. Believe it."

I had to agree with him. And yet, throughout our attack, both ships had kept on shooting, and shooting pretty well. They had no air cover and only two small destroyers to help with the AA problem, but they kept fighting. When I pulled out I'd taken a good look at their topside areas and they were a shambles of broken and blackened metal, ruptured steel plating, leaning superstructure elements, and yet all of it populated by bright yellow and red flashes as those game bastards kept shooting at us. Above all else, *that* fact made an indelible impression on this ex-nugget.

That night Admiral Spruance took the task force north, refueling as we went. The Japs had landed troops on Attu and Kiska Islands, part of the Alaska Territory island chain that extends 1,200 miles into the Pacific Ocean. We pilots spent a lot of time debriefing our exploits to the intel people and then catching up on some much-needed sleep. Down in the hangar deck the mechs worked round the clock to repair damaged or simply broken aircraft. The next morning I had a cigarette out on the edge of the flight deck and watched them push three SBD carcasses over the side. They'd been deemed too damaged to repair, so the mechs had stripped them of all usable parts and then the flight deck crew pitched them overboard.

It was a sad sight. Those warbirds had done their job, so it was hard for me to wrap my mind around the fact that they were as expendable as empty ammo crates. Like us, my disloyal brain reminded me. Somewhere back in the States a crew of aviation assembly line workers, mostly women, had put their everything into making those planes.

Rooster showed up to join me in the morning cigarette ritual. He informed me that one of the planes just sent overboard had been ours. A Jap shell had cracked the keel during the cruiser strike. Good Boeing iron that it was, it held up until I landed and the tailhook caught, at which point the entire fuselage had been torqued ten degrees out of alignment. Damn, was all I could say.

We were halfway up to Alaska and doing strike planning when Admiral Nimitz recalled the entire task force to Pearl. Apparently there was other business to attend to, although, once again, we pilots weren't told any details. The skipper thought our reversal served the Japs right. Why in the world would they invade a couple of remote islands up there near the Arctic, he pointed out, unless to attract some American forces to an ambush. Now they can just sit there and shiver. And starve: rice doesn't do well in Alaska.

Our arrival in Pearl turned into something of a celebration. The Pacific Fleet command had put out a public news bulletin that the carrier fleet had defeated a Japanese carrier fleet at Midway. They were a little sketchy on the details of actual losses in the public release, theirs and ours, but the import was clear: for the first time since Pearl Harbor we'd smacked them hard *and* sent them packing. Among the naval commands at Pearl, however, the "butcher's bill" was beginning to sink in. Still: we'd lost one carrier; they'd lost four. Everyone around the devastated harbor had a little more spring in their step after that news got out.

Bombing Six had flown off the Big E from 50 miles out and landed at one of the new air stations on Oahu. The other carrier squadrons did likewise, and then there was a general rebalancing of three carriers' worth of planes among the two surviving flattops. Pilots were reassigned to bring squadrons up to full strength again. The good news was that about a third of the guys we'd thought had been killed in action had been picked up by a three-day multi-plane Catalina seaplane sweep carried out after the Japs had retired.

To my surprise some of the most experienced and senior pilots were sent back to the States to the aviation training command to teach the next crop of nuggets the ropes of carrier warfare. That served two purposes: the instructors were real combat veterans, and an eight-month tour in the training command was a great way to recover from the strain of carrier warfare. They'd be back to the fleet soon enough, rested, refreshed, knowing the latest technical and tactical stuff, and flying brand-new planes when they did come. The first week back I got to spend a couple of days down on Waikiki Beach at a fancy hotel. Each squadron got some beach time, and that was wonderful. The only thing missing was the sight of bathing beauties. Everywhere you looked there were only hundreds of young men lounging around in khaki shorts, Hawaiian shirts, and all sporting sunburns and exotic drinks involving rum, pineapple, and tiny parasols. I remembered those damned things well and stuck to beer. And thought about my classmate and Mai Tai buddy, who was probably still aboard the capsized *Oklahoma*. *God*damned war.

The next week we regrouped as a squadron and spent our days completing a myriad of admin duties: maintenance, after-action reports, annual inspections, and all the other overburden associated with being a naval officer. The Monday after that the entire squadron, officers and enlisted, were called to the air station movie theater, which we found surrounded by armed Marines. A passing Jap bomber had strafed the air station and put several holes into the ceiling of the theater, so now there were white cotton plugs everywhere to keep out the occasional tropical shower.

Once inside we found out what the big deal was all about. We were there for a highly classified briefing on something called Operation Watchtower. Apparently the Allies were going to seize a couple of islands down in the Solomons chain to prevent the Japs, who were already there, from achieving a stranglehold on the seaborne supply line between America and Australia. The Solomons were a very long way from Pearl, some 3,500 miles. The Japs' main base was at some place called Rabaul, and they had begun construction of an airfield on an island called Guadalcanal, some 660 miles from Rabaul.

These names were exotic and, of course, totally foreign. None of us had even ever heard of the Solomon Islands, much less Guadalcanal and Rabaul. You will, the briefer predicted. Everyone will. Admiral Nimitz was going to send three of his remaining four carriers to support the operation: *Enterprise*, the recently repaired *Saratoga*, and *Wasp*. We'd be under the overall command of Admiral Ghormley, based in the port city of Nouméa, in New Caledonia, which itself was nearly 1,000 miles from Guadalcanal.

I was reminded of the time I'd taken a driving tour out in the great American West. Where's the meteor crater, I'd asked a motel clerk. Just up the road, which in reality meant 200 miles. Just up the road in the Pacific *started* at 1,000 miles.

The high command expected that the Japs would "respond vigorously," as the briefer put it, to our occupation of Guadalcanal, and they'd do that from Rabaul. There'd be a British carrier and an Australian cruiser involved at some point but our Marines would be doing the heavy lifting by taking both Guadalcanal and a Jap seaplane base on a nearby island called Tulagi.

There was silence in the theater when the briefer was finished. I think everyone was really surprised. We were going to stage an invasion? After six months of the Japanese overwhelming everything in their path, from Manchuria to Java, we were finally going to go over to the *offensive*? The skipper raised his hand and asked the most important question: When?

"Carriers leave the first week in July. The invasion is planned for the first week in August."

I did some quick math: if this Guadalcanal target was 3,500 miles away it would take ten days to get there at the fleet's most economical open-ocean transit speed. The skipper told us we'd spend that transit time training all the new guys after the Midway reallocation of planes and pilots. Our short "vacation" was clearly about to end. I realized I wouldn't miss it very much. The "charms" of Waikiki were definitely overrated.

ELEVEN

We hit the seaplane base on Tulagi Island the afternoon before the Marines landed on Guadalcanal. Bombing Six and Scouting Six from *Enterprise* along with Bombing Three from *Saratoga* made successive strikes, apparently catching the Japs entirely by surprise. The seaplanes in question were the *Kawanishi* models, the biggest armed flying boats in the world, almost twice the size of our Catalinas. They carried a crew of ten, had a sea range of 4,400 miles, and were armed to the teeth with the capability to deliver big bombs, depth charges, torpedoes, and to shred the top hampers of any ship or submarine with 20mm cannon and large machine guns. We first bombed the piers and ramps in the harbor and then went down for strafing runs on the planes themselves, flaming every damned one of them. But it was on my second strafing pass that some lucky Jap AA gunner shot the propeller off my trusty SBD. One moment I was climbing through 3,000 feet after shooting up the harbor; the next something flew past the canopy and the engine ran away with an angry howl until the over-speed shutdown functioned as the mill redlined. The sudden silence was horrifying but not as scary as the sensation that our beloved warbird had just turned into a flying rock.

Per training I shoved the nose down to maintain airspeed and yelled at Rooster to prepare to ditch. My first priority was to get as far away as possible from the hornets' nest we'd just stirred up on Tulagi. The weather was relatively clear and the sea calm. I radioed our strike leader and told him I was going in, east of the island, heavily aware that there would probably be no Catalinas way out here coming to pick us up. I was hoping against hope that the Japs hadn't noticed my plane had been disabled. There was no fire and we weren't making smoke, so maybe, just maybe, we'd appear to simply be leaving the party. From the ground it would look like we'd just leveled off and flown away. More strafing runs were in progress behind us, which ought to keep their AA crews' attention. I held her nose down at as shallow an angle as I could to gain distance from Tulagi, and then went into roller-coaster mode: kept her pretty flat until I felt a stall coming on, then dropped the nose sharply to restore airspeed, then eased back into the glide to gain more distance from Tulagi while Rooster ran through the ditching checklist. Truth be told, however, the SBD3A had the glide characteristics of a school bus.

We both slid our canopies back and I made sure the life raft was free of any entanglements. We ate up those 3,000 feet of altitude much sooner than I would have wished. When we were 20 feet above the water and just about to stall again I lifted the nose slightly so that the tail would hit first. Five seconds later I felt the bump of the tailhook hitting the water, and then we were down in a huge crash of seawater, a painful pull on my straps, and the shock of something hitting me in the solar plexus, namely the stick.

Immediately the plane stood on her nose, courtesy of that two-ton engine right in front of me plus a tidal wave of seawater flooding my cockpit. We'd been trained to wait for the initial crash energy to dissipate. The plane rocked its tail high in the air and then settled back down, not quite level, and began to sink. She slowly raised her tail again as our constant nemesis, gravity, discovered all that steel and seawater in the nose. *That* was the moment to get out. I hurled the raft over the side, holding on to its lanyard, unsnapped my straps, and tried to get up. Apparently we'd hit harder than I'd known because I couldn't stand up. I couldn't do anything at all. Worst of all I couldn't catch my breath. I felt like I'd been poleaxed.

"I gotcha, Boss, I gotcha," Rooster shouted in my ear. "Easy there, now."

He dragged me out of the cockpit and down onto the left wing which was already awash. I tried to say something but a wave came up and slapped me in the face. The next thing I knew I was immersed in the warm Pacific, spitting up seawater, kicking my legs to keep my head above water, and coughing my lungs out. Rooster reached around my chest and pulled my Mae West lanyard, which solved the problem of keeping my face out of the water. The plane was definitely sinking now so we pushed away from it, towing the black rubber bundle that was the life raft. Then the tail went perfectly vertical and she slid under the waves in a boil of air bubbles laced with avgas.

We didn't inflate the raft immediately. Other pilots had reported that if Jap fighters came looking and saw a raft, they'd strafe it every time. If it was a *Kawanishi* who found you, they would land, take you prisoner, and deliver you to a higher authority, usually at the headquarters which you'd just bombed. We could only imagine what happened after that, so our training called for us to watch for enemy planes for a little while before actually getting into the raft unless the sharks showed up. Fifteen minutes later we heard a familiar rumble of SBD engines. A pair of them from Scouting Six came overhead at 1,000 feet and waggled their wings. We both made a thumbs-up sign and then they were gone. Our sense of relief was palpable. They knew we were down and alive. What they could do about that we did not know, but, by God, it was a start.

We drifted somewhere east of Tulagi and Malaita Island for almost two days. There were some minimal supplies of food and canned water in the raft, which we rationed carefully. The rest of the time we kept watch for *Kawanishis*. At the first sound of an approaching plane we planned to go over the side and underwater. On the afternoon of the second day we did hear a plane coming. Looking into the sun we saw the silhouette of what had to be a seaplane, so over the side we went and hid under the raft. When the plane passed overhead we saw it was a Catalina, so we popped back up and started waving. The parasol-winged seaplane turned around, landed, and picked us out of the water. One of the guys helping us aboard stuck a big knife into our raft, and then we were off. By policy they weren't supposed to land in the open ocean, but rescuing aviators had an informal dispensation from that rule.

We learned that the Marines had taken the almost-completed dirt airfield on Guadalcanal without much of a fight and, using abandoned Japanese grading equipment, were scrambling to make the runway fully serviceable. A detachment of Marine fighters was expected in the next day or so. The PBY crew told us that they'd flown all the way from Nouméa, a distance of almost 1,000 miles, which was where the big boss for the south Pacific, Vice Admiral Ghormley, had his headquarters. A thousand miles, I thought. That should keep him safe. Maybe he was the Navy's version of Douglas MacArthur.

We flew south of the island of Malaita because capture of the Tulagi base was still in the mop-up phase. Then we flew the long way around to Guadalcanal and landed on the finished half of the dirt strip for fuel. There they found several Navy hospitalmen waiting with some wounded Marines in litters on the ground. That meant we two lost our seats so that the plane could take as many wounded as possible back to the Nouméa field hospital complex. A mud-splattered Marine took us across the red dirt of the airfield and into a pagoda-shaped structure on one side of the airfield, which was serving as a temporary control tower. Down at the far end of the field we could see construction machinery kicking up large clouds of red dust while a couple of stubby tanks kept them company. The occasional thump of artillery made the walk interesting, but our guide didn't seem to notice it.

There was an extremely harried Marine major in the tower room trying to deal with various crises. Our guide pushed us up to the desk and then left. The major finally saw us.

"And who the hell are you guys?" he asked. He looked as if he hadn't slept for days.

We told him our sad story.

"So you didn't bring me an airplane?"

"No, sir," I said. "It was shot down, remember?"

"What the hell am I supposed to do with two aviators and no fucking plane? If you had a bomber *and* fuel *and* bombs, I'd be kissing your boots, but otherwise take two APCs and call me in the morning."

He gestured for us to get out of there and turned back to the three field radios that were all clamoring for his attention at once. Rooster and I wandered out of the chaos into the hot sunlight and sat down on ammo boxes.

"Welcome to Guadalcanal," Rooster muttered.

"Yeah, well, he is just a little busy. Now that they've got wounded there'll be more Catalinas. We'll just have to wait for a seat."

"That something you *know*, Boss?" Rooster asked.

Finally a sergeant stopped to ask who we were and what we were doing there. We again recited our tale of woe. He grunted and took us to a collection of rectangular tents that apparently was the main communications center for the operation. Everyone inside the tent seemed to be really pissed off. We finally learned why: the invasion's support ships, loaded with food, medical supplies, and water, had been withdrawn "temporarily," so things were a little tight right now. About that time a firefight erupted somewhere nearby, with lots of machine-gun fire and the crump of mortars joining in. The sergeant told us to stay there. He then ordered a corporal to find us some weapons and some ammo.

We waited some more, trying to stay out of the way of the beehive of activity going on. We were used to the air-conditioned spaces aboard ship, where everything was clean and nobody was shouting. This was more like a Boy Scout camp where the tender-feet had been turned loose with a serious job. There was no ventilation in the tents, no fans, and conversation was difficult because of the generators roaring just outside. The corporal returned with two 1903 Springfield rifles, both of which had bloodstains on the stocks. He gave us each a handful of ammo, wished us good luck, and disappeared. Rooster went looking for water and found out he had to go about 200 yards to the nearest "water buffalo," a short, squat water tank on wheels. He came back to beg somebody for a canteen and then went back to the "buff," where the guys guarding the tank only filled it halfway. Water was being prioritized for the medics and the wounded. The rest of the troops were advised to catch rainwater in their helmets.

At around two in the afternoon a jeep came up to the Pagoda and debarked a full colonel and what looked like his aide. When he noticed the two of us sitting there in our damp flight suits with rifles by our side, he walked over. I'd heard that Marines were sometimes called leathernecks. This guy's face looked like a picture I'd seen of Sitting Bull, only meaner.

"Okay, I give up," he growled. "What the hell, over?"

For the third time I told our story. He gave the standard Marine sympathy grunt and asked if we'd had water or chow. Rooster said he'd raided the water buffalo.

The colonel nodded. "You have to have water in this heat. Food right now is optional, but I'll try. We had some inbound but the Navy took it back. I'll get the comms people to get word to them that you're here. In the meantime, this island is infested with embarrassed Japs and is by no means secure, so I'm going to get someone to put you in a relatively safe place for the night. Right now, stay put."

We both said yessir like a couple of recruits and sat back down once he'd left. Rooster began examining his rifle and then started to load some rounds into its magazine. I was a shotgun man so he had to show me how to operate the thing. Each rifle had a bayonet folded under the barrel, which we left alone. A few minutes later a Marine showed up and handed us some C-rations and a single bullet-dented canteen. Progress.

That night the Marines seemed to be extremely edgy. There'd been reports that the Japs had landed a large force of infantry somewhere along the island's north coast and were intent on re-taking the airfield. The local commander, General Vandegrift, had set up three defensive lines around the airfield, even though he was convinced the Japs would come over the beaches at Lunga Point, not from the interior. Rooster and I were given steel hel-mets and a pick and a shovel. We were told to dig a slit trench about a hundred yards from the Pagoda.

An exhausted-looking sergeant brought us a shelter half while we were digging in so that we'd have cover from the nighttime downpours. He was a short man, carrying a carbine-style rifle on a shoulder sling. He also had two hand grenades, a canteen, six ammo clips, a first-aid kit, a 1911 model .45, and a large knife hanging off his webbed belt. I wondered how he could even walk. He examined our unimpressive efforts in moving the red Guadal-canal dirt, squinted, and shook his head.

"Gotta go deeper, Ensign," he said. "Think China. You need to be able to stand up in that hole with just your tin hat showing. And make one end deeper than the other so's the rain will collect there and not in your shoes. Then build a lump so's each of you can poke a rifle up over that dirt and kill some Japs. You know how to fix those bayonets?"

We didn't have the first idea. He showed us, trying to disguise the fact that he thought we were hopeless.

"Your hole here is behind two other defensive perimeters," he said, "so you should be okay if the Japs hit us tonight. But you never know. In the meantime, don't shoot at anything or anybody unless they're wavin' a sword or screaming *banzai*. If some shit *does* start tonight, fix those pig-stickers, keep your heads down, and leave the serious business to us."

"They didn't teach us much in the way of infantry tactics at flight school, Sergeant," I offered.

He grinned, squatted down on his haunches and lit a cigarette, then offered each of us a smoke. We eagerly accepted.

"Ain't much to it," he said. "If they come, there'll be a whole lot of noise. Rifles, machine guns, mortars, maybe even some arty. And flares. There'll be lotsa flares. The Brits told us that the Japs give their troops some kinda pill to amp 'em up just before they jump off the line, so they scream a lot."

He paused to take a huge drag on his cigarette, burning it down to a glowing half. "If they make it all the way to the runway, there won't be that many of 'em left. It also means there might not be that many of *us* left, either, so you two might have to stand tall right here and start shooting. The trick is to make each shot count. None of this between-the-eyes shit, especially when your own eyes will prolly be closed. You aim for his knees and fire once. Work the bolt, aim for his knees if he's still upright, and sque-e-e-ze the trigger. Don't jerk it."

"His *knees*?" Rooster asked.

"Everybody shoots high when they're scared. Aim for his knees and you'll hit him in the belly. Then pick out another one and do it again. One round: one dead Jap. That's the way to kill 'em all. Where's your water?"

We had the one canteen, but it was empty. He handed over his canteen and told us to drink up. "I'll see what I can do," he said. "But you gotta understand something: the fuckin' Navy has done a bunk. As in, they cut and run. There was a big sea fight last night and our guys got creamed. Bunch of our heavy cruisers went down. A thousand or more dead. Plus: the fuckin' carriers have left. Without air cover, the transports, which still have half our gear, have also left. So we're on our own here, and there ain't much in the way of chow, fuel, or ammo."

"Left?"

"That's the word the colonel used, when he wasn't cussin' the yellow-bellied squids, no offense to you two flyboys. Listen: You shoot some Japs close to your hole? When things calm down, go out there and scrounge their rice bags. Colonel sez we're all gonna be rice-bellies before this shit's over. Make sure they're dead before you take their stuff, though. You know, just stick 'em with those bayonets. If they move, stick 'em again like you mean it."

I looked at Rooster after the sergeant had left. There'd been just the hint of a gleam in the sergeant's eyes when he talked about sticking Japs. It was possible he'd been putting us on just a little bit. Still.

"You ever heard that expression, out of the frying pan and into the fire?" I asked.

He nodded bleakly and we returned to our dig-down-to-China project. As darkness fell we were exhausted, soaking wet with sweat, but standing in a slit trench with our chins on the top edge. All our excavated dirt was mounded up around our hole. We'd been so busy digging in that we'd forgotten that we needed a way *out* of the trench, so then we had to dig some more to cut steps into that hard red dirt at one end. A corporal came by as we finished up. He was carrying almost as much gear as the sergeant had been, but he had an M1 rifle, not a carbine. He handed over some C-ration boxes and two canteens of water. We drank eagerly, trying to ignore the bitter taste of whatever they'd put into the water to make it safe.

"Use that shelter half to catch rainwater," the corporal said, seeing our faces as we gagged on the treated water. "It tastes a whole lot better. And smear some of that mud on your arms and faces so the skeeters go somewhere else. They got malaria around here. Come morning, head up to the Pagoda. There's scuttlebutt that we'll have a cook tent tomorrow."

We got him to refresh us both on how to operate the Springfields, begged a little more ammo, and then dutifully rigged one edge of the shelter half so that rain would collect. For once we hoped it would rain, because our canteens were nearly empty.

Even at night it was very hot and wet on this godforsaken island. I promised myself that I would never, *ever*, complain about the living conditions aboard a Navy ship.

We heard vehicles moving around as night settled in, their big diesel engines grinding away in the hot darkness. There were no lights showing anywhere, which had to mean that the Marines *were* expecting a Jap attack. Rooster and I checked our rifles to make sure they were loaded correctly. The sergeant had made a big deal about making sure the bullet's pointy end faced down the barrel. We went ahead and put the bayonets on and took a few practice aims over the rim of our trench. The rifles were unwieldy with the bayonets fixed, but we had that dirt mound to rest them on. We looked at each other in the darkness, both of us surely thinking the same damned thing: What the *hell* were we doing here?

We picked our way through the C-rations. Fortunately Rooster knew how to operate the tiny can opener that was glued to one of the cans. We then decided to take two-hour shifts so that one of us would always be awake. Rooster was more tired than I was so he went down first, sitting lengthwise in the trench with his back against the crude steps we'd cut into the earth. The shelter half covered only his head and chest. If it really rained, he'd get soaked, but we'd had to shorten it to catch precious drinking water. Towards the end of my first watch I heard some sporadic shooting off in the distance.

Probably some animal spooking the sentries out in the jungle between us and the sea, I told myself. I know the feeling, I thought. The dark jungle around us was full of small sounds. Then three red flares turned night into day behind us and all hell broke loose.

The sergeant had been *under*stating the noise. A veritable tidal wave of gunfire rose around the airfield and rolled over our little foxhole: the crack of rifles, the deadly, deep-throated chatter of the .50-caliber machine guns, thumps from mortar tubes, and the nasty bang of some kind of field artillery, probably those short

75mm howitzers I'd seen when we landed. I couldn't have said anything to Rooster if I wanted to because of the ear-smothering racket. More flares, white ones this time, and then some red ones that seemed to be farther out. White: Marines—red: Japs? We had no idea, but when a couple of bullets puffed our shelter half up into the air we both did a synchronized deep knee bend.

Bits of dirt began flying off our mound and down into the trench, and, if anything, the noise got worse. Worse meant closer, I told myself, and I pulled back the bolt and jacked a round into my rifle's chamber, closed the bolt, upon which the rifle immediately fired because I'd had my finger on the trigger. Fortunately it was pointed up and out of the trench but it scared the shit out of both of us. There was smoke now, gun smoke and what smelled like burning oil. I *had* to see.

I reloaded and then used my bayonet to cut a small notch into the mound of loose dirt around our trench and peered over the edge just as more flares went off. To my horror there were men everywhere, running, kneeling, shooting, falling down, throwing grenades, spinning around as they got hit. I leveled my rifle over the mound. Rooster was suddenly right there alongside, his rifle pointed out into the smoky gloom, and then some kind of round, probably mortar, went off about 50 feet in front of us. Fragments from the mortar explosion hummed past our heads. I was so scared that all I could do was gawp at the firefight that was going on right in front of us. I wanted to shoot, to do *something*, but there was no way to tell friend from foe. That was until three smallish figures in green uniforms came out of the darkness and ran straight at us, bayonets leveled, furiously working the bolts on their rifles and screaming their lungs out. Japs! Rooster fired immediately and one folded over and went down. I fired next, aiming at his knees just like the sergeant had told us, and the man's face exploded. He fell like a tree. We both shot the third guy, who shot back, blasting a clump of red dirt into my face. He collapsed ten feet from our trench, hitting face-first, and then, sweet *Jesus*, got back up onto one knee and lifted his rifle. We both worked our bolts and fired simultaneously. One of us hit him in the face, the other lifted the top of his skull right off. We'd both aimed at his belly.

Suddenly a Marine appeared, flopped down on his belly next to our trench, and emptied a submachine gun out into the darkness like a Chicago mobster, mowing down more green figures who were coming at us. When he'd taken care of business, he saw the three dead Japs nearby and grinned. Way to go, *squids*, he said. Then he was gone, running into the dark with his submachine gun held sideways on his hip, firing into the darkness.

I rubbed as much dirt out of my eyes as I could and then hunkered down, rifle pointed out, waiting for something to shoot at. Then a heavy .50-caliber machine gun erupted up on the Pagoda and proceeded to sweep the entire area, cutting down green men, trees, bushes, ammo crates, and everything else out there in the weeds. Incredibly we saw muzzle flashes out in those weeds, as dying Japs shot back.

And then it was over. The firing petered out and finally stopped. The flares hissed out in the wet sawgrass. A string of single shots cracked the air for the next twenty minutes, and then we heard a rebel yell from somewhere way out there on the field. It was repeated all around the airfield. Two planes were burning on the edge of the runway, casting the whole scene in bright orange light as they settled into their own demolition. I could see distant figures moving cautiously here and there, using whatever cover there was, kneeling to shoot or stab and then scrambling sideways before somebody shot back.

I suddenly had to sit down, which is when I discovered that I'd pissed my pants. I looked over at Rooster, who was clutching his crotch, aghast at apparently having done the same thing. Aim for their knees, the sarge had said. Aim, hell, I thought. Dive-bombing a Jap carrier was a piece'a cake compared to this shit. Rooster remembered that we were supposed to go get their rice. I said I was willing to wait until morning. Two Marines came trotting by just then, looking for trouble. They saw the dead Japs, saw us, and quickly relieved the bodies of their ration bags before disappearing into the night. And yes, they did stick the Japs in the throat before reaching down to rifle through their combat belts. Oh, well, I thought, hopefully we'll be lifted out of here in the next couple of days. In the meantime, I told Rooster he had the watch. He started laughing, but I was too exhausted to see the humor in our situation. Then it started to rain. Perfect. Nobody would be able to tell we'd pissed ourselves.

The next morning found us both sound asleep in our hole, sitting in about six inches of muddy red water. Our efforts to catch rainwater had been defeated by the bullet holes in our shelter half. We climbed out and walked toward the Pagoda, where a mess tent had been set up. We joined the line and found out they had coffee, powdered scrambled eggs, and canned bacon. It smelled wonderful. One of the guys in line recognized us.

"Hey, it's the flyboys," he announced. "They killed some Japs last night. How about that shit."

There were murmurs of approval from the line. One Marine asked how many we'd bagged.

"Three," I said. "Here, anyway."

"Yeah? That mean you been killin' Japs somewhere's else?"

I nodded. "The two of us dive-bombed the Jap carriers at Midway. We and the rest of our squadron probably killed a couple thousand Japs that day."

There were whistles of appreciation, and then lots of questions about Midway. We got our chow and joined a small knot of Marines sitting on pallets, their rifles across their laps while balancing their mess kits on top of their rifles. While we were talking to the Marines a clutch of R4Ds appeared, escorted by some fighters. Six of the two-engine aircraft in all, which back home were called the DC-3, landed, bringing medical teams and the material needed to set up a field hospital. They also brought ammo, food, and enough avgas to refuel the fighters, who would escort them back to home base. Once unloaded they took aboard grievously wounded Marines for the flight back to the big field hospital at Nouméa. We hitched a ride on one of them for the 1,000-mile trip, both of us sporting USMC utility caps. Hopefully from Nouméa we could get back to the Big E, where we would have some stories to tell.

TWELVE

Two weeks after Rooster and I got back aboard the Big E the ship departed Nouméa and headed for the waters east of Guadalcanal in company with the carriers *Wasp* and *Saratoga*. The intel briefers came to the ready room to tell us what was going on the second day out. The Japanese had mounted a major operation to retake Guadalcanal and they were coming out in force. Two large carriers, *Shokaku*, *Zuikaku*, and the light carrier *Ryujo*, plus an entire herd of battleships, cruisers, destroyers, and even one of their big seaplane tenders were headed south from Rabaul and Truk. A convoy of troopships carrying over 15,000 Japanese troops was close behind.

Our mission was to break this effort up. The main problem was finding the Japanese carrier formations, preferably before they found us. As we all knew, any carrier, theirs or ours, presented a large and vulnerable target to a flight of determined dive and torpedo bombers. Bombing Six and Scouting Six began flying scouting missions, augmented by PBY flights out of Henderson Field on Guadalcanal. We searched the northern sectors of the Solomon Islands for the entire day and found nothing. That night, the *Wasp* was detached because she was low on fuel, so it was just *Saratoga* and the Big E left to take care of business.

Saratoga's scouts got lucky on the following day by finding the light carrier *Ryujo*. A strike was launched immediately to go get her. A PBY had actually issued the first sighting report, which was confirmed a couple hours later. We kept waiting for Admiral Fletcher to launch a strike from *Enterprise*, too, but he wanted to hold our air group back until he knew where the much bigger, so-called fleet carriers *Shokaku* and *Zuikaku* were lurking. At around four in the afternoon *Enterprise* radar detected an incoming strike formation 80 miles out. Fighting Six launched everything that could fly that wasn't already airborne on CAP stations, while Bombing Six aircraft were struck below in anticipation of the attack. The engineers drained all the avgas lines leading to the flight and hangar decks and filled them with CO_2. GQ was sounded and the ship buttoned up. We aviators didn't really have GQ stations, so we gathered in our ready room to await developments. It was an unpleasant wait. We were locked into a space just below the flight deck by fire-isolation doors in the passageways around the ready rooms. The ventilation systems had been turned off for general quarters. Our skipper had gone to the admiral's combat information center to watch the bigger picture. The rest of us could only sit and wait.

We could feel the Big E increasing speed and easing into a gentle turn. A circling carrier was harder to hit than one running in a straight line, as we had learned from the Japs at Midway. We knew there were already dogfights in progress as the outer CAP went after incoming bombers. One of our gunners, who was also a radioman like Rooster, managed to patch in the CAP control radio circuit to a speaker in the ready room, so we got to listen in to the increasingly urgent chatter as our Wildcats went head-to-head with the bombers and their escorting fighters. Every pilot in the room felt the itching in his hands; we wanted to be up there. Our trusty SBDs were dive bombers, but we could knock a Zero or another bomber down almost as well as the fighters if they made the mistake of getting too close to us.

Enterprise's maneuvers became a little more forceful when the five-inch batteries along the flight deck opened up. All of our escorts would be shooting, too, and the sky would be turning black by the time-fused five-inch fragmenting shells. Then we felt a deep, thumping blast somewhere aft, followed by another one which sounded like it went off on the flight deck, followed instantly by a bigger blast. A minute later there was a third hit, again on the flight deck, and this one was pretty close to our ready room. A fine mist of dust and ceiling tile debris bloomed in the ready room and the lights went out for a few seconds. The flight deck guns never stopped shooting, but it felt as if the ship was slowing down. That first bomb had gone deep, and that could be seriously bad news. We got a whiff of smoke coming out of the ventilation ducts. Since they were shut down, that meant fire wasn't too far away.

One of the pilots shouted: Look! He pointed at the door that led to the passageway outside the ready room. The smoke wasn't coming from the vent ducts—it was curling in around the seams of the ready room door, which, being one level beneath the flight deck and way above the waterline, was just a plain metal door. The nearest pilot got up and gingerly touched the door, recoiling immediately. There was a scramble to get something stuffed into those seams. One of the guys pulled down the briefing stage curtains and another poured coffee from the pot all over them. They then jammed the edges into the door seams.

Lieutenant Quantrill got up onto the stage, pulled a chair up with him, and touched the overhead. It, too, was hot to the touch and we suddenly got a whiff of woodsmoke. That meant that the flight deck was on fire above us. The Royal Navy's aircraft carriers had opted for steel flight decks; the US Navy had chosen wood to reduce topside weight and to provide a better surface for landings. A coffee cup began a slow slide off the stage table, which is when we realized *Enterprise* had developed a list. Quantrill, who was the senior officer present, was calling somebody on a sound-powered telephone to let them know we were stuck in the ready room and that we were getting smoke.

Five minutes later the guns went quiet, but we hardly noticed. It was growing progressively hotter in the ready room. The coffee-soaked stage curtains had stopped most of the smoke, but the ship was still at GQ, doing damage control, so there was no ventilation. Then somebody banged on the door and shouted for us to back away. An axe crashed through the door handle side and then a large man wearing an oxygen breathing apparatus kicked the door in. Immediately the room began filling with acrid gray smoke, but the big guy was followed in by several men, each wearing and carrying an OBA. We began putting them on and trying not to screw it up; all of us had been trained, once, how to put on and energize an OBA, but that had been a long time ago. The damage-control team helped us get the systems going, and then we formed a line at the door and followed the team out into the passageway, where we could see absolutely nothing except small cones of yellow light from battle lanterns. They instructed us to grab the belt of the guy in front of you.

They took our little conga line forward, away from where all the blast noises had come from, and finally up and out onto the flight deck, forward of the island structure. We got the OBAs off and gulped down fresh sea air. Behind the island there was a pretty substantial fire, but *Enterprise* was still moving forward under her own power. The gun crews were out on the flight deck helping to snake fire hoses aft to fight the fires. The deck near the five-inch mounts was littered with brass shell casings, which were trying to slide down the hill created by the ship's list. I could see *Saratoga* in the distance. She appeared to be recovering aircraft. The skies were clear of AA bursts and enemy aircraft, for the moment, anyway. Big E was surrounded by escorting destroyers who had formed a ring of AA guns around their carrier. Still, we'd been hit by three bombs, and nobody topside seemed to know how much damage that penetrating bomb had done or even where it had detonated. The list was subsiding as the engineers did some counter-flooding way down below.

We were all surprised to hear the call to flight quarters to recover the planes from Fighting Six. The ship began a slow turn into the wind. That put the smoke from the flight deck fire, which was mostly gray smoke now, off to the starboard quarter. We learned from one of the five-inch gun crews that a bomb had hit the base of the aftermost twin five-inch mount and set off the ready service ammunition inside. That's what was burning, although it was almost out now. Twelve men had died inside the mount and in the handling room just below it. Another bomb had hit between the island and the upper five-inch mount, detonated on the deck, and caused a second fire, including setting some of the wooden flight deck itself ablaze. That fire had been put out as well. The gunners had no word about the first hit, other than that there was smoke coming out of the very back end of the hangar bay. When the Wildcats started landing we headed back down to the ready room. The passageway still stank of smoke but the air was clear now that ventilation had been restored. Lieutenant Cox met us in the ready room and told us to suit up. Someone had located the two fleet carriers who'd just pounded Mother *Enterprise*.

It was nearly five o'clock in the afternoon, which meant a late-day attack depending on how far away the two big boys were. I was halfway into my flight suit when the GQ alarm went again. The Japs had sent a second raid and our fighters were being sent up again. Bombing Six was told to stand down. I elected to go topside, not wanting to be trapped in the ready room again. I watched six fighters get off the deck before that launch was also canceled. Long-range radar had seen the Jap strike formations turning around and heading back north. Our admiral decided that enough was enough and turned our formation south, away from where we thought the Japs' big decks were, after first recovering our fighters.

The ship secured from general quarters, so I took a fresh-air hike to the back of the ship to take a look at the damage. Both after five-inch gun mounts were wrecked and there was a big hole in the flight deck in the parking area near the blackened gun mounts. Thirty-five men had been killed in the gun mounts and handling rooms, and another thirty-five had died way down on the fifth deck, with an additional seventy men injured. The word was already out on the flight deck: we were going back to Pearl for repairs. The ship's welders were already burning away at the hole in the flight deck, but replacing those gun mounts plus whatever had happened down below would take a shipyard.

Saratoga's Bombing Three had been shining while *Enterprise* was under attack. They'd found and wrecked the light carrier *Ryujo*. Then they'd launched a second strike against the bigger carriers but had been unable to find them, but they did find the 15,000-ton seaplane tender *Chitose*, a floating base for those nasty *Kawanishi* flying boats, and obtained enough hits to bring her dead in the water with major flooding. I felt like Bombing Six had been sidelined for this scrap. *Wasp* had left before anything started because she was low on fuel, so *Sara* carried the water during this particular carrier battle. It was not like the spectacular victory we'd achieved at Midway. On the other hand, the Japs had lost another carrier. That meant five since I'd begun actual flight ops. I wondered if all those graybeards in Washington had gotten the message: carriers were not some flashy distraction. Maybe the Japs had done us a favor by sinking the battleships at Pearl. We'd had a battlewagon with us during the past few days, but all she was good for was five-inch AA fire. Give them their due, they could fill the skies with frag shells from all those bristling five-inch barrels clustered along their sides, but those big sixteen-inch guns had remained centerlined.

The skipper called a meeting that night to talk about the future. *Enterprise* was going back to Pearl for repairs, which might take up to two months, if you included the thousands of miles of transit involved. Once back in Pearl, the ship's air group would be going ashore, mostly for yet more training. Some of our pilots would go back to the States to train the next class of nuggets. Others would be cross-decked to a new carrier that was coming out, but her arrival date was unknown. There were two other possibilities, but decisions had to be made before the Big E left the theater of operations, as in, tonight.

The first option was to go to Henderson Field on Guadalcanal. They needed bomber pilots to attack the steady stream of Jap convoys coming down from Rabaul bringing Jap army reinforcements to Guadalcanal. The second was to cross-deck to *Hornet*, who'd missed the battle of the eastern Solomons but needed replacements in both their fighter and bombing squadrons.

I had zero desire to go back to Pearl for yet more "training" while living in Spartan Marine barracks on an increasingly crowded island that was still doing blackout every night. And having already been to the island paradise known as Guadalcanal, I opted for the *Hornet*. I was a carrier dive bomber pilot, and *Hornet* would be staying out here and hopefully sending carrier dive bombers out to kill Japs. Any volunteers for *Hornet*? I raised my hand.

The next morning Rooster and I ferried an SBD over to the *Hornet* to join Bombing Eight. I'd hoped it wouldn't be another episode of nugget-training new guy in new squadron, but I needn't have worried. They greeted me as "Fish" Steele, and the skipper had promotion papers in hand, courtesy of a message from Bombing Six. I was now Lieutenant (Junior Grade) Steele. No more En-swine jokes. Three other pilots from Bombing Six had also cross-decked, so I didn't feel lonely. Rooster disappeared down into the hangar bay with the SBD I'd flown over. I knew I could count on him to get the straight skinny on my new squadron by day's end, but my first impression was of a competent and friendly outfit. It was interesting to watch them try not to think about the pilots and gunners who were gone when they saw all the new faces in the ready room.

We cross-deckers met with their flight officer, Lieutenant "Skivvy" Hastings, for a review of Bombing Eight's formation procedures, tactical radio rules, and other standard operating procedures. There wasn't much that was different from the way we'd been doing things in Bombing Six, but there were still bad feelings in *Hornet*'s squadrons about what had happened at Midway, where her air group essentially missed the show by flying out the wrong way. The fact that I had been at Midway and obtained direct hits led to my being asked what I thought of their SOP, which was quite a contrast from my first days with Bombing Six. For once I had the good sense not to offer any sage advice to my new squadron mates. Midway was still a raw nerve with these guys.

We had about a month to absorb all this before we found out that the Japanese navy was coming in force to settle the Guadalcanal issue once and for all. That was the good news. The bad news was that *Saratoga* had been torpedoed, again, and was on her way back to Pearl, leaving *Hornet* the only carrier in the southwest Pacific. *Enterprise* would be returning soon, but her exact arrival date was unknown. The other big news was that Vice Admiral Halsey had relieved Vice Admiral Ghormley as the overall naval commander in the southwest Pacific. Halsey had an interesting reputation and was known for his aggressiveness. He was also an aviator. The Bombing Eight skipper knew him and told us to stand by for a new way of doing business. True to form, one of Halsey's first fleet-wide messages ended with the exhortation to kill Japs, kill Japs, then kill more Japs. It was a stark contrast to the way the carriers had been handled under Ghormley's command. In late October we got our first taste of Halsey's fondness for offense. The *Hornet* task force was ordered to head northwest to take on a Japanese carrier fleet bearing down on Guadalcanal. *Enterprise* was back and would rendezvous with *Hornet* in thirty-six hours, and then both carriers would begin the deadly scout plane dance.

Two mornings later, we were ordered to suit up for a strike against the Jap carrier formation. *Enterprise* had already launched. *Hornet*'s fighters were being kept back on the theory that the Japs would be coming, while *Enterprise* fighters would accompany her bombers and provide cover from Zeros over the Jap formation. Rooster and I climbed aboard the SBD we'd brought over from *Enterprise*. She was armed with two 500-pounders due to the long range to the targets. Half of the fighters launched ahead of us; the rest were kept back aboard on five minutes readiness so that they'd be fresh and fully fueled if the Japs did show up. We were fifth to launch, but as I brought my bird up to full power the engine stuttered and then lost RPM. I throttled back and tried again. This time the engine wouldn't even go to full power. I hand-signaled the launch crew that I had a bad bird. They signaled me out of the lineup and back down the starboard side to the parking area. Number six in the takeoff order launched without incident, as did the rest of the strike, a total of twelve SBDs. I was cursing the engine as the flight deck crew attached a pusher boom and headed us for the after elevator. I'd never missed a strike. I told Rooster it was all his fault, and he acknowledged that he was, indeed, the guilty bastid. I knew he was as disappointed as I was, but there was nothing we could do about it.

I climbed up to the primary flight deck control center, called PriFly, which was a steel box overhanging the flight deck on the island, much like an airport's tower. I asked if there was another bombing bird. No such luck. Did Scouting Eight have any birds? All gone hunting. Relax, Fish. You hit three carriers; you need to give some other guys a chance to shine. I was making it known that I wasn't too happy about that when an alert came from the combat information center down below: many bogies, inbound, range 55 miles. Launch the CAP. I looked at my watch: 1045. Our strike and their strike were going to pass each other.

There was an immediate scramble down on the flight deck as the rest of the fighters, whose pilots had been sitting in their cockpits, lit off their engines and crowded forward. I told Rooster to lay below into the hangar deck. For myself, I didn't want to repeat the experience of being trapped in the ready room if the Japs got lucky, so I slipped out of PriFly and went down two levels and around to the outboard side of the island, away from the flight deck. I found a small niche on a gallery catwalk between two stacks of the new-model twenty-man inflatable life rafts. It gave me a great view of the action and some protection from the 40 knots of wind streaming over the ship. To my surprise I was joined by Rooster, holding onto his white hat and close on my heels. Apparently he didn't fancy being on the hangar deck during an air attack any more than I did the ready room.

The ship was going to general quarters as the remaining fighters wobbled off the front end and began clawing for altitude. The wind across the bow grew noticeably stronger as *Hornet* increased speed. When the last Wildcat went off the bow she began a slow, shallow turn to port. I could see the escorting destroyers moving in closer, their gun mounts training out in the direction of the approaching swarm of Jap bombers. I moved out to the edge of the gallery deck, found a perch on an equipment box just below the signal bridge, and settled in to watch the show. The skies were partly cloudy, the seas relatively calm, and every gun on the ship was manned and ready. I started scanning the sky for Japs. Rooster stayed back in the notch between the life rafts and sat down on the trembling deck.

Two heavy cruisers in the carrier's screen about two miles back on our starboard quarter opened up first with their five-inch batteries. I couldn't see what they were shooting at until black puffs began to decorate the northwestern skies around the formation. I felt like I should be doing something to help with the defense, but without an airplane, a pilot was just supercargo. I nearly jumped out of my skin when all four of *Hornet*'s twin five-inchers let fly right below me. The ship was now in a slow right turn to bring the five-inch batteries' gun barrels to bear on what was coming, which I still couldn't see. I did see a black speck way up there turn bright orange and fall out of the sky, followed by another. The curtain of flak grew heavier as every ship in the task force got into it, blasting hot steel into the skies from five-inchers and the light cruisers' six-inchers. The side of the battleship accompanying us turned into a wall of flame as her five twin-barreled five-inchers opened up. I still couldn't see the Japs. Then I realized I should have been looking *up*.

And here they came, just like we had done at Midway. Two Vals, carrier bombers, the Jap version of the SBD, had pushed over into seventy-degree dives, engines howling, the planes getting bigger and bigger as they jinked from side to side, buffeted by the aerodynamic forces of a 300-knot drop and near misses from all the AA fire. I stared in horror, very much aware that this was how the Japs on *Akagi*, *Kaga*, *Soryu*, and *Hiryu* must have felt when we hit them. I also realized that coming up here had been a dumb idea. Neither of us had helmets, life jackets, or any other form of protection. The noise from all the guns made my ears hurt so bad I wondered if they weren't bleeding.

I never saw but I did feel the first bomb hit. It was back aft, right in the middle of the flight deck, and it punched a small hole in the deck and went down. A dud, I prayed, but it wasn't. Somewhere in the ship's belly there was a heavy thump and then a thunderous boom. Debris and fire shot up out of that small hole and out the side and stern galleries of the hangar deck. Then a second one, much closer, which went off just behind the island, blasting three planes right off the ship's side and knocking me over in a tangle of limbs and nearly over the side. As I tried to gather my wits we were showered with fragments of shattered wood from the flight deck. I looked over at Rooster, who was curled up in a tight ball, covering his head and face with both arms. Very dumb idea, I thought again.

I let go of the gallery railing and started to crawl over towards that notch between the life raft stacks. Then I heard a sound I couldn't at first comprehend: the scream of an airplane engine well past its red line. I looked over my shoulder just as a Val, his right wing on fire, crashed into the island, just abaft the bridge, maybe 60 feet away, and exploded into a huge ball of flaming avgas. Then a giant clubbed me in the head and I was well and truly gone away.

THIRTEEN

The first thing I noticed when I came to was the quiet. Second, it was evening, with the sun no more than ten degrees from touching the distant horizon. Third: somehow, seawater had washed over my entire right side. Only seawater isn't red. I tried to move and my body convinced me that wasn't a great idea just now. What was bleeding? I felt my scalp, which seemed looser than it had been. There was a long cut on the right side that ran all the way down past my right ear.

Where is everybody, I wondered. Rooster: where's Rooster? I was lying on the deck, my right arm curled underneath me. The deck was warm. Really warm. I tried to focus, but it was hard and my ears were ringing. Then a cloud of hot smoke enveloped me and I spent the next minute trying to cough up my lungs. When I regained control of my spasms the smoke had whisked away. I looked around for Rooster and there he was. Awake, looking back at me, but something was seriously wrong. And why was it so quiet? Where the hell was everybody?

"What happened?" I rasped at him.

He opened his mouth to reply but only revealed a mouthful of blood. He closed his eyes and then his body sagged and seemed to lose definition.

Rooster was dead.

God*damm*it!

I was pressed up against the blackened steel of the gallery railing. I looked out, expecting to see the horizon. Instead I saw the sea, much closer than it should have been. *Hornet* had a heavy starboard list on. There was a roaring fire somewhere down below, probably in the hangar deck. The ship rolled hesitatingly a few degrees to port, then back to starboard a good twenty degrees, where she hung ominously. I remembered that feeling when *Oklahoma* began to give up the ghost.

Good God, I thought: they've abandoned ship! At that moment a thunderous roar came from way down below on the opposite side of the ship. *Hornet* bucked sideways, clearly gut shot. Then a second one, even bigger. A third, and then a fourth. Torpedoes. Big torpedoes. A minute later I could feel the ship settling rapidly into the sea. I was astonished to see two Jap destroyers pulling out ahead of the ship, turning across her almost submerged bow, and then speeding away to rejoin their forces. I heard a great whistling noise building from somewhere forward on the flight deck. I knew what that was: the sound of air being forced out of the hull as she began to fill.

Gotta move, gotta get out of here. I painfully picked myself off the deck. The rack full of life rafts had been upset, with the black rubber bundles scattered all over the gallery deck. The area forward of the life raft stack was wrecked, burned, and shredded, with the wing of a Jap plane clearly visible in the wreckage, that red circle staring back at me in triumph. He'd dropped his bomb, then probably been torn up by the close-in 20mm's and just kept coming, determined to make his emperor proud.

The ship lurched to starboard, as if something big had given way down below.

Life rafts. Get one. Hell, get two, pitch 'em over the side and go in after them. They were heavier than I expected, but I managed to get one, and then a second one up over the railing and into the water, which was now only 20 feet below me instead of 70.

Gotta go. Gotta go. The whole ship was shaking now, as if she was resisting her fate. I would, too. The waters here were four miles deep.

"Boss!" Rooster croaked. "Wait for me."

I turned around. He was alive and crawling towards the railing.

Neither of us had a life jacket, but it was no longer a matter of choice. The whistling noise from the flight deck elevator openings was much louder now.

The vibration got so bad that Rooster and I were shaken off the gallery deck and into the water. I hit the side of one of the life rafts. I grabbed and tried to corral it, and, in so doing, I managed to pull the inflation handle. The raft rewarded me with a punch in the face as the rubber expanded. Above us the dark gray bulk of a 27,000-ton aircraft carrier leaned way over, on fire from end to end now and threatening to roll over right on top of us.

I looked around for Rooster but couldn't find him, so I clambered aboard the raft and then tried again. I saw him, ten feet away and making a feeble effort to swim towards the raft, trying to ignore the looming shadow of the dying carrier that was getting ever closer. I went back into the water and swam over to him, grabbing him by the sleeve of his shirt, and then pulling him back to the raft. He tried to help but he was much too weak. I don't know how I got the both of us onto the raft but I did, and then I collapsed to get my wind. Something big hit the water right next to us. I opened my eyes in time to see things rolling off the flight deck as she started her final plunge: airplanes, push-tractors, even bombs, all accompanied by a sickening number of smaller, dungaree-clad white and red bundles sliding down the ruined deck and slapping lifeless into the sea.

I looked for the paddles. There were supposed to be paddles. There. Strapped to the floor of the raft. I pulled one out and started paddling as hard as I could, which wasn't very hard. When I finally ran out of steam I looked back. The back one-third of the carrier was standing up out of the sea now, her bronze propellers shining in the evening light. I watched in awe as she slid down into the depths. Then I think I passed out.

I awoke sometime later. It was night. Full dark, no wind. Rooster was a gray shape on the netted bottom, out like a light. *Hornet* and all her works were long gone. The sea smelled of fuel oil and char. I looked around and saw the second life raft 20 feet away, bobbing patiently. Somehow that was important. Extra water. Food. I knew I should go back into the water and retrieve it. I closed my eyes for just a minute, resting for the effort. The next thing I knew it was daylight. Something had awakened me. Noise. Engine noise. I looked around and then up. An ominous black silhouette was nose on and getting bigger and bigger. Four engines. Floats out at the wingtips. *Big* seaplane.

Kawanishi.

I rolled into the sea on the opposite side of his approach, popped back up, grabbed Rooster and pulled him, squawking like a chicken, into the water with me. I yelled at him to take a deep breath and then we both went down as far as we could. A second later bright silver slashes appeared in the water as those barbarous bastards strafed the raft. We popped up thirty seconds later as the seaplane rose back into a slate gray sky. We waited for him to turn around but he didn't. He droned away, satisfied with getting a few murders under his belt before breakfast. I longed for the day that we got out of this present fix and back into the business of carrying out Halsey's first law.

The raft had been hit several times, but, being a honeycomb of rubber, there wasn't much real damage. First order of business was to get back in and then we needed to retrieve that second raft. There was no telling how long we'd be out here or if the PBYs would even be sent out. They'd abandoned the ship, so they might think they got everyone off except the dead.

I finally inspected the raft. Food and water were in two long pipe-like canisters strapped to the inner sides. I broke out a water can and punched it open with the can opener taped to the inside

of the canister. We both gulped it down despite the taste of chlo-
rine. Rooster seemed to recover a bit and he was able to help me
paddle over to the second raft. We thanked God there'd been no
wind. We lashed it to our own raft and then relaxed and prayed for
the PBYs. My head wound had stopped bleeding but I could feel
a long, ugly scab forming. Neither one of us had serious wounds,
but we both felt like we'd been steamrolled. I had vague memories
of a lecture at flight school about the effect of a bomb blast on the
human body.

"Should'a stayed in the house," I observed.

"No guarantees that fire in the hangar bay wouldn't have
cooked us," Rooster pointed out. "You see that wing on the signal
bridge? The one with the meatball on it?"

I nodded.

"That's what they'll do one day," he said. "When they run out
of bombs and carriers. They'll start doing that shit on purpose.
Japs're big on suicide."

"God I hope not," I said. "How do you defend against that?"

He just shook his head, winced at the effort, and then curled
up to take a nap.

I stayed awake. I felt bad about our predicament. If we'd stayed
inside the ship we'd have probably been led out to one of those
ropes leading over the side, slid down into the water, and been
picked up by a destroyer. We would have been on our way to
Nouméa by now. I'd told Rooster to go below, but I should have
known he'd stick with me. Nugget mistake, I thought. Believed
I was a big aviator by now. Then I remembered something: if a
PBY did fly over, how would we make him see us? Smoke flares. I
crawled over and past Rooster and opened up the supply canisters.
Time to take everything out and see what we got.

The new rafts were designed to hold up to twenty men, with the
wounded inside and even more clinging to the nets stitched into
the sides and the bottom if necessary. Most ships carried the old-
style balsa-wood-and-netting rafts, which weren't really lifeboats

but more like big flotation devices for men to hang on to during an operational rescue and recovery operation after a ship went down. These things were much better, although once the wind came up they'd go wherever the wind took them, so there was no hope of navigating by the stars and paddling to some island. I hauled all the supplies out, aware that I'd probably never get all that stuff back in. I found smoke flares, wrapped in oilpaper. They worked just like a railroad flare: cut the paper off the top, remove the top, and scratch it hard against the igniter pad. There were some medical kits, a couple of flashlights, food and water packets, a ball of marline twine, two fishing kits, and, buried all the way at the back of the tube, a package of cigarettes and some matches. Hallelujah!

I lit up a cigarette and blew the smoke at Rooster, who woke right up.

"Where the hell did you find that?" he asked. I handed him one and the pack of matches. He lit it reverently, like an altar boy lighting the altar candles.

"For me to know and you to beg, slave," I stated calmly. "I will require that you keep my stateroom spic and span and bring me champagne on demand."

"Y'all got it, Boss," he said with a grin. "You gonna want fish aigs, too?"

"Absolutely," I said, and then looked up. A sudden breeze had come up. The skies were neither clear nor cloudy, but they were a slate color that hadn't been there earlier. "I think we need to lash down all this stuff before it gets rough out."

It was a good thing we did. A squall line rose up on the horizon and within a half hour we were bouncing around in crashing, confused waves, torrential rain, and a wind with a mission. Once again, the rafts proved their worth, because they were equipped with a tarp stitched into one end. We could huddle out of the rain, although unlike on the old balsa rafts, the waves came aboard and stayed, forcing us to bail. We'd brought the other raft in closer and doubled the line attached to it. We'd also re-strapped the supply tubes to the side netting. Even if the wind flipped the raft, all we had to do was hang on and wait for the fun to stop. Rooster suggested we tie ourselves to the raft in case that did happen, so we made a crude rope out of the marline, allowed six feet of slack, and secured the other end to our left wrists.

As things turned out, the squall passed as quickly as it had erupted. We both felt better, having had a fresh-water shower. I tied the two smoke flares to the top line of the side netting. They were waterproof and I made sure Rooster knew how to light one off. It was starting to get dark. Rooster and I each had a ration of food and a can of water. Then we each lit up a precious cigarette and pretended we were on a cruise. Another squall jumped us late that night. This time the fresh-water shower was colder than the one we'd enjoyed earlier. I'd had great plans to use stars to figure which way we were drifting, but the skies were solid overcast. I did know that the northeast monsoon was coming on, which meant we'd go southwest. What I didn't know was where *Hornet* had been when she went down. I gave up trying to figure it all out. We had food and water for several days between the two rafts. What we needed now was a PBY.

We spent our time swapping stories. It turned out that Rooster was not the country boy he pretended to be. He was from Alabama, but from Mobile. His father was an engineer like mine was and he'd had a year of college before coming into the Navy, trying to outrun the looming Depression. He'd actually been offered a commission at one point until he made the mistake of bedding his squadron's executive officer's wife. The XO sought physical retribution, which did not go in his favor. That meant, of course, that Rooster was put on report for striking an officer, which in turn led to a hasty transfer and permanent enlisted status. I asked him if the lady had been worth all that. They are all worth it, Boss, he said. Every one.

The following night, just after sunset, we heard aircraft engines. They sounded different from the *Kawanishi* engines, but they were high, so we really couldn't tell. Whatever it was, it was multi-engine. Ours or theirs? I thought the plane was headed south. That would indicate ours since Nouméa was south of Guadalcanal. We didn't have much time to decide, and a minute later, I scratched off the first flare. The light was dazzling in the ocean darkness. The smoke, almost invisible in the night, blew off to the southwest. We listened for any change in the aircraft's engine noise. Nothing. The plane kept going and finally disappeared. I doused the flare in the sea and tried not to get too disappointed.

"That guy was *way* up there," Rooster observed.

"If it was a PBY or an R4D, he was probably ferrying wounded from Guadalcanal to Nouméa," I replied. "Assuming I have any idea of which way is which."

Rooster agreed. The question neither one of us wanted to bring up was whether or not anybody on that plane had noticed a sudden blaze of light way down there on the sea surface. Not to mention that what looked like a blowtorch to us would have been a pinprick of light if that guy had been at 15,000 feet.

The same thing happened the next two nights. A lone aircraft, *way* up there as Rooster had put it, droning through the night. None of them had reacted to our flares. We'd used up all the flares from the one raft so we raided the supply cache on the other raft for more.

"We can't keep seeing each other like this, Rooster," I pointed out after the next plane ignored us.

"Thanks for reminding me, Boss," he said.

"And this is still all your fault, too," I replied.

He grinned in the darkness.

"I thought you were a goner, back there on the gallery deck. I'm sure as hell glad you weren't."

He nodded.

"Because then I wouldn't have anyone to blame for this mess we're in except myself," I said. "Happily, here *you* are."

"I gotta take a leak," he announced, disrespectfully. Somehow that struck me as really funny, and then we were both laughing, possibly just a bit hysterically. That's when something really big appeared out of the black sea in a great rush of foaming water and suddenly the night was alive with the sound of substantial diesel engines. We gaped like a pair of Bedlam idiots as a submarine approached out of the night and came to a stop, its rounded bull-nose looming right over our raft. Gray figures threw us a lifeline. Rooster grabbed it before I could get to it, and then they pulled us close in to those sloping sides. I found myself tearing up. Some alert aviator *had* seen the flares. Thanks be to God.

FOURTEEN

The submarine was the USS *Hagfish*. We were hustled down the forward hatch, surprisingly wobble-legged, while somebody topside tried to sink the life rafts with a submachine gun. A chief petty officer led us aft to the control room, where the skipper, a lieutenant commander, welcomed us on board. I was amazed at how unsteady we both were. I'd felt we'd been relatively safe in the raft, with food, water, and even a tarp, but the crew members around us were looking at us with obvious sympathy. I introduced myself and Rooster to the captain and told him we'd been on the *Hornet*.

"Word was they got everybody off," he said.

"Everybody who could walk or be carried," I replied. "We were up near the signal bridge when a Jap bomber decided to commit suicide in our faces." Then to my surprise, I asked if I could sit down. My knees were trembling and the lights in the control room had taken on a hazy appearance. There was a sudden stir of people and then we were being hustled forward.

The next thing we knew we were in bunks with a hospitalman first class in attendance. He came over to me after looking at Rooster and appraised my clotted scalp. They're gonna call you zipper head once that heals, he pronounced. A lieutenant who identified himself as the boat's exec asked if we'd be able to tell him what happened to us so they could get a report out. I looked at him for a moment and then said that we'd both been knocked unconscious by a Jap bomb.

"When I came to, the ship had been abandoned," I told him. "I remembered a big yellow flash. Then everything went black. I woke up with this big cut on my head and I could hardly move. Felt like a steamroller got me. Radioman Baynes was bleeding from the mouth and he was unable to move."

On signal from the XO, the hospitalman moved back in and checked us both for concussion symptoms. I was declared okay; Rooster was less so. I explained that we'd probably been left for dead when the ship was abandoned. The island had taken a bomb hit and then a suicide plane, so the structure was a shambles by the time they decided to abandon ship. I also told him about the two Jap destroyers who'd showed up and put four final torpedoes into the *Hornet*.

"Got it," the exec said. "We're here because a PBY pilot reported seeing what he thought was a flare in the area where *Hornet* went down. We were on our way to a patrol area near the Philippine island of Talawan, which is north and west of here. They diverted us to check out the flare report."

"Thank God you did," I said.

"The question now is what to do with you guys. We're trying to arrange a rendezvous with a Catalina somewhere out here while we're still relatively close to Guadalcanal, but they're kinda busy now moving casualties to Nouméa."

I told him I had no idea of where we were at the moment. I'd known that the *Hornet* had been operating somewhere between the Santa Cruz Islands and the Solomons, but, in general, carrier pilots only needed to know where their home plate was in reference to the target they'd flown out to get. The exec nodded his understanding.

"Everything out here is separated by *thousands* of miles," he said. "People have no idea of how big the Pacific Ocean is. I guess what I'm telling you is that you might have to become submariners for a while. We're supposed to take a look at the waters around Talawan, which is like the southernmost island in the Philippines, see what's there, and then head south to Australia."

"Well, hell, XO," I said. "We're fresh out of SBDs, so I'm game. How can we help?"

He grinned. "Get some rest," he said. "We'll figure something out."

The exec found some new dungarees for Rooster and a set of wash khakis for me. Our oil-soaked flight suits had been thrown over the side. I was also provided with a *Hagfish* ball cap and a pocketknife with the boat's insignia. I learned the next day that he hadn't been kidding about distances in the Pacific Ocean. It was almost 3,600 miles between the Santa Cruz Islands and Talawan. The boat could run 20 knots on the surface at night, but during the day we had to submerge to stay out of sight of the Japs' long-range seaplane patrols. That meant creeping along at about five knots so as not to use up something reverently called The Battery, so we were going to be submariners for at least ten days, maybe even longer. The exec explained to us that we were going to the waters around Talawan because Jap warships were supposedly using one of the bays there as an afloat logistics base. It provided a deep-water anchorage and a place to rendezvous with oilers and supply ships before pressing on to Rabaul, their base in the Solomons. The island was thought to be occupied by a Japanese army unit. Foreign occupation was nothing new for the Philippines; I learned that, beginning in the thirteenth century, the Arabs, the Portuguese, the Spanish, and finally the Americans had all claimed it at one time or another. Talawan was a small island, 20 some miles long and 12 wide, pockmarked by volcanoes, some of them active.

"We're gonna go to a patrol area just east of the island," the exec told us. "See if we can get on the route between this anchorage and Rabaul. We haven't had any of our boats in the Celebes Sea so far, so we might get lucky."

It ended up taking twelve days not ten due to a problem with one of the boat's four main engines. We mostly tried to stay out of the way, which was hard to do because there was absolutely no spare room anywhere. Rooster's concussion was receding, but he was clearly uncomfortable in the confined spaces of the boat and especially with being 200 feet underwater half of the time. I didn't really mind being submerged and actually appreciated the fact that, when we were "downstairs," the sea was always calm and the entire boat was air-conditioned.

Hagfish was a relatively new boat and this was her first war patrol. Her crew was a mixture of experienced submariners and brand-new guys. They didn't call them nuggets, apparently, but it wasn't hard to tell which was which. We, of course, were useless supercargo, consuming food, fresh water, precious air, and contributing nothing. The exec had told us that the boat had reported picking us up, but, so far, there'd been no instructions from Nouméa as to what to do with us. Rooster informed me that I was really going to like Australian beer.

Not only was the Pacific a really big ocean but it was also an empty ocean, at least in these parts, which made me wonder why we didn't just stay on the surface to make better time. We didn't encounter a single ship during the transit, and even when we arrived off the coast of Talawan there was nothing but the occasional brightly painted fishing boat. We changed our routine once we entered the eastern boundary of our designated patrol area. The boat maintained radio silence to avoid the Japs' Pacific-wide HF radio listening networks. We stayed submerged during the day after nearly getting caught by one of those monster seaplanes the day we arrived off of Talawan. We would come up every night to recharge the battery and get navigation fixes with the boat's radar, but we stayed away from fishing boats in case they'd been augmented with a Jap soldier and a handy-dandy field radio.

The sub's crew was tense now that we were in enemy waters. In the meantime Rooster and I wondered if we would ever fly again.

Here we were, experienced carrier dive bombers, locked up underwater in a steel tube. The only break we got was at night, when we were allowed to come up to the bridge, a small platform just in front of the periscope stack. Behind the periscope structure was an even smaller platform that housed a 20mm cannon and a steel box marked "life jackets" that looked as if it hadn't been opened in some time. This was called the cigarette deck, where crew members could come up two or three at a time to get some fresh air if the tactical situation allowed. The rest of the crew had to be content with the rush of fresh, if warm and humid, air that was being sucked down into the interior to both feed the diesel engines and flush out a half day's worth of oxygen-depleted air from the all-day submergence. They posted as many as four lookouts up above the bridge platform to make sure we didn't get surprised. In a way we two were privileged characters, being allowed to go topside for a couple hours each night.

We got a scare on the third day, just after dawn. We'd submerged an hour earlier, as usual, but then the Sound shack reported high-speed propellers approaching. The boat went to GQ, which meant that every one of those heavy steel interior watertight hatches was dogged shut. The exec had told us to go to the officers' wardroom when GQ was sounded, yet another reminder that the two of us were mostly in the way. We barely made it; the crew had been drilled incessantly to close all those hatches within sixty seconds of the alarm. The wardroom, unlike the carrier's, was tiny, no more than six feet wide by nine feet long. It had a table which could accommodate only six officers at a time. Rooster, being enlisted, was uncomfortable being in what he called officers' country, but I reminded him that they were being nice to us even if we were useless. He was visibly agitated at not knowing what was going to happen, especially now that we were back to being 200 feet under the surface. Then I remembered that ships at general quarters communicated among the various battle stations via sound-powered phones. There was one of those phones mounted under the captain's end of the wardroom table, complete with a selector switch allowing one to dial into any of the boat's battle circuits.

I removed the handset and then began cycling through the selector switch buttons until I heard voices. They couldn't know that I was listening as long as I didn't press down on the handset's press-to-talk button. This way I could listen in to the stream of orders and acknowledgments, and tell Rooster what I was hearing. The ventilation shut down all at once and the word came over the phones to rig for silent running.

"They think it's a Jap destroyer, transiting through the area," I told Rooster. "He's going fast enough that they don't think he's sonar-searching, which is good news for us, apparently."

"So what's the big deal?" Rooster asked. "Why GQ?"

"Captain thinks something big is coming into that anchorage and that this destroyer is headed out to escort him back into the bay. The skipper has ordered the boat to periscope depth once this tin can goes by."

It became very quiet in the boat with the ventilation off. We could actually hear the propeller sounds of that destroyer hurrying by up on the surface. It was a scary sound. Rooster mouthed the words *what are we doing here?* at me. I just shook my head. Diving down into a Jap carrier formation through the AA bursts and with Zeros flashing by had been exciting, even scary, but in the air we could evade, jink, bob, and weave. Being down here underwater with a Jap destroyer passing overhead was much scarier because there was *nothing* we could do about it. The name "destroyer" originated from their mission, torpedo boat destroyers. Initially the torpedo boats they had in mind were German PT boats, but it still applied, since *Hagfish* was certainly a torpedo boat.

Hagfish began to tilt in the up direction. We were running on the battery-powered electric motors so there was no noise from the machinery rooms, just the creaking and crackling noises of the hull as we came up from depth. Those noises were probably comforting to the submariners, but not to us. They reminded us of where we had just been, deep in the ocean, which was no place for a couple of flyboys. Our nemesis was gravity; theirs was something called hydrostatic pressure.

The ventilation was restored once we came up to periscope depth, whatever that actually was. The good news was that we could no longer hear that destroyer. It had to be midmorning, but would we surface? No, hell, no—it was daylight. I longed for a cigarette and some fresh air, as incongruous as that sounds, but I knew we wouldn't expose ourselves in broad daylight. Sure enough, the boat tilted down as we again sought safety in the depths of the ocean. There was a depth gauge in the wardroom, positioned where the captain could see it. Past 100 feet the hull began to acknowledge the pressure outside, as if glad to be back in its proper element.

They finally secured from GQ and now we were condemned to yet another day of sitting around trying to stay small. I hung around the control room, talking to the officers and enlisted men who cycled through the nerve center of the boat. They were interested in hearing about Midway and Guadalcanal, since all they knew about those battles was what the fleet broadcast news service told them, and those contained enough propaganda to make even the crew wonder if any of it was true.

We surfaced that night well after sunset. It was, as usual, a great relief to have fresh air streaming down through the conning tower hatch into the boat. This was the time the cooks could prepare meals for the entire crew without filling the submarine with heavy-duty cooking smells. People could smoke as much as they wanted to. Rooster had become a popular figure down on the crew's mess decks as he related stories of carrier warfare and his own adventures at Midway and other carrier battles. I found that the boat's officers, on the other hand, staunchly believed that they, the submarine force, had been doing more damage to the

Japanese navy than anyone else. As I learned of their exploits it occurred to me that their determination to be the *Silent* Service had probably denied them the credit they deserved.

There was one other aspect to submarine service that was unique to them: if an aviator got shot down and seemed to have survived the crash, other aviators would probably see it happen, so there was at least a chance that a PBY or a friendly destroyer would come looking for you. If a submarine was mortally damaged and went down, that was that. Nobody would be looking for you. The boat simply became "overdue and presumed lost." I could see where that stark fact could create a certain fatalism in their beloved Silent Service. I didn't share any of those thoughts with Rooster, who was already antsy enough being in a sub.

I was about to request permission to go topside to the cigarette deck when there was a sudden commotion in the control room. The last half-hourly radar sweep had shown two contacts to the east of us, about 12 miles away. The captain was being extremely cautious with his radar, believing that the Japs, whose ships didn't appear to have radar, *did* have the ability to detect a radar signal. That meant that the radar operators would take a single sweep once every thirty minutes but no more than that. The two contacts put an end to our fresh-air extravaganza. Once again we stood back out of the way as the boat submerged and began to make preparations for a torpedo attack. The exec pointed Rooster and me towards the wardroom and then Control sounded the GQ alarm for battle stations, torpedo.

There was some more of what my Marine buddies on Guadalcanal had called hurry-up-and-wait while the fire control team up in the conning tower developed a torpedo-firing solution on the approaching contacts. The exec had shown us how they computed a solution for the torpedoes. I'd been surprised at how close they had to get to ensure a good hit. If their target happened to do a zigzag turn away at the last moment the whole firing solution would be compromised and the target might get clean away.

I eavesdropped again and learned that the target appeared to be a Jap cruiser of the *Nachi* class. Ten minutes later we felt the mushy thumps from the forward torpedo tubes as the boat fired three torpedoes. Finally we heard two distant explosions, and then the boat tilted down and began a light banking turn away from the scene of whatever they'd done. It wasn't long before we heard the swishing sound of approaching propellers and then, more ominously, the high-frequency pinging noises of a destroyer sonar. Just like someone who's never seen a rattlesnake recognizes the sound of one immediately, both Rooster and I knew what was probably coming next, but it was a whole lot more violent than we'd expected.

We both found ourselves rolling around on the wardroom deck with the chairs after the first ashcan went off. The explosion had knocked the boat sideways and created a wet mist of fine particles, dust, and bits of insulation raining out of the overhead. My ears were ringing and Rooster had that same stunned look he'd had up on the lifeboat deck on *Hornet.* The second one was not as bad, but the third went off below us and I thought I felt the whole boat try to bend in half. A fourth blast sounded like it was off to one side, which is when I realized the boat was in a hard turn and headed in the down direction. On purpose, I hoped.

I got up and pulled the wardroom curtain aside only to get hit in the face with a sharp spray of seawater strong enough to sting my skin. A pipe union had cracked. At depth, what would have been a weep on the surface became a water-drill. The lights flickered out and then the battle lanterns came on, illuminating a dust-filled passageway with a morbid yellow light. I was getting pretty tired of seeing battle lanterns. I pulled myself back into the wardroom when I realized the down angle was increasing. There was a lot of shouting out in the passageway, but it sounded like disciplined shouting, officers giving orders and subordinates reporting what they were seeing or doing. Another series of depth charges started going off but nowhere near as close as the first four. Even so, I winced every time one of them boomed into the sea. The hull was creaking and groaning in earnest, which didn't do much for our confidence. Finally we felt the deck starting to level off.

I saw Rooster huddled up in one corner of the wardroom, his eyes white with fear. "We got away, Rooster," I said. "They're bombing where they think we are, but the skipper turned, went deep, and we got away."

I wasn't sure he heard me but then he wet his lips and nodded. I made a mental note to not let Rooster back up onto the cigarette deck tonight because I thought he might be ready to just jump off. A third series of depth charges boomed nearby but these were even farther away. I began to relax. *God*, I thought. How do these guys stand this shit?

Then there came a different booming sound, followed by several smaller explosions. This symphony of destruction lasted for over a minute before subsiding into a hideous cacophony of rupturing steel beams, imploding compartments, and great gushes of steam escaping underwater. Some of the sounds were almost human: deep groans, the shriek of metal structures being torn apart, and then a frighteningly familiar rumble of air being forced out of a sinking ship. This had to be the cruiser. It was horrible. I kept thinking I could hear men screaming but I knew that wasn't possible.

The boat's propellers thrummed suddenly as we bolted from the area. I had no idea of how deep we were and was afraid to look at the depth gauge. It felt as if the skipper had ordered full power, something I'd not seen during any of our long daytime submergences, because it meant the battery would be depleting rapidly. After a few minutes we felt a small up-angle. Soon the hull's complaints began to diminish. I looked over at Rooster, whose face was regaining some composure as those crushing noises diminished. I felt so useless that I began to pick up the pieces of broken crockery and right the chairs. Then the ventilation came back on, which was a wonderful relief. It wasn't fresh air but it was *chilled* air that drove away the stink of seawater which had come in from all the broken gauges or other piping leaks in the boat. The propellers finally slowed after about twenty minutes and the boat began to tilt upwards again. I thought I heard more distant underwater explosions but I couldn't be sure.

It was an hour before we came back up to periscope depth. Apparently the boat's radar revealed only one small contact, 15 miles to the west of us and headed in the away direction. The men in the control room were celebrating, much like we had done after the first day at Midway. I overheard the captain telling the exec that the Japs would be out in force at daylight so we needed to run at full speed to clear the area while recharging the dangerously depleted batteries. The navigator pointed out that there was a deep-channel strait between Talawan Island and an even smaller island to the south. We could run on the surface tonight, cut through that channel, and take up a patrol area on the other side of the island, which had the advantage of being even closer to where the Japanese anchorage was. The captain wondered aloud whether that channel could be mined. The navigator said that the water depths in the strait ranged between 400 and 1,000 feet deep, which argued against there being mines. Navy Intel claimed that 200 feet was the Japs' depth limit for placing moored mines, so the skipper agreed. We would make the passage from our current position about an hour and a half before first light and then submerge.

Rooster and I found out later that the target had indeed been a Jap cruiser. Since the skipper never saw it actually go down he couldn't claim more than damage, but everybody was convinced that she'd sunk, especially after hearing those horrific noises. He said that our torpedoes were almost puny compared to the Japs' fish but they still packed a punch—when they worked. I didn't pursue that comment. I couldn't imagine taking all those risks to get set up for a torpedo attack and then wonder if the damned thing was going to work. Rooster reminded me that not many of our torpedo bombers' fish worked, either, like at Midway. That's because they all got shot down before they could get their fish away, I replied. The slaughter of Torpedo Six was still very fresh in my mind, especially after we'd found out that Admiral Halsey had vetoed any more torpedo bomber attacks against carriers. Trouble was, Halsey hadn't been there on the big day and Admiral Spruance felt he had to throw everything he had against a force of four fleet carriers.

The cooks took advantage of the open hatch to make hamburgers and deep-fried potatoes, so everybody ate too much. Those who could hit their racks. I slept for maybe four hours but then something woke me up. I think it was the sound of voices from the control room as they began the task of navigating through the strait by radar. In peacetime there would have been channel buoys or a lighthouse or two, but the Japs had doused every navigation aid in their blood-soaked Greater East Asia Co-Prosperity Sphere. The strait was only about ten miles long and four to five miles wide, so this transit shouldn't take long, although the skipper slowed the boat down to 10 knots as we entered. He took station on the bridge, along with the torpedo officer, who was standing officer of the deck, and four lookouts. I asked the exec, who was down in the control room, if Rooster and I could go topside and watch from the cigarette deck. He hesitated.

"If we get jumped by a Jap gunboat, we might have to crash dive," he said. "The fewer people on the bridge, the quicker we can do that."

"Please, XO," Rooster said. "I'm . . ."

He didn't finish, but the look on Rooster's face told the exec that this aviator was desperate to get topside, if only for a half hour.

"Okay," he relented. "Cigarette deck. No smoking, though—

the Japs are always watching and a ciggy-butt can be seen literally for *miles* at sea on a clear night. Any shit starts, the two of you drop, and I mean *drop*, down that conning tower hatch, because the captain, the lookouts, and the entire Pacific Ocean will be right behind you, got it?"

With a chorus of yessirs we gratefully climbed the ladder up into the conning tower, ignoring the mildly surprised stares of the navigation team, and then one more ladder up to the bridge itself. That hatch was held open with a small hank of rope which the last man down was supposed to yank to seal the boat in the event of a crash dive. The current of fresh air coming down through the hatch made our eyes water. To our surprise, there was a full moon, which was probably why the skipper had slowed the boat down to minimize our wake. He was busy talking to the navigation team so Rooster and I crawled as quietly as we could around the periscope stacks and down onto the cigarette deck. Just being on the cigarette deck made me want a smoke but I wasn't about to do anything that might jeopardize our privileged position. The platform had a grating for a deck, so we could actually see our wake bubbling pleasantly alongside.

The shoreline on either side was invisible, even in the moonlight. I wondered if the Japs posted sentries on the shore itself, because our diesels seemed really loud out here on the calm waters of the strait. The radar antenna squeaked into motion every ten minutes for a couple of revolutions. I knew about radar from carrier operations, but it had never occurred to me that a submarine might have one. The antenna on the carrier had been the size of a baseball backstop. *Hagfish*'s radar antenna was a small, curved piece of metal only about three feet long.

The diesels suddenly shut down and the boat began to slow. I wondered if Rooster and I should start making our move toward the main hatch but none of the other shadowy figures up on the bridge were moving. After a few minutes we could see that the boat was still moving, so we must have been using the electric motors now. The wake astern had almost disappeared. The captain and his OOD were staring intently through binoculars at something in the dark on the port bow. Had that last radar sweep detected a surface contact?

Suddenly I experienced what felt like a sinking sensation and then I noticed that the black water sliding by on either side of the boat was washing *across* her main deck instead of below it. Rooster's eyes got wide as he saw it, too, and yet there'd been no Klaxon alarm for a dive. One of the lookouts perched up on top of the sail said something into his sound-powered phones, and both the officers down on the bridge swung their binocs to the right a little. The boat seemed to settle even deeper down into the sea but then it came back up. It was as if she was skimming the surface through some balancing operation between being surfaced and submerged. Rooster quietly un-dogged that metal locker marked "life jackets" and fished out two bulky kapok life jackets. He dogged the lid back down and handed me one of them. He put his on, but I kept mine off, thinking that I'd never fit down that hatch with one of those on if they did call for an emergency dive. Besides, the jackets reeked of mold and dry rot. Rooster didn't seem to notice.

We slowed even more to maybe just a few knots of forward movement. There came a sudden rush of bubbles all along the hull and we could feel the boat rising back up to a normal surfaced level. Then we began a slow, very slow turn towards whatever it was out there the lookouts had locked on to. That made sense: put the boat's silhouette bow-on and there'd be a lot less to see of her if there *was* a gunboat or a destroyer out there, searching for us. I wasn't sure whether I wanted to be up here or down in the confines of the boat, safely behind that thick, steel hull if a gunfight erupted. I wondered why we didn't just submerge but then realized that submerging would mean spending a whole lot more time in the confines of the strait, possibly with unfriendly company. There was just so much I didn't know about submarines. I saw one of the lookouts above looking at his watch as we drifted silently, barely maintaining steerageway, and then remembered we had to be out of the strait and safely submerged before the sun came up.

And then the sun did come up. Right under the boat.

FIFTEEN

I have never felt such pain in all my life. It was as if God himself had swung a sledgehammer against the grating under my feet, sending a white-hot lightning bolt up both my legs, thighs, and straight into my spine. My body bent completely in half the way someone who's been groin-kicked does. I was unable to breathe, scream, or even grunt. Coincident with the blast the entire submarine rose up at least ten feet, causing me to crash down on that steel grating with enough force to imprint the metal grid on my forehead. The only things that saved me were that I had been holding that lump of a life jacket against my chest and the fact that the grating deck had bent down almost thirty degrees. Stunned, I was only able to just lie there and try to get a breath into my bruised lungs.

A sleek, black column of water rose on either side of the boat like the jaws of a vise. I saw Rooster go flying right overboard. The only reason I didn't go too was that my head was stuck under one of the steel railings. Then I was literally buried in tons of falling seawater as the column collapsed. I hurt so bad that I wanted to just die and get it over with. Then something wet and heavy hit the back of my legs and immediately rolled off, probably one of the lookouts. As that thundering cataract subsided on either side of the cigarette deck I opened my eyes long enough to see another one of the lookouts, his head lolling on his shoulders at an impossible angle, slide between the railings and into the maelstrom below.

But not that far below, I realized. The boat was going down like a stone. A roar that sounded like a ship's boiler lifting safeties was coming from the conning tower hatch as the flooding down below drove every bit of air out of the boat. She didn't tilt one way or the other. She just went down, straight down, and when that howling column of air changed over to a column of debris-laden water shooting 50 feet into the air, I knew I had to get away from her. I screamed soundlessly at my body to move but nothing worked, and then a heavy swirl of warm seawater tumbled onto the cigarette deck and swept me off the boat like a piece of trash.

I went under, knowing this time that this was it, I was going to be sucked down with the sinking submarine. Once again, the life jacket saved me. For some reason I hadn't ever let go of the cluster of strings with which you tied the thing onto your body, and I felt my left arm tugging the rest of me back to the surface. Right into a large whirlpool, where I began to go round and round, sinking deeper towards that central cone. The moon was still out so I could see other faces on the other side of the whirlpool, some obviously dead, and a couple struggling to breathe and escape the pool.

Then it was over and there was only silence. I felt myself sinking and thrust the life jacket between my legs, which promptly dunked my face underwater. I tried again, hugging it this time, and that was better, much better. *Everything* hurt. My joints felt like hot and painful jelly and I was bleeding from my nose and the forehead print job. I closed my eyes and tried to just hang on to my new best friend, that grayish life jacket with the words "Deck Division" stenciled on it. I found myself mouthing the words *Deck Division* softly as the letters went in and out of focus right in front of my face. I thought to myself: Live or die? That's easy, said my badly rattled brain. Relax. Sleep a little. You'll feel a whole lot better in the morning. Just let go of this stinking life jacket and this will all be over. Then Rooster bumped into me and I yelled with pain.

"Boss," he said. "*Boss!* It's me, Rooster. Stop fighting me."

Fighting? I wasn't fighting anybody. I *couldn't* fight anybody. I was Rubber Man, desperate to be gone from this horror. Then Rooster pulled the life jacket out of my death grip and put it on the way it was supposed to go, and now I didn't have to struggle to keep my face out of the water. I began to calm down until a huge bubble of air filled with bright shiny diesel oil burst about 20 feet from us, filling the night air with the oily stink of a dead ship, especially when some bodies started coming up. Lifeless, boneless apparitions from Davy Jones' locker flopped around in the confused sea, many with their innards projecting from their mouths. We both looked on in horror as we recognized some of the faces that were popping up around us—the exec, Hospitalman Morris. All dead. All drowned. Their expressions seemed to accuse *us* of the crime of still being alive. I began to weep. Rooster slapped the shit out of me.

"C'mon, Boss," he said. "We gotta get ashore before the sharks come."

Sharks, I thought. Good God. Then something bumped into me from behind.

Shark! I screamed, but it was the body of the captain. His facial expression was one of great sadness, as if in his final moment he'd realized what had just happened. The intel had been wrong about that 200-foot depth limit. The Japs *had* mined the strait.

Rooster pushed the body away and I bristled momentarily at the lack of respect.

"Boss!" he said, almost shouting. "It's gonna be daylight soon. We gotta get to the beach. We gotta get out of sight. Japs'll be out in the morning, looking to see what the hell happened."

"Okay, Rooster," I replied, suddenly filled with a sense of calm logic. I looked around. The moon was headed down by now. "But which way?"

Good question, his expression said. Neither of us had any idea of which way to go to get out of the strait and onto a shore. *Any* shore. We'd been heading generally west to get around to Talawan's west coast, but then we'd turned to point our skinny nose at that gunboat, if that's what it had been out there.

"Boss, look," Rooster said. He was pointing over my shoulder. I couldn't turn around. Just tell me, I mumbled. But finally I wrenched myself around and looked while trying not to throw up with the pain of moving. There was a light in the distance. Reddish, not white. Flickering. A torch, maybe? Had someone come down to the beach to see what all that noise had been about? A Jap coastal sentry, already gabbling away on his radio?

"Okay," I sighed. "Better than nothing. Let's go."

Easier said than done. I'd never tried swimming with a kapok life jacket on; as pilots we'd only been trained on the inflatable variety. The best I could manage was a clumsy dog paddle. Rooster kept one hand on my life jacket but I was obviously holding him back with my rubbery efforts. Then we heard a voice.

"Hey," someone called in the darkness. "Help."

We stopped our feeble efforts to swim and looked around. A white face emerged, swimming awkwardly. It was Lieutenant (JG) Teller, the boat's torpedo officer. He closed in on us and grabbed onto my life jacket to catch his breath. "I think both my legs are broken," he announced and then passed out. As he began to sink I grabbed his shirt front and just managed to hold his head above water. Then we heard splashing noises nearby and yet another face emerged. A very young face. One of the lookouts? He latched onto Rooster's life jacket, tried to say something, but then just started crying.

We just floated for the next five minutes, pretty much unable to do anything. The youngster finally stopped his sobbing and tried to get control of himself. I wanted to offer some words of encouragement but my mind was a blank. Lieutenant Teller came to finally and then took in a huge breath as the pain from his legs made itself fully known. I was hurting, but not like that. His face was gray. I realized he was in shock.

"Boss," Rooster said softly. "We still gotta get ashore."

He pointed with his chin to our right. I looked over and now I could actually make out a darker mass on our local horizon. Then it hit me: if I could see that, daylight wouldn't be long in coming. Rooster was right. In an hour even a sleepy Jap sentry on the beach would be able to see us. A second thing hit me. We were much closer than we had been to that torchlight. The current must be pushing us ashore, which was a godsend, because our little four-man jacket-raft of broken humans didn't have much of a powerplant available. Even so, Rooster and I began kicking in the direction of the beach. Teller couldn't help, but the youngster could.

Then we heard the sound of a diesel engine approaching from out of the darkness. It was much smaller than *Hagfish*'s big mains, but it was definitely coming our way. We stopped thrashing around in the water and tried to make ourselves small. The engine slowed down and then searchlights switched on about 400 yards away, maybe even less. If it was a gunboat they'd be searching for survivors. We turned our white faces away from the lights as they swept in our direction but then, thankfully kept going. Then we could hear shouts coming from the gunboat which was still invisible and her engine went to idle.

"Go," I whispered. "They've found debris. They'll stop to pick stuff up, see what their mine killed."

We pressed on towards that dark beach with marginally increased energy, fully aware that the more of it we could see, the more the crew of that gunboat would be able to see. An exhausting half hour later I felt my right foot hit something solid. Ahead of us was an impenetrable wall of dark jungle with maybe a five-foot-wide dark sand beach. I stood up and promptly fell over with a loud splash. Rooster stood up into a crouch and began dragging the rest of us up onto the sand, me first. The youngster crawled out of the water on all fours, lay down, and closed his eyes. Rooster and I worked together to pull Lieutenant Teller out of the water on his back, where he collapsed with a silent grimace. Rooster sat down in the sand with a thump and tried to catch his breath.

I don't know how long we just sat there. A part of my brain was telling me we couldn't just stay there, exposed as we were on the sand. Not with that Jap gunboat out there. But that meant moving, and moving was out of the question for a while. Until we heard the sound of airplane engines. I opened my eyes to find full daylight was upon us. I sat up, rolled over, got up on my hands and knees, yelled in pain and fell right back over. Rooster managed to get to his feet, as did the young seaman, who looked as if he was about to sprint into the jungle until Rooster snapped at him. They dragged me and then Teller into the undergrowth at the top of the beach. I scanned the seaward horizon, looking for that gunboat, but she'd gone. We could still hear the drone of a multi-engine plane farther out in the strait, but there was some haze now and I couldn't see it. It sounded like it was running a search pattern of some kind. We needed to get farther into all that undergrowth.

The youngster looked like he was still ready to flee until I told him to help me with the lieutenant. All three of us ended up pulling him, still on his back, ten feet into the cover of the jungle, while he gritted his teeth and tried not to scream. The engine noise grew louder. I hoped they wouldn't be able to see where we had disturbed all that pristine sand but I thought they were going too fast to see that level of detail. Plus that black sand wouldn't show that it had been disturbed like white sand would. I hoped.

A minute later one of those damned *Kawanishi* flying boats roared by, not 50 feet over the water, positively bristling with cannons and guns, but, happily, he was a couple hundred yards offshore. We waited to see if the thing would turn around but it kept on going down the strait. Teller groaned.

I crawled over to him and gently slid his khaki trouser legs up his shins. His lower legs were red and swollen, but I couldn't see any obvious fractures. I gently touched his shinbone and he nearly jumped out of his skin. There were angry purple stripes running from his knees all the way down to his insteps on both legs.

"I don't think they're broken," I said. "Bruised all to hell, but not broken."

"So you decline to operate, then, Doctor?" he asked.

I looked up at his face. He'd attempted a joke. Good sign.

I looked over at Rooster, who was nodding. I sat back on my haunches and tried to think of what we had to do next. Water. Food, if possible. Get deeper into the jungle before the Japs sent a squad out to see if any survivors had made it to the beach. One of us would have to go back down to the beach and erase all signs of our landing. My head hurt. Hell, *everything* hurt. I looked at the three other faces and realized that I was now in charge.

Good deal, I thought. My first command.

SIXTEEN

All aviators go through survival training, either at Pensacola or in the snake-infested countryside down in the Florida Everglades. I sat there, trying to organize my thoughts until the light changed. I heard a wall of rain approaching us through the jungle, making quite a ruckus. The sound reminded me I was dying for a drink of water. God was sending us some.

I got up and began snatching great big green leaves off various plants, twisting them into crude funnels, and handing a funnel to each man. Point the wide end up into the falling rain and drink from the other end. The shower swept past in five minutes, by which time we were no longer thirsty. Now if I could only find some young bamboo and a really sharp machete, we'd be able to store water. Great idea, of course, but it only made our situation more poignant because we had *nothing*—no machetes, matches, survival food, first-aid kits, weapons, or even a compass. If you managed to survive a crash on land and your plane didn't burn you'd have all of those things. On the other hand, having experienced what happens to a sub when it hits a sea mine, I could understand why they didn't bother. Lieutenant Teller had told us those life jackets we found were only used when deckhands had to go out on the main deck to work in heavy seas. No wonder they reeked of mold.

"Everybody okay with my being the man in charge?" I asked.

"By all means," Teller said immediately, wincing as he tried to move his right leg. He'd been trying to do that for some time now and hadn't gotten very far, so maybe my medical diagnosis had been off the mark. If so, and if the Japs found him, they'd just bayonet him where he lay. I sent Rooster and the youngster, who turned out to be an engineman-striker named Cory Macklin in one of the sub's main engine rooms, down to the beach with instructions to sweep it clean. That *Kawanishi* flying boat hadn't spotted us, but we knew that they'd found the inevitable oil slick and debris field where *Hagfish* had met her ghastly end. It would only be a matter of time before they'd send an army patrol out to see if anyone had made it ashore; the Japs wouldn't miss an opportunity to murder some helpless survivors.

I laid out my plan when the beach sweepers got back to our little hidey-hole. "We need to move away from the beach," I began. "Hopefully find some place that'll give us both shelter and fresh water."

"And then?" Teller asked.

"Hunt for food."

"How?"

For some reason his reply pissed me off. "Beats me, Mister Teller," I said. "So first things first—we need to figure out a way to move *you*."

We spent the next twenty minutes trying to solve that problem because Teller's swelling legs still wouldn't support him. I pushed into the jungle for a good three feet before giving up, having encountered a green tangle of liana vines, large, hostile-looking plants, and the sounds of something substantial slithering away. There was no way we could get through all that without machetes. I still had my *Hagfish* penknife in my pocket, but that wouldn't impress this jungle very much. Then Rooster had an idea: send one man down the beach, and a second man in the opposite direction. Look for a creek or a river coming down to the sea. Then we could pull Teller into the surf, such as it was, and drag him in the water to the creek and then upstream. Let the water support him and then all we had to do was pull. Rooster and Macklin headed off in opposite directions with instructions to keep just inside the jungle line if possible.

That left Teller and me to wait for some results.

"Look," he said. "Way I feel, I'd be just as happy to crawl out into the sea and take a deep breath. Then you guys would have a better chance."

I sighed. "Our chances of getting out of this are pretty small," I said. "Having to deal with you just makes it interesting. You think we hit a mine?"

He nodded. "We were in just under three hundred feet of water, so we should have been safe. I guess nobody told the Japs." He coughed then and spat out some bloody saliva. "My innards feel like they're all detached from their moorings," he said. "The captain and I both were hammered at least five feet into the air. Neither one of us had a chance to even bend our legs. I think he broke his neck when he came back down. I didn't swim off—I was washed off. Don't know why the hell I didn't just drown."

"And all the folks down below?"

He shrugged and then winced. "That blast broke the boat literally in half. She would have flooded end to end in about thirty seconds. All the interior hatches were open, although that wouldn't have made much of a difference. Even if someone survived the explosion, he would have been pinned to the overhead by the flooding."

"Does anyone know we were headed through that strait to the other side of the island?"

"Nope," he said. "Skipper never sent out a message on his intentions. Still scared of their listening nets. They'll wait two weeks back in Pearl and then declare *Hagfish* missing and presumed lost. Welcome to the submarine service."

"I guess we aviators are spoiled," I said. "We go out in a flock.

Someone gets shot down, someone else will see it. Then they send PBYs out to look for the pilot. Sometimes, when you see the guy going down in flames and no chute, you know he didn't make it. They'd still send out a PBY."

"That must be comforting," he said. "When one of ours disappears in the Pacific, there's no point in searching. Most of this ocean is miles deep." He eyed the skies around us. "Pray for rain, there, Boss. My throat is really dry." Then he went to sleep.

Rooster was the first one back. He'd found nothing. Macklin came in an hour later and reported that he'd found a small-ish creek coming down from higher ground beyond the jungle. I turned to tell Lieutenant Teller, but then discovered he'd gone to find his shipmates, entombed in the straits about two miles away.

Shit, I thought. On the other hand, his dying meant we could move a lot faster, and going up that creek seemed a better bet than taking on this jungle.

Fireman Macklin asked what we were going to do about Lieutenant Teller.

"There's nothing we can do, Macklin," I said. "We have no way to bury him."

"Jesus, we can't just . . ."

I put a hand on his shoulder. "That's not Lieutenant Teller anymore, Macklin. That's a corpse. Lieutenant Teller is back down on what's left of *Hagfish*, commiserating with the rest of them. God will take care of them, and Nature will take care of—that. Now *we* gotta go."

Four hours later we found exactly what we'd been looking for. The big surprise was that the jungle wasn't very much of a jungle once we crept over the bar and sloshed our way up the creek bed. We'd walked in the surf line the whole way to the creek, which slowed us up a lot but left no tracks. The stream widened out once we moved away from the shoreline. We finally realized we were going *up* in elevation as the jungle thinned out. After the first hour, we came out onto semi open ground. There were trees and some scrubby vegetation but they grew sparse as we continued to climb into low hills above the coast. I felt it was safe enough now to continue on dry land but, even though we'd left the jungle behind, there were still vines snaking through the grass everywhere. We all tripped over the damned things on our way up. I fell once hard enough to make my eyes water.

The skies were clear and it was hot. We were all sweating pretty hard which wasn't a good thing without fresh water. We'd tried the creek water, but it had been brackish. Hats would have been nice, too; that sun was medium ferocious. We finally heard and then came to a thin waterfall which was pouring out of a narrow gorge, maybe 50 feet above us. There was a shallow pool at the bottom of it. We all just climbed in and luxuriated in the cool water after first slaking our thirst. The rocks encasing the falls were black and porous, probably ancient lava. Looking back down the slope we could see the broad band of the coastal jungle and even a glittering ribbon of blue water where the straits were. Along with what looked like a gunboat.

"I guess they know," Rooster said. "Shit!"

"Yeah, I suspect they do," I replied. "Hopefully they'll find Teller's body and decide no one else made it out."

I was basing my wishful thinking on the fact that we'd gone up the beach but stayed in the shallow surf the whole way. Our situation was better, but only minimally so. We had water but no food. Even if we caught fish or small game, we had no way to cook it. None of us knew enough about the flora of Talawan to be able to say that such and such plant was safe to eat. We were certainly hungry, but I wasn't sure if I was ready to eat raw fish or game. Then Macklin surprised us.

He'd taken off his watch, which had stopped working after being in the water. He pried off the lens cover and then began to gather tiny bits of dry grass and leaves into a small pile. Using the lens cover and that intense southwest Pacific sun, he soon got a fire started, which Rooster and I fed with dry sticks collected from around the waterfall pool. For some reason, that little fire was the most comforting thing I'd seen since the disaster in the strait. I speculated that there must be fish in that waterfall pool, but Rooster just shook his head.

"No way to git those suckers," he pointed out. "Gotta do it another way."

He took Macklin with him and went back downstream about a hundred yards. They collected an armful of the thinnest of those maddening vines and tied up a crude gill net, which they placed across the stream. Then Macklin went back up to the point where the pool funneled down into the stream and began throwing rocks into the water. Rooster waited at the homespun net and collected a half-dozen fish as they fled from the disturbance upstream. None of them was a trophy, but all of them were pretty good eating that evening, cooked on hot rocks next to the pool.

Two out of three ain't bad, I thought as darkness descended. The next thing we needed was some kind of shelter. I'd been hoping for a cave near the falls like I'd seen in all the Hollywood castaway movies, but there wasn't one. Just worn volcanic rock which looked like it had been through smallpox. There was warm black sand around the pool, so each of us burrowed down into that for the night. Strangely there weren't too many insects, or at least nothing like down in the coastal jungle. I wondered how high we'd climbed.

My body still ached and I was saddened by the loss of Lieutenant Teller and all the rest of the *Hagfish* crew. Teller had tried to keep a brave face, but when he said all his organs felt like they'd been torn off their moorings, he must have known he was dying. Rooster seemed to be in better spirits and was probably relieved to be out of that claustrophobic steel tube masquerading as a warship. Macklin was still pretty jumpy, but he was young and strong, so the three of us had a pretty good chance of surviving. It would depend on how many Japs there were on this island and how hard they looked for us.

But survive to what end? I didn't want to spend the rest of my life on this island, and yet, having seen the charts, I couldn't imagine how in the world anyone would find us and bring us back into the fold. We were a *very* long way from carrier task groups, PBYs, and with *Hagfish*'s loss, no American submarines would be sporting about in these waters anytime soon. I drifted off to sleep with the comforting smell of woodsmoke, determined to rethink our problem in the morning. Maybe build a big raft and sail it off to the east. Or south to Australia. Get those saws, hammers, and nails going, and big canvas sails to catch the southwest Pacific trade winds. Right.

I think it was the woodsmoke that betrayed us, because when I woke up the next morning we were surrounded by about a dozen figures with decorated Asiatic faces. They wore what looked like a combination of tribal clothing over tan or black shorts. Every one of them had a rifle of some kind. They were squatting on their haunches and looking at us as if we were some kind of interesting new food prey. Rooster heard me exclaim, sat up, and stared at them.

"Aw, *shit*," he growled. "Don't tell me—cannibals?"

SEVENTEEN

The sound of a man laughing softly came from behind me. I turned to find a Filipino man leaning against the black rock wall which flanked the falls. He was taller than the others and had a look of authority about him. He was wearing khaki trousers and a white shirt, leather boots, and a sweat-stained pith helmet. A large pistol supported by one of those Sam Browne duty belts decorated his right hip. He looked to be in his late thirties, but it was hard to really tell.

He casually launched himself off the lava rock wall and came down to where the three of us, still in our shallow sand graves, were staring in amazement. I halfway expected him to say: Dr. Livingstone, I presume?

"Welcome to Talawan," he said. "And, no, these are not cannibals. They are native peoples of this island and their ancestors include people from all over this part of the world, including China. More importantly we are members of the Philippine resistance. I assume you are Americans? From whatever ship that was that exploded out in the straits?"

I was almost too surprised to answer. The contrast between his clearly Asiatic heritage and the quality of his English was remarkable. Looking at his face I wondered if he was only part Filipino. "You got it," I replied. "And who might you be?"

"I am Domingo Abriol, formerly of Manila. But enough talk: right now we need to get you three out of here before a Jap beach patrol gets a whiff of that smoke and comes up to have a look."

The three of us climbed stiffly out of our sandy bunks. Two of the native militiamen doused our smoldering fire while others tore off branches and began sweeping away all evidence of our overnight stay. I took off my shoes and socks and walked into the pool to rid myself of all that sand. Rooster and Macklin followed me in. In five minutes we were off, walking single file with Domingo Abriol in the lead. We climbed up and around the outcropping that had created the falls, while three of his men spread out behind us to make sure we'd left no obvious sign. Above the falls was a fairly level plateau about a half mile wide. From that we filed down a narrow trail leading into a shallow, grassy canyon. The trees were getting sparser up here and there were house-sized boulders scattered up and down the ravine. Above us was another black rock cliff which looked to be at least a thousand feet high. In the distance off to our right the unmistakable cone shape of a volcano pushed a thin grayish plume straight up into the hazy tropical air.

"I didn't know there *was* a Philippine resistance," I said to Abriol's back. I was puffing now, out of shape from those days of sitting around in the sub, plus some of my leg muscles still hurt from the mine explosion. Rooster was beginning to really drag, while Macklin kept looking furtively at the Filipinos and their rifles. The ground was tricky, with lots of rocks scattered everywhere.

"Much bigger operation up north on Luzon, the main island," he said over his shoulder. "Talawan is not exactly an important island, so we are very small potatoes compared to the Luzon resistance. The big islands have regular army organization—colonels, battalions, companies. Down here on Talawan it's just me and my friends here."

One of the villagers walking ahead of us gave a sudden shout, startling Macklin, who'd been walking behind him. Macklin stepped sideways and then tripped over a rock and went face-down onto the ground, where a thick, light brown snake with a hood behind its head struck him right in the face—twice, before the villager who'd yelled stepped forward and removed its head with a wicked-looking machete. Everyone in our group froze for a moment before leaping to Macklin's aid. We rolled him over. I gasped when I saw his face. It was as if someone had thrown acid into his eyes, turning them a grayish, egg-white color. There were two clear bite marks, two holes on his right cheek, the other two on the right side of his neck just under his jaw, clearly red puncture wounds. The ones on his neck were bleeding. Macklin took a deep, straining breath, then a second one, harder than the first, tried for a third, and then his eyes lost focus and he went mortally still. I was speechless.

"Spitting cobra," Abriol said, peering down at the dead snake. "They shoot venom at their prey's eyes which blinds them immediately. And a neck bite right there, well, that's where the carotid artery is. That's always going to be pretty quick. One of Talawan's scarier snakes, I'm afraid."

I sat back on my haunches. I didn't know what to say, or do. Rooster looked as shocked as I was. The lumpish body of the snake was still writhing slowly on the ground, as if in search of its head. It was about four feet long.

"We must go on," Abriol said. "My men will hide the body, and the wild dogs will take care of the remains. I'm very sorry. Was he religious?"

I stood up, took a deep breath, and said I didn't know. He wasn't wearing dog tags. Abriol nodded. The villager who'd shouted the warning came up to Abriol and began apologizing in Tagalog, but Abriol waved him away in a sympathetic fashion with only a few words.

I wanted to ask a hundred questions but decided to save my breath, especially if we were going to take on that looming escarpment in front of us. It had looked to be *right* in front of us, but two hours later we were still climbing toward the base. I thought I heard Rooster groan quietly as we finally closed in on that sheer black wall. It looked like Abriol was heading directly for another one of those giant boulders, partially buried in deep black sand, but when we reached it he simply walked around it and into a narrow passageway that led right into the rock face.

I glanced up as we made our way into the passage. It looked as if the entire side of the mountain, if that's what this was, had split apart, leaving a ten-foot-wide crack that went up at a slight angle, with sides that were black and shiny, reminding me of obsidian. The trail curved around to the right and then back to the left for almost 200 yards before we stepped out into a huge bowl-shaped formation, obviously the crater of an extinct volcano. The crater was perhaps a half mile in diameter and perfectly symmetrical, with walls rising at least 500 feet all around. There was a purplish lake at the bottom a hundred feet or so below us, but no vegetation anywhere.

"Welcome to the Tambagi crater," Abriol said. I was still taking it all in when I got a whiff of sulfur and then felt a warm, wet sensation on my right pants leg. I looked down to discover a tiny fissure in a rock next to my leg that was weeping barely visible steam.

Not extinct, I thought.

Abriol nodded when he saw me work that out. "That lake down there is mostly acid of some kind. My people showed me by taking me down there and throwing a coin in right at the edge. It boiled away in about sixty seconds, so we don't go down there, okay?"

"You bet," I said. "So where—"

"Please, follow me," he said. We turned left and walked along a two-foot-wide ledge for a hundred yards, trying not to look down, until we came to another hole in the crater wall. This one was roundish and maybe 20 feet in diameter. It appeared to be a tunnel of some kind, with walls of more of that shiny black rock. I noticed that our escort of native resistance fighters had melted away once we'd entered the crater. There was now only one older-looking guy taking up the rear of our little column.

"This is an ancient lava tube," Abriol said, stopping to explain what we were looking at. "It goes all the way through the crater wall to a sheer cliff on the western slopes of the mountain. It's about four hundred feet long, with a downward curve to it. We've made our base here. It's perfect, because from the air, if any of our campfire smoke escapes, any passing Jap pilot will think it's the volcano. Their patrols don't come in here because the locals have told them that there is poison gas in this crater and that the slopes are home to some really bad snakes."

Tell me about it, I thought. Poor Macklin.

"Is there really poison gas?" I asked as we started single file into the tunnel.

"There probably is a layer of carbon dioxide hanging above that acid pool down there," he said. "And you've seen the snakes firsthand. Are you hungry?"

He grinned when he saw two heads nodding vigorously. We had gone 50 feet when the walls began to vibrate to a deep rumbling noise. It lasted twenty seconds, followed by a fine mist of black dust that seemed to materialize out of nowhere and settled on our clothes in almost microscopic particles. There was a surprising amount of sunlight coming from the entrance, and the motes of lava dust created a momentarily beautiful scene.

"Earthquake," Abriol observed. "Comes with the territory. You'll get used to it. The locals tell the story that the last time this volcano let go, their shaman knew it was coming because the daily earthquakes stopped completely for a couple of weeks."

Suddenly I was exhausted and I could see that Rooster was even more tired than I was. I just wanted to sit down, but our guide insisted we go farther into the lava tube. After a few minutes we could smell something cooking. Finally we walked through what I recognized as crude blackout curtains, a panel of fabric on the left, then one on the right, then one more on the left. We zigzagged through them to discover that the "camp" was really nothing more than a line of bamboo pallets leaning against the tunnel wall, each with a cotton blanket and a tied cylinder of straw for a pillow. Farther on was a makeshift table, some benches, and a stone firepit. A trickle of water wept out of the tunnel wall and headed down the long curving floor. A tin pot intercepted some of the water and there was a dimpled metal cup hanging next to the pot. Two old women were squatting next to the fire, tending some battered pots hanging over a bed of coals. There was a faint movement of air through the tunnel that took away what little smoke there was. At the far end of the space two young girls were sitting, trying not to stare at us.

Dinner turned out to be some kind of mystery-meat stew and rice, served in clay bowls. There were hot peppers in it but it was still wonderful. I made a signal to Rooster to hold back to make sure there would be enough for everybody else but Abriol told us to eat our fill and not worry about it. "They'll be back tomorrow," he said. "With another version of that gilly-gilly and maybe even some homemade beer, if we're lucky."

He then turned to the sole remaining resistance fighter and spoke to him in a native language. The man nodded, picked up his rifle, and then helped the two women to gather up their stuff. The girls sprang up and helped. One of them got the giggles when Rooster burped. She was very pretty and trying hard not to make eye contact with Rooster, who was too tired to notice. Her mother did, however, causing a rapid departure.

Then it was just the three of us—two American naval aviators, survivors of a submarine sinking, and this odd individual who had set up a resistance cell in a volcano. There were three kerosene lanterns hanging from a pole on the wall. He extinguished two of them and then sat down on one of the mats with his back to the curving tunnel wall.

"Where'd all your soldiers go?" I asked, still sitting on the other side of the primitive bamboo table. Rooster had taken down one of the straw pallets and was busy setting up a bunk.

"They go back to their villages at night," he replied. "We only come here when something happens and we go out to see. Like rumors of a big explosion in the south channel."

Somehow he'd managed to light up a pipe. The smell of the tobacco made me hunger for a cigarette. Where the hell did he get tobacco out here in the Philippine Islands, I wondered. The surreal nature of our circumstances made me sigh out loud.

"What?" he asked, as he puffed on that pipe to get it going.

"I am Lieutenant Junior Grade Robert T. Steele, US Navy," I said. "I am—was—a Navy carrier dive bomber pilot. Rooster—that's Radioman Second Class Billy Baynes over there—is my gunner and co-pilot. Less than a month ago we had been busy attacking Japanese carriers in the Solomon Islands area with the rest of our squadron. Then my carrier got bombed and eventually sank. The two of us went into the water as our carrier went down. We were eventually picked up by one of our own subs, but then she had to make a long transit under radio silence. Once here she attacked a Jap cruiser, and then we got depth charged for a while. They decided to go around to the other side of the island and chose to go through that strait. Apparently we hit a mine and Rooster, Macklin, the lieutenant who was standing OOD, and I ended up in the water. The lieutenant who was the officer of the deck died on the beach once we got ashore. Macklin you know about."

"Go on," he said.

"Well, now I'm sitting here *inside* a fucking volcano with a Filipino guy who speaks damned good English and who says he's in charge of a bunch of Filipino natives running some kind of resistance operation against the Japanese army. I'm not complaining, mind you, but I am just a little bit bewildered, Mister Domingo Abriol."

He laughed quietly. "That's *Father* Domingo Abriol," he announced. "I also happen to be a Catholic priest."

I shook my head. "Of course you are," I said. "I think I really need some sleep."

"Great idea, Lieutenant," he said, gently. "And for what it's worth, this really isn't much of a volcano, as Philippine volcanoes go. The real McCoy is thankfully about twenty miles away. We'll get everything sorted out in the morning. At least you're alive, right?"

Man had a point, there, I thought, as I got up to go assemble my bed for the night. Rooster was already asleep.

EIGHTEEN

The next morning we were awakened by the rumble of yet another small earthquake. The sound seemed to echo, as if it ricocheted from one end of the lava tube to the other. Father Abriol was sitting right where I'd left him, already awake. When he saw we were awake he got up, stirred the embers of the fire, and plopped an odd-shaped pot down on the flames. Soon the smell of coffee permeated the tunnel. Coffee in the Philippines, I thought. And tobacco. Boy, did I have a lot to learn.

He showed us to the latrine a hundred feet or so down the tunnel, where the floor cracked open, revealing a seemingly bottomless chasm. We walked back up to the camp, washed up, re-stowed the pallets, and then we gathered around the firepit, munching on some kind of flatbread he'd produced from a wicker basket and drinking some truly wonderful coffee. I asked about the coffee.

"Been here in the Philippines since the sixteen hundreds," he said. "Spanish friars brought it in from Mexico. Most of it's grown up in the highlands of Luzon to the north. There's one tiny plantation on the slopes of that smoking volcano you saw. We Filipinos are addicted to it, especially in Manila."

"I can see why," I said. "I thought Navy coffee was good, but this . . ."

He nodded, obviously pleased that we approved. Then he grew serious. "From what you told me, the Navy doesn't know what happened to your submarine or even the fact that you are alive, correct?"

"We weren't privy to what messages were being sent or received when we were on the boat. They said they reported picking us up but never got an answer back as to what to do with us, as I remember. We were mostly trying to not be a burden."

"I'm asking because there's a radio down in one of the villages. I think we need to tell Manila about you. Maybe they can send another submarine to pick you up."

The expression on Rooster's face revealed exactly what he thought about getting on another submarine. He quickly steered the conversation away from that really bad idea. "What kind of radio?" he asked.

"It's a radio, that's all I know," Father Abriol replied. "Uses a telegraph key. It runs on a hand-cranked generator and I'm the designated operator since I've begun learning Morse code. We get our instructions from the resistance headquarters near Manila once a week. In turn, if I have something to report, I do it precisely at one in the morning. I report as to what Japanese ships are here or whenever anything changes. They told us to move the radio immediately to another village every time I use it."

"And what are your instructions, Father Abriol?" I asked.

"There's only one deep-water anchorage on Talawan Island," he replied. "The Japs landed earlier this year and went to work on making Orotai, which is not much more than a large fishing village, some kind of temporary base. Right now, my orders are to report any Japanese shipping that comes here, especially warships.

"When the Japs first arrived they built a walled compound down near the fishing boat pier in the town. They rounded up every able-bodied man they could find in the town, disassembled some of the town's buildings for materials, and created their fort. The garrison isn't large—perhaps two hundred fifty or so. They have barracks, gun towers, and some warehouses, all surrounded by a twelve-foot-high wall."

"Not much of a garrison," I said.

He shrugged. "There's more: three months after they arrived, they began building another compound across the river from Orotai. We thought it was to be a second fort for the army troops who'd landed, but then we found out it was going to be a prisoner-of-war camp. A month later a transport arrived and they boated in about two hundred or so British prisoners from their Malaya campaign."

"Wow," was all I could muster.

"By then they'd built a barbed-wire-and-bamboo-log enclosure for the prisoners, and then some barracks for their men and a small house for their commandant, a lieutenant colonel named Tachibana. They then cleared all the land around the enclosure down to bare dirt and mounted machine-gun towers at three corners. They put the word out in the town that anybody coming within sight of the camp wall would be killed. Then they went through the town and the nearby countryside and took all the food. If anyone resisted, they were killed on the spot. They took young women, too."

"And you reported all this to Manila?"

"I actually went up there in one of the bigger fishing boats we have here," he said. "When the Japs landed I knew *I* had to disappear. They're known to kill priests on sight. I brought the radio back with me, along with a crate of old rifles and some ammunition."

I thought about that. So if these guys had a radio, it was probably an HF set of some kind. Maybe I could get Rooster to key a message to Manila that the local resistance had two American pilots, and also the news that the *Hagfish* was no longer with us. I wondered what the resistance up in Manila would do with that news. If they'd sent a hand-cranked radio down here to the boonies, they'd certainly have even better radios near occupied

Manila that could get through to the American high command in Australia. Which begged the obvious question: Would the Navy do anything about it? They'd already diverted one submarine to look for us after Santa Cruz—and subsequently lost it. Would they do that again? Or would we need to start learning the local language?

"How many Japs are on this island?" I asked.

"We think about two hundred fifty soldiers, all based in Orotai. They've also got one gunboat. They keep an old freighter anchored close off the town which I think provides communications and a secure base, since there's no electricity in the town."

"How are they treating the locals?"

"Like the barbaric bastards that they are," he said with some heat. "Their commandant, Tachibana, is a real monster. Brutal is an insufficient description for him and his officers."

"Why are they *here*?" I asked.

"Talawan is a small island, with three tiny villages and then the town of Orotai, which itself is pretty small. Most of this island is uplands like where we are, with lots of volcanic features, impassable terrain, and very little flat ground whatsoever. We don't know why they chose Talawan, except maybe for that anchorage. Mindanao, that's the next island up and northwest from Talawan, has a much bigger occupying force and an airfield. And a much bigger armed resistance, too. The prisoner-of-war camp may have been an afterthought. There's really no port, as such. No docks, piers, warehouses, or rail connections. Just a protected anchorage, for now."

I remembered the *Hagfish*'s XO telling us that they suspected that Talawan was a way-station base. They'd anchor a tanker and some supply ships here and then transiting fleet units could come in, refuel, rearm, replenish, and then get back on the road to the Solomons. Like that cruiser. I told all this to Father Abriol.

"That makes some sense," he observed. "You must remember, the Japs are a long way from home. It's over two thousand miles to Tokyo. Perhaps they're going to build all of that infrastructure for their navy one day. Oil tanks, food warehouses, ammunition storage, although an airfield would be really tough."

I remembered what the Marines and Seabees had accomplished on Guadalcanal, using Japanese equipment and works in progress to get Henderson Field up and running. But that ground had been flat, and the Japs had already done the ground preps for an airfield. From what I'd already seen, Abriol was right. There really wasn't much flat land on this island.

"They've rounded up about two hundred men from the town and put them into a forced labor camp," Abriol continued. "As I said, they also picked up some of the young women from Orotai and any in the villages who hadn't run for purposes that you can imagine. It wasn't difficult for me to organize a resistance force after that, let me tell you."

At that moment, a sweaty and puffing young native came down the tunnel. He gabbled away at Father Abriol for a minute. The priest replied and the young man took off back up the tunnel.

"Trouble?" I asked.

"There's a Jap patrol squad at the waterfall," he said. "They've brought dogs."

"Uh-oh," Rooster said. "You got any extra guns?"

"Not here," he said. "But we probably won't need them. We've talked about this eventuality and made some plans. Come with me."

Father Abriol, who still had that hoss-pistol strapped on, gave us each a bamboo canteen to fill at the wall weep. He produced some binoculars and then we went out of the tunnel. We retraced our steps to that crack in the rim. Coming out of the crack, we turned right, went about a hundred yards, dropped into a small ravine, and then lay down behind some of those big lava rocks. Below us the valley stretched out in the rising sunlight. The cone-shaped volcano in the distance was no longer sending smoke into the air.

"I keep patrols of my own going in this area and all around Orotai," he told us. "As I said before, the Japs usually don't come near this place. But if they've brought dogs, they must suspect that somebody from that submarine not only survived but escaped into the interior, and they'll also know *we* had to be involved in that. Two birds with one stone, if they can find us."

"So what happens now?" Rooster asked.

"We wait for the bait," he announced, making a rhyme out of it.

"The bait."

"Keep your eye on that clump of trees that extends out into the valley. There, on the right. Watch for a runner."

We waited. And then we waited some more. The air above the valley was beginning to shimmer. Obviously Abriol was going to tell us what the plan was as soon as he saw that it was actually being executed. With Japs, one never knew. I decided to find out some more about Father Abriol.

"Tell me, Father. How did *you* end up here?"

"I'll give you the short version," he said, taking another sweep with the binoculars. "Simply put, I was banished by Holy Mother Church. I made the grave mistake of falling in love with a lovely but married young woman in my first parish assignment. I not only fell in love, I managed to get her pregnant. When her husband found out, the monsignor found out and he went to the bishop. The cardinal bishop was in his eighties and had a predictably medieval reaction to this situation. He sought Rome's help in exiling me to the 'ends of the earth,' as he quaintly demanded. The 'ends of the earth' turned out to mean the very bottom of the Philippine Islands chain, namely the island of Talawan. In all fairness, they needed a priest. It was a tiny congregation, much more animist than Catholic and as far from Manila as one could get, so down I came. This was ten years ago."

"Couldn't you have just resigned from the priesthood, and, I don't know, stayed there in Manila?" I asked.

He shook his head. "One doesn't 'resign' from the priesthood," he said. "You undertake Holy Orders, as it's called, you're a priest for life in the eyes of God. Or at least the Church, which is much the same thing. Besides, the husband was a member of the provincial police. The Diocese was informed that an 'accident' was in my future, like the one that had befallen his unfaithful wife, so, suddenly, exile started to look pretty good. Ah, there he is."

"There *who* is?" I asked, shielding my eyes from the morning sun to search that long valley again.

"Paulino Magsay," he replied, staring through the binoculars. "He's a village elder and an expert tracker. Probably fifty years old and tough as a mahogany railroad tie. One of his daughters was kidnapped by the Japs. For the past hour or so he's been trotting in this direction laying a scent trail for those dogs, probably using some urine."

"He's bringing the Japs *here*?" I asked, trying not to reveal my concern.

"Not quite here," Father Abriol said. "He's taking them to a small cave below us. You can't see it from here. He'll drop little bits of urine as he runs. The dogs will get on his human scent, of course, but that urine will be the brighter trail for those amazing noses. And if those dogs go into that particular cave, they won't be coming back out."

"What's in there?" Rooster asked.

"A pair of Samar cobras are known to nest there," he said. "Those are the spitting cobras. You've seen what they can do."

Indeed we had. Poor Macklin. I'd already forgotten all about him.

"I thought cobras were something you only found in India," I said. "Or Africa."

He smiled. "We have cobras, green pit vipers, and some of the world's deadliest sea snakes here in the Philippines. You have to *want* to provoke a sea snake, but all the others are easily provoked. We also have some truly large pythons, but they don't bother people unless people bother them—the usual story with snakes. But if the patrol leader orders his men into that cave, they'll probably die there, too."

"You make that sound like you don't want that to happen," I said.

"Well, personally, I don't. First, because I'm a Catholic priest—I don't want to see anyone die unnecessarily. Second, if the Japs figure out that this was a setup, they'll exact retribution against the entire local population."

"All the more reason for them *all* to die," I said. "By the way, I was at Pearl Harbor."

"Oh," he said, suddenly at a loss for words.

"That him?" Rooster said, pointing down into the valley. "I thought I saw somebody running."

Father Abriol swept the area with his binoculars again and then steadied. "Yes, that's him. He'll run to the cave, throw in the urine pouch, and then disappear. Everybody keep down now—the Japs have pretty good binoculars of their own."

We heard the dogs before we ever saw them. They came about thirty minutes after our sighting of Magsay. We kept our heads down while Father Abriol crawled along our parapet to watch through a crack.

"There are two dog handlers and four more soldiers," he reported softly. "The handlers are out in front with the dogs and the soldiers look to be struggling to keep up. I think one's wearing a sword."

"That'll be the officer in charge," I said.

The sun was getting hotter and I was grateful for the primitive canteen. Rooster was giving me that "what in hell are we doing here" look again. Twenty minutes later Father Abriol started giving us a whispered play-by-play report. The dogs and handlers are at the cave entrance. The handlers are waiting for the guys with rifles to catch up. Everybody waited some more. Then: they've loosed the dogs into the cave. I halfway expected to hear screams of agony from the dogs but we didn't hear a sound.

Looks like that officer is telling two of the squad to go in there, Father Abriol continued, changing his position to get a better look. That cave was a couple hundred feet below us but those sheer stone walls carried the sound of voices straight up. It sounded like an argument, although all the newsreels I had ever seen featuring Japanese army officers talking to each other sounded like they were getting ready to kill each other. They don't seem to want to go in there, Father Abriol reported. Then we heard the crack of a rifle or a pistol—I couldn't tell which.

"Wow," Father Abriol said softly. "The officer just shot one of his own men. I guess that's what happens when you don't obey an order. The other soldier *is* going in. He's mounted his bayonet. The dog handlers are getting out of the way. They don't have guns. And—"

This time we did hear a scream, but not from a dog. Father Abriol gasped.

"What's happened?" Rooster asked.

"That soldier came back out," he said in a shocked voice. "There was a snake hanging from his *throat*. Now he's down on the ground and writhing around. The officer is going after the snake with his sword. Holy *Mother!*"

"What are the rest of them doing?" I asked.

"Backing up. Backing *way* up. *Oh!*"

I put my index finger up to my lips—the priest was getting loud.

"He cut that snake in half," he said, back to whispering. "But then he picked it up and—and—I think it struck him, right in the face. That's a cobra, all right. They're very aggressive. Now the officer is down. God, what a mess!"

I sat back against the warm stone, realizing now that Abriol had set a trap that worked much better than he'd anticipated. So now we had an officer and presumably two soldiers probably dead or dying, plus two tracking dogs who never came out. I remembered being told as a kid: never pick up a "dead" snake. Some of them aren't willing to admit they're dead. I wondered what the Japs would do when the remains of the patrol got back to their base in town—send up a whole company? We didn't need that. I asked Father Abriol if he could see anyone using a radio.

"Not that I can see," he said. "Now there are three men on the ground down there and *no*body's moving except the front end of that snake."

I tried to cast that image out of my mind. Father Abriol said the handlers were each picking up a rifle. One of them bent to retrieve the officer's sword but that snake tried to strike him.

"They're leaving," Father Abriol said. "And so are we. Jesus wept."

NINETEEN

That evening four of us went out through the lava tube's other end and headed west down the mountainside. Father Abriol took the lead; I brought up the rear. Rooster and one of the Filipinos were in the middle and each was carrying a bolt-action rifle that looked like a weapon left over from World War One. Father Abriol had asked if I wanted a weapon but I'd declined. My legs still weren't a hundred percent after the mining, so what I really wanted was a stout walking stick to deal with all that volcanic sand and slippery gravel. The lava tube thumped out a friendly goodbye earthquake just as we emerged into the twilight.

We walked for a little over an hour into the scrublands that surrounded the volcanic area. Ahead we could make out the dark line of thicker vegetation. As we got closer we could see a pond of sorts, surrounded by trees that were taller than all the rest. The pond was like a small oasis in these dry upland rock gardens. Three tall volcanic boulders stood guard over a small clearing next to the pond, where some more of Father Abriol's people were waiting, their rifles leaning up against the big rocks. I asked him what we were doing.

"We're going to meet with the competition," he said. When he saw my consternation he grinned. "It's a long story," he said. "First let's sit down. Hopefully my friends here have brought food."

They had. It consisted of a clay pot full of golf-ball-sized rice balls, containing bits of smoked fish and some vegetables I couldn't identify mixed in with the sticky rice. It was, if anything, spicier than the stew we'd had last night, but we hadn't eaten since dawn and thus made short work of it. This time Father Abriol joined in. My mouth was stinging a bit when we were done so we were each offered a piece of freshly cut sugarcane, which mollified the fires pretty well if you chewed and sucked on it long enough.

Some of the other scouts had built a low fire up against the biggest of the boulders. After we'd all eaten, the four of us sat down on the ground near the fire while the scouts slipped away into the forest, leaving one man to tend the fire. He went into the nearby woods with his machete and came back with a tube of bamboo, maybe five inches in diameter and two feet long. He filled that from the pond and parked it upright against the big rock. Then he went back out, apparently to find more wood for the fire. A half moon hung in the tropical sky, providing weak light.

"The competition," I said, still baffled.

"Yes, well, the Spanish came to the Philippines in the sixteen hundreds and established the One True Faith as the official religion, but these days it's one of *three* religions practiced in these islands: Catholicism, Animism, and Mohammedanism."

That last floored me. *Mohammedanism?* Here? I could understand animism—local gods, ancestors, tribal customs and taboos, house spirits, animal spirits, the volcanoes—things the natives had either feared or believed in since long before Christ and His missionary hordes. Father Abriol saw my disbelief.

"Oh, yes," he said. "Arab traders came out of the Indian Ocean in the *thir*teenth century, almost two, three hundred years before the Spaniards got here. When the Spanish became aware of them, they pushed them down mainly into Mindanao Province and called them Moros."

"As in, the Moors."

"Yes. As you may remember from school, the Spanish have some unpleasant history with the Moors."

At that moment a small, brown-faced man stepped out of the forest and made a hand signal to Father Abriol. He then melted back into the darkness.

"Okay," Father Abriol said. "They're coming. We will be speaking in Tagalog; I'll translate later. You two relax and make no sudden moves, okay? These people fought a long war against the American occupiers at the turn of the century. The one I'll be talking to is an important and revered figure on Talawan, so if you can, look respectful. They won't be happy you're here."

"Makes two of us," Rooster muttered, but we both acknowledged the warning. If my memory served me, the Moros were the reason the 1911 Colt .45 was invented. They were the guerillas who'd charge American forces and *keep* coming despite being hit several times.

A few minutes later six figures dressed in white emerged cautiously from the woods. They looked different from the local tribesmen. Each of them wore a white headdress, either tied around their heads or in the form of a full turban. They wore a white sash around their waists and baggy loincloths that looked like diapers over their bare legs. Their expressions were grimly hostile. They wore long knives at their waists and all but one also carried a rifle. That individual was older and taller than the rest, with a more elaborate headdress, robes instead of the loincloth, and he was using a tall walking stick.

The men with rifles stopped short of the firelight and spread out into a semicircle, where they squatted down to keep watch, their rifles across their legs. They were calm but guarded. The older man came forward and greeted Father Abriol in Tagalog. In the firelight we could see that he was indeed old, with skin like brown parchment stretched over a hatchet-shaped face, a hooked nose, and fierce black eyes. He bowed formally to Father Abriol, who bowed right back and then stepped forward and pressed his forehead against the old man's outstretched hand. They then both sat down cross-legged on the ground and began to talk.

The old man asked a question and Father Abriol responded at length. When he was done the old one responded at an even greater length. His tone was emotionless and he stared into the fire as he talked. Father Abriol waited until he was sure that the elder was done, and then he spoke for about five minutes. It went on like that for half an hour before the elder nodded once and then got up with the help of his walking stick. He politely inclined his head to Father Abriol. Then they all walked back into the forest.

Father Abriol let out a sigh of what sounded like great relief. I asked him what he'd been worried about.

"I called them the 'competition' earlier," he said. "When some American priests visited our seminary in Manila, they jokingly referred to the Protestant churches as 'the competition.' Here it's no joke, and that's because of the bloody history between Philippine native Mohammedans and foreign Christians. They're mad at the Church for two reasons: the Koran says Christians are unbelievers and therefore worthy of death. They also consider the Catholic Church and its priests to be occupiers, even though the Church hierarchy in Manila today is entirely Filipino. We agreed to a truce of sorts when the Japs came. *Every*body hates the Japs."

"'The enemy of my enemy is my friend'?" I asked.

"Sort of," he replied. "I told him you were here to help with the resistance and that you were not the advance party for another American occupation."

"These guys live in Orotai?" I asked.

He shook his head. "No, their territory is the northern half of Talawan, beyond the central volcano fields. That's the part that's closest to the province of Mindanao and its islands, where the Moros are. Their relationship with the Moros is complicated, because these people are Shia, and the Mindanao Moros are

Sunni Mohammedans. Shia and Sunni do not get along, but they hate foreigners, especially Christians, more than they hate each other."

"And everybody hates the Japs," I echoed.

"Now you understand, Lieutenant," he said. "I told you—it's complicated. I was told that he, Emir Mohammed al Raqui, already knew that there were Americans on Talawan, so I asked for a meeting to head off any possible problems. I wish I could claim that we coordinate our 'resistance efforts,' but a wary truce is more like it."

"And emir is like the chief?" Rooster asked.

"He's much more than that," Abriol replied. "He's an extraordinary healer. As you could see from his looks, he is definitely descended from the Arabs of long ago. Our people on this side of the volcanoes both revere him and fear him. The Moros are violent people. They tend to settle disputes with guns. And yet, when a mysterious fever swept through Orotai and the surrounding villages, he came down from the north with strange medicines and stopped the outbreak."

Okay, I thought. I'm impressed. "What happens now?" I asked.

"Now I think it's important we get to our radio and notify Manila that you're here, preferably before al Raqui decides to inform the Japs that there *are* Americans on the island."

"He'd do that?"

Father Abriol hesitated. "I'm not sure," he said, finally. "When the Japs came, he met with them and told them Allah did not permit them to help either side. Basically, that they'd stay out of the conflict as long as the Japs left them alone. The Japs promised they would. They exchanged some more pretty lies like that, and so far, that's how it's working. It helps that the Japs are down here and they are up on the northern end, where there's nothing the Japs want."

"But they know that you and your men are watching and reporting to the resistance in Manila?"

He nodded. "Using that radio kind of gave it away," he said. "As I said, we use it sparingly, and only at designated times. Then we move it quickly. My limited skills with Morse code keep me on the air longer than I'd like."

"I could get Rooster here to send the message—he's an aviation radioman as well as a gunner. He's like lightning on the Morse key. When's the next window?"

"Tonight. By the way, he also knew that you two were survivors from what happened out in the strait."

"But not about what happened to that Jap patrol today?"

"Not yet," he said. "He will, in time, of course. He has eyes and ears in Orotai, as I have up-country. That incident will get out quickly. What happens after that depends on whether or not the Japs think it was an unfortunate accident or that *we* were involved."

My head was spinning: What the hell had we got ourselves into on this tiny remote island? Mohammedans fighting with Christians and also with each other. Both of them, Shia and Sunni, were fighting the Japs. And of course there was always "Dugout Doug" MacArthur safe in Australia vowing "I will return," which undoubtedly angered the Mohammedans and all the rest of the Filipinos no end.

TWENTY

Two hours later we were met somewhere out in the forest by two women, who apparently had been told to bring us into the village where the radio was hidden. There was still some moonlight and also a well-defined path, but our route to the rendezvous with the women had been anything but straightforward. The village was dark when we got there, and except for some very thin dogs there didn't seem to be anyone up and about. The women took us to a longhouse, a rectangular-shaped shed with no walls and some bamboo tables and benches inside. One of them lit a single, small candle and gestured for us to sit at one of the tables. She then bowed and retreated into the darkness. I wanted to ask what was next but I realized that all of this was pretty much prearranged.

After a while four men carrying what looked like a stretcher came towards the longhouse from the opposite direction we'd come from. The radio came in two parts: the radio itself and the generator, which was powered by a set of hand cranks like bicycle pedals on either side. Father Abriol met the men and instructed them where and how to set up the device. He unreeled a long wire from the back of the radio and gave the end of it to one of them, who walked out of the longhouse and into the forest with it. I was surprised at how long it was, but when it finally began to tension up, Father Abriol gave two sharp tugs on it.

"He'll take that end and climb a tree to get it off the ground," he explained. "I've taught them how to run the generator and maintain the required voltage. Now we have to write the message and then code it."

Code it, I thought. Well, of course. Father Abriol asked me what I wanted to tell Manila. I thought for a minute. Who were we talking to and who were *they* talking to? We needed to tell the Navy high command in Nouméa that we were there on Talawan and that *Hagfish* had hit a mine.

"Try this," I said. "'Inform American high command two Navy aviators rescued by USS *Hagfish* are on Talawan. *Hagfish* sunk by a mine. Aviators are only survivors.' That short enough?"

Father Abriol nodded. "The code is pretty basic," he said, producing a pocket notebook and a stubby pencil. "It's based on the numerical day of the month. I write the message on double-spaced lines. If today is an odd-numbered day of the month, say, the thirteenth, I offset the message letters by seven to the right. So 'a' becomes 'h.' If it's an even day, say the eighth, I offset the message letters to the *left* by six. So 'a' becomes 't.' I start the message with the number of the day I'm using in the clear so they can break it. Then I send the rest of the message as a stream of letters."

Rooster was fascinated by this so Father Abriol had him help with the encoding process while I held the candle. They made the calculations and wrote the substituted letter above each letter in the message. I then "broke" the message to see if it came out right, which it did. At the appointed time one of Abriol's men sat down next to the generator and began rolling the pedals while watching a needle on the face of the transmitter to keep it slightly above the required eighteen volts. Rooster said the radio was pretty basic— it could transmit on one frequency only. He sat down with the key pad and began tapping out the letters of the code. It took only a couple of minutes, and then Father Abriol held an earpiece to his right ear and waited for Manila to acknowledge. Then he nodded.

"Good," he said. "Now we pack it all up." He rattled off some

Tagalog and his troops retrieved the antenna from its treetop, packed the whole kit up on the stretcher, and walked off into the woods with it. Father Abriol tore the page out of his notebook and held it over the candle. Then we went back into the woods in a different direction from which we'd come, with a guide in front.

"Where we going now?" I asked.

"Orotai," he said. "It's only five, six miles away from this village, which is called Lingoro. I've had word there are Jap ships in the anchorage."

It was not quite breaking dawn when we finally stepped into what looked and smelled like a restaurant. We'd come down a maze of back alleys containing some interesting wildlife, including a huge snake that had a rat halfway ingested. We walked by lots of trash, stacks of bamboo logs, bundles of firewood, bags of charcoal, the occasional water buffalo, and chickens penned up in wire crates. From the last alley we ducked through a gate into a fenced dirt yard and, dodging more chickens and ducks, into the kitchen area. There were four women in the kitchen, all busy preparing things I couldn't identify. We walked through the waiters' passageway, past the dark dining area, and then up some stairs to the second floor, which turned out to be one big room. The windows were shuttered with bamboo curtains and there were beds along one wall, each enveloped by mosquito netting, as well as a large table in the middle.

We were met upstairs by two Filipino men wearing dark cotton trousers and short-sleeved white shirts. They greeted Father Abriol warmly, shook hands with us, and then gestured towards the table, where we all sat down. One of the women from the kitchen brought up some coffee and bread. I needed the coffee— we hadn't really slept since the night before the snake cave. I marveled at Father Abriol: he didn't seem to have been fazed in the least by being up all night and walking several miles to boot. He introduced me to the two men.

"This is Vergilio Santos; and this is Benny Himalan. They are both policemen in the town. Vergilio is the de facto chief of police."

I shook hands with both men. Vergilio could speak limited English, courtesy, apparently, of Father Abriol. "Welcome to Orotai," he said. "Bad place now."

"Thank you," I said. "Thank you for your protection."

He beamed. "Japanese bad people," he said. "Hurt Orotai people."

"They hurt everybody," I said. "All over the Pacific."

Father Abriol had to translate that one. Vergilio nodded solemnly. Then Abriol took over in Tagalog and I sipped some coffee. Rooster just watched while discreetly checking out how we'd escape from this room if we had to. And if we had to, what would be the point of that, I wondered.

Father Abriol and Vergilio talked at length. Benny Himalan just listened, nodding every time Vergilio made a point. Father Abriol made one last statement in Tagalog and then turned to us as the cops took their leave.

"The incident at the cave is out on the streets," he said. "The Japs rounded up a group of Filipinos and made them go out to carry back the bodies. So far there's no talk of reprisals—the dogs made a mistake and the soldiers suffered. Second, there *are* two Jap ships in the anchorage. Warships, from what my people are telling me. That means there'll be Jap officers in the town tonight. They come ashore bringing cases of *sake*, get drunk, and then at midnight the ships' boats come in and haul them all back to their ships."

"Where do they do all this carousing?" I asked, and then, almost immediately, I knew the answer.

"Right here, Lieutenant," Father Abriol said. "Vergilio and I both thought that the best place to hide you, for tonight at least, was here, the last place the *Kempeitai* would be searching if they somehow got word you'd been smuggled into town."

"What's a *Kempeitai*?" Rooster asked.

"The Japanese version of the German Gestapo. Bad news, all around. Even the Jap army officers are afraid of them. If a *Kempeitai* agent questions the loyalty of an officer, that officer might as well kill himself. There's four of 'em here in Orotai."

"Lovely," I muttered.

"The owner of this place will be up shortly. It was originally the only bar in the town. The Japs took it over and told him they would be his only clientele. The Jap officers come here every night. When warships come in, their officers come here as well."

"Their version of an O-club," I said.

"Something like that. Then they made him build a Jap bathhouse of sorts out back. There are showers and one of the cooks is a good barber. We'll get you some plain black trousers and white shirts—those uniforms have to go."

"Officers in civvies behind enemy lines are automatically considered spies and shot," I pointed out.

"If the *Kempeitai* catch either or both of you you'll be praying to be shot. So, right now I need to get out and down to the church tower to see what's here. Then I'll have to send another radio report. And, finally, I need to say Mass."

"Doesn't that bring a crowd?" I asked. "Don't the Japs notice?"

He smiled. "There's a small river that empties out into the bay here," he said. "I go upriver a few miles and set up an altar on the shore after dark. My 'parishioners' come in banca boats; they hear the Mass from out on the water. Then I distribute the Holy Eucharist to them. I give them extra consecrated communion wafers to take back to their families in the town and the villages."

"I gotta ask," Rooster said. "Where do you get communion wafers in the Philippines?"

"Oh, right here," Father Abriol said blithely. "They bake them downstairs."

I thought Father Abriol was taking the old adage about hiding things in plain sight a mite far. On the other hand, if this *was* the official watering hole for the occupying army officers, those

Kempeitai bastards probably wouldn't be tossing the place. Unless, of course, somebody informed. Like a certain emir.

Father Abriol put on a loose flowing white shirt to hide the Sam Brown gun belt and then donned a small Moro-like headdress. "After you get cleaned up they'll show you where you're going to hide for the night," he said. "Tomorrow we'll go take a close look at this POW camp. I've been hearing some terrible things about it. Oh, by the way, we need to do something about those pasty white faces of yours."

I had no answer for that. Aviators normally have sunburned faces from all the sunlight burning through our canopies at altitude, but we'd been cooped up on that submarine for long enough to begin looking like the submariners, who had had complexions like the underside of an oyster.

Four hours later we'd been transformed. First we'd been taken to the bathhouse with our heads covered in a towel by three giggling Filipino women. The walls of the bathhouse were sheets of corrugated steel sunk vertically into the ground and supported by bamboo frames. The roof was made of the same stuff. We were shown the primitive showers and given bars of sandpaper soap, or at least that's what it felt like. After we'd showered and de-grimed, the girls led us in all our naked and red-skinned glory to the warm bath pool. The "baths" were basically square holes in the ground lined with lava rocks and then filled with water.

The girls removed melon-sized lava rocks from a charcoal burner with a stable fork and dropped them into the water, with lots more giggling, especially in Rooster's direction. Apparently they'd never seen a man with red hair before. Then the hot bath, where we were given safety razors with which to shave. Then the cool bath. As I luxuriated in the waters I had to wonder: in a few hours there would be Japanese officers in here. What would they think if they knew their restorative baths had been contaminated by US Navy fliers? I felt like pissing in the water, but I knew that would upset our Filipino hosts, upon whom our lives depended utterly.

That raised an interesting question: What if the report of our being here had *not* been relayed to American military authorities, whether in Nouméa or Australia? Or, if it had, what if they'd decided that retrieving the two of us wasn't worth hazarding another submarine? It was a reasonable question, given what had happened to *Hagfish*. That hadn't been our fault, of course, but still: Talawan had proved itself to be a dangerous place for US submarines. Rooster and I kicked this around while soaking in the wonderful warm water. It was not an optimistic discussion.

Before we got out we had to retrieve the lava rocks, which went back onto the charcoal grate. The girls gave us some short-skirted bathrobes and took us back to the second floor of the restaurant. By then some amazing smells were drifting out of the kitchens. If this place had been closed off to everyone except the garrison, then the Japs themselves must be supplying the food. It was early evening and the Japanese officers would soon be arriving if the scurrying and chattering staff were any indication. In a normal restaurant, the staff would have been excited at the prospect of a full house, but from what I could see, these people were actually afraid. Then the face-maker showed up.

An elderly lady came up to the second floor, bearing a tray. We thought it might be some of the food being prepared downstairs but then we saw the small vials on the tray, along with a collection of brushes. She bade the both of us to lie down on the mats, put almond-shaped pieces of damp cloth over our eyes, and then proceeded to paint our shaven faces with an amazingly soothing solution of I know not what. When she was finished she sat back and nodded approvingly. There were no mirrors in the room, so I had no idea of what I looked like now, but apparently my pasty white skin was no longer a problem. I wondered how much it would help, though: our beards would be evident in just a few days, especially

Rooster's. His face didn't look all that much different, but when he saw mine he mimed the word: wow.

An older man came upstairs after our makeup artist had left. He had some pidgin English and showed us where we'd be hidden during the night. The walls of the second floor appeared to be made of split bamboo logs. He showed us how to open a section of one wall, which revealed a long hidden room, more like a long closet than a room. There was a two-tiered line of bunks mounted along the corrugated-iron external walls. The whole thing was 30 feet long and maybe 4 wide. If there was any ventilation I couldn't see it, and a rush of hot, humid air reeking of stale cigarette smoke hit our faces when he opened it up. He left the door open and then told us they'd bring us food as soon as Father Abriol returned.

"*Hapon sundalo* here chop-chop," he told us. "Gonna be much noise. Here is water. Now: you go inside. Be quiet."

He slid the wall section back into place and then it sounded like he was hanging some sort of fabric on the wall outside. We were startled by a sudden roar of rain on the metal roof, but it had the effect of cooling all that tin and making the air inside the hidey-hole more bearable. It stopped almost as soon as it had begun. Rooster found a crack between two floorboards through which we could see down into the big, open dining room downstairs. We spread some mats on the floor and took turns watching the festivities getting underway below us. This was as close as either of us had been to actual Japs.

Neither of us was up to speed on Jap uniforms, but we assumed that the guys wearing khaki shorts and carrying swords were army and the ones in gray uniforms and without swords were from the warships. They filed in over a noisy half hour while three tiny Filipino women rushed about bringing small containers of some kind of booze to the short-legged tables. *Sake?* The officers were sitting cross-legged on thin pillows down on the floor, lighting up smokes, guzzling down their drinks, while calling lustfully to friends at the other tables and offering a toast a minute in every direction. Then there was a sudden pause in the ruckus as a very large Japanese officer sauntered into the room and took a seat at the center table, where the older officers were sitting.

"Man, that's a *big* sucker," Rooster muttered. He wasn't kidding. I almost wondered if he was one of those sumo wrestlers we'd seen in movies about Japan, except he didn't seem to be sporting those enormous fat rolls. His khaki uniform fit him like a tent, and his hair was longer than any of the other army officers' and tied at the back in a greasy bun. He carried an extra-long samurai sword, and it looked like he had another, shorter version stashed along his waist. The rest of the officers were obviously deferring to this guy, whose hoarse voice was louder than all the rest and sounded like someone who could double as a foghorn if he wanted to. This had to be the garrison commandant, Tachibana. The serving girls brought him three vases of liquor, which he downed directly, not bothering to pour them into the miniature cups the others were using.

The atmosphere down below was getting pretty thick with cigarette smoke but then we smelled food. Some of the Filipinos we'd seen earlier down in the kitchen appeared and began putting bowls on the tables along with more of those little vases. There was lots of bowing and scraping on the part of the Filipinos as they backed out of the room.

We got tired of watching the Japs stuff their faces and suck down whatever they were drinking until it was apparently time for speechmaking. The two older naval officers each stood up, made a short speech, bowed and sat down. That was followed by an approving chorus of bowing Japanese from the assembled multitude. Finally Tachibana heaved himself to his feet, his sword upsetting some of the tableware. He launched into what sounded like an angry tirade but the crowd was loving it or at least pretending to and responding with *banzai*'s and *hai*'s. Just like Hitler's crowds, I thought, and they're both in the same bloody business.

The officers began to mingle after the speechmaking. The entire room was filled with bowing men, while the three serving girls tried to clear the tables and bring out tea. As one of them reached under Tachibana's arm to remove a bowl she spilled something on his uniform. He expelled a huge hiss and the officers at the tables closest to him went rigid. The girl began apologizing profusely but it was clear that the commandant wasn't having it. He reached down and snatched her upright by her right forearm, and then, using both of his massive hands, he broke that arm over the back of one of the chairs. The snap was audible and the girl screamed.

An older Filipino came rushing out of the kitchen area and literally ran to the table to retrieve the crying girl. Tachibana let him pick her up and turn to go and then stuck the tip of his sword scabbard under the old man's feet, sending him and the girl sprawling, evoking new shrieks of pain from her. Tachibana yelled something at the old man and then spit on him. The old man literally dragged the girl along the floor by her other arm like someone trying to do the sidestroke on the floor until he reached the kitchen door. Tachibana hurled more furious epithets in their direction and then turned to the crowd of officers. I knew perhaps three words of Japanese, but it didn't take a genius to understand what he was saying: *this* is how you treat these filthy Filipino dogs. Then he raised one of those little vases and roared out a *banzai*, which the crowd dutifully echoed, although, to their credit, some of them didn't seem to have their hearts in it.

We watched for a little while longer, but sickened by how Tachibana had treated the Filipino girl, we pulled a scrap of fabric over the crack and lay down on the cots. The hidden room was really warm by now and the cigarette smoke actually stung both our eyes. I thought they were smoking some kind of animal dung. I finally fell asleep only to be awakened some time later by the sound of the hidey-hole door being opened. There was Father Abriol, peering into our sweat lodge.

"Dinner," he announced, in his best butler's voice, "is served."

As we feasted on the leftovers from the party, very glad to be out of our little oven, he told us that the big guy we'd seen was indeed Lieutenant Colonel Hiroshi Tachibana, and that what he'd done tonight was completely in character. He apparently considered the British POWs across the river as toys for his barbarous amusement, having lost all vestiges of soldierly honor by surrendering instead dying for *their* emperor. He'd recently instituted a rule that once a month he would go into the town and personally behead a random water buffalo to show how bad his sword was. The carcass would then be dragged away to feed *his* troops. The Filipino family who'd lost their water buffalo might or might not be able to feed themselves, since the beasts were the "tractors" of the entire rice farming infrastructure.

"Actually that kind of behavior helped to solidify *my* role here on the island," Abriol said. "I've organized a crude barter system to make sure that no family goes entirely without rice. But every time he kills one, another farm is crippled."

"Can anyone help that little girl?"

He shrugged. "Maybe, maybe not," he said. "There are no doctors here on Talawan, and the few shamans can only deal with fevers and the like. Once the anger dies down in Orotai we'll get her out of the town. Then, if she's well enough, we might be able to take her to the Mohammedans. But I have news."

"Oh, shit," Rooster said.

The padre grinned, but it quickly faded. "There's a story going around the town that a damaged Jap ship was coming in. One of the bar girls who works in a 'tea house' up near the Japanese compound speaks, or at least understands, Japanese. She reported that a Japanese cargo ship that had been torpedoed was trying to make it into the harbor. They were trying to get her into shallow waters and run her aground before she sank, because she had a cargo of rice and canned food for the big base at Rabaul. She was also carrying prisoners of war who were being sent back to Japan to be used as slave labor. Supposedly there were some Americans among them."

Well, that got our attention. "They gonna put 'em in the camp here on Talawan?" Rooster asked.

The padre shook his head, with a sigh. "The ship didn't make it and sank about ten miles offshore in very deep water. The sergeant she was 'attending to' told her that the ship's crew had locked down the hatches before the ship went down to inhibit the flooding. The crew got away on lifeboats. The prisoners did not. The officer thought that that was an appropriate fate for soldiers who had surrendered."

"God*damn* their eyes," Rooster swore. My sentiments exactly.

TWENTY-ONE

Just after two in the morning the three of us took our leave from the makeshift Japanese O-club. The kitchen staff gave us some rice balls and water. There was a partial moon and the dirt streets smelled of recent rain, which was a great improvement over the usual stink of fresh manure. The two Filipino policemen led us on foot through a warren of back alleys and unlit, unpaved streets. Twice we had to jump into the shadows when Japanese military police vehicles appeared, creeping through the town in first gear. One was an army truck, complete with a squad of soldiers sitting in two rows facing each other under the canvas tarp covering the cargo bed, their bayonets glittering in the dim moonlight. The other was a boxy, green sedan with two men inside, both of them wearing those round spectacles featured in so many of our propaganda posters. The patrols explained why, wherever we were going, we weren't taking a straight line to it. There was no conversation but even at that hour of the morning, I had a sense that we were being watched from behind closed shutters the whole time. Scruffy-looking dogs would skulk along the street behind us, but they didn't bark. Abriol explained that barking dogs ended up on the menu in Orotai.

We finally arrived at the riverbank just outside the town, almost completely hidden in dense vegetation. One policeman lit

a cigarette with a flourish of his lighter. Moments later three of
what the Filipinos called banca boats appeared out of the gloom
and came alongside the muddy banks, each with a single paddler at the back. Father Abriol had told us that banca boats were
hollowed-out tree trunks. If the boat was intended for seagoing
use, it would be equipped with outriggers. Otherwise it was just a
really heavy canoe. Each of us climbed carefully into a boat, and
moments later we were being paddled upstream and away from
Orotai. The river water near the town smelled brackish, with more
than just a hint of sewage. There didn't seem to be any opposing
current or else the guys paddling at the back were really strong,
because we seemed to be making good headway.

We went upstream into the forest for about fifteen minutes and
then crossed over to the opposite bank, where the paddlers nosed
into the reeds along the shore. Father Abriol gestured for us to get
out. He put a finger to his lips for silence, and then indicated we
were to follow him into the dense bamboo thicket growing along
the riverbank. It was hard to tell in the darkness, but we seemed to
be going back *towards* the town we'd just left. I was careful about
where I placed my feet. At one point he stopped and just listened
as something thrashed its way through the bamboo and into the
river. Then he turned and explained what we were doing.

"There's a creek that joins the river up ahead," he whispered.
"The prison camp is just across the creek. We must be very quiet
and move slowly. They have three guard towers with spotlights
into the camp *and* searchlights pointing out over the river and the
creek. The camp has one high barbed-wire fence all around it. The
prisoners are apparently much too weak to climb it and they'd
be shot if they even tried. Let's go."

We smelled it before we ever saw it. The latrines for the camp
were plank stages hanging over the creek but it was obvious that
not everybody was able to make it to a latrine. The air was filled
with the reek of raw sewage, contaminated mud, unwashed bodies, and maybe even some unburied bodies. We got down on our

hands and knees to make the final ten-yard crawl to the edge of the
bamboo, where the spotlights pointing into the compound shone
with a fitful yellow glow. The only sound we could hear was a diesel
generator running somewhere in the camp. Based on the way the
lights were flickering, it wasn't a very good generator, but we still
took great care not to show our faces. The prisoners were barely
visible. The Japs had made them build long bamboo shelters with
frond roofs and no sides. The captives were visible as gray shadows lying on the ground under the roofs, with a few in low cots.
No one was standing or walking and they looked mostly like a
collection of shockingly thin, pale ghosts.

"How many?" I asked the padre.

"There were a couple hundred when they first came. Now?
Maybe half that. The Japs are starving them. They take the gar-
bage that's left after they've eaten and boil it in a trash can. They
throw in a couple of handfuls of rice and that's what they feed the
prisoners. Nothing fresh. Everyone has scurvy. I think they'll all
just die off if this goes on; they're almost skeletons as it is."

"Any way the resistance could get food in there?" I asked.

He frowned. "It would be really difficult—each tower has three
guards. And machine guns. Certainly not in daylight, and they do
random searchlight sweeps at night."

"I saw lots of fresh fruit for sale in the town," Rooster said.
"We could creep up to the wire and just throw it in there."

"First we would have to make contact with the prisoners,"
Father Abriol said. "Let them know we're out here and that we're
going to try to smuggle in some food. It would be very dangerous, for us, and for them. Any of them caught with smuggled food
would be sent to one of Tachibana's sword demonstrations."

"Does anyone know if the Japs have mined the perimeter of
that camp?" I asked.

The padre shook his head. "My people don't think so. The
prisoners are made to go outside the wire twice a month and clear
away brush."

"And nobody's tried to escape?" Rooster asked, as we backed away from the creek.

"They're much too weak. One time one of them slipped in the mud and fell into the creek. He grabbed onto the bank and tried to crawl back out as the guards came running up. He simply couldn't do it, so a guard bayoneted his hands and then watched him slide back into the water without so much as a bubble."

"One less mouth to feed," Rooster muttered.

"Exactly," Father Abriol said. By then we'd reached our banca boats. "If we're going to help them, we'd have to do everything for them. Let's head back."

"Then you'd need to kill every Jap on the island," I said, as we pressed our way through all the greenery. "*Then* you could go into the camp, get them fit to be moved, and your people could disperse them up-country before the Japs could send in reinforcements."

"Maybe," he said. "Killing all the Japs—that's a tall order."

We came back out onto the main riverbank and got into our bancas. The paddlers pushed back and then turned to continue upstream, away from Orotai, while we swatted mosquitos in the hot, wet night and tried to maintain our balance in the bancas.

We went upriver for at least an hour before they finally turned into the left bank of the river, which by now was no more than 30 or so feet across. My eyes were fully night-adapted by now, which was good because no one was showing any form of light. Abriol got out and then helped us out of our bancas. They immediately backed out into the stream and disappeared downriver. Three Filipinos were standing nearby, one of whom was much older than the other two. Father Abriol greeted him quietly and then all of us started off into the jungle down a well-worn path. The two younger men were carrying bolos, the Filipino name for what I'd been calling a machete. The jungle soon gave way to scrub forest as we began to climb. I had no idea of where we were, but our guides surely did; we struggled to keep up with them. Finally we came out of the woods and onto the edge of a long, shallow valley that led up to what looked like yet another truncated cinder cone. Father Abriol explained to us that the entire island of Talawan was the top of one really big volcano which rose from the ocean floor from a depth of about three *miles*.

We trooped down to where a vigorous stream cut its way along the bottom of the valley and sat down on its banks with some large boulders at our backs. I estimated that we were five miles or so outside of Orotai, but I wouldn't have bet my ass on that. Father Abriol sat next to our guide and cooled his feet in the stream, so we did likewise. The water was surprisingly cold and smelled faintly of sulfur, but it felt wonderful on our sore feet. The two of them talked in Tagalog for about five minutes, while Rooster and I sat there wondering why we'd come to this particular spot.

They finished up their conversation and then Father Abriol asked the old man something while pointing to the bolos the other two were wearing. They promptly handed them over to the priest along with their bamboo-section canteens, and then they left, headed back towards the woods. Father Abriol handed each of us a bolo and a canteen and then showed us how to attach the sheaths to our belts. The bolos were about 16 inches long with wooden handles covered in some kind of hide. They were surprisingly heavy and clearly very sharp.

"Better than nothing," he said. "Sometimes better than guns. They can kill without a sound."

With that lovely thought we asked him why we'd come out here instead of heading for the lava tunnel hideout.

His face turned grim. "Because I received word last night that the Japs in Orotai do know about you two. When I went on the air last night I got an immediate reply, as if they'd been waiting for me to contact them. Apparently someone told the *Kempeitai* in Manila that you two were here on Talawan. Probably under torture. Then they said that rescue now was not possible. And third, they want me and my people to execute stage two."

"Rescue referring to Rooster and me?"

"Yes."

"And stage two?"

He sighed. "The Philippine resistance envisions three stages: stage one, form networks of trusted people, collect arms and other supplies, and create safe places to hide. Watch and report what the Japs are doing. In our case stage one meant mostly watching the harbor and reporting what ships came and went. Stage two means we're to begin *active* resistance. The Japs have to live off the land here. Food and water. We can make those supplies dry up."

"What happens when the Japs figure out what's going on?" Rooster asked.

"Yes, that's the rub," he said ruefully. "There *will* be reprisals, and if what we've heard about up in Luzon and Manila, they will react like the barbarians they are. Many people will die, I'm afraid."

"And when that starts happening, how strong will *your* network be?"

He shook his head. "I can't answer that," he said. "The Japs will start rounding people up in Orotai and torturing them to find out who's operating against them and where we hide. The people on this island are simple fishermen and rice farmers. I don't think they're ready for what the Japs are capable of, especially this Tachibana monster. He's killed kids in front of their mothers."

"Jesus," Rooster said.

"I also don't know whether or not such outrages will lead to mass fury or a mass betrayal. The only advantage we have is that there are only two hundred or so in their garrison. There are perhaps fifteen hundred Filipinos on this half of the island."

"But mostly unarmed, right?"

"Exactly. To mount a real resistance, we'd need guns, ammunition, training, and medical supplies. The resistance network on Mindanao already went to stage two and now they've got their hands full. They're facing regular Jap army troops, not prison guards."

I took a deep breath and then exhaled. I was pretty sure I could see where he was going with this. When the bad stuff got rolling, the only solution *would* be to kill every single Jap on the island. And then what? Evacuate Orotai and then have the entire population run for the hills and the lava fields? Tall order indeed. For one thing, what would they eat?

"You should go back to your bosses and tell them you can't start stage two until you have all that stuff," I said. "Delay things and give yourself more time to get your people ready."

"I'm a Catholic priest," he protested. "I'm no guerilla fighter. When the Japs first landed here, they immediately rounded up all the rice stores. Went house to house in Orotai and took all useable food—rice, preserved fish, dried fruit and vegetables. They even uprooted the vegetable gardens. We found out later that the garrison had been landed with *no* food supplies because everything the navy had was being sent to Guadalcanal."

"So the garrison has had to live off the land right from the beginning?"

"Yes. As I told you, I went underground as soon as they landed. After a while people came to me and told me that the town was starving. I organized a small team of thieves to hit the godowns where the Japs were storing all their loot. They hadn't really set themselves up as a functional garrison yet, so we managed to steal back some of it and distribute it as best we could. Word got around that *I* was responsible for that. Suddenly I was chief of guerillas on Talawan."

"So how *are* the people getting food now?" I asked.

"The Japs landed in early forty-two. In the year since then the people have managed three rice harvests. Some of it's grown in the traditional paddies, in full view. A lot more is grown in tiny patches and hidden here and there. The Japs send out foraging parties and take everything they can find, so we've learned not to store all the food *in* the villages. The fishermen have become adept at avoiding that Jap gunboat. But still, it's hand to mouth here. The people feed and hide me, and now you, because I keep telling them the Americans will one day return to liberate the Philippines."

"*Are* we winning on Guadalcanal?" Rooster asked.

"According to my source in the 'tea house,' the Japs have started calling it Starvation Island, so you are not losing, at any rate. But the fighting remains fierce."

"Which means that liberating the Philippines might take another year, or even two."

"Everyone is hopeful, and now there are *not* so many Japanese warships stopping here at Orotai. Manila tells us that the Japs might just abandon Talawan, that MacArthur has moved to Port Moresby and is pushing them back."

I suspected that the resistance in Manila was probably swallowing too much propaganda from MacArthur's new headquarters in New Guinea. And there was still the unspoken question: Did they *want* MacArthur back? His father, Arthur MacArthur, had been a governor of the Philippines. His son, the current general, had been senior advisor and a field marshal in the Philippine army before being evicted by the Japanese in the early days of the war. I wondered how the emir would react to seeing Douglas MacArthur back in Manila.

"The liberation of the Philippines still might take a long time, Father," I said. "It's not like the Japs are quitters; Rooster and I are living proof of that. We hurt them bad at Midway, and yet they sank our carrier *and* the sub that rescued us. This is gonna be a long slog, Father. Years, not months, I'm afraid. Right now I see the two of us as an additional burden that you don't need, so maybe the best thing for us to do is build a boat and try for Australia."

"Darwin is almost two *thousand* miles from here, Lieutenant. Are you that good a sailor?"

"If we stay here we're just gonna be two more mouths to feed. And, like you we're not guerilla fighters, either. We're dive bomber pilots."

"Your navy must have a lot of those these days," he mused. "Dive bomber pilots, I mean."

"Hunh?"

"Otherwise they'd send someone to pick you two up."

I stared at him. "That's a low blow, *Father.*"

"Guilty, Lieutenant," he admitted, sheepishly. "But you must admit there's a smidgen of truth in what I said. Someone senior has decided that retrieving the two of you isn't worth the effort, especially if they now know the waters around Talawan have been mined."

"So it's up to us to find our way back, then, right?"

"Maybe," he said. "On the other hand, the two of you could make a huge difference here if you'll join forces with us. Me, I suppose, is what I'm saying. You are professional fighting men. I'm just a priest. I believe the Americans *will* win this war and that the Philippines *will* be liberated, but as you point out, it may be a long time in coming. Having actual Americans here with us would help morale immensely."

"Until the reprisals begin," I pointed out. "Then having actual Americans here might be viewed as the *cause* of the reprisals. Tell me: if the Jap garrison knows we're here, what will they do now?"

"They'll hunt you," he said. "It doesn't take two hundred men to guard those prisoners of war. If nothing else, the rest of them probably need something to do."

"What about those Mohammedans we met earlier—will they help? They looked like fighters to me."

"They *will* fight," Father Abriol said. "But only on one condition: that the people they'd be fighting for would have to renounce the Christian faith and become servants of Allah and his Prophet."

Now I began to understand. Father Abriol had two masters: the resistance movement bosses in Manila, but, more importantly, the Roman Catholic Church. If Father Abriol struck *that* particular bargain with the Mohammedan pagans, he'd have more to worry about than the Japs.

Rooster was quietly shaking his head. I could see that the boat idea was beginning to look better and better to him. Then what sounded like a church bell rang three times from the direction of Orotai, causing Father Abriol to look up sharply.

"We need to go," he announced. "First drink water, as much as you can. Then fill your water tubes."

TWENTY-TWO

I thought we'd be headed back to the lava tube, but instead we pressed up the valley. Father Abriol told us that the three bells meant only that part of the Jap garrison was on the move and headed out of Orotai. Where and what for were not included in the bell signal, but of course Rooster and I assumed that the hunt for us was on. Father Abriol kindly refrained from confirming that prospect.

The first thing we did was to cross the stream and walk perpendicular to it until we reached a line of scrub trees and more of those bizarre-looking lava outcroppings. He then peed on that spot. Then we retraced our steps back to the creek, stepped down into it, and walked upstream for a couple hundred yards while trying not to break an ankle doing it. Then we stepped back out and continued on up the valley before stopping. "Your turn," he said to me. "Just a splash. I think they'll bring dogs again."

"Got another cobra cave in your bag of tricks?"

"Something even worse," he said, cryptically, and then increased the pace. False dawn was showing in the east, where that smoking cone-shaped mountain began to take definition. Ahead was a bulky ridgeline that seemed to cover the entire northern horizon. And every step was up—it seemed that every time we evaded Jap patrols, we *had* to go up. Rooster and I were again puffing after the first half hour. Father Abriol seemed unaffected. I guessed that two years as a fugitive and limited food supplies probably led to a high degree of physical fitness. We all took turns leaving scent markers on the way up.

The land became increasingly bleak as we climbed towards the head of the valley. There were more of those giant, black boulders and then patches of what had to be volcanic ash. The stink of sulfur became stronger the higher we went. I wondered if it wouldn't overwhelm any dog's tracking ability. The ground was so hard we didn't seem to be leaving any footprints. I finally asked Father Abriol where we were headed.

"That ridge up ahead is actually the edge of a mostly dormant caldera," he said. "It divides the island. I think I told you that this entire island is one huge volcano, rising all the way from the seabed. We're headed for the southern rim of the main crater, which bisects the entire island."

"Another lava tube?"

"No, but if a Jap patrol tracks us up here I have a surprise for them. I'll explain when we get there." He eyed the two of us. "In the meantime, let's take a quick rest and get some more water. This stream is going to disappear soon."

Any break was appreciated. We slaked our thirst, washed off our sweaty faces, and refilled the canteens. We'd come to the stream's origin, a dark pool welling up from the sides of the caldera. Beyond that was only a steep slope of black rock. All the vegetation had pretty much disappeared. Looking back down the valley I wondered how far up we were. High enough to see the blue of the Pacific and the straits where *Hagfish* lay. To the east that single cinder cone was well defined but nowhere near as large as the formation we were climbing. And a couple thousand miles east of that was *Hornet*'s grave and our former lives as carrier pilots. I looked around for Father Abriol. He was sitting on a rock and quietly reciting prayers from a small black book as the sun came up.

We marched for another hour. He took us to a crack in the rim wall, through which we walked single file. The sides of the crack had been terraced on one side by decades of erosion. At the other end it opened onto the vast, misty panorama of the caldera itself, which was perhaps five miles in diameter. The rim wall fell a few hundred feet to the crater floor, which was a featureless sea of ancient ash. I saw no obvious vents or plumes, nor did there seem to be any wildlife up here. There was a shallow dry wash leading from where we stood down to the floor of the crater. It would be the obvious way down, assuming one would *want* to go down there. The walls on either side were like black glass, just like the lava tube.

"Rest here," Father Abriol announced. "I'll take the first watch at the entrance to the crack. When I get sleepy I'll come get one of you. See those terraces above us?"

We nodded.

"There are handholds and foot pockets just to the left of the main fissure. We will climb up those to that first terrace if the Japs actually come. Now, before you lie down come with me back to the entrance."

He told us to find some round, basketball-sized rocks. We spread out on either side and within ten minutes we had four. He chose two and we carried them back to the other end of the crack. He positioned one at the top of that dry wash, and the second one he wedged onto that glasslike slope leading down to the crater floor. He then invited us to urinate on both of them. Satisfied, he went back to the entrance.

"Okay," Rooster muttered. "What the *puck?*"

"I have no idea, other than he *wants* the Jap patrol to follow us up here. After that, I'm in the dark."

"You think we should just tell him goodbye, head for the coast, and go into the boat-building business?"

"With no food, uncertain water supplies, no compass, and no idea of where we'd even find wood for a boat?"

He sighed. "Just a thought, Boss. But I signed up to kill Japs with thousand-pound bombs, not goddamned bolos."

Me, too, I thought. But: I'd concluded that the padre was right: Our beloved Navy probably did have an ample supply of SBD pilots and gunners, so if we were going to fulfill Halsey's first law it might as well be here as anywhere. I told Rooster to grab a nap while he could, and then, being the exemplary leader that I was, I showed him how to do that.

Minutes later, or so it seemed, Father Abriol was rousting us out. "They sent a whole squad this time," he said. "And more dogs."

The sun was already past high noon, so he'd taken the burden of sitting there, watching, all morning.

"What do we do?" Rooster asked, fingering the handle of that big bolo knife.

"You two climb up to that first terrace," he ordered. "There is a pile of rocks up there. Pick out the six biggest and bring them to the edge of the terrace. I'll join you as soon as I set the trap."

"What trap?" I asked.

"That dry ravine over there goes down to the floor of the crater. The bottom part of it turns to black glass. I'm going to roll those two rocks down the slope. One will go all the way to the floor. The other will roll down the ravine, taking the scent. It should look like more than one man went down there."

"But what's the trap?" I asked again.

"The floor of the caldera?" he said with a most un-priestly grin. "It's volcanic ash. Looks solid, but it's not. I'm hoping the dog tracking team starts down the ravine following the scent. They'll hit the slippery part and slide out onto the ash-field, which is God knows how deep. Get going."

Handholds and foot pockets, the man had said. A mountaineer I was not, but with a lot of awkward effort and a couple of breathless moments, Rooster and I made it up to that first terrace. The terrace was 20 feet wide and littered with rocks and gravel on mostly level ground. Then I saw the rocks the padre had been talking about, stacked like cannonballs. I realized that Nature hadn't done that.

Then I realized why the padre wanted *big* rocks. Not all of that Jap squad would go down into that dry wash. We positioned six of the "cannonballs" next to the rim of the terrace. I thought I heard a dog bark down below. We crept to the edge of the terrace, lay down, and peered over the edge just as Father Abriol slipped up over the rim and joined us on the terrace.

I counted eight soldiers total coming cautiously out of the crack. Two were barely managing to hold back two large tracking dogs who seemed to be determined to jump into that ravine and follow the scent trail. The officer in charge of the group, identifiable by his sword, was issuing rapid-fire orders that sounded like he wanted everybody to stop for a moment and regroup, but it was no use. Both dogs and their increasingly overwhelmed handlers plunged into the narrow wash in a clatter of gravel and excited Japanese. Three more soldiers followed them down, their rifles at port arms, obviously trying to be more careful. The officer and his two remaining soldiers stopped short to see what happened next as the dogs, handlers, and the three soldiers clattered a couple of hundred feet down through the narrow ravine.

What happened next was that the dogs, their handlers, and the three soldiers bunched up when the going got really steep, about 50 feet from the bottom. There they encountered the really slippery rock. Then suddenly both dogs started barking frantically as they lunged forward. The entire crew ended up sliding down to the bottom of the slope on their backsides, the soldiers yelling excitedly as they lost their rifles, and then all of them shot out onto that formless gray expanse, into which they promptly disappeared without so much as a puff of ash.

The sudden silence was appalling. The three remaining Japs at the top of the wash were momentarily transfixed. Father Abriol picked up a rock. "Now," he said in a soft, lethal voice.

While the Japs stood stunned at the top of the wash, we three drop-launched our rocks from our perch 80 feet above them. I threw first. My first rock hit the officer on top of his right shoulder. He screamed in pain and went down, just as my second rock hit him in the head with a satisfying whack. The second soldier was so shocked at seeing the officer with his head stove in that he made an easy target for Rooster, who dropped him with a direct hit at the top of his spine. He lurched sideways onto the motionless officer and then the both of them rolled down into the ravine, gathering speed as they headed for the bottom like two out-of-control rag dolls, limbs flying until they, too, zoomed out onto the crater floor and submerged.

The remaining soldier had by then figured it out. He swung his rifle up and fired one shot at us before the padre flung down a jagged black rock that hit him square in the face as he frantically worked the rifle's bolt and looked back up in time to see his doom. He collapsed onto his back even as he fired, the bullet ricocheting off the stone wall of the crater. Father Abriol flung a second rock, which hit the man square in the chest, a blow that probably stopped his heart.

Once more, there was total silence. Then Father Abriol surprised us. There were two rocks left. One at a time he picked them up and launched them to hit the lone body directly below. The look on his face was pure murder. Without a word he went to the edge, turned around, and started down the handholds. We waited for him to get all the way down and then Rooster went. He was slower than the padre, which is when I came to the realization that Father Abriol was no stranger to this place.

By the time I got down to the bottom of the terrace, I was surprised to see blood everywhere. Rooster gave me a look and then nodded sideways at the priest. Father Abriol had taken Rooster's bolo and opened the throat of the motionless Jap. Only then did he sit down and catch his breath, that bloody bolo dripping a pool

of blood onto his lap. Rooster and I were too shocked to say anything.

The stink of fresh blood suddenly overcame the sulfur in the
air and I thought I was going to be sick. It was one thing to watch
an entire aircraft carrier blow up over my shoulder as I pulled out,
incinerating hundreds if not a thousand men, but a mile below
me. It was quite another to revert to Neanderthal warfare and
then have to walk around in the puddles of gore. Unlike in the
movies, the smells were pretty bad.

An hour later, we stashed the two rifles we'd recovered in a tiny
lava pocket not far from the rim. The rifles seemed to be a pretty
small caliber, not much bigger than the .22 rifles of my youth,
although the powder cartridge was much longer. The officer's
sword and pistol had come off on their way down, along with a
single ammo belt. Rooster had taken a momentary interest in the
officer's sword but it turned out to be some kind of cheap imita-
tion samurai piece. Father Abriol kept the officer's pistol. We'd
left the body where it lay. I'd wanted to drag it down to the crater
floor, but Abriol had pointed out what should have been obvious:
How would you get back up?

We left the caldera and trudged back down to the spot where
the stream bubbled up from the earth. I had a dozen questions
for Father Abriol about that place, but he was definitely not in a
talkative mood. Having blood on his forearms up to his elbows
probably had a bearing on that. When we got to the spring we all
stripped down and bathed in that pool for longer than was probably necessary. The water felt wonderful but the act of cleansing
ourselves from our murderous, caveman ambush felt even better.
At one point I looked over at Rooster, who was completely submerged up to his chin. The look he gave me said it all: we're in it
now. I didn't think he meant the pool.

Three hours later we were in Lingoro village, sitting around
one of those bamboo tables in the longhouse which Abriol called

a *torogan*. I thought it was the same one we'd done the first radio message in, but I'd become completely disoriented by our various treks. The villagers provided food—boiled rice with "things" in it, a large bottle of local beer which Rooster and I split, and some straw pallets to sleep on. The padre didn't partake of anything; I had the sense that he had shocked himself up there on the volcano. I decided to sound him out on that ambush site, if only to see if he was okay.

"The Arab traders were here first," he told us. "In the long history of occupation, that is. They go back five, six hundred years. Then there were the Portuguese mariners, the Dutch spice hunters, the Spanish missionaries, and finally the Americans. There were Filipinos here before any of them, of course, but apparently the Europeans thought their role was to be subjugated."

"Where'd the Filipinos themselves come from?" Rooster asked.

"I was taught that they came from the Indonesian Archipelago, for the most part. For some reason lost to history, the southern part of Talawan became Catholic and the northern part embraced the Mohammedan beliefs. The occupiers of the day always made their religion mandatory. There were times the Spanish tried to eradicate the Mohammedans; other times, the Moros returned the favor. Both sides sent raiding parties to capture slaves, women, rice, and, of course, prospective converts."

"And that big volcano ridge was no-man's land?"

He smiled. "After a fashion," he said. "But on 'our' side of the big caldera our ancestors took advantage of some natural terrain features to construct ambush killing grounds, like you saw today. There are others, even some in the forests. For instance, there's a lava bubble up near our tube hideout, where the ground appears to be solid rock but in fact is eggshell thin. Lead someone out onto it and they'll fall through. Inside the walls are as slick as glass. No way out. In the old times, they didn't have much in the way of long-distance weapons, so they used natural features as places to kill invaders."

"And the cave with the snakes?" I asked.

"The cobra cave was somewhat opportunistic, of course, but the idea of salting a confined space with snakes and then luring in your enemy is an ancient Talawan tactic. Throw an irritated cobra into a sleeping hut. Or a green viper into the village well—draw up a bucket, get a terrible surprise."

My face must have revealed my horror.

"We don't raid each other's territories anymore, especially since we have brand-new occupiers. But this hostility is very old and will never change. When your enemy is fierce, you turn Nature against him."

As good a strategy as any, I thought. But then I had a question. "Today we took out an entire squad from the garrison. Will they come looking for them?"

"I would think so," he said. "Especially after the cobra incident. Once could be an accident. Twice?" He shrugged.

"How will they know where to look?"

"That depends on whether or not they have more dogs; if they do, the remaining dogs will track that squad's dogs up to that crack in the caldera rim. The vultures may or may not take care of the bodies, but the signs . . . well. Pray for rain."

"So what do *we* do now?" Rooster asked.

"We hide out here in the woods and see how the Japs react. Now get some rest. I apologize for making you murder those men. Now I must pray for forgiveness."

"Father Abriol?" Rooster said. "Don't apologize. Killing Japs is our primary mission."

"Good to hear," Abriol said. "But, as a priest, it's not *my* primary mission, is it. I'm not asking forgiveness for killing Japs. I'm asking forgiveness for so completely losing control of myself. And for enjoying it so much."

TWENTY-THREE

We woke to the sound of running feet. Rooster and I sat up in our pallets while the padre went to the steps to see what was happening. A breathless villager ran up to the longhouse and spoke urgently to him. By then a few of the village elders were coming out of their huts. Father Abriol yelled something to one of them and suddenly everybody sprang into action. Two women came and got us.

"Japs are coming here," Father Abriol shouted after us. He pointed us toward the women. "They'll hide you."

The women took us to a very large tree that stood on the edge of the village circle. Using a stick, one of them moved aside a six-inch-thick and very hairy vine, one of several that snaked up the trunk and disappeared into the canopy, and then opened a perfectly camouflaged narrow door in the trunk. She made it clear with hand signals that we should *not* touch that vine as we turned sideways to get inside. She closed the door behind us.

We stood there in perfect darkness. Or almost perfect. There was a partial moon up, and as our eyes adjusted we discovered there were small slits in the trunk, big enough to admit slivers of moonlight into our living cave. The tree had to be 15 feet at the base, so there was plenty of room for the two of us. The floor of our chamber felt like hard-packed dirt and I thought I could see some boxes and bags stored around the circumference, along with three rifles stacked up against the inside wall. I scanned the interior for snakes, then realized I couldn't have seen one if I tried. Then we heard straining automobile engines approaching, and our slits began to turn yellow-white as headlights lit up the village. We each found a slit and watched as the entire village came out of their huts to see a Japanese jeep-like vehicle followed by a covered dump truck mashing down the vegetation on either side of the main trail leading into the village. It felt like it was two in the morning, but I had no idea.

The jeep drove right into the center of the village, its yellowish headlights illuminating a frightened crowd of village men gathering around one of the older men, whom I assumed was Lingoro's headman. There were three passengers in the jeep. We could just barely see women and children with their eyes out on stalks peering out from the entrances to their family huts and then drawing the bamboo curtains across the doorways.

The truck came into the circle, its engine straining and pursued by a cloud of exhaust smoke. It stopped, shut down, and then disgorged a dozen soldiers, armed with what looked to me like submachine guns. They quickly formed a rough semicircle behind the jeep and then assumed a ready position. Both the truck and the jeep left their headlights on, so we couldn't see faces, only silhouettes. For a moment, nothing happened. Then a small figure got out of the jeep and approached the headman. I couldn't tell what language he was speaking but he seemed to be pretty angry. Everybody jumped when there was a sudden thump of thunder nearby.

The small man kept going while the headman just stood there, nodding occasionally, but saying nothing. It looked to me like the village men were getting increasingly nervous. When the small man finally stopped his yelling, the elder seemed to have nothing much to say, opening his hands in a gesture of ignorance and shaking his head. "Don't know nothin'" was what it looked like. Then a familiar figure stood up in the jeep. Even though we couldn't see his face in the headlights, it had to be Tachibana. He bellowed something in Japanese. The small man acknowledged and then slapped the elder in the face, hard, twice, and then started yelling again. The old man staggered but held his ground. The men surrounding him began to surreptitiously back away, obviously sensing great danger.

In the meantime, Tachibana got out of the jeep. We could see the vehicle's lights bouncing up and down when he stepped down. The driver stayed put. Tachibana stood for a moment, adjusting his uniform and his swords. He really was a huge man, probably fat but with a frame that could carry it. He was wearing an army cap, but since he was in silhouette because of the headlights we couldn't see his uniform. He spat out a command in that hoarse voice and the little guy backed away, bowing and scraping, as Tachibana approached the headman. He stopped about three feet away and started to harangue the elder in Japanese. He looked like a figure from the Apocalypse, his round face in deep shadow, as wide as he was tall, his feet slightly apart, and his hands out of sight. He stopped speaking and then cocked his head to one side as if to say, well?

The elder said nothing, still shaking his head. In one violent motion, Tachibana drew that long sword, raised it above his head, and then brought it down on the top of the elder's head in a flash of glinting steel, hitting the old man so hard that the two parts of his head flopped down onto his shoulders even as Tachibana whirled completely around and took a horizontal swipe with that big blade that sent the two halves of the elder's head flying out onto the dirt. It happened so fast that the headman's body had barely begun to collapse before that second cut happened. The other village men quailed and backed away from the headman's remains.

Tachibana gave another order. Two of the soldiers handed their submachine guns to an adjacent soldier and headed into the terrified crowd of Filipinos, grabbing one and hauling him before Tachibana. This man was older than the rest, but not by much. A soldier stood on either side of him, obviously holding him up because his legs were shaking so badly that he would have fallen down. Tachibana approached him, with that long sword held before him in two hands, its tip just off the ground. He started in again, as he'd done with the elder, roaring at the pale-faced Filipino, who clearly couldn't understand a word. Finally Tachibana pointed straight up. The man looked up instinctively just as the colonel drove that sword into the man's gut so hard that half of it came out of his back. Then Tachibana twisted the sword ninety degrees and began sawing at the man's innards, evoking screams that made me sick to my stomach. He withdrew the sword and the man folded in half, collapsed, and began convulsing on the ground with a whimpering, gargling cry that I'll never forget.

Tachibana flicked the sword out in a sideways motion to remove the excess gore, and then leaned down and wiped the blade clean on his victim's shirt. The dying man was crying now, making a liquid, sobbing sound that was horrible to hear. Tachibana made a sound of disgust and passed the blade over the man's throat, ending it in a surge of dark blood. He backed away from the carnage in front of him and looked around the village. He began roaring again, as if talking to the entire village. The remaining villagers were crouched down on the ground trying not to attract his attention. Fat chance, I thought. And then he saw something, as if out of the corner of his eyes. Someone in one of the huts had pushed the bamboo curtain over the door to one side, peered out, and quickly closed it.

Tachibana roared another order, and the semicircle of soldiers raised their weapons and immediately opened automatic fire on that hut. There were so many guns and so many bullets that the hut began to collapse in the jeep's headlights in a cloud of bamboo splinters and straw dust, accompanied by screams from inside.

Tachibana gave a hand signal and the firing stopped instantly. A small tongue of flame appeared at one edge of the hut and quickly began to grow. A thick bolus of whitish smoke formed at the hut's door and then grew larger and larger as the entire hut became engulfed. Finally a young woman, obviously wounded and dragging two small children, tumbled out of the door with her clothes smoking. She immediately fell down, bringing the children down with her while she frantically beat at the flames. Tachibana waddled over and almost casually pushed the tip of his sword into her throat, and then did the same to the two crying children crouching next to her.

I heard Rooster curse, felt him start to move, and grabbed him. In front of the colonel the woman's hut flamed into a large but brief fire. Tachibana stood there, the sword's tip pushed into the dirt in front of him, and watched the family's death throes until they were finally still. Then he turned around and roared at the village for about a minute before signaling that they were leaving.

The soldiers got back into their truck and Tachibana heaved himself into the jeep, where the first questioner waited nervously. The vehicles turned around and ground their way out of the shocked village. From out of nowhere a young Filipino boy ran at the back of the truck and threw a rock into it. A brief blast of automatic weapons fire flickered from the darkness in the back of the truck and the boy whirled around, crumpling into a bleeding heap.

The villagers stood transfixed in the light of the burning hut as if in some hellish tableaux. Then two women hurried toward the boy lying at the side of the trail, gently turned him over, and began wailing. The rest of the villagers went to where the elder and the other victim lay.

"Jesus H. *Christ*, Boss!" Rooster exclaimed. "Did *we* cause that?"

That same thought was echoing in my mind. It was one thing to read about what the Jap army did to the civilian populations they conquered, but quite another to witness it.

"No," I said. "That Jap colonel caused this. Can you see the padre?"

We both peered through the slits and watched the villagers trying to deal with the catastrophe in their midst. I, of course, had no idea of where they'd hidden the priest, but assumed he was going to remain hidden in case the Japs had left behind a lone sentry with a radio to see if anyone came out of hiding. I explained that to Rooster and told him we'd stay put too until the villagers thought it was safe.

That took a full hour, and then someone was prying open the hatch in the tree trunk. We stepped out warily, both of us feeling like we needed to find someone to apologize to. In the end we just stood by the tree, not knowing what else to do. We finally spotted the padre, who was kneeling on the ground at the side of the woman from the burned hut and her two children, prayer book in hand. I carefully, very carefully, scanned the faces of the villagers as we stepped into the firelight. The two women who'd run to the boy were still wailing and not paying any attention to us. I thought for a moment I recognized one of them—the young girl who'd been with her mother or grandmother in the lava tube. The girl was especially distraught.

Everyone else seemed to be equally busy, trying to attend to the victims. An invisible water buffalo nearby began bellowing in protest against all the noise. Then we heard men's voices, raised in argument. Over to one side of the village circle five middle-aged Filipinos were in a hot discussion about something. I could just about guess what that was about. Father Abriol finished his ministrations, covered the bodies with a sheet, and then joined the group.

He talked with them for ten minutes and then came over to where we were standing, his face a study in hatred. Rooster jumped the gun and asked him if *we* were the cause of this atrocity. I think Father Abriol had anticipated that question.

"No," he said. "They were looking for *me*, not you. That first

Jap was *Kempeitai*. He went first because he spoke Tagalog. None of these people speak or understand Japanese. When he told Tachibana that the people were saying they knew nothing of my whereabouts, the colonel took the opportunity for some killing."

"Why weren't they looking for us?" Rooster asked. "You said they knew we were on the island."

"They probably do, but the Japs are nothing if not efficient. They know that two American pilots couldn't survive very long here unless someone was harboring them. That someone has to be me. Catch me, and the two of you would eventually starve in the forest. No, this was all about finding the treacherous priest. You should know, sadly, he's done it before."

Rooster seemed to be mollified, if only temporarily. I gave the priest a look that said: Thanks for that. He nodded. I think he understood our predicament perfectly.

"I've told the villagers that we will leave immediately, and that we are going north, to the big volcano fields. I asked them to send a runner if the Japs come back. But in the meantime, something interesting happened. Those men, who were arguing? They told me it was time to kill all these bastards. That's a big step."

"Stage two?" I asked.

He nodded. "Yes, I think so. They'll give us food and water, and then we'll actually go to the lava tube. Telling them we're going north is a precaution, in case someone weakens. Then we must make plans." He turned around, saw more people grieving. "But first, I must attend to them."

As the priest walked back towards the lamentations, Rooster had a comment. "Love that 'we' shit," he muttered, bitterly.

"You know what?" I said. "I think I'm ready to help these folks. Those guys are right: it's time to kill *all* these fucking Japs. Just like Halsey wants."

"C'mon, Boss: How we gonna do that? We don't even have a sidearm."

"I've got some ideas," I replied. "But the first thing we have to do is let those POWs know we're gonna try to rescue them. The second thing is to get some rations in there so they'll be *able* to get rescued."

TWENTY-FOUR

Four nights later Rooster and I were hunkered down in that stand of bamboo across the creek from the POW camp. Not much was stirring over there and the guards all appeared to be keeping inside their tower huts behind mosquito netting, depending on their random spotlight sweeps to maintain security. Father Abriol had taken us up to the lava tube in the wee hours before sunrise, where runners from the villages appeared from time to time to make reports. We learned that Tachibana had visited the other two villages that night and terrorized everyone there, too. I'm making this sound like the town and the villages were organized civic centers. They weren't. Of the three villages on the southern half of Talawan, Lingoro, the one where we'd been hidden, was the largest, with about five hundred inhabitants. The other two were much smaller and more like coastal fishing camps than proper villages.

The same was true of Orotai. The padre called it a town, but it was more of a makeshift, ramshackle waterfront with one main street wrapping around the actual shoreline. Behind that was that warren of dirt paths and bamboo huts we'd walked through, which included small vegetable patches, homemade enclosures for livestock, and a single communal well at one end of the main street. Sewage was handled by night-soil wagons. There were no commercial piers, as such, but only two wooden piers where the local fishing fleet landed and sold their catch right off the boats. The Japanese had appropriated the larger one for their fleet landing when transiting Jap warships came in for supplies. The fishermen had been relegated to the other one, which was much smaller and barely standing upright. The "restaurant" where we'd been hidden had been more of a community center than a real restaurant until the Japs took it over and made it into a primitive O-club. The clear area in front of their compound wasn't really a town square but more of a place where the weekly market would be set up.

Beyond the town and the villages there were other clusters of families and even small tribes who lived mostly along the west coast of the island. Unlike on the tropical islands I'd visited, such as Hawaii, all life here was coastal, because the interior consisted of a half-mile-thick band of snake-infested jungle which then evolved into a second band of hardwood forests and finally into an upland savannah overseen by moody volcanoes. There was no island-wide government, as such, and even the police in Orotai were pretty much self-appointed with the approval of village and town elders. Father Abriol and his Catholic Church had been the one entity whose web of influence extended over the entire southern half of the island. It was no great wonder that the Japs were anxious to find and eliminate him. I was by now convinced that the Japs knew the loss of their two scouting forays could not have been entirely coincidental. Even if they didn't, those two incidents had given Tachibana an excuse to indulge in his fondness for mayhem. It was definitely time to return the favor.

My plan, which I'd discussed at great length with the padre, and through him with some of Lingoro's elders, was to first let the POWs know that they had friends outside the compound and to actually show our faces to them. The best way to convince them of that was to get them some food, especially fresh fruit to deal with the scurvy epidemic. Then Father Abriol suggested we'd graduate to rice balls with fish emulsions. I made the mistake of asking what a Filipino fish emulsion was, which turned out to be a mixture of fish oil and salt. Rooster then compounded my error by asking how they made the fish oil.

Almost reluctantly, he told us: first, catch fish, then tie the individual fish to slanting sheets of corrugated iron nailed onto raised platforms. They'd then leave them to decompose under the tropical sun. The decomposing fish would eventually begin to leak streams of "oil" down the valleys of the corrugated iron. They'd collect that, add salt and some secret ingredients, pour it into stone jars, and then let that ferment for a few weeks. They'd strain the result into even smaller jars and sell it.

The process smelled so bad that the tribe that made it had been permanently exiled to a promontory up the coast and well away from all the other villages. Abriol said that a few drops of that stuff in a rice ball was the protein equivalent of a small fish; when times got tough, as they were now, it was the only "meat" many of the villagers could get. For the prisoners, it would probably be the first protein they'd had in a few *years* other than the occasional rodent who zigged instead of zagged. I was unable to look at a rice ball thereafter without visualizing the process.

The plan tonight was for some of Abriol's fighters to float an unmanned raft of some sort down the river past the POW camp on the ebb tide. Before the river's final turn leading down to Orotai and the bay, they'd set it afire and let it go with the tidal current, hopefully on the Orotai side of the river. The burning raft would distract the guards long enough for us to cross the small creek, crawl up to the wire, and see if we could make contact. If we couldn't catch anyone's attention, we'd shove the bags of fruit under the wire and hope the prisoners found them before the Japs did.

Suddenly there was a stir in the camp and a searchlight up on one of the guard towers lit up and swung out over the river. That was our signal. We crept up the creek bank until we were upstream of the latrines and then waded into the water, which was only about waist deep and about ten feet across. As the commotion rose on the river side of the camp and more searchlights lit up, we climbed the far bank and scuttled over to the perimeter wire, praying that, unlike *Hagfish*, we'd been right about mines. The fence was made up of horizontal lines of barbed wire, spaced 12 inches apart and stapled to bamboo posts. We could barely see the glow of the fire from our vantage point all the way at the back of the compound as our sacrificial raft floated down on the outgoing tide. Four of the prisoners' huts were end-on to us, not more than 20 feet away. We could see white-faced figures lying on what would have been a porch but was just bare earth. Naturally they were all looking down towards the river.

I pulled a lemon out of my sack and lofted it into the compound, hoping to hit one of the huts. Instead it rolled under a hut. Rooster fished in my sack, stood up, and pitched one right into the clump of figures outside the hut. At first nothing happened, but then several pale faces turned our way in the gloom. I waved both hands at them then signaled them to come to me. Down by the river some of the guards were shooting rifles at the burning boat. Then I saw one man crawling painfully as fast as he could, which wasn't all that fast, towards the fence. When he got to the fence we pushed both sacks of fruit through the wire.

Under normal circumstances he would have been a big guy. Now he was skeletal, with a face like pale parchment, sunken, dry eyes, patchy hair, and showing sores on his skin beneath the rags that had been his uniform.

"Bloody hell," he whispered in a weak, raspy British accent. "Round eyes!"

"We're American Navy pilots, stranded here on Talawan. We're working on a plan to spring you guys out of this hellhole."

He stared at us for a moment, as if the idea was totally preposterous. "I hope there're more of you out there, then," he said. "What's this?"

"Fresh fruit. We got word that there's scurvy in there."

He grunted, looking back over his shoulder. "Scurvy, dysentery, beriberi, even leprosy, for all we know."

There was more shooting from the river side, but it didn't sound like they meant it. Still, if some sergeant figured out that the boat might be a diversion he might turn out the entire guard company.

"How many of you are left?"

"Forty-two lads as of this morning. We were a hundred eighty strong when we got here. Blokes are giving up, I'm afraid. There's a rumor that more might be coming in. Staff Sergeant William Mason, here, Welsh Grenadiers."

I introduced myself and Rooster and then noticed the shooting had stopped. "We gotta get out of here," I said, conscious now that the burning boat had drifted past the camp. "But we'll be back with more. Hide that stuff, now."

He managed to put a grin on that grimy face. "What stuff?" he asked. "It'll all be gone in thirty minutes. How shall we know when to meet you at the wire, Leftenant?"

"We'll get one of the Filipinos to tie a dead bird on the wire. You see that, we'll come in after midnight. Keep the faith, Staff Sergeant. We mean to kill *all* these bastards before this is over."

"Save some for us," he said, a wicked gleam in his parched eyes. "We'll have some ideas about how to do that."

He backed away from the wire, still crawling and now humping the two small sacks. We did the same, went back across the creek and then to our starting point, where we found our Filipino guide waiting. I was pretty sure he was one of the older men we'd seen at the massacre in the village that night. He raised his eyebrows at us.

"We made contact," I said, giving him a thumbs-up. He grunted and then turned into the jungle, motioning for us to follow.

Father Abriol was already there when we got back to Lingoro, which was a far more somber place than during our previous visits. The charred ruins of the burned hut lay accusingly in shambles as we met the padre at the center hut. The usual sleepy faces peering through doorways as strangers came into the village at night were absent.

"We'll sleep here tonight," Father Abriol said, after we'd briefed him on what we'd managed at the POW camp. "Tomorrow we'll spend the morning rebuilding that hut. It's the least we can do. I said Mass earlier this evening for the victims. I've told the people holding the radio to take it to the fish-oil camp. Nobody goes there."

"Did you report the massacre here to Manila?" I asked.

"Yes," he replied. "They use reports like that to keep the resistance angry. I sent a report, and asked for rifles, ammunition, and whatever medical supplies they can spare."

"If they don't come?"

He shrugged. "Talawan people hunt with spears, bows, and poisoned arrows. We'll start picking off Japs that way if we have to. There's nothing here to really sabotage, so it's going to have to be more basic than that. Killing the occasional Jap while making it look like an accident, if possible. Turn vipers loose in the garrison's barracks. Contaminate their drinking water. Poison their rice stores. Of course we'll have to scatter the women and children into the upland forests once this starts. Leave behind poisoned rice stores in the villages."

"Whatever it takes," Rooster said.

"Whatever it takes," Father Abriol said, grimly. "I keep telling myself there aren't that many of them. A Mindoro fisherman and his family came into the harbor two nights ago with news that the Japs have been driven off Guadalcanal and are retreating up the Solomons chain to Rabaul in the northern Solomons. I'm hoping that means that this garrison is on its own."

"Or that they might be recalled to help defend their base in Rabaul."

"God willing," he said.

I wanted to say that if the garrison *was* recalled to Rabaul, they'd probably execute all the remaining POWs and burn Orotai, but I held my peace. We had enough to worry about. Rooster was less reticent.

"You know they just won't pull out," he said. "They're Japs— they'll do something horrible."

"First they'll need to come out of that compound," Father Abriol said. "And then into the human jungle behind the town's one street."

"Injun country," Rooster said, with a wolfish grin.

Rooster and I made three more night visits to the POW camp, almost getting caught on the third one. We got what seemed like a very meager amount of food and fruit into those walking skeletons behind the wire, but they treated each delivery like the miracle of the loaves and fishes. On our way back across the creek some large waterbird started shrieking an alarm, and the creek- side tower guard swung a searchlight in our direction. We both had to submerge and watch that shimmering patch of light tra- versing the surface of the water above us until it finally switched off. We climbed out of the creek and lay gasping like landed fish on the other bank. Our Filipino guide had decamped when the light flashed on, but we knew at least how to start back to the village. He emerged sheepishly out of the jungle to take us back. He was barely a teenager who'd probably witnessed Tachibana's outrage, so we forgave him.

It was probably close to two in the morning when we got back to the village, which had become used to our nocturnal forays. Father Abriol, Rooster, and I had done our best to rebuild the murdered woman's hut. We'd gone out into the woods and cut down bamboo poles and collected palm fronds. I think the villa- gers appreciated our efforts, but once we left they tore it all down and rebuilt it properly. Then they gave *us* the hut to sleep in, which Rooster and I agreed was much better than pallets in the village "hall."

It wasn't as if life had returned to normal in Lingoro. There were sentries posted in the woods and along the trails leading into the village. Father Abriol and the elders had laid out a plan for the villagers to scatter if another Jap patrol came across the river. There were people watching the harbor and the garrison's compound. Each hut in the village had an emergency sack of rice and other necessities parked by the front door. They'd built corrals in the woods away from the village for the water buffalo, and they'd moved all the communal food stores to hides in the woods. The fact that Rooster and I had been risking our lives to get food to the POWs had apparently made a big impression.

Morning came with a torrential downpour of rain. We couldn't even see the longhouse from the doorway to our hut. Even so, an old woman, covering her head with an oversized rattan hat, brought us a metal pitcher can of coffee and some kind of rough bread along with two bananas. God love them. Every morning I felt guilty for how the US Army had treated these people back in the early part of the twentieth century. I reminded Rooster that our knowledge of history focused on the twentieth century. These people had been dealing with "occupiers" since the 1300s. His response was interesting. "Then they'll win, Boss, because they're still here, and most of the occupiers are dead and gone."

The rain stopped midmorning as if God had closed a valve. One moment a downpour. The next moment we could watch the back of the squall thrash its way into the forest. A runner from Father Abriol trotted up to our hut and gave us a small bamboo tube, in which there was a message written on a tiny scrap of paper. Rooster hated bananas so I offered his to the young Filipino, who took it eagerly. Food was still a problem here on Talawan, I gathered.

The message was printed in tiny characters: MANILA SAYS:

MINDORO FISHING BOAT DID NOT RETURN. DO WHAT YOU CAN. THINGS VERY BAD HERE. DESTROY RADIO. GO WITH GOD.

"Wow," Rooster said, as he read it. "So what's the bad news?"

I had to laugh. He and I looked at each other. A million years ago we had been part of an American carrier task force, delivering death and destruction to entire Jap carrier formations, and then, if we hadn't been shot down, returning to our carrier for coffee and fat pills in the wardroom. Now we were crouching in a primitive hut, bearded, long-haired, smelling of creek mud, with nut-stained faces except for our eyes, which Abriol said made us look like raccoons who'd lost their masks. Instead of flying lethal, modern dive bombers off of 26,000-ton flight decks, we were trying to figure out how to evade a Jap garrison, free a bunch of half-dead POWs, exterminate all the Japs on the island, and prevent an island-wide massacre in the process. As Rooster would say, piece'a cake. Lately now he'd quit saying that.

There was more bad news later that day. The two biggest fishing boats operating out of Orotai, and by "big" I mean that they could go 25 miles offshore and back in a single day, had been intercepted by that Jap gunboat, which had confiscated their entire catch. Normally the Jap garrison had been taking half of what every fishing boat brought in, with the gunboat patrolling offshore looking for fishermen trying to evade it and sneak a catch into one of the coastal hamlets. If they caught one doing that, they'd take the entire catch.

This time they'd taken every boat's entire catch, leaving the town's meager food stores in real trouble. Before the Jap occupation, the people had had the luxury of preserving some of the fish while consuming the rest. Now they were living day to day on what got by the Japs and preserving nothing. Rooster and I knew this meant that supporting the two large round-eyes might not be so popular. Maybe it was time for us to get some bows and arrows and go monkey-hunting.

Father Abriol came into the village right after sunset, bearing some good news for a change. The Mindoro fishing boat *had* gotten through. They'd delivered a case of hand grenades, two captured Japanese machine guns and some ammo, a small box of signal flares plus a single flare gun, and the news that American frogmen had been seen on Leyte Island. He hadn't heard about the gunboat incident, which dampened his enthusiasm. As long as that damned gunboat was out there on patrol, the Japs had their boots on everybody's necks, and we couldn't do a damned thing about it.

Or could we?

"How big are those grenades?" I asked.

Father Abriol shrugged. "They're grenades," he said. "A metal ring at the top, about the size of a baseball with grooves cut all around the middle, and heavier than they look."

"I think I know a way to sink that gunboat," I said. "But I'll need a fishing boat and some Filipino volunteers."

He looked at me in surprise.

"You're the one who said it was time to go on the offensive," I pointed out.

"But attack a Jap navy gunboat?"

"Gotta start somewhere," Rooster said. "Hell, we've sunk Jap carriers. A gunboat? Piece'a cake."

I liked the sound of that.

TWENTY-FIVE

Five days later Rooster and I found ourselves back in the strait where *Hagfish* lay in pieces. We were on one of several 20-foot-long coastal fishing boats departing the Orotai anchorage an hour before dawn. The owner and skipper of our boat was ancient but willing, since it had been his granddaughter and her children Tachibana had slaughtered that bloody night in Lingoro. His crew of four looked to us like teenagers but were actually men in their early twenties. They were actual fishermen, too, but not the ones usually crewing this boat.

The boat had a curved, half-height bamboo-and-rattan shelter over the back ten feet, but the rest of it was open. Amidships was a galvanized metal fish tank for whatever they managed to catch. The rest of the boat was piled with nets, poles, and several of what Rooster called trotlines. The gasoline engine was mounted right in front of that shelter where the man steering could tend to it. There was a single mast whose function I could not discern. Some small pennants decorated with what looked like religious symbols flew from it. The boat had slots for outriggers on one side to aid in stability in case bad weather ambushed them, which happened often. Fortunately there was a breeze, because the boat reeked of spoiled fish.

Rooster and I were stowed away out of sight in the shelter

behind the owner, who did the steering while smoking a truly noxious cigar. Between the fish-stink and that cigar in the hot, close confines of the "cabin," we were both starting to get seasick, even though the sea was flat calm. The owner's name was Emilio and he spoke no English. One of the deckhands, named Tomaldo, did speak some English, courtesy of a course that Father Abriol had been running before the Japs invaded. His mother had been killed six months ago by an injured water buffalo after Tachibana had flubbed the killing stroke out on the main street; the bellowing beast had run over her trying to escape. Of all our volunteers, Tomaldo had been the most insistent on coming with us.

Nothing would happen until late afternoon when the local fishing fleet began returning to port. That gunboat wouldn't even bother to come out until midafternoon, waiting until there was a chance that there'd be fish to confiscate for the garrison. The rest of the day it was moored to Tachibana's communications ship. Our plan was to sink the gunboat with a surprise grenade attack when the Japs boarded us to help themselves to some of our catch. Emilio had told Father Abriol that the gunboat would usually hail and then stop the fishing boat that seemed to be sitting lowest in the water on the return trip, an indication of a full load. They'd come alongside, throw over a line, and then send down two unarmed sailors with baskets.

The gunboat was about 90 feet long and armed with a twin 25mm antiaircraft gun mount up on the bow. In a former life it had probably been a deep-sea fishing trawler that the Japs had converted to a coastal patrol boat when war broke out. The ones that patrolled the Jap mainland coasts carried a crew of thirty or so, but this one was manned with only ten men. They were used to dealing with a thoroughly cowed bunch of fishermen, and reportedly these days didn't even bother to take the canvas cover off that AA mount.

Our plan was simple if chancy. The gunboat normally tried to intercept the fishing boats about 10 miles offshore before they began to scatter to avoid having their fish confiscated. We were not going to evade. Once it came alongside and bent on a line, we'd wait until they put two of their crewmen down into our boat to root around in the midship fish tank. On my signal, Tomaldo would dispatch the two crewmen with a lethal-looking short spear called a *sibat*. Rooster and I would come out and begin lobbing grenades into the gunboat's open pilothouse and any other openings to the boat's interior. Our crew would then break out the three captured Jap rifles and shoot anyone who appeared on the gunboat's deck. Rooster and I would then clamber aboard the gunboat under their cover and heave grenades down ventilation scoops, the main stack, and any other openings that might lead below the waterline. Once we *knew* all 10 crewmen had been killed, we'd scuttle the gunboat, taking any small arms and ammo we could find. Then instead of going back in to Orotai, we'd make for a small cove where a party of villagers would be waiting for us to offload any fish we'd caught and then hide the boat for the night.

Easy enough to describe, but we were on thin ground when it came to what we actually knew about the gunboat, its crew, and their level of readiness. None of us was trained in close combat, although Tomaldo, who had that *sibat* stashed next to the fish tank, was clearly chomping at the bit to kill some Japs. Those initial grenades to the pilothouse would be crucial, because that's where an officer would be and probably the boat's radio. Rooster, who'd been the pitcher for the Big E's softball team, would be aiming at the pilothouse, while I looked for openings in the side. The gunboat's gunwales were at least four feet higher than our little fishing boat and it wasn't like anyone was going to hand us a sea ladder. I was the one tagged to initiate the attack, and that would depend on whether or not there were enough open hatches, portholes, windows, etc. through which we could get grenades *inside* the gunboat and maybe punch holes in the bottom. If it showed up with all guns manned, armed sentries at both ends, and in an obvious state of alert, then we'd abort it.

Lots and lots of "ifs," but I knew that this had to be a case of the gunboat going out and simply not coming back. Missing at sea and overdue. If the Japs contemplated any other scenario, life on Talawan would become even more violent than it already was. Father Abriol had spent a lot of time talking to village heads, the Orotai police chief, and what served as an informal town council in the town. He hadn't told them *what* we had in mind, only that we were going to do something. He'd learned that there were quite a few islanders who were ready to organize a general uprising, especially once word got around that American frogmen had been seen on Leyte Island. Somehow they knew that frogmen meant a landing was in the offing. I didn't have the heart to tell them that frogmen meant that a landing was coming *some*where, but not necessarily at Leyte. In the end, the Filipinos decided they were with us. The more I got to know these people, the more I admired them. They were stoic, brave, and tireless, and this was their home.

At around four in the afternoon we saw the other boats beginning to turn for the harbor. Emilio had enjoyed a pretty good day, although none of the fish had been much over six inches long. He added extra water to the fish tank to lower our waterline and then we headed in, deliberately trailing the other boats. A half hour later we saw the gunboat lying alongside another fishing boat about two miles ahead of us. There was a dirty column of engine smoke curling off its stack. Emilio made a course change as if to take advantage of the fact that the gunboat was occupied. For a few minutes I thought maybe we'd outsmarted ourselves, but then the gunboat began to move away from the smaller fishing boat and head in our direction, with even more smoke streaming out of its flimsy-looking stack. Emilio pretended not to notice her until she tooted her horn, a clear signal to stop. Rooster and I took a deep breath and waited to see how it would play out.

We saw one crewman in a shabby uniform standing on the high bow of the ex-trawler as she closed in. He had a coil of rope in his hands. Another man was standing amidships with a boat-hook. Since we were looking into the setting sun we couldn't see how many faces there were in the pilothouse windows, nor could I see what the doors and windows situation was behind the pilothouse. Emilio stopped his engine and then the shadow of the gunboat began to block out the setting sun and we heard a heavy rope land next to the fish tank. I looked through a crack in the rattan roof and saw a single bored-looking officer standing in the doorway of the pilothouse, smoking a cigarette and seemingly paying zero attention to what was going on down on the main deck. He pitched his cigarette butt over the side as I watched, and sauntered back into the pilothouse.

The crewman who'd been in the bow of the gunboat walked down and opened a gate in her lifelines and then climbed down to our boat. He didn't use a ladder; there were toeholds welded onto the side of the gunboat, just like the ones we used getting up into our cockpits. There was a single door open in the superstructure amidships but I was too close to the hull for me to see what was inside. I looked forward to find Tomaldo staring holes in my face. By now the single Jap was head down in the fish tank, grabbing up squirming fish. I nodded at Tomaldo.

Rooster and I had four grenades each, standard-issue Army grenades we'd both handled in basic training, and with a single spare sitting in Emilio's hat next to the steering wheel. Once I gave the signal, Tomaldo was supposed to uncover the spear and stab the fish thieves. Rooster would step out and throw two grenades up into the pilothouse, one after the other. By then our crewmen would have hopefully uncovered the rifles. Once the pilothouse grenades went off, my job was to step out and start throwing my grenades. That was the plan, anyway.

The first thing that went wrong was that the guy who'd been standing in the bows of the gunboat had handed off the other end of the rope to the crewman holding the boathook. He alone climbed down into our boat, while that other man just stood there, holding the end of the rope to keep us alongside. We hadn't counted on one of them remaining behind but Tomaldo solved the problem for us. He stabbed the man at the fish tank twice with two vicious, short thrusts into his abdomen, then stood up and hurled the spear into the line-holder's stomach. The first man simply collapsed over the fish tank, while the line-handler crumpled slowly to the deck, letting go of the rope and staring at the thing sticking out of his stomach as a waterfall of blood erupted from his mouth.

By then Rooster was out on deck and our other crewmen were extricating rifles from under a pile of nets. Rooster pulled a pin and lofted his first grenade up at the pilothouse doorway. It hit the edge of the door instead and, thank God, bounced *into* the pilothouse and not back down on us. Rooster didn't wait for the first one and threw another one, overhand this time, which sailed right in just as the first one blew up. Once that first grenade went off I stepped out on deck and lofted two of my grenades into that open hatchway amidships, just as Rooster's second pineapple went off up above. Mine both went true and clacked against what looked like a companionway ladder hatch that was open and latched back inside the athwartships passageway. Since I could see the hatch I knew the grenades could see me, so I jumped back into the steering pit, seeking the unlikely protection of its bamboo wall. Both of my pills went off, one really loud in the passageway, and the other one more muffled, where I hoped it had dropped down that ladder and gone off in the engine room below.

Rooster was standing next to the fish tank, a grenade in each hand with their pins pulled and his fingers clamped around the spoons. One of our rifles forward cracked and a sailor with a rifle tumbled into the sea from the gunboat's stern. Rooster saw more movement back there so he threw his third grenade onto the fantail of the gunboat. Someone screamed a warning back on the stern and then it went off. A piece of metal came through the bamboo, past my face at the speed of heat, and then chipped some wood off the mast. Rooster, with one grenade left, clambered one-armed up those footholds, through the opening in the life-lines, and then extended a hand to me. I followed with my two remaining grenades, one in my left hand, the other jammed into my waistband. We heard more rifle fire from behind us but I was too busy looking for a way to get grenades belowdecks. I felt the heat of a fire on my cheek and looked up to see the wooden pilot-house entirely engulfed in flames.

A porthole to our left exploded as someone inside fired a weapon right through the glass in our direction. Rooster didn't hesitate: he pushed his last grenade into whatever room lay behind the shattered porthole, and then jumped back down into our boat. There were two seconds of frantic shouting inside and then that grenade went off, followed by a chorus of men screaming in pain. I looked back down into the boat and saw Emilio still sitting at his steering wheel, chewing on that cigar. He was like a man at a football game, just enjoying the show.

Right above me was a vertical ventilation funnel. It had a small weather vane on its back which would point its mouth into any rela-tive wind and thus force air down below. I pulled the pin on one of my grenades and pitched it into the funnel, where I could hear it rattling down the air duct before it exploded somewhere beneath the waterline with a satisfying thump. I decided to throw my last one down the same funnel, hoping that it led to the gunboat's en-gine room. That one produced a sheet of flame and smoke belch-ing back up the main smokestack. Moments later there was more smoke rising up out of that hatch in the athwartships passageway.

Then everything went silent, except for the crackling fire en-gulfing the pilothouse and a sucking noise as whatever fires were burning down below clawed combustion air down the inside pas-sageway.

The radio. One of us needed to find the boat's radio and make sure nothing was getting out. I told Rooster where I was going and he positioned a couple of men with rifles to cover me. I ran to where a slanting stairway led up to the level of the pilothouse. There was a single small structure behind the burning pilothouse which had two antenna wires leading up to the boat's mast. That had to be the radio room. The only weapon I had was the handgun Abriol had taken from the Jap officer up on the caldera.

I crouched down behind a small lifeboat to pull the slide and see if it was ready to shoot. I saw brass, so at least it was loaded. Apparently in my excitement I'd kept my finger on the trigger, so when the slide rammed forward it went off, sending a round ricocheting into the smokestack. Feeling stupid I scuttled forward until I was alongside the door to the radio room. That's when I realized I should have brought along our spare grenade. Rooster read my mind, went back and got the spare, and lofted it to me on the upper deck. Realizing I needed two hands to catch it I dropped the pistol, which went off again when it hit the deck, this time blowing the heel off my left boot. But I caught the grenade, pulled the pin while holding onto the spoon, and crept up on the door to the radio room. I slowly operated the handle. Locked.

Rooster saw the problem and motioned for me to get away from the door. Then he had his three riflemen open fire on the door handle, which fell entirely off after six splintering rounds. I picked up my handgun and approached the door to pitch the final grenade in, but it suddenly swung open and a terrified young Jap came tumbling out, bleeding from a dozen wounds. When he saw me standing there with a pistol in one hand and a grenade in the other, his eyes rolled up and he simply passed out. I guess I was supposed to shoot him but I couldn't. I could drop a 1,000-pound bomb on a ship and kill everybody, but I couldn't shoot an unconscious wounded man. I took a quick look and then went into the radio room. It was a complete wreck. There was a single internal door that led forward out to the pilothouse. It had apparently been open when the grenades went off out there. By now the pilothouse had collapsed and the heat was diminishing. There were *three* radios, not just one, and each of them had multiple holes in them.

Okay, I thought. They probably did *not* get a message out.

As I stood there trying to figure out what to do next I remembered I still had one grenade left. I pitched that one into a ventilation funnel on the other side. A moment later an explosion down below rocked the entire gunboat. She bucked up in the water and then began sagging to port. Time to go, I thought.

I scrambled across the upper deck to get back to that ladder when a single rifle shot hummed past my head, followed by a loud blast from down on our fishing boat. I hit the deck, just short of the ladder, and I looked down. There was Emilio, standing up at his steering wheel, cigar clenched between his teeth, and with a smoking double-barreled shotgun aimed towards the back of the gunboat. I looked aft and saw a headless corpse roll through the lifelines and into the sea between the gunboat and our fishing boat. I started to slide in the same direction, which is when I recognized that the gunboat was about to capsize. As if to make the point, Emilio backed the fishing boat away to avoid becoming entangled in the mast and funnel of the sinking gunboat. For the second time in my short but exciting navy career I found myself scrambling up the overturning side of a sinking ship. This time I just kept going and ended up in the water on the other side of the gunboat.

I hastily backpedaled away from the now almost overturned hull, which quickly slid out of sight in a rush of blowing air followed by massive, oil-filled bubbles. Emilio steered the fishing boat in my direction. Soon strong hands hoisted me aboard. For a long minute the only sound on the boat was the putt-putt of the engine as Emilio headed for the cove rendezvous he'd arranged. I now thought I knew how the Minutemen had felt when they drove the British army off the Old North Bridge. We'd done it. It hadn't been pretty, but we'd managed to sink a Jap ship. Now, what were going to be the consequences?

Tomaldo came over and asked for my handgun, which I'd shoved into my pocket. He then stood in the bows as Emilio drove the boat through the debris field from the gunboat, looking for floating bodies. He found three and shot each one of them in the chest. I think they were all dead and wondered why we were bothering. Tomaldo explained that the extra blood would bring sharks, and the sharks would leave no evidence of what had happened. Of course, I thought. Why didn't I think of that.

Rooster and I took our seats back in the steering pit.

"We did it," he said, almost wonderingly. "Now all we need is a fuselage to paint a gunboat silhouette on."

I tried to grin but couldn't manage it. All I felt right now was increasing dread. "I hope to Christ that none of the Japs in Orotai heard all those grenades," I said. "Or any local fishermen, for that matter."

"Someone might have seen that fire when the pilothouse went up, but we were a long way offshore. If they come looking they aren't gonna find anything. Tomaldo reminded me that the water is miles deep out here."

But there'll be fuel oil, I thought. Father Abriol had told me the *Hagfish* was still leaking diesel oil, much to the irritation of close-in coastal fishermen. The strait's latest casualty would, too. It had been satisfying to sink a Jap warship, however small, but I couldn't help wondering if we hadn't overplayed our hand.

TWENTY-SIX

For the next two days and nights Rooster and I hid out by ourselves at the lava tube. No one knew, or would say, where the padre was off to. The same grandmother and granddaughter took care of us with food twice a day. One of us kept watch on the trail we'd originally come up after the sinking during daylight hours. If Abriol had posted sentries in the forest we never saw any signs of them. More importantly, there were no Japanese patrols, either.

The granddaughter, whose actual name was quite complicated but who went by the name Tini, was indeed the young woman I'd seen running to the dying boy the night of the massacre. She was very pretty, shy but with obvious intelligence, and apparently fascinated by Rooster. The grandmother played the part of a Spanish duenna, outwardly very strict and highly protective, but probably aware that Rooster had noticed Tini. She, it turned out, was twenty years old and not the teenager I had thought she was. It was part of the charm of the Filipinos that they kept their youthful looks well into adulthood. During our time of waiting she appeared reserved and a little sad, as were most of the villagers down in Lingoro. It was Rooster who took to talking to her and discovering thereby that she spoke some English, courtesy of Tomaldo. I wanted to quiz her on what they were hearing in from the jungle drums, but the words Tomaldo had taught her had nothing to do with Japs and gunboats.

I had time to seriously consider our situation while keeping watch over that long valley. Rooster and I had taken three rifles with us to the tube, along with that hair-triggered handgun. We had twenty-seven rounds among the three rifles. Father Abriol had kept back three grenades, so that constituted our "arsenal." I had been impressed by Tomaldo's *sibat*, but even a squad of second-rate infantrymen with submachine guns would clean our clocks in a New York minute.

On the third morning we enjoyed another small earthquake, except that it was followed by a low, booming roar coming from some distance away. We checked the Orotai end of the tunnel. I was halfway expecting to see flashes from Jap artillery but there was nothing to be seen. The east entrance was a different story. That volcano east of us which had been sending up a lazy column of smoke when we first arrived was now in full eruption. A muscular column of red smoke, fire, and ash rose through the low clouds. Its base was a fierce glow of red, and silent lightning bolts flickered through the column. Above all this a big, dirty cloud was building its way up into the stratosphere. I guessed that the volcano was 10, maybe 15 miles away, but still we could hear it rumbling and roaring.

After the first booming eruption we had earthquakes in our vicinity on an hourly basis. Finally, at about noon, that cloud got too heavy for the atmosphere to support it and it collapsed down in a great dark mass and then flattened out at what used to be the base of the cinder cone. God help anyone within about five miles of that, I thought, as we glimpsed red rivers following it down the cone's slopes. While we were perched on some rocks just outside of the tube, mesmerized by the scary spectacle, one of the villagers appeared in the tube entrance and indicated we needed to follow him back in. He looked scared.

We saw why when we followed him back into the lava tube. Father Abriol was sitting on a bench with his back to the sloping wall of the tube, obviously exhausted and injured. He was a mess: red-stained bandages on his head, both arms, and one hand, all complemented by a swollen black eye and a nasty purple bruise on his neck. One leg was extended straight out, the other bent back under the bench. The grandmother was tending to him, trying to give him water and having a hard time of it, while giving Tini a string of orders. Tomaldo was among the villagers in the room. He told us an alarming story.

Apparently the Japs *had* sent out a patrol to a place where the three paths that led to the three largest villages converged at a large freshwater spring. There they'd laid an ambush in the surrounding jungle, hoping to catch members of the resistance or even the priest himself. A woman had come to the spring to fill two water jars and smelled cigarette smoke, which told her there were Japs lurking in the surrounding bush. She'd pretended not to notice and had walked back to her village where she informed the elders. They sent a runner to the village where Father Abriol was hiding, alerting him to the danger. He and three others had decamped immediately and headed for the crater where we'd done our Neanderthal number. They took a different route than the one we'd taken, which involved crossing a shallow crevasse in an old lava field. He stepped onto an invisible bubble in the lava field and had broken through, falling into a conical-shaped pit that sloped down 20 feet to a pile of sharp rock rubble. It had taken his three-man escort two hours to go find some vines, make a rope and crude harness, and get him out of there.

The whole point of heading for the ash crater was to lead any Jap patrols away from the lava tube, especially if they had dogs with them, but there was no other option after his accident. They'd made a bamboo litter and carried him to the west side slope of our volcano and then summoned help. The villagers had their own form of herbal pain-killers, so he wasn't hurting as much as he should have been, but he was definitely out of action for a while. He gave us a wan smile when we came into the hidey-hole.

"Nice day for a hike," he said through cracked lips. "Or so it seemed."

Another rumbling boom from that distant volcano squeezed our ears. I half-expected our volcano to answer with a sympathetic earthquake. Rooster, ever the claustrophobe, looked uneasy. The lava tube was beginning to remind him of scary times on *Hagfish*.

"We got the gunboat," I told him. "Do you think the Japs know what actually happened yet?"

He shrugged and then winced. "The villagers know that it wasn't an accident, but so far, they're telling me the Japs haven't reacted. They hauled in some fishermen for questioning, who told the Japs they'd seen the gunboat, but that it was heading out to sea. After that, they paid no attention. The Japs let them go. Someone reported they'd seen one of those big seaplanes flying around Orotai the next morning and then out over the sea. Other than that, my town sources are all silent. And nervous."

"I figure they'll commandeer some fishing boats and go out and take a look," I said. "See if there's wreckage, bodies, anything."

The floor gave a little shudder, producing a fine cloud of dust in the tunnel.

"These goddamned volcanoes talk to each other?" Rooster asked nervously.

"Remember, Talawan is all one big volcano," Father Abriol said. "With many mouths. That eruption over there is a good thing. It means the entire island isn't going to be blown into the sky, at least not just yet."

"Not yet," Rooster said. "Great. That's really great news."

"What's our next step?" I asked.

"Next I'm going to fall asleep for about twelve hours. After that, it will depend upon the Japs. If the *Kawanishi* reports an oil slick and they take the gunboat's disappearance as an accident or perhaps the work of an American submarine, not much will happen. If not, God knows."

"That's not exactly what I was asking, Padre," I said.

"I know," he said with a painful yawn. "Why don't you two think of something. I'm going to sleep now."

He closed his eyes and then his whole body relaxed on the bench. For a moment I thought he'd just died, but then I saw his chest moving. I asked Tomaldo what the woman had given him. He grinned.

"The Moros to the north grow opium on one of the higher inland volcanoes," he said. "They trade it for our fish sauce. What do you want us to do?"

I realized then that we'd just crossed a very important threshold. The padre was out of action. The Americans were now in charge, especially since we'd lit the fuse on stage two. If only one terrified fisherman told the Japs that they'd seen the gunboat in pursuit of Emilio's boat, and that's when shooting started, things here on Talawan would come to a sudden and violent head.

"Can you go into Orotai safely?" I asked him. He nodded.

"I need to know what the Japs are doing, and what rumors are going around."

He nodded again. "You will not stop, then?"

"*We're* not going to stop, Tomaldo," I replied. "After the gunboat, *we* must not stop." He got the message, loud and clear.

He came back just after sunset, while Tini and her grandmother were preparing food. He was really upset.

"What's happened?" I asked him. He slugged down some water before replying.

"Tachibana ordered his troops to burn all but two fishing boats in the harbor," he reported. "The boats came back in at the usual time and there were soldiers everywhere. They drove all the Filipinos off with bayonets, took *all* the catch, and then started setting the boats on fire. Next morning he put his men on those two boats and sent them out for fish—but only for the Japanese. He claimed the fishermen were not telling him the truth about what happened to the gunboat. Two fishermen were bayoneted for objecting and thrown into the bay in front of their families."

"So he's figured it out," Rooster said.

"Maybe," Tomaldo said. "It may be something else. If it was an accident, then Tachibana is responsible as the commander. An act of the resistance? He is safe from blame. He saves face by punishing the people."

Face, I thought. I'd heard that expression before, and now I knew why it was important. So: maybe use that concept against Tachibana? I asked where the Japs stored all their food supplies in their compound. He said in two heavily guarded godowns, inside the compound itself. Like everything else in Orotai, it would be built of mostly bamboo, except perhaps for a metal roof.

"I have an idea," I said. "But it will remove all doubt about what's happening."

Tomaldo, still fuming over what had happened, made an impatient gesture. "Tell me," he said.

"Do you know what a fire arrow is?" I asked him.

He frowned and then his face lit up. "I have heard stories," he said. "From the old times. When the Moros first came, they invaded by sea. The hunters took the points off their arrows and then covered the point in the sap of the *hayan* tree. Then they would wrap a piece of cloth around the sap and soak it in plant oil and a secret powder. When the Moros' boats closed in the hunters fired many flaming arrows, setting the boats on fire. When the Moros abandoned their boats, the hunters would kill them all in the surf."

"This will take planning," I said. "But we must strike quickly, before Tachibana realizes he's facing an uprising and calls for help from Rabaul or Mindanao."

"Our people understand," Tomaldo said. "No fishing boats, no food."

"Good. As soon as you can collect the men who can handle bows and arrows, I'll come in and show them how to make the new arrows. When we're ready, we'll go into Orotai at night. I want to attack the Japs' food warehouses in the compound and set them on fire. When the defenders come out with guns, I want archers to kill as many as they can from hidden positions around the compound."

"We have hunters who use the bow, but 'archers'? What are archers?"

"Hunters who shoot men instead of animals. In this case, they will be shooting Japs."

"Animals, Japs," he said with a shrug. "Same-same."

"Not quite," I said. "Hunting arrows have points which go up and down; war arrows have points that go sideways."

"What?" Rooster asked.

"Animals on four legs have vertical ribs; humans walking or standing upright have horizontal ribs."

Rooster, Southern city boy that he was, gave me a horrified look.

"Learned that in Scouts," I said, proudly. "Along with how to make a fire arrow."

TWENTY-SEVEN

Once again I discovered that there were lots of things I *still* didn't know. Such as: Filipino bows and arrows didn't much resemble American Indians' bows and arrows. For one thing, their hunting bows looked more like the English longbows used at Agincourt, almost dwarfing the hunters who were using them. I tried pulling one and it took all my strength to get it started. Secondly, the hunting points were much smaller, almost round instead of the familiar triangle shape of American arrows, so the orientation on the shaft didn't matter. The points, however, were designed to break off inside the victim, and that was because the points had been dipped in the sap of the *camandag* tree just before firing, thereby injecting a lethal poison. Getting a hit anywhere on the body meant inevitable success. Thus there was no need to construct "war" arrows.

Fire arrows were even easier in the day of gasoline; it turned out they already had them. They used them occasionally to start large brush fires on the upland savannahs to drive larger game into the arrows of a hunting team. They cut a spiral groove into the shaft of the arrow behind the point and filled that with a flammable extract from the Philippine version of a pine tree. Then they wrapped a gasoline-soaked film of cotton on top of that as the igniter. The big surprise was that they also used blowguns both as hunting and defensive weapons. The darts they fired were also poisoned, and they were amazingly accurate out to 20 feet or so.

The men who used the weapons were full-grown men, if only because they needed to be taller and strong enough to handle those extra-long bows. The first night I went to the village I met ten of them, with Tomaldo translating. We were surrounded by several teenagers, who seemed eager to join in. They showed me the armory and demonstrated some of it. One Filipino was clearly in charge of the hunters. He was much older than the rest, with a strong physique and gray hair. His name was Magron, and he seemed to command unusual respect. He made a crucial suggestion. There were two guard towers overlooking the Jap compound, each usually containing three sentries. They had spotlights and light machine guns and were similar to the ones across the river in the POW camp. We would have to neutralize them first before attacking the buildings with fire, because the Japs had cleared the area around the compound and the fire shooters needed to be closer.

The Filipinos kicked this problem around while Magron stood there, arms akimbo, waiting patiently. I'd noticed he'd been giving Rooster and me the once-over the whole time, with an expression that said we'd have to prove ourselves before he'd join us. Once the hunters had stopped arguing, he announced the solution: use the fire arrows on the guard towers first. They were all made of bamboo trunks lashed into tower frameworks and, best of all, they had thatched roofs. When the guards bailed out, some of the archers would go after them while the rest tried for the storage buildings.

They decided that they'd go into Orotai the next morning and reconnoiter the best firing positions for both the towers and the buildings inside. With Tomaldo translating, I observed that, with only ten of them, it might be difficult to get enough arrows on target to keep ahead of Jap efforts to douse the fires. He pointed out that the Japs had to go to the town's single well to get their water, usually twice a day, just like everyone else. If they used it to put out fires, and something was done to shut down the well, what would they drink? Magron's demeanor was that of a man who was looking forward to this little expedition.

But that raised my final concern: What about the townspeople, or for that matter, the villagers nearby? Shouldn't we be thinking about a quiet evacuation of the town *before* the attack on the compound? And what about the POWs? Rooster asked. Surely the Japs would order the guards across the river to machine-gun all the POWs the moment a whole-scale attack was mounted on the compound in Orotai. More animated discussion and even some arguing followed those two questions. Tomaldo and Magron finally came up with the solution—we would either have to neutralize the prison guards at the POW compound first, and *then* attack the main compound, or do it simultaneously. With just ten shooters? I asked.

Frowns everywhere. I finally raised a hand. Everyone politely went quiet.

"It is obvious," I said, as Tomaldo quietly translated, "that we have much more thinking and planning to do. The Japanese did not conquer all of East Asia because they were stupid. If they feel cornered, they will come out of that compound with every man willing to die for his emperor, as long as he takes every Filipino man, woman, and child on Talawan with him. They are Japanese: that is what they do. Yes?"

There were reluctant nods all around. Reluctant because the Filipinos wanted blood. Of course they did, but this nugget was beginning to understand why the generals got paid the big bucks: I didn't know the first thing about planning out a campaign of attack, or how to solve all the what-ifs that even we amateurs had already identified, so we had to proceed slowly and carefully.

Magron finally raised his hand and then spoke up. Tomaldo listened for a few minutes and then translated. "Magron says there is an old Chinese expression that makes sense here," he said.

"And?"

"That expression is: slowly, slowly, catchee monkey."

Right, I thought, nodding. "What does Magron suggest?"

"We do this thing in pieces. First, get most of the people out of Orotai. Not in one night, but over several nights. When most of the people have gone, do something to the town's well. Not poison, but perhaps fill it in. Then, the English prisoners: do not attack the guards. Wait for heavy rain, then cut the fences instead. Get them out and get them to safety. Send two men for each prisoner—they are very weak. Then when Orotai is empty, and the water is gone, and the prisoners are safe, then burn the two remaining fishing boats. We do not have to attack the compound. When there is no more food or water, they will come out, screaming *banzai* and all of them ready to die. Then we help them do that."

"But they have rice stored in that compound," I said. "They can fish from the shore if they have to. Don't we still have to burn the godowns?"

Tomaldo asked Magron.

"No," was the answer. "The rice they stole is still in the open baskets they took from the people in Orotai. All we have to do is get a small boy into the godown one night with some tubes of water. Pour some water into each basket. It does not take much; by morning all the rice in the basket will turn green. Ruined."

Mold, I thought. Magron was right: in this heat, wet, sticky rice would propagate mold rapidly throughout each basket.

I sat back and thought about all this. Forget the all-out frontal assault, bows and arrows against machine guns. Do it in pieces. Quietly. The town's population diminishing, while whoever was left behind made themselves visible, as if all the townspeople were still there.

It made sense. I finally realized that these nice people here on Talawan, simple fishermen and farmers that they might be, also had a tradition of stubborn defensive warfare against *centuries'* worth of invaders. The Japs were just the latest chapter and the locals had finally had enough. I looked over at Rooster. He was nodding.

"Magron is right," I declared. "We will do it his way."

I waited for Tomaldo to translate and watched Magron slowly beam.

"Now," I said. "You are many. Rooster and I are just two. How can we help you?"

Tomaldo posed that question to Magron and the others. Magron answered for them all. Tomaldo suddenly looked like a man who didn't want to translate what he'd just heard. I tried to help him out.

"Let me guess," I said to him. "Stay out of our way and let us take care of this problem?"

Tomaldo looked quite relieved, if a little embarrassed. "He said to tell you that, yes, but to be polite. He does not want you two to lose face."

"Got it," I said. "I think we need to get back to Father Abriol. Can someone lead us back to the lava tube?"

Tomaldo began setting that up, but Magron apparently had one more idea. He buttonholed Tomaldo for another minute or so, who then turned to me.

"He asks if you can help with the English prisoners, once we get them out. You speak their language, know their customs. Perhaps one of you can go with the men who will set them free, so that they will know we are their friends."

"We can both go," I said. "Tell him that is a good idea." Then I remembered something my skipper had told me. "And by the way, there is another old saying that applies here."

Magron looked over at me once Tomaldo translated that, and raised his eyebrows.

"Tell him that in any plan for a battle, the enemy always gets a vote."

Magron didn't get it at first, probably because the word "vote" was unfamiliar, but then he did. He laughed out loud, and nodded. Then the war conference broke up as he took charge and began to issue orders. A few minutes later we were on our way back to the mountain to tell our warrior priest that life was about to get really interesting on dear old Talawan.

TWENTY-EIGHT

Father Abriol was not in great shape as it turned out. His swelling was down but his bruises were now in Technicolor. Tini and her grandmother had been replaced by two much older women, who'd arrived with baskets of herbs and potions. Abriol was mad at them because they'd begun to cut back on the opium-based stuff while they switched him over to less addictive remedies. More importantly, he was horrified that we had "allowed" the Filipinos to take things into their own hands for an attack on Tachibana and his compound. Between the pain and his concern for what might happen now, he was definitely not pleased with the two of us.

"First of all," I protested, "I did not 'allow' them to take charge. That Magron fella was already in charge. He brought his own people when he showed up and those guys didn't look like farmers to me."

Abriol sighed and tried to get more comfortable on his cot. His caretakers glared at us; they clearly didn't approve of our even being there. "Ignacio Magron," he said, "is at least eighty years old and is my counterpart, so to speak, in the spirit world beliefs here on Talawan."

"Like a shaman or high priest?"

"Both of those things, but first and foremost he is a warrior. He's old enough to remember the Filipino insurgencies against the Spanish *and* American occupiers. He claims to have fought against the American army as a young man, alongside the Moros."

"Wow," Rooster said. "No wonder he wanted us to butt out."

"Perhaps," Abriol said, squirming on his pallet, still trying to find a more comfortable position. He groaned when he hit a sore spot and then glowered at the two old women crouching near the fire. They ignored him.

"No one can verify that claim, of course, since most of the Moros who fought the American army died doing so. The problem is that the Moros believed their spirits would keep them physically invulnerable. Magron was young at the time and may still believe some of that."

"I don't think so," I replied. "Rooster and I were kinda flailing, trying to think of ways to go after Tachibana without getting the whole town of Orotai wiped out. Magron's the one who suggested doing it in stages. I think he's as concerned for the townspeople as you are."

"I still think I need to talk to them," he said, grimacing when his injured leg started to slide off the pallet.

"Wouldn't hurt," I said. "One of the problems was that we don't speak Tagalog; Tomaldo had to interpret everything, back and forth. In any event, Rooster and I will start working on how to get the POWs out. Right now we need sleep."

There was a basket of the ubiquitous rice balls, which this time had been dressed with soya sauce. I liked them better than the fish rice balls, now that I knew how that stuff was made. We ate some and effusively thanked the two crones, who cackled their appreciation. Rooster set up his rack down at the end of the chamber, while I set mine up nearer Abriol in case he fell out of his cot during the night. The women departed after brewing up a pot of that wonderful coffee.

Some time in the wee hours Abriol needed to make a visit to that fissure in the floor of the tube. I helped him hobble down and back, where he collapsed painfully and then just lay there, breathing heavily and groaning occasionally. Unable to sleep, I asked him if he would tell me his history. The long story, so to speak. At first he said nothing, making me wonder if he'd even heard me. Then he sighed and began.

"I was born on Luzon, not that far from Manila. My mother was Filipina; my father was a Spanish navy sailor who'd stayed behind after the Americans destroyed their fleet and became the new occupiers. He told us he'd swum ashore near Cavite in the chaos after his ship was set on fire. There were many Spaniards who 'failed' to return to Spain after the defeat at Manila Bay in eighteen ninety-eight. He was a good man, and he took good care of our family. He was the son of a blacksmith back in Spain. His entire family back in Spain were metalsmiths and wheelwrights of one kind or another. He was also a very devout Catholic, so we had strict observance of Catholic rules in our house. It was a strong family, and we were respected in our town."

"How did you end up becoming a priest?" I asked.

"I of course first learned our native language from my mother and our neighbors' children. It was my father who made it a point to teach me basic Spanish because, when I was growing up, Spanish was still important in government circles. The Church ran the town schools where I continued to learn Spanish. There was an English missionary nun at the school and she taught us English for four years because our new rulers spoke English. I did well in school and especially with languages, but I was useless as a metalworker. I could do basic carpentry and metal finishing, but I just wasn't strong enough to work a forge and hammer out real steel. My father was very patient but the writing was on the wall. My skills lay elsewhere.

"My parents, especially my mother, then pointed me towards entering the Church. When I applied to the San Carlos seminary in Manila, the fact that I had a grasp of three languages, especially English, led to acceptance. At seminary I added Roman Latin to my inventory, and after eight years in San Carlos, I was ordained a deacon and then, one year later, a priest. My family was very proud of me, as you might imagine. Our entire neighborhood celebrated the ordination of one of their own."

"And then . . ."

"Yes, and then. Exile on Talawan. For a while I missed the big city and seeing my family, although my father turned his face from me. I missed things like refrigeration, electric lights, trains, doctors, and the like, but there was no going back. My neighborhood had been disgraced by my indiscretions, and while my mother wrote letters for a while, it seemed best to just become a memory."

"Did you get that church in town built?"

"That building had originally been a godown. One day about a month after I first arrived they were having a festival celebration which involved fireworks and it got away from them. The building burned, along with several children who were caught in a stampede. I gathered the townspeople around the ruin and said Mass for the children. When some fishermen who hadn't attended asked if I would say another Mass, I did so and then asked the elders if I could rebuild it as a church."

"By yourself?"

"Well," he said, "that's how I started. Clearing away the wreckage, salvaging what materials I could. I was new, and I think the people wanted to see what kind of man I was."

"Did they know why you were there?" I asked.

"I don't think so. The Manila Diocese had occasionally sent a missionary priest to Talawan Island, mostly, I think, because of the Mohammedans in the north, but they never stayed, even though the serious Catholics kept asking."

"So when you showed up it was 'prayers answered.'"

"Something like that. Anyway, when I was ready to begin building, I went out into the nearby forest and cut down a tree to make my first building post. It took me all day. Some villagers took pity on me when they heard what I was trying to do. That grew into a community effort and we got our church. It's not much by Manila standards, but memories of what had happened there made it a special place. Until the Japs, of course. By then I was well established, but so were their instructions from Tokyo as to what to do with priests."

I had more questions about the local people, but he was obviously tiring. Finally I asked him if I could get him some water. When he didn't answer I looked over and he was fast asleep. I decided it was time for me to see if I could manage that, too. I was really tired, but sleep had been evasive during this surreal experience. That one constant question rambled through my brain at all hours: What in God's world am I doing *here*?

At dawn, one of Abriol's sentries came trotting down the lava tube. He reported in Tagalog: No Japs in the forest. Then he had more to say, which got Abriol's immediate interest. I heard the word "Negritos." Abriol dispatched the young man and then told me that four Negritos had appeared, which was very unusual. They were members of the Batak tribe which lived mostly on the northeast coast of the island, above the central volcano range. For them to be down here on the southwest coast was unheard of, and when the sentry brought the group in he kept his distance, clearly afraid of them.

When they appeared I thought that they resembled African Pygmies. They were not quite five feet tall, with black skin, almost emaciated bodies, and kinked hair. They wore loincloths, sleeveless tunics, and bamboo sandals. Each had a different headdress and they carried long, thin reeds with them, along with a smaller but nastier version of the bolo. The reeds were two feet taller than they were and had a mouthpiece of some kind on one end. Everything about them, from their faces, to their stained, almost pointed teeth, to the charms and tokens worn around their necks, proclaimed primitive. The reeds, I finally realized, were the dreaded blowguns.

Abriol greeted them in Tagalog but got blank looks. Then he

tried Spanish, and that worked. Our sentry brought them water, which they accepted. Then they squatted down to talk to Abriol. I'd taken Spanish in high school and again at the academy, mostly because it was one way to unload the academy's heavy engineering course load. That said, this form of Spanish had some Tagalog or other Asian dialect intermingled, so I understood only bits and pieces. When they were done, Abriol thanked them several times, and then they left, as quietly as they had come. Our sentry chose to stay behind with us.

"As I said," Abriol began. "They are almost never seen south of the volcano range. Not to say they haven't been here, because if *they* wish to remain invisible, they surely can. They're an ancient tribe and their news is unsettling. They came to warn us that their main village had been bombed by two of those big Jap seaplanes that fly out of Mindanao. No warning, and for no apparent reason. They appeared from the sea and everyone, men, women, and of course, children, came out to see them because they were so big. Then the bombs rained down, killing many of the tribe. They flew over twice, the first time to drop bombs and the second to use their guns. By then those who could had fled into the forest, but they've lost about a third of the people in that village."

"Wow," Rooster said. "Are they part of the resistance?"

"No, they're very secretive, hunter-gatherer people. They exist at a bare subsistence level. They're skilled with natural medicines but also poisons and do not like strangers coming around."

"So what brought the *Kawanishi*?"

He wiped his brow which I realized had become sweaty. I wondered if he had a fever. "I suspect a Jap patrol blundered into them," he said. "And was quickly killed. Otherwise I can't think of a reason for the Japs to bomb a Negrito village—there's hardly anything to bomb. There are many different Negrito tribes up on Luzon, and even there, no one bothers them, and for good reason."

"Are they going back?"

"Not quite yet," he said. "They told me they wanted to see these Japs who had bombed their villages. There's no telling what they have in mind."

"Why would they come to warn *you*?" Rooster asked.

Abriol had to think about that. "Good question," he said finally. "But if Tachibana thought there was an island-wide insurrection building, he might well call in those seaplanes on the villagers here, or even Orotai. We must warn the people: if they hear planes coming, run into the forest immediately. In fact, I will do it myself."

He made to get up and began tottering. Rooster caught him before he fell and propped him back up against the wall next to his pallet. He's getting worse, not better, I thought.

"Or maybe not," he groaned. "You two please go to Lingoro at once. Danilo here will take you. Warn them, and they will send runners to the others."

"And how about Orotai?" Rooster asked.

"I think if Tachibana is there, he will not bomb himself."

I didn't have the heart to tell him that those *Kawanishis* were perfectly capable of bombing Orotai without touching the Japs' compound, or that they routinely carried 4,000 pounds of bombs.

TWENTY-NINE

When we arrived at Lingoro it became obvious that Magron had wasted no time. There were feverish preparations throughout the village for what might be coming from the Japanese. Families with young children were packing up and disappearing into the forests. Hidden food stores were being dug up and distributed. We'd seen lots of sentries on our way into the village; Magron had found a role for the village's teenagers. Tomaldo was sitting in the longhouse drawing a map of Orotai with possible places for archers to get close to the compound without being seen. He got up and came to greet us.

"Father Abriol sent us down here," I said. "We had a visit this morning from a small group of Negritos."

He seemed surprised. "Negritos? Here?"

I told him about the *Kawanishis* bombing their village. He had the same question that Rooster had had: Why warn us? Before I could answer we heard the low drone of approaching airplanes. Four-engine airplanes, from what I was hearing. I told Tomaldo to get everyone out of the village, *right now*. He blinked but then began yelling in Tagalog. Whatever he said worked. People dropped what they were doing and sprinted into the forest, some dragging small children behind them like rag dolls. Tomaldo, Rooster, and I joined the mass exodus as that menacing thrumming sound grew louder. More than one, I shouted to Rooster, who was out-running me.

We suddenly encountered a pile of rocks which looked like the spine of some buried prehistoric animal and dropped down behind it, only to find Magron and five of his archers already there. The "archers" were armed with rifles this time and they looked like they were itching to use them. Then the bombing started.

We were only a few hundred yards from the center of the village, which was apparently the aiming point. There were two planes and they dropped eight bombs, 500-pounders from the sound of them. The blasts compressed our skin and, even behind the rocks and a couple of football fields away, we could feel the heat flash of each blast. Instantly the air was full of dirt, shards of wood, sections of galvanized tin, and parts of human beings. It rained this horror for a good ten seconds after the last plane lifted out of its bombing run, followed by the sounds of them coming right overhead.

We'd clamped our hands over our ears, but even so, I could barely hear anything and all of us were sporting nosebleeds. A human hand had landed on Rooster's back as he tried to become one with that odd ridge of lava rock; one of the archers swatted it off his back. All five fingers began to curl in when it landed on the ground. Then one of the archers shouted something and pointed up. Both of the seaplanes were circling back, bent on making an-other pass. They'd used their bombs; this would be the 20mm cannons on a strafing run, hoping to catch any survivors who were standing up after the bombing run.

One of the Filipinos, aghast at seeing those moving fingers, dropped his rifle and ran into the deep woods. Magron yelled after him but he was gone. Rooster grabbed up the man's rifle.

"C'mon," he yelled. "Let's fight back."

With that he went down to the lower end of that rocky spine, sat down, rested the barrel on the rock, and aimed it into the air while inspecting the rifle's works. Magron and the four remaining men did the same, creating a firing squad of crouching men. By then the *Kawanishis* were making their final turn to come back for a second run at the village. Rooster, with Tomaldo translating, showed the others how to lead the target and to shoot high rather than fire right at it. I looked at the rifles, which were more bolt-action antiques, except that they had clips hanging from under the action. I took one final up-periscope look as the *Kawanishis* made their final inbound turn and throttled back to descend. Definitely a strafing run, I thought, having done the exact same thing.

"Shoot at the *second* plane," I shouted to Rooster, who understood and told Tomaldo. If we shot at the first plane, the second one could make a slight turn and treat *us* to a hailstorm of high-explosive 20mm rounds.

Even throttled down we could hear the distinctive up-Doppler sound of reciprocating engines coming at us, and then the ground around the village erupted in a thousand puffs of smoke and whining projectile fragments. The sound of the guns themselves followed an instant later. The *Kawanishis* were really low this time and now it was my turn to make love to that rock. I never heard the rifles go to work, but I could see hands and arms working furiously as the second plane flashed by.

To my total astonishment, they hit the damned thing, for there was now a bright yellow fireball trailing the inboard engine on the plane's right side. We stood up and watched as it disappeared over the trees. At the last second in which we could still see it, the plane's right wing tore right off. Moments later we heard the sound of a plane crash, followed by a black and orange mushroom-shaped cloud rising above the forest. The bottom of the cloud was illuminated by a huge gasoline fire somewhere below it. Despite knowing what we would find in the remains of the village, there were fierce grins all around at the sight.

The lead *Kawanishi* had turned around and was circling the crash site at about 1,000 feet, perhaps a mile away from us. It did two orbits and then straightened out and headed back north toward Mindanao. The boiling black smoke of a gasoline fire continued to pump into the tropical air before a breeze finally caught it and bent it toward the sea. I grabbed Tomaldo's arm and told him we needed to get to the crash site, leaving Magron and his shooters the grim task of going back into what was left of the village. He nodded, informed Magron of what we would be doing, and then we headed west along an existing trail. We didn't exactly run but we did hurry, conscious that the Jap garrison would be coming out as well. Rooster asked me why I wanted to go to the crash site.

"I thought I saw the tail come off right when the wing flipped up and over the fuselage," I said. "If it's not in that fire I want to find it."

Rooster looked puzzled but then he understood, gunner that he was. The *Kawanishi* HK-8 model carried a twin-barreled .50-cal. machine gun in a blister on the tail. If that had survived the crash, we might finally acquire a weapon which would go a long way to leveling the playing field when we attacked the Jap compound. Anyway, it was well worth a look-see.

It was no problem to find the main crash site, given the size of the fire, which had also managed to set several bamboo trees ablaze as well. The engines were recognizable through the flames but not much else. The smell of roasting bodies was startlingly vivid. It took us another forty minutes to finally find the tail section, which had landed upside down in a small stream. And there, sticking up in the air, were the twin barrels of the *Kawanishi*'s stinger, embraced by the still and bloody arms of the plane's tail-gunner. *Only* the arms, though—the rest of him was gone.

It took much longer than I had hoped for us to get that gun mount out of the wreckage. First we had to punch our way into the tail fuselage using bamboo sticks because the normal access tunnel back to the tail blister was embedded in the creek. Then we had to get the bloody bits and pieces of the gunner's remains out of the way, which was a truly nauseating task. The machine gun was built into a ball-shaped cage that allowed the gunner to train, elevate, or depress the two barrels in an almost 360-degree sphere of action.

We had no tools other than our bolos, which fortunately had heavy steel blades, capable of smashing through all the lightweight aluminum. In the end we managed to cut the entire ball cage out of the tail cone, letting it fall into the soft ground on the banks of the creek. Two belts of glistening brass-cased ammunition came with the gun assembly. We paused at frequent intervals to listen for sounds of a rescue plane or, worse, Tachibana's men coming. The big fire was starting to burn itself out. If that towering smoke cloud dissipated, Tachibana's men would have a hard time locating the wreckage without air support. We hoped.

Then we had to decide what to do with our prize, which weighed a whole lot more than I'd expected. Rooster said the guns were in good order after he had carefully unloaded and then cleared both of them. The trouble was that the guns themselves were hard-mounted onto a framework within the ball cage, and we had no way to dismount them without tools, and power tools at that. Rooster estimated that the whole assembly weighed about 350 pounds. Since there were three of us, I suggested we rig a travois, roll the gun assembly onto it, and drag it away from the tail as far as we could manage, and then hide it. We could then gather up a working party back at the village and haul it somewhere where we might be able to take it apart. How, where, when were open questions, but if we could acquire a working and transportable twin-fifty it would surely be worth the effort. Each of the ammo belts carried 150 rounds, and there were incendiary tracer rounds every fifth link, just like ours. We might not even need archers.

THIRTY

Lingoro was a heartbreaking scene when we finally got back, hours later. It had pretty much ceased to exist. Where the houses had been was now just an expanse of dirt with 15-foot craters everywhere. All the nearby trees were down in heaps of firewood, and even the giant where we'd been hidden had had its top two-thirds blown over. Most of the people had managed to flee, but there were some, the very old or women with infants, who had not escaped. They were now reduced to bits of red spattered all over the flattened grass and bushes. Magron and some of his men were sitting in a circle where the longhouse had been, attending to Father Abriol, who'd been parked in a litter laid on the round side of a bomb crater. The village was silent, as if the very earth was still in shock at what had happened. What the bombs hadn't flattened, the 20mm cannon fire had shredded. I didn't see *any* of the villagers. We walked into the rubble and sat down with the rest of them.

Abriol looked at us with a tragic face. He'd been weeping and still was. Magron's face, on the other hand, was a study in cold fury. I told the padre what we'd accomplished; when Tomaldo translated that news to Magron, his old eyes gleamed with sudden murderous interest. I was surprised that this old medicine man even knew what a twin fifty was, but then, there was a lot we didn't know about him. Rooster had to explain the significance of our newly acquired treasure to Abriol, and I couldn't tell if he was pleased or afraid. He still looked feverish, but he'd quickly realized that the plans for attacking the Jap compound were now certainly going to proceed. Being a priest, he was still consumed with the magnitude of the human disaster all around him.

"The Negritos know something we don't," I speculated. "I think it all means that the Japs are getting ready to bail. That means the prisoners, what's left of them, are probably dead ducks. We definitely need to get those POWs out if we can *before* we attack the Japs in their compound."

After Tomaldo translated for Magron he became very agitated. We sat back and waited for their tense exchange to conclude. Tomaldo turned to us.

"Magron wants no delay," he said. "He wants to attack the compound tonight. If they can have that machine gun, he will use it. But this bombing must be avenged immediately. As long as Tachibana is still alive on this island, he will continue to attack the people here, who are defenseless. Those prisoners should not have surrendered. They should have fought to the death, as we are prepared to do."

"That's a very Japanese concept," I replied. Tomaldo hesitated, not wanting to translate that. I indicated he should.

Magron was taken aback when he finally parsed what I'd just said. Then he got really angry, but Abriol raised his right hand and began to speak to him in Tagalog. This time Tomaldo started to translate for us but Abriol gave a sight shake of his head. That's new, I thought, until I remembered: they were speaking Tagalog, which meant that whatever Abriol was saying, *we* couldn't understand it, thus saving Magron's face, especially if Abriol was arguing with him. It soon became clear that whatever the padre was saying, Magron wasn't having it. In an obvious case of disrespect Magron interrupted Abriol. He spoke for about a minute in short, clipped sentences. Abriol asked him a question, probably along the lines of: Are you sure? Magron grunted one final word and then got up, summoned his war party, and stomped off into the still-smoking forest. Tomaldo just stood there, eyes closed, shaking his head.

"Well?" I asked.

"Well, he said if you insisted on saving the English prisoners, do it yourselves. They were of no concern to him or the people of Talawan Island. He was going to punish the real enemy, the Japanese, and kill them all."

I sighed. Then I became aware there were villagers creeping back into the circle of craters and splintered trees that had been their village not an hour ago. None of them was speaking. They just wandered around the wreckage, being careful not to step on the bloody bits. Some of the older women began to wail softly in their anguish. Small children buried their faces into their mothers' skirts, refusing to look. One woman gave out a hysterical shriek and threw herself down into one of the craters, which had already begun to fill with muddy water. She lifted up the blackened corpse of a toddler, holding it up in the air and screaming at the sky as if she was cursing God for letting this happen.

Abriol turned to us. "You should leave now," he said quietly. He told Tomaldo, whose immediate family lived in a nearby hamlet, to take us back to the lava tube. He would have to stay to say Mass and comfort these people in any way he could.

"If Magron attacks the Japs," I said, "the *first* thing they will do is order the camp guards to shoot all the prisoners."

"I know," he replied. "But what can *we* do about that?"

"I have no idea right now, but if you can find Rooster and me a couple of rifles and some ammo, I want to be taken to the POW camp as soon as it gets dark."

He began shaking his head. "No, no, *no*," he said. "Those prisoners can barely get up to make it to the latrines. Even if you single-handedly wiped out all the camp guards, what then? How would you get those walking dead out of there? How would you get them to safety? Feed them? Shelter them? You're not thinking, just like Magron is not thinking."

It was becoming clear that Abriol's injuries and the shock of the village bombing had completely unnerved our heretofore warrior priest. I tried a different tack. "Magron's going to help us," I said.

"Oh, yes? Since when?"

"You get word to Magron that the Allies are going to defeat the Japanese and drive them all the way back to their home islands by killing them until they give up. After that, there will be many questions asked wherever the Japs occupied territory. Those who helped defeat the Japs will be honored. Those who helped them will be hanged. Tell Magron that his decision to abandon the POWs to their fate will end up in the second column. Tell him to think about that and then to bring many boats and men to the POW camp tomorrow night. Unless, of course, he is afraid."

"He will never do that," Abriol protested.

"Then the two of us will give it a try," I said. "Yes, we'll probably fail, but we'll go down fighting and Magron and his men will be known as the ones who ran away."

"I can't tell him that," Abriol said. "He is likely to cut *my* head off for saying such a thing."

"*I* can," Tomaldo said. "And I will. The lieutenant is right. If we let those men die we will become like lepers in the eyes of all Filipinos."

Father Abriol wrung his hands. "Please, *please*, stop this insanity, the two of you. All this killing! It's madness!"

"It's war, Father," Rooster said, gently. "The Japs started all this shit because they *like* war. It gives them a chance to be samurais again and to die honorably. It's our duty to help them accomplish that. I swear that's all they're fighting for."

Abriol threw up his hands and limped away, talking to himself. Tomaldo said he'd leave immediately to find Magron; they couldn't be that far away and his own scouts in the forest would know where they went. I told him we'd stay here until he got back,

and then we'd head for the POW camp tonight to make a reconnaissance.

That didn't happen. Tomaldo did not come back that night.
Rooster and I wondered if Magron hadn't exercised some elder
power over the youngster after he gave the old man my message.
Now I was getting depressed—every time I initiated something,
more Filipinos got killed. Standing there among the stinking
bomb craters and grieving villagers, I began to think that maybe
Rooster had been right all along about building that boat. We
sure as hell weren't doing much good for the people of Talawan
Island.

After a while, though, people from the other villages started
to come in. They brought food and water and the men brought
tools. The only good thing about living in a bamboo-framed hut
was that even a 500-pounder would mostly blow it down. The
villagers were supremely practical. They went poking through the
wreckage and picking up the useable bamboo framing logs. They
then began reassembling the village huts. Several teenaged boys
were put to the task of filling in the craters with picks and shovels.
Others were sent into the woods to get the vines they used to lash
together the logs. Rooster and I helped where we could while trying not to get in their way. At one point Rooster went over to the
remaining bottom half of that big hollow tree and stepped inside.
He came back out a minute later with good news: those three rifles
were still there. They were 1903 model Springfield bolt-action
rifles, and one of the boxes contained ammo. Even they would beat
a bow and arrow.

Two hours after sunset and still no Tomaldo, so we asked for
a guide through pidgin and hand signals. Two boys volunteered
to take us. The British prisoners had been getting fresh fruit and
a little bit of cooked rice passed through the perimeter fence on
an every other day basis. We had nothing to bring them after the
bombing but the news that we were going to try to spring them
from the camp tomorrow night. It took an hour to get down to

the camp itself, and then another half hour to choose our moment to get across the creek and up to the back fence. The prisoners had set up a watch routine, posting one man at the back fence as soon as the evening head count had been made. It was nearing midnight when we finally made contact. As it happened, this night the man posted was the same sergeant we'd spoken to on the night of first contact, Staff Sergeant Mason. We crouched in the dark next to one of the fence posts.

I told him that things were coming to a head with Tachibana, as evidenced by the village bombing. He said they'd figured as much because the compound guards had seemed extremely nervous lately. The good news was that the POW camp garrison had been cut in half after Tachibana ordered several of them back to the compound at the port. There was only one sentry at each of the gun towers instead of three, and they were spending an awful lot of time in the tower shelter, as opposed to being out on the platforms with the guns and the lights. The prisoners had been careful to disguise their improving health by continuing to drag themselves around their huts.

"Can they walk on their own?" I asked him.

"If not, those who can't will be carried by those who can," he said. "But: the Jappos definitely have the wind up. One of our lads understands some Japanese, and he says the guards are talking about leaving Talawan and that the prisoner problem has been solved by orders from Tokyo."

"I think I know what that means," I said.

"Not too bloody hard to suss out, is it?" he said. "Tomorrow may be cutting it close."

"Best we can do," I said. "But I'm hoping we'll have some help coming tomorrow night. Boats and men to help move each of you once we get you out."

"You *hope*?"

I explained our problem with Magron and that it might come down to just the two of us and any men I could talk into helping.

"We'll sort it, somehow," he sighed. "If you can get this bloody wire cut and knock out the tower guards, we'll make it work. They change guards at midnight, by the way."

The nearest tower's spotlight came on and began one of its random sweeps of the camp yard, buildings, and fence lines. Mason melted away and so did we. It occurred to me that I had no idea how we were going to cut that heavy-gauge barbed wire.

The men of the village were still working on erecting shelters when we got back, working by the light of makeshift torches stuck in the ground. We were surprised at the progress they'd made. The bomb craters were mostly filled in and there were several shelters already up, most consisting of four poles and the beginnings of a palm-frond roof. All the shelters were filled with sleeping forms. A small group of women were tending a fire over to one side over which hung a black kettle. We were welcomed to partake in the hot stew and it was wonderful. Rooster and I had stopped asking what was in these concoctions; when you get one meal a day you're mostly just grateful and the local monkeys are nervous.

We asked after Father Abriol; they took us to that giant tree trunk and led us inside. He still looked to be in bad shape. The women tending to him were speaking in hushed tones. When he heard us come in he turned his face toward us.

"Infection, I'm afraid," he said in a feverish voice. "It's my leg."

Rooster and I examined his leg and then looked at each other. The proud flesh and the noxious smell when we removed the bandages told the story, even if neither of us had ever seen it: gangrene. The swelling and toxic colors had reached the middle of his shin. If he was going to live, the leg beneath the knee would have to come off. We stepped back outside. By then Abriol had drifted back to sleep.

"What the hell are we gonna do, Boss?" Rooster whispered.

At that moment a file of men entered the village, led by none other than Magron, followed by Tomaldo and what I'd begun to think of as the archers. Magron approached me and signaled for Tomaldo to translate.

"You are right and I was wrong," he announced.

I knew immediately that this was yet another occasion for "save face" strategy, so I improvised. "I am honored that you are here, and we need your help. First of all for Father Abriol."

He didn't expect that news and hurried into the tree sanctuary. He came back out in less than a minute and began issuing orders. His people ran to get some of the torches to build a fire near the tree trunk. Magron pulled out his bolo and a tiny black stone and began to sharpen it.

"Magron will cut off the leg," Tomaldo said. "Then he will seal the cut with hot steel. He has done this before."

Magron was watching us to see our reaction. I bowed to him and then told Tomaldo that we agreed, this was the best thing. Magron gave some more orders which sent some of the old women hustling this time. They returned with a cup fashioned from bamboo, which Magron took into the sanctuary. Then he came out and handed his bolo to one of the women who carefully placed the blade in the wood fire, turning it periodically to heat it evenly. Rooster asked me if we should back out. I said: no. A Filipino is going to amputate a white man's leg; we should stay to show our approval.

The women brought Father Abriol out of the tree base on a crude litter and set him down on the ground next to the fire. A small crowd had gathered by now, and several of them were praying. Abriol was clearly out of it. His lips were moving but with no discernible sound. Magron directed one of the women to place a bamboo log high under Abriol's thigh. As soon as it was in place he pulled the red-hot bolo from the fire and cut Abriol's right leg off just above the knee with one powerful chop. He then pressed the glowing blade against the stump and cauterized the big artery and any other bleeders in a horrific cloud of bloody steam. Abriol's whole body went rigid and then his head lolled to one side as the smell of burning meat filled the air. Rooster and I finally remembered to breathe. One of the women carried the diseased leg out into the forest. Others moved in with ointments, crushed herbs, and clean cloth to cover the burn. Rooster grabbed my arm.

"Boss," he said in a trembling voice.

"If he survives that shock, he'll live," I said, quietly. "Magron knows what he's doing and so do those women."

Magron heard me say his name and turned to look our way. I nodded vigorously, signaling: good, very good. Tomaldo translated and Magron acknowledged. The women carried Abriol back into the tree shelter, while Tomaldo, Magron, and I walked over to a downed tree trunk and sat down to talk about tomorrow. Obviously Tomaldo had managed to change the old man's mind about a preemptive attack. How, I didn't know, but I thanked him privately.

THIRTY-ONE

By sunset of the next day we were about to put our plan into motion until a runner from Orotai trotted into the village with news. Tachibana had sent squads of soldiers into the town to go house to house in search of food—and hostages. There were now between twenty and thirty women and children being held inside the Jap compound and the town itself was being patrolled. Our informant had no news of the POW camp but he did tell us that those four Negritos were waiting outside the village for permission to come in and talk. Magron sent him back out into the forest to bring them in. Tomaldo and Magron sat down with them while Rooster and I went to check on Abriol.

The padre was conscious but well under the influence of whatever the women had given him this time, which was a good thing. The cavity in the tree trunk smelled of honey, which the women had applied to the massive burn. Abriol was breathing normally and his face had regained some of its usual color. He lay back on his cot, mumbling parts of the Catholic Mass in Latin. The women shooed us out after a minute, so we joined the conference outside. Tomaldo said the Negritos had agreed to help us at the POW compound, especially when they realized that this village, too, had been bombed by the Japs, just like theirs.

"They will kill the guards in the towers for us," Tomaldo told us. "Then they will go to the guards' hut and kill anyone who comes out."

"That'll be a lot of shooting," Rooster said. "Surely they'll hear all that over in Orotai."

"Blowguns make no sound," Tomaldo said. "Once the guards in the towers have been silenced, banca boats will gather along the creek and then take the prisoners upriver. There is one new problem: the Negritos saw a Jap patrol in the forest while they were making their way here. They said there were five men, and that they were being very quiet."

I groaned out loud. Tachibana had put patrols out into the forests, confirming that old rule about the enemy getting a vote when you made a plan. "What's Magron think about that?"

"He says we cannot go tonight. We cannot make the attempt until we know how many patrols are out there. When we do make the move he has asked the Negritos to take the lead when we go down to the camp. He says they can sense the presence of Japs in the woods and give us warning. We will then have to evade or silence that patrol, hopefully without using guns."

The next day was one of more feverish preparation for the night's operation. Magron had sent out four patrols, each made up of five Filipinos and one Negrito. Their job was to make sure the villagers hadn't been discovered assembling banca boats, food, and bamboo canteens for the POWs. I was getting increasingly concerned about what messages Tachibana had sent off to his superiors up on Mindanao Island from that communications ship. Rooster asked Tomaldo how they were going to cut the barbed wire; Tomaldo said they had no tools for that, so they would cut through the base of several bamboo poles holding up the wire, and then collapse the fence when the time came. It looked to me that Tomaldo had become Magron's second-in-command, so he was busier than a one-armed wallpaper-hanger. We decided to, once again, get out of their way. Then Rooster had an idea: let's go get that twin fifty mount.

"And then what?" I asked.

He thought for a moment. "Mount it on a banca boat, or maybe two banca boats lashed together, with outriggers on both sides. If I can figure out how a Jap fifty-cal works, we could bring it along tonight down the river. Might come in handy."

I wasn't so sure about mounting that heavy beast on banca boats, but it certainly would be nice to have a gun like that if Tachibana caught us in the act and sent a bunch of troops across the river to wipe us out. We caught up with Tomaldo one last time. He agreed to send us out with six strong teenagers to hump the gun back to the village.

It took damn near all day to accomplish that, but at last we got back to the village around three in the afternoon with the gun mount suspended between two poles like a dead pig. Rooster and I had taken turns carrying the two belts of ammo, draped around our necks. I never want to have to do that again: those things were *heavy*, and they clinked incessantly the whole way, which made us all nervous. By nightfall Tomaldo and our teenagers had married two banca boats together, lashed a bamboo platform between them, and fitted outriggers for stability on both outboard sides. Rooster had removed all the unnecessary parts of the ball turret, reducing the two guns to a single unit which still could be trained and elevated. He checked the headspace with the gauges conveniently wired to the barrels and then loaded up the two belts. He wanted to test it, but we decided that the distinctive boom of a fifty would carry a long way and surely alert any Jap patrols.

The four villager patrols came back in at nightfall in time to eat and then get a nap before we all went out at 2200, two hours before the guard shift change at the camp. Our flotilla of banca boats had set sail earlier to get down to the main river before tying up to the banks upstream to wait for the signal to approach the camp. Rooster and two rowers were assigned to our "battleship," while I went with Magron and Tomaldo to make first contact at the wire. We had, of course, no idea of what we might find: all the

POWs dead by execution, an entire company of Japs waiting inside the wire—or many other nasty possibilities. Tachibana clearly was fully alerted once his patrols reported that Orotai was practically empty and that the jungle was alive with people coming and going furtively. His taking of hostages into the compound confirmed that.

The weather and the moon were on our side. The night was warm, as usual, and there were periodic rain squalls blowing in from the straits. The moon, such as it was, flitted in and out of low-flying scud. The four Negritos led the advance party, just in case the Japs had sent out night patrols. They usually didn't because that's when the green vipers came out to hunt. I shared their concern on that score.

By 2330 we were crouching in the dense bushes lining the creek and scoping out the camp. There were dim lights over by the guards' hut and we could hear that creaky generator running. The prisoners' huts were dark as usual. The odor of the latrines hadn't improved. We were waiting for one of the spotlights to make a sweep of the perimeter before making our move, and that took what seemed like forever. Once the tower nearest the creek lit up and jerked its yellow beam around the entire camp and then switched back off, we would send in the Negritos while we made the break in the fence.

The moment it was switched off the Negritos slipped into the creek and headed in. Magron had told them to take one tower at a time, beginning with the one nearest where we would cut down the fence. The way they moved was amazing to watch. One moment they were right in front of us; the next they were simply gone without a single sound. The forest had gone silent when we'd first approached the creek banks but now the night insect orchestra was back in full cry, which should mean we were alone out there.

I heard Magron grunt as he pointed at the target tower. A black shape was going up one leg of the tower like a snake. He wasn't using the ladder for some reason, until I remembered that the ladders were attached to the gun platform. Anyone climbing the ladder would shake that platform, alerting the sentry. Once the black shape reached the actual platform it merged with the shadows underneath. Then: silence. I'd half-expected a cry of pain or an exclamation from the sentry as he got hit by a dart, but there was no noise at all. We didn't see the Negrito again until he stepped out from under the platform and headed for the next tower. The other three had been told to surround the guards' hut in case an alarm was sounded.

It took them just over a half hour to neutralize the sentries, during which there were no alarms or spotlights lighting up. A light was still on inside the guards' hut and we could hear a radio playing some strident Japanese music, if you could call it that. Magron decided it was time to get to the fence. He had left a small handsaw with the sergeant major with instructions to cut halfway through the backs of the fence posts at the rear of the compound, the line that faced the jungle. We couldn't be sure they'd managed it but it would save us a lot of time if we didn't have to make the entire cut through the eight-inch-thick bamboo poles. We stepped down into the creek, which was deeper than I remembered it. It was probably high tide in the river. Coming up the opposite bank we lay still for a few minutes, listening for any sounds that might indicate waiting guards. Or dogs.

Finally Magron made the birdcall they'd agreed upon. Nothing happened. He waited for a few minutes and made it again. Shit, I thought. Had they executed the prisoners? No—there were still guards in the towers, although they were now sleeping the long sleep. There was 25 feet of cleared dirt we had to cross to get to the base of the actual fence. Magron decided we'd go to the fence and try the call again. It was the longest 25 feet I'd ever crawled, expecting a sudden glare of spotlights and a blast of machine-gun fire. When we finally reached the wire it was really dark. We felt around the base of the fence poles for cuts but found none. Magron signaled that we needed to crawl along the fence, away from the creek. After another tense 15 feet we found the first cut. Obviously we'd gone to the wrong part of the perimeter. There was a dark shape sitting by the fence which turned out to be the staff sergeant.

"Cheerio," he said, softly, handing the saw through the wire. "Tonight the night?"

"Yes, it is," I told him, while Magron got to work on the fence poles. I told him the plan was to bring them through the wire, one by one, help them cross the creek, and put them on litters, after which two Filipinos would carry them into the woods on the other side of the creek.

"What about that lot?" the sergeant asked, pointing a thumb at the nearest tower.

"They're all dead," I said.

He grinned in the darkness, then experienced a coughing fit. He clamped both hands over his mouth, bent over and suffered a full minute of excruciating chest spasms. I waited for the fit to subside, realizing we'd made the right choice in allotting two bearers for each prisoner. Sergeant Mason had put on a good front but he was very sick. They probably all were. Hardly any food, dirty water, crude sanitation, the heat, mosquitos, and the sheer hopelessness of being prisoners half a world away from England. The little bits of fruit and rice we'd smuggled into the camp were probably why they were still alive. Magron, finishing the first pole, looked up. The generator had stopped.

We held our breath. Was this the normal routine? Turn it off after midnight to save fuel? But what about those random spotlight sweeps? We heard a door bang open down by the guards' hut and saw the wobbling beam of a flashlight. We couldn't see the soldier carrying it, but he was headed for that little shack where the generator lived. Halfway there the soldier spat out what sounded like a curse. A moment later the flashlight went down on the ground, where it remained motionless. Now what, I wondered. Was there anyone else awake in the guards' hut? Would they all turn out to see what was going on?

Nothing happened. The flashlight lay there on the ground, illuminating a tree stump. Magron resumed sawing on the next pole. Mason crept back to the nearest prisoner hut and soon we could see figures stirring in the darkness. Once Magron got three poles cut all the way through the fence sagged almost to the ground. I thought he would cut one more, but instead he produced a tree branch with a Y-shaped crotch in it and propped the bottom wire up about two feet, enough for a man to crawl under it.

The silence was a bit unnerving. I kept waiting for the off-duty guards to wake up as their subconscious minds realized something important was amiss. Then the four Negritos were at the wire, appearing so quietly that I almost shouted an alarm. The headman pointed back to the guards' hut and puffed out his cheeks five times in quick succession. Clear as a bell, I thought. They'd gone *into* the hut and taken care of business, which should mean there were no more Japs on this side of the river. Magron made a different bird cry in the night and the banks of the creek were suddenly crawling with villagers, bearing their litters and slipping down into the water.

It took much longer than I'd anticipated to get them all out, some forty piteous souls by my rough count. We no longer had to worry about making noise and that helped move things along. Magron let the Brits organize themselves under the urging of Sergeant Mason, while we went through the camp collecting Jap weapons. We took the machine guns and their ammo off the towers and some rifles and pistols from the guard hut. It took four Filipinos to carry all this loot, which left Magron looking very satisfied with the night's activities.

Once everyone was accounted for he and I went back across the creek to join the Filipinos as they carted the POWs down to the main river and set them on the waiting banca boats. I had wanted to burn the camp once everyone was out but Tomaldo had pointed out that a big fire over here would bring out the Orotai garrison. I wondered what he and Rooster were doing. As we climbed out of that miserable creek, hopefully for the last time, we found out. The unmistakable sound of a twin fifty erupted out in the Orotai harbor.

THIRTY-TWO

Immediately I knew what they'd done. They'd paddled down the river and gone after that communications ship anchored in the harbor. From the controlled rate of fire, even at this distance, I could tell Rooster was doing the shooting. Disciplined bursts, never rapid-continuous fire, he always told me. The barrel jumped when it was fired, so you wanted to let it settle back on target between bursts of three to four rounds. After not much more than a minute, the racket ceased. If Rooster had succeeded in wrecking the Japs' communications ship, Tachibana and his remaining garrison were now isolated in beautiful downtown Orotai.

Moving the POWs to safety in the surrounding forests took the rest of the night. Villagers from the smaller settlements had been called into service to bring food and clean water. Others had been tasked to build small encampments up on the edge of the lowland forests where they gave onto the volcanic fields. There wasn't all that much food to go around, but the POWs were used to surviving on a cup of watery gruel per day. Now they were getting clean water, fresh fruit, and the ubiquitous rice balls flavored with protein-rich fish sauce. They were also getting the first baths they'd seen since arriving in Talawan. Heretofore they'd had to stand or lie out in the tropical downpours; now there was the miracle of soap. These were simple things, but a vast improvement on their prior conditions. Above all they now had hope of survival. For all our success, however, I was still mindful of Tachibana and his hostages once he discovered what we'd done.

A hue and cry awakened me just after dawn as bearers brought two men in on litters. I first thought we'd missed a couple of POWs, but then I realized it was Rooster and Tomaldo they were bringing in. I hurried over to see how bad it was. Tomaldo had been shot twice, once in the hand and a second wound on the side of his neck. He was conscious and anxious to tell me what happened. Rooster had a bullet wound to his chest. The bandages someone had put on were blood-soaked to the point of saturation and his face was a frightening gray color. He was in and out of consciousness. I leaned in close to see if I could hear the sounds of a sucking chest wound, but his breathing appeared to be nor-mal if very shallow. The entry hole indicated that the bullet may just have clipped the top of his right lung. I couldn't find an exit wound, and that spelled trouble. The healing women immediately surrounded him, including Tini who cried out when she saw all the blood. I asked Tomaldo what had happened.

They'd been able to surprise the floating comms station under cover of a rain squall. Rooster had wanted to get in as close as pos-sible and then shoot half the ammunition into the single, center deckhouse and then use the rest to punch a hundred holes in the ship's side right at the waterline. The remains of the ship's crew climbed out of the smoking wreckage of the deckhouse while Rooster was busy opening her hull to the sea and fought back. They were using rifles and Tomaldo had been hit twice almost immediately. Rooster had then lifted the barrels of the fifty and mowed down the Japs, firing at them on the deck until he'd run out of ammo. One lone survivor then stepped out of the trawler's pilothouse and shot Rooster in the chest before losing his balance as the ancient ship lurched over onto her starboard side, prepar-ing to capsize. A moment later she rolled completely upside down while the Filipino paddlers backed the banca boat away from the scene as fast as they could. They stopped their frantic paddling once the trawler disappeared into the darkness to tend to To-maldo and Rooster and to dump the fifties over the side.

Having done what they could they then paddled back into the river, keeping as close to the far bank as they could. The Jap gar-rison in Orotai was by then fully alerted. There were searchlights everywhere amid the sound of police whistles and even a bugle carrying across the dark water. They knew that their communica-tions ship had been attacked but that was about all they knew.

Magron appeared while Tomaldo was telling me all this and began to talk to Tomaldo in Tagalog. Magron was clearly excited, so much so that Tomaldo couldn't get a word in edgewise. I inter-rupted and asked Tomaldo what was going on.

"He wants to attack the garrison in Orotai immediately," To-maldo said, sitting down now as the pain began to sink in. "Before Tachibana kills all the hostages. There is word that Jap soldiers were seen in the POW camp at daybreak, so Tachibana now knows they've escaped."

I knew what that meant: there would be no more doubts about a general uprising of the Filipinos on Talawan. The question was: What could he do about it? Killing the hostages might make *him* feel better, but it wouldn't change his tactical situation, especially now that his radio links had been severed. The problem was that a dawn attack on an alerted garrison would produce more casual-ties on our side than theirs, and would certainly seal the fate of the hostages.

"Tell him *I* think he should spend the day moving his people into position around Orotai. He has some machine guns from the towers and some rifles now, plus his fire archers, but it will take hours to get his men assembled and into position. Tachibana will put patrols out during the daylight hours, so you will need pa-trols of your own. Take the Negritos with you on patrol; they can probably mount an ambush better than you and your people can."

Tomaldo was translating all this as I spoke. I could see Magron was frustrated. He was a man of action, not delay. Tomaldo kept going after he'd translated what I'd said. He used a respectful voice while arguing for my plan over some sudden charge of our very light brigade against the compound.

"Ask him if his men can operate the POW camp machine guns," I interjected. Magron frowned when he heard the question and then shook his head.

"I can show them," I said. "Even two or three machine guns would be very useful if they make one of their *banzai* charges. A man with a bow cannot shoot fast enough to kill a twelve-man squad that does not fear death."

Magron grunted. I realized he was tired, if not exhausted. I'd been able to snatch a couple hours of sleep after the POW camp raid. He had not. He nodded his head once, emphatically.

"As you say," Tomaldo announced. I told him that Magron should get some food and then a few hours of sleep. He would need to be wide awake tonight.

Magron didn't take well to that suggestion, declaring he was not tired and just because he was old, he was not weak. He then stomped off towards the cook fire for some food. I told Tomaldo to ask the women to attend to him and to get him to sleep for a little while.

I then went to check on Rooster. The women had him on a cot in one of the newly rebuilt huts. Tomaldo followed me over there. The women told him that the American had lost a lot of blood but that the bullet appeared to have gone right through him. They had given him some water and a few sips of their pain-killing witches' brew. Tini sat on the ground at his head, wiping his brow and trying to be brave.

I noticed that Tomaldo was starting to look a little gray around the edges. When I pointed this out to one of the women he, too, was immediately taken under care. I came out from the shelter to see Magron sitting against one of the broken tree stumps, sound asleep. There was a bowl next to him, and one of the really old women was sitting next to him, keeping the bugs away with a palm-frond fan.

Good, I thought. Then finally I went to check on Father Abriol. He was still laid up in the tree cavity and asleep or, more likely, doped. His color had returned and when I put my nose down to the bandaged stump there was no smell of decomposition. Maybe, I thought. Just maybe.

All the principal fighters were now hors de combat. I went to find some water and then I started asking via hand gestures where those captured Jap machine guns were.

THIRTY-THREE

By the day's end nothing was ready. Nothing. Magron had slept for four full hours, waking up and transitioning to an embarrassed, towering rage in the blink of an eye. He began yelling at everybody, which accomplished little more than scaring his people. Thirty minutes later one of his patrols came back to the village. Their report was chilling. Tachibana had indeed sent out patrols and this group of ten archers, alerted by their Negrito that soldiers were coming, had set up an ambush with their bows. When the Jap squad entered a small clearing the Filipinos unleashed a storm of poison-tipped arrows, taking down seven soldiers, the entire squad, without making a sound. The only problem was that the Japs had stationed a tail-end-Charlie guard to walk 50 yards behind the main squad. This guy appeared out of nowhere and opened fire on the Filipinos with a submachine gun. Three Filipinos went down dead before the Negrito put a dart in his throat. As he began to collapse, he stitched the Negrito from top to bottom, killing him instantly. Then he seized up and fell over.

The remaining Filipinos helped the wounded back to the village while one man was left behind to collect all the Jap weapons and ammo belts and hide them in the nearby forest. Magron deflated when he heard this bad news. I thought maybe his success at the POW compound had made him forget that the Japanese army had conquered China and then the whole of Southeast Asia. Jap soldiers who'd been through all that were not to be taken lightly. The other two Filipino patrols had encountered a second Jap squad. They had elected to lie down in the jungle and just let the Japs go by. They had heard the chatter of the first squad's submachine gun in the distance. As soon as the Japs were out of sight and sound, they'd headed back to the village. Magron wasn't thrilled with them, but they at least were all alive and present for duty, unlike some of their brothers-in-arms. The three remaining Negritos had vanished.

Magron and I needed to talk so I went to see if Tomaldo could translate for us. I discovered that he was running a fever and that his wounded hand was almost hot to the touch. The women were feeding him small sips of some other medicinal brew. God, I thought, if Tachibana had any idea how bad off we were he'd turn out his entire garrison and end all his problems right here in Lingoro. My last hope was Abriol. I went back to the tree trunk and found him awake.

"Can you translate for me?" I asked. "I need to talk to Magron."

"I'll try," he said, weakly. One of the women began clucking her displeasure but Abriol shushed her. I sent one of the other women to bring Magron. He stepped through the hidden door a few minutes later.

"This has been a bad day," I began, while Abriol translated.

Magron looked at me like I'd just said something particularly stupid. I went on.

"We cannot attack the garrison tonight until we are better prepared. We lost archers today. This will frighten the rest. There are more weapons to be recovered. I tried to teach some of the archers how to use the machine guns but they could not understand me. Tomaldo is down with a fever. The Negritos have disappeared. The Japs are out in the woods."

"What shall we do?" he asked.

"I want to go into Orotai, with you, to see what the Japs are doing."

That last bit surprised the priest. "Tonight?" Abriol asked. "Just the two of you?"

"Yes," I said. "Our fighters need time to recover. I want to sneak into the town and see if we can cause some trouble for the Japs. Make them pull their patrols back into the town. Take a couple of fire archers. Frighten the garrison."

Abriol translated and Magron's eyes lit up. I think he then said the Tagalog equivalent of: Now we're talking!

Abriol warned me that this was a very dangerous thing to do. The town was by now almost empty. Anyone creeping around the streets would be immediately suspect. I watched Magron, who I think understood that Abriol was trying to talk me out of this.

"Tell him we should do this tonight," I said. "It will encourage the people we need tomorrow to know that their leaders are not afraid to fight the Japs."

"But—"

"Please, Father. I need to do something *he* wants to do; otherwise everything's going to turn to worms."

Abriol translated and Magron got up immediately to organize things. I went to check on Rooster. They'd cleaned him up considerably and they had smeared the wound site with honey. He appeared to be sleeping rather than unconscious, but I sure wished I could get him to a real sick bay.

Magron, six archers, and I slipped out of the village just after dark and headed for the town in banca boats. Without the Negritos to sniff out Jap patrols Magron thought we'd be safer on the river. Our little flotilla smelled of pine pitch or whatever the Philippine equivalent of that was. The fire arrows were interesting. They were thicker than the ones I had seen before. One of the archers showed me that they were hollow. The entire shaft had been stuffed with that tarry substance, plus a bigger blob on the point.

The sky was fully overcast so we enjoyed almost perfect darkness out on the river. The boats made no noise whatsoever going downstream because Magron had timed our sortie to join the ebbing tide. I sat alone with a single paddler in the middle of our banca fleet. I'd pawed through the pile of captured weapons and discovered an American submachine gun, a US Army .45-caliber M3, commonly called a "grease gun" by the Marines on Guadalcanal. There were only two clips for it. It had obviously seen some rough service and may even have been captured on Guadalcanal. I'd fired one at the academy rifle range and mostly torn up dirt, but as a scare weapon, it was pretty convincing.

We landed upstream of the town on the town-side bank, just outside of the shabbier precincts of Orotai. There were no streets, per se, just crooked paths and crude, stinking drainage ditches. Magron led the way, followed by his archers, with me being tail-end Charlie this time. We stayed away from that single paved street along the harbor, keeping instead just behind it and using the more substantial buildings on the street as cover. I was worried about stray dogs, but we didn't see or hear a single one.

We moved more carefully the closer we got to that blunt point of land where the river joined the harbor, because that's where the Jap compound was. We passed behind their makeshift O-club, which was now dark. A glow of lights rose as we closed in on the compound. The Japs had put up spotlights, all pointing outwards along the top of their compound fence. Originally the fence had been barbed wire, but now it was a solid wall of bamboo stakes, maybe ten feet high. The dark silhouettes of a couple of gun towers kept watch over the perimeter fence, their gunhouses almost invisible in the dark shadows caused by the bright spotlights. To the left was the town's fishing boat pier, now bereft of boats. We could hear a generator running inside the compound, but no other sounds.

Magron pulled his team together and began issuing instructions, none of which, of course, could I understand. In one sense, it didn't really matter. They were going to do whatever they were going to do; I was along mostly to show respect and moral support for Magron. His somewhat hostile demeanor had softened a bit ever since I'd proposed we go into the town and raise some hell, especially after I'd shut down Father Abriol's objections. It was disheartening to see Abriol soften from his formerly steely resolve. Pain does that, I reminded myself. He'd hurt himself badly in that fall and then had tried to tough it out. Now, minus his leg, he seemed truly defeated. The bombing of the village hadn't helped his morale, either. It was one thing to entice a Jap patrol into an ancient man-trap, quite another to be the most likely cause of a *Kawanishi* social call.

Magron took my elbow and led me to a large but half-dead tree right next to where the town's main drag ended at the fishing boat piers. He pointed to the first crotch of limbs, almost eight feet off the ground. Then he pantomimed the perimeter fence of the compound, the gates in the now solid wall, those gates opening, and many men coming out. He touched my M3, pointed me up into that crotch, and made a sweeping motion with an imaginary gun. I nodded my understanding. It was clear as a bell: get up in this tree with that thing. If the Japs come out, give them a nasty surprise.

He grinned. We were going to kill some damned Japs tonight, you American occupier, you. I grinned right back at him, suppressing the sudden desire to tell him that any Japs coming out of that compound would have their own version of the M3. But, I thought, what the hell. Rooster was down, maybe even dying. Abriol had been sufficiently shocked by what those seaplanes had done and the subsequent amputation as to be out of the game, perhaps permanently. Tomaldo, Mister Energy himself, was wounded and down with a fever that might or might not require the same treatment that Abriol had gone through, and he had to know that. The villagers were being very brave, God bless them all, but underneath all that bravado they were sick with grief at what had been done to them and terrified at the prospect of what horrors might follow. Even the fierce little Negritos probably had had enough. And, there were hostages.

Magron was right: it was time.

I managed to get up into that tree without dropping my weapon but it hadn't been exactly a quiet effort. Fortunately the Japs didn't appear to have any patrols out in the town, itself. I settled down to wait.

And wait. Then wait some more.

I almost began to believe I'd been directed up into my tree to ensure I wouldn't interfere in whatever the hell Magron was plotting, but then I understood. There were noises rising in the compound, which was some hundred yards distant from my position. There were sounds of men moving in response to verbal orders, and I could just barely make out small figures climbing up those towers and then others coming down.

Changing of the guards. Was this what Magron had been waiting for?

I felt rather than heard something go flying over my tree, arcing high into the night air and trailing a yellow glow. A fire arrow! The missile curved up and then down, trailing a few sparks, and disappeared behind the fence.

Suddenly the night was filled with fiery trajectories, each one rising higher than I would have thought possible, before curving downward in a gentle arc and disappearing. This went on for almost an entire minute. I'd been so busy watching the arrows go over that I forgot to look back at the compound, which was now no longer dark at all.

Or quiet.

There was a sudden upsurge in shouted Japanese behind the wall and then the now familiar sound of police whistles. The thatched roof of one of the towers suddenly burst into flame, revealing the spectacle of three Jap soldiers crowding the top of the ladder in an effort to get away from the burning embers that were falling down on them. Even better, as they went down the ladders some stopped suddenly, shrieked, and then fell with arrows sticking out of their bodies. Behind the towers there was a larger conflagration rising. A machine-gunner in one of the other towers began firing into the town, but it was clear from the tracers that this was more a panicked response than a search for specific targets. Three fire arrows from three different archers converged on that tower, and a moment later the machine gun went silent. Then I heard deep popping noises from inside the compound, followed seconds later by thumping explosions out in the town and along the main street.

Mortars.

Tachibana had anticipated an attack and had registered mortars on the most probable positions that any attackers would take up. Soon there were fires in and along the front street to match the blazes lighting up the sky within the compound. The volley of mortars was answered by a shower of fire arrows from places nowhere near the mortar blasts, and this time, the wooden walls of the compound were the target. The arrows stuck into the walls but then sagged down, which let the entire length of the fuel-stuffed shaft lie vertically on the bamboo wall, almost guaranteeing that it would catch fire. By now the three guard towers were fully aflame, lighting up the entire area in front of the compound like giant tiki torches.

I was acutely aware that all the fires had lit up my tree pretty well, too. I shifted my position so that I could point the grease gun at the compound's main gate. Part of me couldn't believe the compound defenders would open that gate and come out fighting, but, then again, these were Japs. When in doubt, start screaming *banzai* and then charge your enemy. Which is exactly what happened. The front gates swung backwards and a small horde of Japanese soldiers came streaming out, bayonets fixed, and yelling at the top of their voices at as yet invisible enemies.

You're on, Nugget, I thought.

I brought the grease gun to bear and began to sweep the stream of Japs charging out of the compound. This is for Rooster, Tomaldo, and the battered priest, I shouted, as I cut them down. I purposefully aimed at their knees just like the Marines had taught me. When the slide finally locked open, there were fifteen motionless bodies piled up in front of the gates. I jammed a second clip into the M3, raised it, pointed it, and then relaxed my trigger finger until two of the soldiers lying on the ground tried to sit up and point a rifle at me. Two bursts and that effort was quashed. Two more poked rifles around the main gates and started shooting blind. I let off a burst at the part of the gate they were hiding behind which suppressed that problem.

By now no one else was moving. I could smell the oily heat coming off the barrel of my grease gun. The gates to the compound remained open, framing what was now a major conflagration behind them. How hard could it be to douse a flaming arrow stuck into some wood, I wondered. Really tough if you didn't have fire-fighting water to begin with, I realized. The Japs had probably been subsisting on rainwater ever since the townspeople had disabled the only freshwater well in town.

I waited for Magron to make the next move while continuing to scan the front walls of the compound for snipers, but Tachibana moved first. He fired another volley of mortar rounds which began landing in the plaza area in front of the compound and among the nearest buildings facing the main gates. Some of them fell close enough to my scraggly tree to chip pieces of bark away. I crouched down in the crotch of the tree and hoped for the best. Behind me I could feel the heat of new fires as the adjacent structures went up. Tachibana was clearly trying to drive the archers out of their bow range as he concentrated the mortar fire into the area from which most of the fire arrows had come. After shooting two dozen or so rounds, he checked fire, at which point a volley of arrows came from the *other* side of the compound walls. These weren't fire arrows, so I presumed they were poison-tipped war arrows. I only caught a brief glimpse of them as they arced over the walls and were briefly illuminated by the fires within. The archers seemed to be concentrating on a specific area in the compound, so one of the archers at least knew the compound layout and where the mortar battery was. The barrage seemed to work because there were no more rounds popping out of there.

Once again silence reigned except for the crackling of the fires in the compound and behind me. With several sections of the wooden walls aflame it might as well have been daytime. I could see a couple of wooden buildings in the compound starting to collapse but I didn't see a single human figure moving in there. I wondered where Magron had taken his position. It had to be within sight of the gates. Then he suddenly appeared. Incredibly he'd stationed himself at the far right corner of the compound wall, where it cut back toward the riverbank. He'd probably been able to see *inside* the compound through a crack in the bamboo wall during the whole fight. I saw two Filipinos behind him, peeking round the corner of the wall.

Then we heard a familiar voice: Tachibana himself, beginning some kind of exhortation to his remaining men. Each time he finished speaking they roared their approval, but there were definitely fewer voices in his rabidly loyal garrison.

Now what, I wondered. Another charge? I had only the one partial clip left, but I could thin them out as they bunched themselves getting through that gate. Then a whole section of the wall came crashing down in a flurry of red embers, revealing the whole interior of the compound. I could see Tachibana atop a mortar ammo box in front of a couple dozen or so soldiers. The soldiers were standing in ranks with their rifles, ignoring the hot smoke and flying embers swirling around them. Three officers stood right behind Tachibana. The colonel himself wore that enormous samurai sword which bobbed at his side as he worked himself up.

Then he stopped and turned around to face the gate. He made a motion with his right hand. One of the officers bowed and then trotted toward the main gate, carrying what looked like a three-legged wooden stool under each arm. I sighted the M3 on him as he came through the gate but held back. The officer walked 30 feet out in front of the gates and set the stools down, one in front of the other. He then yelled something in Japanese at the cluster of burning buildings, did an about-face, and stamped back into the compound to join Tachibana and his formation.

Two stools, five feet apart. Tachibana wanted to *talk*?

I began to make like a snake to get down out of that tree. If all those soldiers made it through the gates I didn't want to be treed like a raccoon and also shot like one. By the time I got down on the ground Magron was walking nonchalantly out toward the stools, acting as if nothing much was going on. A cloud of smoke obscured the gate for a moment. When it cleared here came Tachibana and his troops. I got the M3 ready from behind the trunk of "my" tree, expecting to have to protect Magron once Tachibana got close enough to unlimber that big sword, but that's not what happened. The colonel, dressed in his ample khaki uniform and high leather boots, stopped and stared at Magron with an expression of pure contempt. This seemed a bit much given the current state of the Jap compound. His guards came to a rigid parade rest behind the colonel and planted their rifle butts in the dirt.

Tachibana sat down on one of the stools and gestured for Magron to sit on the other. He then snapped his fingers and one of the officers came running over and knelt down beside the colonel. Tachibana said something and the kneeling officer translated into what sounded like Tagalog. Magron responded in kind and I thought I heard him say his own name. Introductions were being made. I suspected that these proceedings were being observed by Magron's archers, although there was so much smoke along that line of smoldering buildings behind me that I couldn't be sure. Another section of the wall collapsed in a shower of sparks, startling me but neither of the two antagonists. Tachibana launched into a long tirade, getting louder and angrier the more he went

on. When he was finished his interpreter started to translate. He'd
gone about halfway through what the colonel said when Magron
raised a hand and spat out a single word. The officer seemed
taken aback, as if he didn't want to repeat what Magron had said.
Tachibana snarled at him and the officer made the translation.

Tachibana straightened up and looked as if he'd been slapped
in the face. When the interpreter saw the colonel's expression he
began backing away, still down on his knees. Magron remained
seated, arms folded across his stomach. Tachibana ordered his
guards to go back into the compound, or what was left of it. Maintaining parade formation, they turned as a unit and marched back
through the gates. The colonel started to walk after them but
then halted and turned around. Magron was still sitting on the
stool. Tachibana yelled at him. Magron only shrugged and then
began picking his nose, as if he didn't give a damn what the en-
raged Japanese colonel had to say about anything. That apparently
was the last straw; Tachibana drew that gleaming sword, raised it
high over his head, and advanced on a defiant Magron like a two-
legged thundercloud.

And then stopped short. All of a sudden there was this diminu-
tive black figure standing in his way, cradling what looked like
a thin walking stick in his armpit, almost like a Marine drill in-
structor.

Tachibana lowered his sword so that the tip touched the ground.
He stared at the Negrito and then began to laugh, gesturing to
Magron as if to say: This is going to protect you? *This?* The Negrito drew back and spit on Tachibana's mighty sword, and then
in a move so swift that a rattlesnake would have been impressed,
he fired a dart directly into Tachibana's right eye. The colonel
howled in pain and took a step backward, trying to pluck the dart
from his eye. Then he went rigid, his good eye looking around as
if it was trying to figure out what was happening. He collapsed
a moment later onto his knees, leaned forward on the haft of his
sword, rolled slowly to the right and expired in a huge sigh. The

Negrito slipped his blowgun back into his belt and pulled out his bolo, the one with that wicked hook on the back of the blade. He stepped forward, yanked the dart out of the dead man's eye, and then used that hook to remove the remaining, "good" eyeball. In full view of his stunned audience, he popped it into his mouth and began chewing. I could hear the collective hissing gasp from the guards inside the compound. Then he just walked away into the shadows, vanishing like the lethal ghost he was.

I expected the remnants of the garrison to rush back out in full cry, guns ablaze, but they just stood there, looking over at one of the remaining two officers, when another section of the wall collapsed down by the fishing boat pier, as if trying to punctuate the fact that there *was* no more Japanese compound.

Magron had remained seated throughout this entire confrontation. Now he stood up, dusted off his clothes, took one last look at the bloody heap on the ground, spat at the still kneeling officer, and walked into the compound itself, not even looking at the group of cowed Jap soldiers. He disappeared all alone into the swirling cloud of smoke and sparks, as if he was looking for something. Then I remembered: The hostages. Oh, God, I thought.

I stayed behind my tree, ready to even the odds if the Japs decided to keep fighting. Which, of course, one of the officers did. He drew his sword, unimpressive compared to the one lying next to the colonel, and walked over to where the trembling interpreter knelt. He yelled at the man, who shook his head and closed his eyes. The officer raised his sword as if he was going to execute him but then turned on his heel and called back to the one remaining officer. That worthy ignored him. This time he spat on the ground, turned around, raised his sword over his head, and issued what was an obvious challenge to the flickering darkness beyond the compound. Seeing no takers he advanced toward the burning buildings, still yelling, until an arrow appeared in his stomach. He collapsed, bent double in obvious agony, his sword lying on the ground.

I trained the M3 in the guards' direction, but they had apparently decided *not* to follow him in an honorable if suicidal charge. They put down their rifles and gathered into a tight knot of frightened men. I realized they were mostly teenagers. Suddenly there were men behind me, emerging from the hot ashes of the town's main street buildings, and advancing quietly on the compound. At that moment Magron reappeared out of the smoking interior of the compound. His eyes were bulging in fury. He yelled something to the archers, who began nocking those longbows.

Wait, I thought. They've surrendered. The six archers continued walking slowly toward the gates, forming themselves into a wide arc. Then they stopped. Clamping their quivers between their legs, they began firing into that clump of trembling soldiers, killing every last one of them in under a minute of ruthless, silent slaughter. I was astonished to see the two remaining Jap junior officers, who'd finally drawn their swords, make an attempted charge at the archers. By then all six archers could shoot at the two of them and they went down on their faces looking like pincushions.

Magron approached the bloody pile and drew that captured pistol. He walked among the dead, kicking each one between the legs, and then shot one of them in the head. He approached me once he'd checked each one. I think he understood the look of horror on my face, because he said something in Tagalog and then beckoned me to follow him back into the smoke. It was not one of my best decisions because he took me to what looked like a small cattle pen between the smoldering godowns, where the bodies of the hostages were strewn like so much trash. The Japs had bayoneted every one of them, probably to save bullets.

Okay, I thought. This had been a massacre. Just like the one out front. Summary justice if I ever saw any. I turned around, leaving Magron alone to mourn the consequences of his attack on the compound. As I walked back toward the gates I took one last scan around the remains of the compound walls, looking for any lone survivors who might pop up for some revenge. This had been too easy. There should have been more Japs in here.

I stopped in the middle of the compound and looked hard between gusts of wood smoke. There was one remaining unburned shed at the end of a line of four; the others were just blackened mounds.

I looked close. It was just a wooden shed with miniature barn doors on the front and no windows. This one had a metal roof, which is probably why it hadn't caught fire.

Something's in there, I just *knew* it. While I was staring I thought I heard a sound coming from that direction. A metallic clink. Barely audible, but then I was 15 or so feet from away from those doors.

A clink? I was really tired, but something was telling me that I knew that sound.

A clink. And then I remembered: when Rooster and I were humping those .50-cal. ammo belts through the jungle, the cartridges had bumped into each other as I struggled to keep them off the ground, making that identical clinking sound. I saw Magron coming back out of the hostage pen area out of the corner of my eye, but I knew I couldn't wait. I lifted the barrel of my trusty grease gun and emptied that thing into the front of that shed, concentrating on the lower half of those wooden doors. Apparently I'd had most of a clip left so when the noise stopped the bottoms of those doors were well and truly splintered.

Magron came running, yelling something in Tagalog that sounded like *what the hell?* The other Filipinos who'd come into the compound were all down on the deck, staring at me like I'd gone berserker. Still pointing the grease gun, even though it was empty, I walked over to the shattered doors and kicked them aside. There, surrounding a water-cooled, .50-caliber, antiaircraft machine gun on a tripod were four Japs. Two were obviously dead; the other two were moaning and trying to crawl away. Magron appeared behind me and finished them off. Then he stared at that big machine gun, which looked like the ones the Marines had been using on Guadalcanal, only bigger. Tachibana must have known, I thought. Once the fires started, he must have known that he and his garrison were finished. So he'd posted one final detail of soldiers. I could just imagine his orders: When it seems to be all over, they will come into the compound to look and spit upon our dead. Once there's a crowd, open the doors and even the score.

Magron tried to speak but only managed a croaking noise in his throat. His face was as white as a mahogany-complexioned man's could get. Then he looked over at me with my still-smoking grease gun and bowed.

"My pleasure," I said, bowing back. "It's the least I could do."

I backed out of the picture as the other Filipinos came over and saw that machine gun. There was a rising chorus of chatter in Tagalog. I walked back to where the gate had been and out into the street. Forgetting my M3 was empty I scanned the remaining portions of the compound wall, but my brain told me it was over, well and truly over. I was pretty sure there were no more live Japs on Talawan Island. The metallic stink of fresh blood mixed with woodsmoke reminded me once more of Guadalcanal.

I knew we might not be out of the woods yet, especially if Tachibana had had a radio in the compound and that there might now be an entire regiment of Japanese soldiers from Mindanao en route to straighten things out. Still, I felt a great satisfaction. Bows and arrows against 60mm mortars, rifles, and machine guns. Primitive traps from centuries past lurking out in the countryside, snakes in caves, a rock barrage from the dawn of time wiping out the remains of a Jap infantry squad. All of this because they were occupiers, just the latest round, and heartless monsters at that.

I looked up. Magron was standing not far behind me, nodding at me approvingly, as townspeople began to creep out of the woods around Orotai.

THIRTY-FOUR

There was a small crowd around the hut where Rooster lay when I got back to Lingoro. I hurried over, fearing the worst, but was intercepted by Tini's grandmother. She took my hand and diverted me towards the big tree hide and Father Abriol. He looked about the same and the dressings around his stump were weeping some blood. There was still no hint of gangrene, however, and his eyes were a little bit brighter.

"I forgot to tell you," he said, as I sat down on one of the ammo crates. "When your gunner came back wounded I sent a messenger north and asked if Mohammed al Raqui could come down and tend to him. He arrived by boat two hours ago. Word got around, and that's why there's a crowd over there. He's a famous healer and they want him to tend to them, too."

"What's Rooster's condition?" I asked.

"Well," he said, "he clings to life, but I'm very glad the emir is here. The women said the bullet went straight through, but the emir said they were wrong and that he would have to find it and take it out."

"That's what I thought," I said.

"He brought two other healers with him, probably apprentices. I thanked him profusely for coming and then got out of his way. What happened in Orotai? The rumors are incredible and spreading like wildfire."

I told him of what we'd achieved, including the massacre of the hostages and what Magron and his archers did about that. He grimaced, but nodded his reluctant acceptance. "I would expect nothing less," he said. "So it's true? All the Japs are dead?"

"Unless there's a patrol skulking around out here, I'd say yes. Once Tachibana went down, the enlisted troops gave up. Their officers insisted on doing their duty and thus became *good* Japs. By luck we discovered one final ambush in place."

He sighed. I knew that he was probably appalled at what had happened, and yet he'd been with these people for ten years. Surely he saw the justice of it. I certainly did.

There were sounds of people approaching outside so I went to open the door. The emir stepped in, stooping to clear the doorway, followed by two others who looked like full-blooded Arabs, not Filipinos. His robes were bloodstained, as were the shirtsleeves of his assistants. He bowed formally to Abriol, who tried to bow back and had to stifle a groan. Then he bowed to me. Surprised, I awkwardly returned the gesture. Then he began to speak to Abriol. I held my breath. When he'd finished Abriol nodded and turned to me.

"Your gunner will heal, God willing," he began, translating literally. "The emir found the bullet just under the skin of your friend's back. He removed it and did some other things, something involving needle and thread that I didn't quite understand. He's attended to Tomaldo's hand and will now examine my leg. He was impressed that you two joined our cause and, because of that, he will send us some help to rebuild."

"That's good news, isn't it?"

"Yes, it is," he said with a wry smile. "Although they will come to make some converts if they can."

"You did call them 'the competition' as I recall," I said. "I'm going to see Rooster. Please tell him the Americans appreciate his help very much. We are in his debt."

Abriol translated my message and the old man replied. "He says there is word spreading from Luzon, Samar, and Leyte that the Americans are coming soon to drive out the Japanese. He asks that this time, once that has been accomplished, you go back to America. He insists that you tell your government that."

"I will indeed tell my government that. Actually, after this war is over, the Americans will want nothing more than to go home. We now understand that the Philippines belongs to the Filipinos."

The emir seemed pleased with that answer. Father Abriol shot me a knowing look. I wished it was true, but in my heart I knew it probably wasn't and so did he. But I was getting better at telling people what they wanted to hear and thus preserving that all-important "face."

Rooster looked a little worse for wear after the emir's ministrations and the sight of one of the women carrying out an entire basket of blood-soaked cloths wasn't reassuring. On the other hand he seemed to be sleeping peacefully and breathing regularly and without the liquid-lung sounds I'd heard before. Young Tini was by his bedside, holding his hand. Then I looked again: Rooster was holding *Tini's* hand. Oh, my, I thought. I backed out, conscious of the women's total awareness of what was happening there. Whatever it takes to pull him through, I thought; whatever it takes. Then I went to find Tomaldo and through him, Abriol's radio if it still existed.

The weather was miserable for the next week as the northeast monsoon began to take hold, with rain, a vigorous, steady wind, thunderstorms, and high seas that made fishing almost impossible. I went into Orotai while waiting to see if they could find Abriol's radio. The British prisoners of war, who had been dispersed throughout the forest after the big escape, were being brought back into Orotai, where they were housed in the remains of the Japanese compound. The godowns and the Japs' perimeter wall were gone, but several smaller buildings were being disassembled to make one large one. The townspeople had returned to pick up the pieces after the Japs' mortar barrage, and there was even a feverish community boat-building operation going on when I arrived.

The POWs were being cared for by women from the town. One had died out in the forest, but the rest were looking much better, which wasn't saying much. They couldn't have looked much worse. I was initially worried that if the Japs did dispatch a retribution force to Orotai, gathering them into the town might be a bad idea, but there really was no other alternative. They couldn't stay hidden in the bush forever and Lingoro village had its own problems with rebuilding, not to mention scarce food. One place was off-limits in the compound: that shoddy corral where the hostages had been executed. There were already crude crucifixes, flowers, and crossed palms adorning the fence that surrounded a large dirt mound. Apparently Magron had ordered all the bodies burned and then buried right there. The Church would have disapproved, but, again, there wasn't any other alternative. In the evenings family members were allowed to come in, pay their respects, and grieve.

The bad weather eased up the following week and the first of the newly built fishing boats were able to get out to sea. The town's morale really improved when an interisland cargo sailboat arrived with rice and salted fish, courtesy of the Moros in the north, along with two "missionaries of the one true faith," who set up shop near the compound. Father Abriol, getting used to bamboo crutches, had returned to his quarters in the church; he stopped to talk with "the competition" every morning. By then I was staying in the erstwhile Japanese O-club as life began to return to Orotai. The menu had been much depleted but at least we did eat once a day. Rooster remained in Lingoro after telling me he thought it was his duty to help Tini and the villagers rebuild. I solemnly agreed that he was probably right about that while trying mightily to keep a straight face.

Magron and his hunter-archers had gone proudly back to their part of the island to a hero's welcome now that the Jap menace was gone. We never saw the Negritos again; they had simply disappeared, as was their wont. I was going to miss them, especially after that display of primeval defiance in the town square. I think that spectacle had been the final straw for the Jap soldiers.

The radio and its generator arrived in town a week later from wherever it had been hidden, smelling faintly of fish oil. By then Rooster was able to walk into the town with the help of his "nurse," the redoubtable Tini, so I drafted a message that I hoped would bring someone to Talawan to pick both us *and* the POWs up. We sent it out in plain English to save time and effort. By then the American Army had landed near Leyte Gulf, and there was word of a general uprising in and around Manila. It had been a long time since we'd reported in, so, as I expected, there was no acknowledgment at first. I had Rooster send it out three times more at different times of the day, in hopes that somebody might hear it, but there was still no reply. Even more frustrating was the fact that the radio would only transmit on that one frequency, so there was no way we could come up on one of the US Navy freqs.

We kept trying for two more days until the radio's generator suddenly smoked and all its dials dropped back to the zero position. So that was that, we told ourselves, until ten days later a US Navy destroyer showed up outside the harbor at Orotai. They sent a boat into the fishing pier while the ship, guns trained in our direction, remained out of small-arms range in the harbor. A young lieutenant wearing a steel helmet and a gray life jacket over his khakis stood up once the boat tied up. He wanted to know the whereabouts of the two American pilots and some British prisoners of war who were supposed to be on this island.

Rooster and I were standing on the rickety pier, along with Father Abriol, who was sitting in a homemade wheelchair they'd fashioned out of bamboo and bicycle tires. I spoke up and told him who we were. The expression on the lieutenant's face as he

looked the two of us over said we might have a lot of explaining
to do. I asked Father Abriol to send someone to the compound to
start bringing out the POWs who were most able to walk. Once
they began limping out of the compound the lieutenant relaxed
and spoke to one of the boat's enlisted crew, who produced a por-
table flashing light and began signaling the destroyer. He told us
the ship was an APD, which was a destroyer that had been turned
into a high-speed transport ship.

Maybe, I thought, as I watched the embarkation begin, just
maybe we were finally going home.

THIRTY-FIVE

My defense counsel met me at the Makalapa headquarters main entrance. It had taken the entire week for me to get through my story because we didn't stay in session all day. Apparently there were several other courts and boards of various kinds being held at PacFleet headquarters. Besides, my voice tired easily.

We headed past the decorations and flag stands of the formal main entrance and past the attending Marines and then walked down a long corridor leading to a back door. I'd been able to find a pair of slacks and a white shirt and tie at the Lucky Bag in the bachelor officers' quarters, so I was a bit more presentable now. I'd had my hair cut and the beard shaved, so now my walnut-stained face, highlighted by that long white scar, was fully visible. Other officers were in the corridor, some carrying charts and others briefing folders, and all wearing worried expressions. Apparently the Philippines operation was touch and go and there'd been rumors of Jap battleships ambushing a formation of our carriers. Not surprisingly, the fleet headquarters was the virtual Grand Central Station for rumors.

"Well, I'll be damned," a voice said behind. "*Fish*: is that you?"

I turned to recognize a three-striper stopped in the corridor. It was Channing Cox, my skipper at Midway in Bombing Six. "What in God's name happened to your face?"

He walked over and shook my hand while I stood there, speechless. "You're alive," he said. "We thought you went down with *Hornet*. Where the hell you been, Lieutenant? And what're you doing here at Makalapa?"

My defense counsel rescued me. "He's the subject of a court of inquiry," he said. "He was picked up on the island of Talawan in the Philippines, along with a bunch of Brit POWs. The Navy didn't—doesn't—believe he is who he says he is."

"Are you shitting me?" Commander Cox asked.

"No, sir."

"Bobby," he said. "Surely you've told them—"

I pointed to my face. The first time I'd seen it in a mirror onboard that destroyer I wouldn't have believed it either. "I've spent the past week telling my story. Is there any chance . . ."

"*Hell* yes," he said. "Is that where you're going? To this court?"

I nodded. He handed his folders to a lieutenant commander who'd been walking with him and off we went. Within an hour my legal ordeal was over. The president of the court told me to report to the CO of the naval air station at Ford Island for reassignment. Then he said he wanted to speak to me in private. We left the courtroom and walked down to the CincPacFleet dining room and coffee mess. The stewards brought us coffee and then we sat down at one of the tables.

"I have to tell you, Lieutenant: I was very impressed by your testimony. I think you deserve official recognition for what you and your radioman-gunner did there on Talawan. I urge you to write this all down before you forget it."

"I'm not likely to ever forget it, Captain," I said.

"Yeah, I understand that. I'm talking about details, times, places, dates if you can manage it. Write it up, then get that report to me. I think it's important, both for the navy and your own career."

My career, I thought. That word hadn't crossed my mind once in the past, what, almost two years? *Career*?

"I have one question, which I deliberately didn't bring up in open session."

"Yes, sir?"

"Where is Radioman Baynes?"

"Missing," I said, promptly, and then told my preplanned fable. "He went back to the village once the destroyer showed up. It took us two days to get the POWs out to the ship. When it was time for me to take a boat out there I sent a runner to Lingoro to get Rooster. They said he'd gone upland because of a report that a Jap patrol had been seen. The captain of the destroyer said he *had* to leave that morning. And, so . . ."

The captain looked at me. "And that's your story, is it?"

I looked down at the table, a bit ashamed. He'd seen right through it. Captains often did that. "I think he earned it, Captain," I said quietly. "He was never going back into a cockpit after all he'd gone through. I think he'll do more good in that little village than he could ever do in what remains of this damned war."

"Is that so," he said. He finished his coffee. "Okay, I will officially take that thesis under advisement. I recommend that you make his disappearance a little more mysterious when you write up what happened there at the end."

The look on his face was officially stern, but there was a twinkle of sympathetic humor in his eyes. He understood perfectly.

"Thank you, sir," I said. "Thank you very much."

"You're welcome, Lieutenant. Now: how's about getting into a proper uniform, now that you're back in the land of rules and regulations. By the way, I know a skin doctor here up at Tripler who might be able to fix that face of yours. Get up there and ask for Doctor Jack Hall. He's really good. Unless of course you want to keep it?"

"I hadn't thought that far ahead, Captain," I said. "I'm still pretty tired."

He nodded. "You did well out there, Lieutenant. Very well. Take the next week off before reporting to Ford Island. Get up to

Tripler. Write up your story, and then get it back over here. You know where to find me."

Suddenly I was at a loss for words. The tapestry of all that had happened began to parade before my eyes. The room was suddenly blurred. The captain put a hand on my shoulder. "You did good, son. You did *real* good. And here's something you might not know. After what you went through, especially aboard *Hornet* and then *Hagfish*, not to mention Talawan, you'll be officially offered the option of simply going home. You've done more than your share of fighting this war. We *are* going to win this thing. We know it, I think the Japs know it. And then, it will be time to get on with the rest of your life. Trust me when I say *no* one would gainsay your decision to simply go home."

Again I didn't know what to say, but the idea of going home had never occurred to me. He looked at his watch and said he had to go; yet another court was in the offing. I sat there for a few minutes and then went to find the shuttle back down to the BOQ at the naval base.

Interestingly, my room in the BOQ was just about identical to the one I'd stayed in waiting for the Big E to come back into port. This time, however, there was no seabag and no orders packet. At some point I'd have to go find a paymaster, a uniform shop, and an ID office to reestablish who I was. Or at least who I'd once been. In the meantime, I had some writing to do.

The only souvenir from Talawan was an ornately carved bamboo tube Magron had brought down to the pier as I was waiting for the next and last boat out to the destroyer, whose stacks were puffing with impatient steam. It was not quite four feet long and slightly curved, but it had been signed or at least marked by all sorts of people from Lingoro and Orotai. It was heavy for bamboo, but it was also almost three inches in diameter, which probably accounted for the weight. I'd carried it all the way back to Pearl like some oversized baton, much to the consternation of some of my fellow passengers.

I went over to the closet and rousted it out. I read through the signatures, touched the carved totem faces and figures, most of which I couldn't recognize. I smelled the wood and all the sights, sounds, and memories of Talawan came flooding back. I laid it down on my bed and then noticed there was a thin green line about ten inches from one end that went all the way around. I hadn't seen that before.

Then it hit me: Was that a seam? Was there something inside?

I picked it back up and shook it. It didn't feel like there was anything inside, but that green line was marginally wider now. The ends of the tube had been carved into complex handles, like a rolling pin. I gave one a hard pull and by God, it popped off. Inside was a roll of what looked like saw grass leaves, wrapped so tightly I could barely pull them out, after which I raised the tube to see what slid out.

Tachibana's great sword fell out onto the bed. I almost stopped breathing. The sword wasn't very clean, with green stains from the leaves on the mother-of-pearl-encrusted handle. There was also a faint odor of something truly nasty rising from it. I stared at it for a moment and then grasped the handle and tried to pull the blade out of its scabbard, but it seemed to be stuck. Then it moved. When I saw why it was so sticky I quickly pushed it back in to the hilt.

Just a friendly little reminder from Magron, I thought. This is what becomes of occupiers on Talawan Island.

My brain tilted for a moment, and then I made a decision. The captain had been right. It was indeed time for me to just go home. Enough was enough.

AUTHOR'S NOTE

Talawan Island is fictitious and not to be confused with the very real, and much larger, Palawan Island in the Philippines. This story is based in part on a true incident in the Philippines, however, when a US submarine struck a Japanese sea mine and broke in half. There were initially fourteen survivors but only a few made it to shore, where they were picked up by the local Filipino resistance group. Eventually they were captured by the *Kempeitai* and imprisoned in a POW camp on Palawan Island for taking part in guerilla activities. After a bombing raid by US carrier aircraft, the commandant of the camp had the four submariners pushed into a ditch, doused with gasoline, and burned alive. One of them was the son of the admiral who'd been in command of the Pacific Fleet when the Japanese attacked.

There have been many books written about the battle of Midway and for years I thought I knew what had happened out there, but I was wrong. Find and read a book called *Shattered Sword*, by Jonathan Parshall and Anthony Tully, for a different account, different because it's based on Japanese primary sources.

The carrier USS *Hornet was* sunk at the battle of the Santa Cruz Islands. The ship was abandoned once the fires caused by Japanese bombing attacks got out of control. Their escorts managed to get almost everyone off and then left her to burn. Two

Japanese destroyers came upon the burning hulk and dispatched her with torpedoes.

The *Kawanishi* H8K flying boats existed as described in this story. They carried a crew of 11, as well as torpedoes, bombs, and depth charges, and they bristled with 20mm cannon and .50-caliber machine guns. They could range 4,000 miles on a single mission and if the seas permitted, they could land at dusk and just float around all night to save fuel.

I chose the name Tachibana as the chief villain of this story because a Japanese army lieutenant general named Yoshio Tachibana was hanged in Guam after the surrender for war crimes against Allied POWs, including the ghastly ritual cannibalism that occurred on the island of Chichi Jima, where the Japanese beheaded captured pilots and consumed their internal organs. To the Japanese militarists, a soldier who ran up a white flag lost all of his personal honor and most of his humanity. Allied POWs under Japan's boot were treated so miserably because, in the eyes of their captors, they had become despicable creatures for not fighting to the death as any real warrior would.

And, finally, you might think I exaggerated the ocean depths around the Philippines, but the so-called Philippine Trench is 34,580 feet deep at its deepest point, or just shy of seven *miles* deep. The country has some of the biggest volcanoes in the Ring of Fire, including Pinatubo, which evicted the entire American base establishment when it erupted in 1991 in the second-largest volcanic eruption of the twentieth century.

I've personally been to the Philippines often during my naval service, and our family has wonderful memories and connections to those amazing people. My mother and father were married in Manila when he was a young naval officer and her father was the Studebaker Automobile representative for the entire country. She had a Filipina *amah* during her childhood so my mother spoke a mixture of Spanish and Tagalog characteristic of Manila. My older brother was born in Manila just before the family moved to Shanghai, eight years before war broke out.

My last time in Manila was when I was assigned to the US embassy as the head of a US Navy mobile training team in 1966, teaching Philippine navy crews how to operate Swift-class gunboats. LBJ had given the Philippine government three Swift boats in return for his being able to claim that the war in Vietnam was an "Allied" endeavor. During the at-sea phase of that training we operated their three Swift boats in the waters around Corregidor, chasing pirates. The boats would come rumbling in at sundown to the Manila Yacht Club where I was billeted. They'd pick me up and we'd go out for night operations in Manila Bay. I stayed in the same club guesthouse building where my parents had honeymooned thirty-four years previously.

The pirate problem was real. They'd come out onto the waters of Manila Bay at night and pretend to be fishermen, just two men and a small light in a banca boat. Tipped off by corrupt customs officials in Manila, they'd wait for a specific cargo ship to come through, headed for the city. On signal, a dozen of these "fishermen" would light off 75HP outboards on their banca boats and swarm the ship like iron filings to a magnet. They'd climb aboard, slaughter the entire crew, and then run the ship aground and loot it. We engaged in several nighttime firefights with them; they could outrun our boats but not our radar and our lovely 81mm mortars.

One night the Philippine commander of the three-boat division, whom I was "advising," got fed up and decided to attack the two seaside villages where most of the pirates were known to be based. They shelled the villages and the piers and then machine-gunned the whole burning shoreline, Magron style. The next day I went to see the naval attaché to inform him of the incident, and to suggest that perhaps our usefulness was at an end. The horrified ambassador quickly agreed and the next day my crew and I flew over to Saigon from Clark Air Base to join a Swift boat division based on the Long Tau (or Saigon) River. I think we saw more action on Manila Bay than we did for the next year in Vietnam.

During the Second World War the Filipinos suffered badly, both from the conquering Japanese and then the eventual battles when the Americans returned to drive them out. They were some of our staunchest allies against the Japanese invaders and the Japanese knew it. Thousands died, both in Manila at the hands of the *Kempeitai*, and out in the countryside and the outlying islands, but they never wavered. Our history books make it sound like they were staying fiercely loyal to America in hopes of eventual liberation. I think they were simply continuing their dogged determination to evict, one way or the other, the latest group of foreign occupiers.

PTD